# Like a Child
# at Home

# Like a Child at Home

By Audrey Siegrist
Artist: Peter Balholm

Rod and Staff Publishers, Inc.
P.O. Box 3, Hwy. 172
Crockett, Kentucky 41413
Telephone: (606) 522-4348

Printed in U.S.A.

ISBN 0-7399-2374-9

Catalog no. 2301

1 2 3 4 5 – 15 14 13 12 11 10 09 08 07 06

To
"Mack" and his family,
whose faithful lives
were the inspiration
for this book.

# 1

On this early-April morning, Linda Faith Asbury sat dreamily on her window seat, gazing out the long, old-fashioned window, over the acres of farmland that she could see in every direction. She had gotten up early, even before the alarm clock, set for five-thirty, had awakened her. She wondered how anyone could sleep on such a beautiful spring morning, when the sun was already reddening over the horizon and the early morning shadows had long retreated before the coming day.

Propping her elbows on the windowsill, she thought of the past and dreamed about the future. She thought of how she had lived for all her sixteen years on the Asbury farmstead two miles north of town. Springville was home, on the beautiful eastern shore of Virginia. There was no other place she would rather live—no place in all the world! Here were Mom and Dad—Lester and Alberta Asbury—and big brother Larry and younger sister Loretta.

The farm, with its rolling sand hills and green pine forests, and the town, where all her friends lived and where she had shopped with her mother for as long as she could remember, were the center of her life—of work and play, of dreams and aspirations. Bordering the farm and the town, the Sinapuxent River rippled by. It was a place to play in, fish in, or dream beside.

In the distance, across the vast flatness dotted here and there with farm buildings, Linda could see plumes of smoke rising from factory smokestacks near town. In the mid-1960s, Springville was a growing town. Large factories in the town proper and others on the outskirts of town provided jobs for many of the Springville working class. And new industries kept moving in, bringing more workers into the area. One factory built modular homes; another one, farm machinery. Pap-pap Jones's company built baby grand pianos.

Mom often talked about her father's business, glorying in the knowledge that her family, the Joneses, was one of the most prosperous in the area. Linda chuckled to herself, thinking about Mom's aversion to farm life. She often wondered why Mom had ever married Dad, if she so much hated farming! She could hear Mom now, making it clear to Dad that never, under any circumstances, would she help in the barn. *Her* father was the president and owner of Jones Manufacturing Company, Incorporated, and she would not ruin her beautiful hands milking cows in a smelly barn! Nonetheless, Linda thought, Mom did quite well as a farmer's wife. She was an enthusiastic gardener—with gloves, of course—and a good cook. And Mom and Dad loved each other; Linda felt secure in that.

As Linda gazed into the distance, she thought she could see the uppermost point of the steeple on the ivy-covered Episcopal church, on Main Street. The Episcopal church had the highest steeple of all the churches in town, but their church—Mt. Olive Methodist Church on Townsend Street—had the sweetest sounding bell, Linda thought. She thought of their church, where she had gone with her parents for as long as she could remember. It had been rebuilt in the last twenty years and was now a comfortable brick building with a bell tower and steeple. The bell rang proudly every Sunday morning, promptly at 8:00. Linda often heard it, even two miles out of town—especially if the wind was in the right direction.

Springville High. Linda could not see it, but it was in her thoughts. For Linda, much of life revolved around Springville High School. She had been going there nearly every day, 180 days a year, for almost four years. She was a sophomore now and was enjoying every minute of learning. The high school had been built long ago on a large lot on the south edge of town. For seventy-five years, its red brick face had broadly stood, solemnly facing the row of maple trees across the street, defying prevailing west winds. Occasional northeasterly winds with a sting of ocean salt had scoured the back side of the building, but that was in the days before the new additions had been added.

On most school days, Larry drove to school in his little blue Corvair because often one or the other of them had band practice, a club meeting, or some sports event or practice after school. But some days they rode the bus. On those days she and Larry and Loretta met bus #15 at the end of the lane at eight-fifteen. At three-thirty in the afternoon, the bus dropped them off again at the end of the lane as it made its country circuit. Larry was a senior, and Loretta was in eighth grade.

A hawk suddenly flew out of the maple tree in front of Linda's window, arresting her attention. In its wicked-looking claws, it carried a smaller bird. *I hope it was only an English sparrow!* Linda's thoughts protested. She loved the many songbirds that made their homes in the trees and shrubs around the house, and she always resented the intrusion of hawks into their quiet sanctuary.

It must be almost time to go to the barn, Linda thought when she heard Dad bumping around in his bedroom. She knew that Larry had gone past her door a few minutes before, for she had heard his characteristic whistle. He was often whistling merry tunes, which fit well with his upbeat, happy personality. How Linda loved her big brother!

The alarm clock suddenly began its jangle on the nightstand beside her bed, violating the stillness. This was Wednesday morning, so of course there was school that day. Quickly she jumped up to turn it off. Then, after dressing for the barn, she hurried downstairs and into the early day.

Breathing deeply of the spring freshness, she looked over the greening farmland. Ah . . . the farm, and in the spring! Their farm had been in Dad's family for four generations. Over two hundred acres were on the west side of Route 104. The farm buildings nestled on that side too, comfortably situated inside a white board fence. Around the house were huge old maple trees, planted many years before by Dad's great-grandfather.

Linda walked backward down the walk as she looked at their house. Her friends always talked about how huge it was. And it surely was more house than they needed for their family! It had been built in the days, Dad had told the children, when large families were the norm. Its six bedrooms and two baths upstairs, and the living room, formal dining room, library, and large kitchen downstairs were reminiscent of earlier generations. On two sides of the house was a large screened-in porch. Linda and Loretta had spent many happy hours on that porch, playing doll or school, when they were little girls. Now it was a wonderful place to visit with friends or to read a book on a warm summer day. On another side was a sunroom with long floor-to-ceiling windows. That was where Mom often entertained the local garden club.

In the front yard, among trellises and rosebushes, was a fish pool. Linda could see it in her mind. Around the pool, slabs of stone, hauled from a great-uncle's farm in West Virginia, formed a lovely patio. That rose garden was Mom's delight. Linda remembered helping Mom plan and lay out those rose gardens.

Linda had been so excited when Dad had finally filled the fish pool, and the little goldfish were swimming around, their bright colors flashing in the golden sunlight. As a child, she had lain along the edge of the pool for hours at a time, head propped on her hands, watching the movement of the colorful fish. And when she got older, Mom sometimes let her feed the fish. What a delight that was!

Behind the house was a large garden, bordered in the back by rows of raspberries trained up on fences. Linda could see the onions poking up stiffly in straight rows and the lettuce and radishes beginning to show green against the sandy, brown soil. Beyond the garden was the orchard, with its promise of loveliness, as in every springtime. The peach, pear, and apple trees were already beginning to show their tender blooms.

Linda walked through the gate of the white board fence into the farmyard. Tiny jumped up from his nest under the fig tree and wiggled over to greet her, stretching and yawning in his characteristic way. Linda picked up the little black terrier and scratched behind his ears as she listened to the chickens singing themselves awake in the nearby chicken house. Probably Dad had gone there to check on the chickens before starting the milking, she thought. How those Leghorns sang when someone came into their pens. Sometimes it was almost deafening!

She set Tiny on the ground and meandered slowly to the dairy barn, turning her gaze from the old-fashioned chicken barn to the equally old-fashioned dairy barn. They looked very much alike, and probably sometime in the past had been quite imposing! Now they were simply the dairy barn and the chicken barn. The chicken barn had been an old horse barn that was converted to serve their present need. Dad had built two floors in what had been an old hayloft, to house a thousand hens. On the ground floor were several of the original horse stalls, a place for pigs (when they had any), the egg-packing room, and the feed room.

At the back edge of the farmyard was a large pole shed with equipment arranged conveniently inside it. A corncrib was adjacent to another building where Lester stored and mixed feed for the chickens and cows.

Just then Dad came out of the chicken barn and headed toward Linda. "You look like you are still dreaming, Linda," he greeted her pleasantly. "Are the cows in yet?"

"I'm enjoying our farm and seeing it through the eyes of spring," she answered out of a happy heart.

"Everything looks prettier in springtime, doesn't it!" Dad laughed. "Even barns and fences in need of paint!"

"I guess I *am* dreaming a bit," Linda said, laughing with Dad. "But I'd better go for the cows, or you will be ready to milk before the cows are there!"

Linda climbed over the fence while Tiny crawled through a hole at the bottom, and they began their long walk to the woods for the cows. Dad had long ago put up sturdy, woven-wire fences, beginning at the dairy barn and following the now-greening pastures out to the pine woods. He had included some of the woods in the pasture, which provided shade for the cows on the hot summer days and a place to bed down overnight. Hayfields and rye fields lay adjacent to the pastures. The pine forest covered many acres, all the way back to the Sinapuxent River. Linda thought of the many pleasant times the family spent in the woods and at the river. Close to the river were acres of marsh where beautiful cypress trees grew, their knees poking up out of the spongy moss and marsh. White-tailed deer abounded there also and provided good hunting for Dad and Larry and their hunting friends every fall.

Linda looked across the road to the east side of the highway, where there was an additional one hundred acres of cropland. Dad usually planted corn and soybeans in those fields and, in years with adequate rainfall, harvested adequate crops.

The sandy soil was rich in nutrients, but it dried out very quickly. Since only the very wealthiest farmers and those who grew many acres of sweet potatoes or watermelons could afford irrigation, most of the farmers took the weather as it came and made the best of it. Linda thought of all the acres that her father needed to run over with his equipment each growing season. She did not consider their farm as being large, till some relative from another area mentioned it. Then she realized that most of the farmers in this part of Virginia needed to farm many acres to grow enough feed for their cattle or chickens.

On the east side of the highway, at the edge of the cropland, were two tenant houses. Pansy and Pug Patterson lived in one, and the Northams, Shem and Louise, lived in the other. How Linda loved their friendly black neighbors. Pansy cleaned every week for the Asburys, in lieu of rent, since Pug did not have a steady job and could not always pay the bills. The Northams were good renters. Mr. Northam was the minister at the black Methodist Church down the road, and he always paid his rent, regular as clockwork, on the first day of every month.

Linda noticed that their windows were still dark in the early morning. But soon Pansy would be up and about, Linda knew. Pansy was always busy and industrious, working hard to make ends meet for herself and her husband.

All around the Asburys were other devoted farmers. Like the Asburys, many of the families had been in the area for several generations, drawing their livelihood from the soil. It was a farming community, and Linda was happy to be a part of it.

For many generations, life had rolled on, just like this, in and around the town of Springville, even as the Sinapuxent River, which bordered it, rolled on day after day—its waters ever moving down to the sea.

# 2

Saturday had come, and Linda was glad for a break to be at home and help around the farm and the house. Spring was too special to sit in a stuffy classroom and study Latin or participial phrases.

Linda did not understand how anyone could not love farm life: the vastness of the fresh outdoors, the sweetness of the early morning breezes, the smell of a freshly mown hayfield, the song of the meadowlark on the pasture fence. There was nowhere Linda would rather have lived or worked! Next to her school studies, gardening and field work were her greatest joy. She also loved the thirty-two gentle Jerseys that composed their dairy herd.

This gorgeous spring morning, Linda again headed across the pasture toward the woods, where the cows always bedded down at night under the pine trees. Tiny followed behind, ready to nip the heels of any straying cows. Already the sun was well over the eastern horizon and was sending long shadows through the pine trees into the pasture.

"Come on—come on," Linda chanted, her voice carrying easily in the stillness of the early morning. She could see the cows slowly getting up, rumps first. Soon Buttercup, the established leader, was moving along the path toward the barn, and the rest obediently followed, heads nodding up and down, up and down.

Linda walked along near the middle of the line, her hand on the back of Beauty, her very own little Jersey. Near the end of the line were two of Beauty's daughters, Annie and Pearl, which also belonged to Linda. Beauty had been a 4-H project long ago, when Linda was still in elementary school. Tiny trailed at the end of the line, occasionally giving a sharp bark.

Bringing in the cows was usually Linda's job because she enjoyed the leisurely walk morning and evening. Dad and Larry did the milking then while she fed the calves and heifers. Each morning and evening, Linda mixed and carried bucket after bucket of Calfmaker, a substitute milk, to the young calves in pens in a large open shed behind the barn. How she enjoyed the lively little Jerseys! She started at the first pen. Eagerly Daisy plunged her soft little nose into the warm milk, snuffling and slurping her way to the bottom of the bucket.

Linda laughed delightedly as she hung onto the bucket. Daisy butted and slurped, her little tail pumping contentedly. Suddenly the milk was gone. With a toss, the little head thumped the bucket. Linda hung on. "You never get enough, do you," she said. She rubbed the little bumps on Daisy's head that would someday be horns. Daisy tossed her head and tried to get Linda's fingers in her mouth. "Oh, you little rascal!" Linda exclaimed, pulling her hand away from Daisy's rough tongue.

After feeding the young calves from buckets, Linda carried grain to the heifers. They jostled each other eagerly as they saw her coming, each wanting to be first at the feedboxes.

By the time Linda had finished feeding the young stock and putting fresh bedding down for the calves, Dad and Larry were finishing up in the barn. She hurried up the back walk, hungry for a hearty breakfast.

Loretta was lifting luscious, brown sausage patties out of the frying pan. Mom got a pan of cornpone out of the oven and set it on the table. "Oh, yum!" Linda exclaimed as she peered around the kitchen door from the washroom, where she was washing up. "Sure looks and smells good!"

Loretta tossed her strawberry blond curls. "Just plain ol' country fare," she retorted with a laugh. "But I would sure rather cook than work in the barn, with all its animal smells!"

"That's why we get along so well, sis," Linda returned, smiling at her younger sister.

Linda brushed out her long, auburn hair. Large brown eyes in a fresh, healthy face looked back at her from the mirror. *If only I wouldn't have those freckles on my nose,* she thought, bending nearer the mirror to scrutinize them more closely. Yes, they were still there! And come summer, when she would be in the sun day after day, they would be even more noticeable. *But looking won't change my plainness,* she thought ruefully. She knew that she looked like Dad, with his big, plain features—not at all like her dainty mother.

She tied her hair back with a fresh band and hurried out of the washroom in time to make way for Larry and Dad, who were just then stomping in the back door.

There was a moment of silence as they all bowed their heads at the table. For as long as Linda could remember, this had been a custom in her family. When her friends came, they sometimes laughed about it, but they never seemed to think less of her for it.

"What's on the agenda for today, Dad?" Larry asked. "I have baseball practice at one o'clock. But I can help with work at home this morning."

Dad scratched his ear. "Well now, we should finish planting corn. There are fifty acres on the other side of the road to plant yet."

"Is everything ready to go? I'll get right to it, if you wish," Larry said, quickly pushing his chair back from the table.

"And there's feed to mix," Dad added. "But maybe one of the girls will help with that . . ." Dad's dark eyes twinkled at Linda.

"You know I'd rather do that than clean, any day!" she returned with emphasis.

"Pansy is coming to clean today," Mom injected. "So you can have both girls if you need them, Dad."

Loretta looked up, horrified. "Me!" she exclaimed. "I don't want to work with the feed!"

"Well now, it won't hurt you for once," Dad said in his slow drawl.

"Thanks, Mother," he added. "I'll be glad for both girls' help if you can spare them. With the spring planting taking my time, I've gotten behind with the other chores. There's a lot of outside cleanup that needs to be done too."

"Oh, Dad," Linda said as she got up from the table, "Red Ziller asked me the other day if you are hiring help for the summer. He is looking for work."

Loretta guffawed. "Is he that red-haired fellow who keeps trailing you all the time?"

"I don't know about the 'trailing.' But he is definitely a redhead; that's where he got his nickname. If I remember right, his name is really John Ray; but if a teacher calls him that, Red doesn't even know that the teacher is talking to him!"

"His name *is* John Ray," Larry affirmed as he stood by the kitchen door, "and I think he ought to go by that name. *Red* seems like a slam against his hair color. But I doubt my calling him by his right name would make much difference."

"Well, at any rate, I think his hair is a nice color. And he's nice—and sensible too," Linda added.

"Is he the kind we would want around the place?" Dad asked, drumming his fingers on the tabletop.

"I don't think you would mind having him around, Dad," Larry returned. "I happen to know him pretty well, even though he is a junior, because he is in my P.O.D. [Problems of Democracy] class."

"And he's in my geometry class," added Linda. "He's a good, diligent student."

"Is he the one whose father died suddenly of heart trouble a number of years ago?" Mom asked.

"Yes, he is," Linda responded. "He and his mother live alone, and he has been trying his best to support her since his father's death. He doesn't like it that she needs to go out and clean office buildings; he thinks he should make the living, especially now that he is older. He has a lot of determination. Works after school wherever he can get work. But he says he would rather work on a farm than anywhere else because he loves being close to the dirt."

Dad rubbed his chin thoughtfully. "Is this Red Ziller anything like the Clyde Tilghman who was looking for work awhile back?"

"Oh, no, Dad!" Linda asserted emphatically. "They are as different as day and night. I was hoping you wouldn't give Clyde work. He is such a bully at school, always trying to get attention." Linda carried a stack of dishes to the sink.

"Hmm. I can't understand that," Dad said thoughtfully. "I've always appreciated working with his father. In fact, it was his father who asked me if I could give his boy work. And I thought I would, till you girls told me how Clyde acts in school."

Linda thought of Mr. Tilghman, who for many years had been on the deacon board of the Mt. Olive Methodist Church with Dad. She did not know him well, but she did know his son Clyde well! He was rough and crude, usually the one who laughed the loudest at anything funny and was the most boisterous in games. She recoiled in horror as she thought of the time a year or so ago when he had asked her to a library club social. For weeks after she had refused him, he kept taunting her and bullying her. "Red Ziller and Clyde Tilghman are as different as day and night!" Linda reasserted with feeling.

Larry took up the conversation. "Remember when Clyde was expelled from school for three days last fall?" Linda nodded her head.

"You remember why?" Larry continued. "He pulled a chair away from behind Jane West, and she sat suddenly on the floor, injuring her back. And Clyde stood there and guffawed, even when he knew she was hurt! That's the kind of character he is!"

Dad rubbed his chin again, a habit of his when in deep thought. "Well now, I could use a good worker to help get our fencerows trimmed back. And the yard fence needs paint again, and there are a hundred and one other jobs that are always coming up," Dad said finally. "Tell Red to call me, if he asks again."

Loretta winked at Linda.

"Oh, Loretta," Linda scolded, "get your mind off the boys. You'd better concentrate on your studies for a few more years."

"Your sister is right," Dad said, looking sternly at Loretta.

Linda knew that Dad and Mom were concerned about Loretta's penchant for hanging around the fellows. And her falling grades this year gave them even more reason for concern.

"Thanks for the good breakfast, Mother," Dad said, standing up and stretching his muscular arms behind his back and up over his head with a big sigh. He seemed suddenly even taller than his six-foot height.

"And I'll be ready for help, girls, as soon as

you can come out," he added.

Linda enjoyed working with Dad. He was usually cheerful and patient, with a ready smile. She often thought she worked much better with Dad than with Mom. While Mom was slim and girlish and still lovely, she was also quick-tempered and often hard to please. Dad was just Dad—a big, plain, kindly farmer. He was mannerly and gentle, with none of Mom's sophistication. Dad was loved by everyone, even Mom, who was so opposite from him in so many ways.

For while Lester was a farmer, Alberta was a society lady. She had a degree in nursing, and she still enjoyed getting together with her colleagues. Somehow, Linda did not feel at home with the social gatherings that her mother often hosted in their home. Mom felt very much at ease with the businessmen's wives and the doctors' wives. Linda did not; she would rather spend a couple of hours chatting with Pansy, the cleaning lady, than with Dr. Boyer's prissy wife.

Sometimes Mom would scold Linda after she purposely avoided an afternoon tea. "You'll never amount to anything if you don't choose the right friends!" she chided her. "I'm trying to help you girls into the right social circles, and you, Linda, don't even appreciate it!"

Linda resented her mother at times like that. She was capable of making her own friends, and she had friends in plenty—of the nice girls around town. Pastor Baker's daughter, Andrea, was her closest friend. Besides, she did not even like the "high-class" girls at school. They were snobbish and mean, and you had to be like them to fit into their cliques. But it did not do a bit of good to tell Mom how she felt; Mom just did not or would not understand.

One thing that did please Mom though, Linda knew, was her consistent 4.0 grade point average. She also followed with interest the various sports events and school programs in which Linda and the other children participated, glorying in their accomplishments. She kept encouraging Linda to excel so that she would have a chance at being valedictorian of her graduating class.

Linda's thoughts continued to run as she helped Dad shovel the ears of corn into the corn sheller. Yes, she could pick her own friends, and she was not the least bit interested in the kind that Mom would like her to keep company with!

Meanwhile, Loretta bagged the shelled corn. When they had forty bags, Dad drove the Farmall tractor near the feed room. He connected one end of the huge belt to the Farmall power pulley, ran it through the hole in the feed room wall, and connected the other end to the feed mixer.

Linda could see Larry across the road, running the other Farmall with the corn planter slowly back and forth across the long field. She could see his jacket flapping behind his back. In the stiff spring breeze, clouds of dust swirled up from behind the corn planter. Even though she could not hear him, she guessed he was whistling merry tunes that fit his mood at the present. Then Dad revved up the Farmall, and the sound of the grain being thrown around inside the big metal bin of the feed mixer drowned out all else, even Linda's thoughts.

By noon Dad was finished with the most necessary jobs. Linda took a shower and rode into town with Larry. She spent the afternoon in the public library, working on a research paper titled "Church Divisions During the Reformation." When Larry came to pick her up at four o'clock, she hastily gathered her papers and cards together and stuck the research books back on the shelves.

"What are you doing tonight?" Larry asked as they drove home.

"I didn't make any plans. I'll be at home," Linda said. "But what about you?" She turned to smile at Larry, enjoying the roguish twinkle he turned on her from his merry brown eyes. She thought he was the nicest boy she knew, even if he was her brother.

Larry turned his attention back to driving, occasionally glancing at the passing farms as he followed the straight, level road through the countryside. "I think I'll go over to Ron Bradford's tonight," he said after a while. "I'm still trying to beat him at table tennis! Actually, though, we want to try to finalize where we will be going to college next fall."

"Haven't you decided yet where you are going?" Linda asked, realizing it was high time to make such a decision.

"I think we've narrowed down our choices. But we still need to decide between the University or Madison. We want to stay together, and I think both of us will register for premed."

"Where do Mom and Dad want you to go?"

"Mom, of course, prefers an Ivy League college!" Larry scoffed, putting undue emphasis on the *Ivy League*. "But Dad is more sensible. He would prefer that I go into agriculture and get a degree at East Carolina, where he did, or Rutgers; but he won't stand in the way if I want to be a doctor. And he feels the same way Ron and I do—find a decent campus that has some moral standards, even if it isn't a top-rated school. He would like it best if I could afford the higher tuition costs to go to a Christian college, such as Wofford or Pfeiffer. But I don't want to go so far from home."

Linda shivered. "It scares me silly to think of going through those decisions soon myself! Maybe I'll decide to stay home and be a farmer," she said pensively. "I love nature and can't bear the thought of being cooped up in a stuffy building all the time. But I suppose I probably will go into science of some kind. Wouldn't Mom be embarrassed to have a farmer for a daughter!" Linda laughed at the thought.

"Why must girls go to college anyway?" Linda asked after a while. "Probably all I'll ever be is a housewife, and if I marry a farmer, I'll help my husband on the farm. Just like Mom. What do all her years of study profit her now?"

"Oh . . . you need *culture,*" Larry quipped, "or you'll be a nobody! Or, like our teachers all cram into us, you have to get a good education to be able to make a *living!*"

"Don't you believe that?" Linda asked, observing Larry's sarcasm.

"Oh, I suppose; I guess we have to. That's all we ever hear!" Larry turned his Corvair up their long lane.

Linda was gazing out at the row of pointed poplar trees that lined the lane. "Do you ever think about God? Or about finding God's will for your life?" she asked suddenly. "You know, Pastor Baker preaches like that. And sometimes I read the Bible, and I wonder what part it should play in a person's life. If we are Christians, shouldn't we think more about things like that?"

Larry hesitated a bit; then he said, "I must confess, I don't think too much about it. I believe in God, but I always thought He expects us to look out for ourselves the best we can. I suppose He is too busy to worry about the petty little things that trouble us humans, the things we should be figuring out for ourselves."

"This research paper I'm doing—I've uncovered some interesting facts," Linda responded. "Today I was reading about a group that came out of the other Protestant groups during the time of the Reformation. They were called Anabaptists. From what I was reading, their one desire was to live according to the Bible. Many of them were killed for their faith because they refused to go along with the state church. I had to wonder if they have descendants around anywhere today."

"I wouldn't know," Larry said thoughtfully. "There are lots of Baptists, but I don't know who the Anabaptists would be. But come now, we're good, church-going folks; isn't that good enough?" Larry drove carefully into the garage and parked his Corvair.

Linda lapsed into silence as she collected her research papers off the seat beside her. Why did she often feel that her church did not completely satisfy? She was sure that her pastor was a good man, and she loved his dear daughter. And she was happy. Life was good; she had many friends and a wonderful family. But something was missing. She often thought about it. But if she spoke about her feelings to others, it seemed they did not understand. Would she ever know what that something was that seemed to be missing in her life?

# 3

Sunday mornings were always lazy mornings at the Asbury farm. Sunday school did not start till nine-thirty, so the usual weekday morning rush was missing. It was the one morning of the week that Linda slept in—if sleeping till six o'clock instead of five o'clock could be called sleeping in! She had always been an early riser, while Loretta could sleep till noon if Mom would let her. One thing that Dad and Mom definitely agreed on was that lying in bed was nothing but laziness. And as for Linda, she could never lie in bed when she could be outside enjoying the sights and sounds of nature, especially on such a wonderful spring morning as this.

This Sunday morning Linda dressed quickly and took a walk out through the orchard. A robin was singing at the top of a pear tree, and a mockingbird went through his repertoire from a maple tree in the yard.

Linda climbed onto her own perch on a huge, low-hanging horizontal branch of an old, sprawling apple tree. Ever since she was a little girl, this apple tree had been her private refuge. Here she often brought a book for a leisurely Sunday afternoon of reading. Or here she often came just to be alone with her thoughts. This was her tree. She looked protectively at the gnarled branches poking stiffly upward all around her. Her father had often threatened to cut this tree down. It hardly bore any fruit anymore, and he said it was not worth the space it took up. But always Linda had pleaded for it; this tree was like a personal friend. How could she bear to see it made into firewood?

Hugging her jacket around her, she let her thoughts drift again to her never-ending fascination for *spring!* As far as she could see, new green grass shoots were springing out of the remnants of last year's thatch. Everywhere, buds were bursting into pastel pinks and rosy reds. In the distance, she could see rows beginning to show where Dad had planted corn two weeks before. As she sat silently, a rabbit sprang to life almost directly under her and nibbled daintily among the leaves in a clover patch.

*What is the meaning of all this?* she wondered, as she often did. *We learn in church that God set all these laws of times and seasons. And yet at school the science books teach that all this wonderful creation just happened to come to be after eons and eons of time . . . How could anyone believe such far-fetched fantasy as that? To me, all nature seems to speak of a wonderful and loving Creator who wanted to give the best gifts to a people whom He made to love Him in return . . .*

*What is life?* she continued to muse. *Is it like Shakespeare says in* Macbeth? She thought of the words that the literature class had recently needed to memorize:

Life's but a walking shadow, a poor player
That struts and frets his hour upon the stage
And then is heard no more: it is a tale
Told by an idiot, full of sound and fury,
Signifying nothing.

Linda's thoughts continued. *Life is more than that; life comes from God. It is a gift to us, to be filled with meaning and purpose and finally to return to Him. It can't be that we all came about just by accident!* Linda reached up and broke off an apple twig, decorated up and down on each side with delicate pink buds. *I can't believe that something so wonderful and intricate as this came about by happenstance.* She carefully peeled open a tiny bud, revealing petal after petal of delicate beauty. *In this bud is the apple and all the life of future trees, each bearing fruit after its kind,* she pondered, remembering a Bible verse she had read. *If God took so much interest in the intricate beauty of an apple blossom, which is just for a little time, how much more must He be interested in* me—*in all people, who, the Bible says, are made in His likeness! But why was I born? What purpose is there for me in life? How can I find that out, and how can I know Him?*

The apple twig dropped to the ground, and the startled bunny raced away. Linda hardly noticed. *If only there was someone I could talk to,* she thought, *someone who would understand and help me find answers.* She thought of Andrea, the pastor's daughter and her closest friend. They shared many things and occasionally even talked about spiritual things. But there was always a sort of stiffness when the conversation drifted to spiritual matters, as though this was not quite familiar ground to either one of them.

Some of her friends at school talked about being "born again," especially some that went to the Revival Tabernacle on Center Street. Well, even Pastor Baker used that term occasionally in his sermons, as though everybody ought to know what it was all about. But what *did* it mean? Would the people out at the Revival Tabernacle know something about it? But then, Mom mocked the people who went there. She said that it was only the lower-class people who went to that church, and she would not allow Linda to go when her friends from there invited her to special meetings.

And Linda wondered sometimes what was really different about the people that went to the Revival Tabernacle. They did not smoke, drink, or go to dances or the movies, but in other ways they did not act any different from many others. Some of them got angry or talked back if insulted, some cheated, and some were wild in other ways. So really, what was the difference? Mom said that their religion was just for Sundays, when they would get all excited and jump around in the aisles, shouting and crying and singing. But come Monday, she would scoff, they acted just as sinful as anybody else. *Is Mom right?* Linda wondered.

Larry's whistle quickly recalled Linda to reality. She hopped out of her perch and stooped under the apple tree branches to see the house. Larry was standing on the back porch, looking her way. Seeing her, he motioned for her to come in. It must be time for breakfast already! The church bells began to ring in the distance as she walked back through the orchard to the house.

As usual, they got to church promptly at nine-fifteen. To Dad, any time after that was not acceptable, even though Sunday school did not start till nine-thirty.

After the Sunday school hour, Linda looked down from her place in the choir loft at the rest of the extended family in the Asbury pew. It was seldom that Linda's family got to sit together with the others. Linda and Larry both sang in the choir, and often Mom played the organ. Dad was one of the deacons, so sometimes he had business to take care of that kept him busy during part of the service. But there were always Grandma and Grandpa Asbury, and Great-aunt Hettie, and Uncle Bob and Aunt Evelyn. Loretta was sitting between Grandma and Grandpa, as she often did, especially if none of the other family members were able to be there. Sometimes some of the married cousins also helped to fill the pew when they came for visits.

Across the aisle from the Asburys was Mom's family, the Joneses. And they were the kind—Linda thought again of the old saying—that people tried to keep up with! She noticed Mam-mam's carefully styled hair and her expensive, tailored suit. Dangling white pearl earrings and a pearl necklace set off her dark ensemble. How aware of herself she looked as she gazed steadily forward, her head lifted high on her graceful neck. Mam-mam was at least sixty-five, Linda knew, but she tried her best to keep a youthful look. Linda smiled inside as she thought of Mam-mam tottering around on her spike heels, determined not to be outdone by the fashionable young girls. Pap-pap sat rigidly beside her, scarcely less proud. After all, was he not one of the most successful businessmen in Springville?

Mam-mam and Pap-pap Jones were not the sweet old couple that Grandpa Asbury's were. Somehow, Linda never felt comfortable at the Joneses' house; it was far too fine for children, or even teenagers, to feel at home in. Their house was one of the elegant, old, ivy-covered homes out at the end of Main Street, complete with cook and gardener quarters in the rear.

Linda had always felt happier running around the gardens and flower beds, where Joe was usually busy working. Old Joe and Mamie had been almost as dear to Linda when she was a little girl as her stiff and proper grandparents were! How she had always loved the old black couple. When Mam-mam and Pap-pap were busy entertaining their important guests, Joe would gladly entertain the busy little girl with his many stories as he pulled weeds in the gardens or trimmed the flowering shrubs. Or Linda would follow Mamie about the huge old kitchen, watching her roll out biscuits or crusts for sweet potato pie. Mamie had been "Mammie" to Linda's childish tongue, and Mammie she always was thereafter, to the consternation of Mam-mam!

It was different with Grandpa Asbury's. They lived in a bungalow not a mile from the farm, and Linda remembered many a pleasant day helping Grandma with her various gardening tasks or with her little chores about the house. The house always smelled wonderfully of cedar and mothballs. Surely a moth could never survive in that house, Linda remembered thinking many a time as a young girl. And Grandpa kept a horse in the little barn behind the house—a gentle one, just right for the grandchildren to ride.

Below the long, sloping yard was a pond. Linda had many memories of fishing there with Grandpa. And she remembered the first time that she rode the horse by herself. For some reason, old Maude had taken the notion to gallop down to the pond and take a good, long drink. Linda hung on for dear life, fearful of sliding down the mare's long neck into the water. Even now she could remember how funny she had felt, and she squelched the laugh that wanted to rise up in her. Grandpa's yard was a wonderful place for romping and playing. A long swing hung from a high branch of a huge old maple. And the croquet game or horseshoes were set up many a Sunday afternoon.

These thoughts flitted through Linda's mind as she sat with the other sopranos in the choir loft and watched the worshipers file into their pews. There came old Grammy Riley with her hat on as usual, Linda noticed. *Many of the older women wear hats to church, but the younger women don't. I wonder why. And all the women wear dresses to church, even though I know many of them wear pants through the week.*

Suddenly Andrea nudged Linda. "What are you thinking about?" she whispered with a grin. "Get ready to sing!" Immediately Mom, who was sitting at the organ, broke into a prelude. Choir robes rustled as the choir stood up to sing the two opening numbers. Soon the beautiful strains of the song "Oh, for a Thousand Tongues to Sing" broke over the gathered worshipers.

The highlight of the service that particular morning was the announcement Pastor Baker made at the end of his sermon. "There is something I would like to share with the congregation this morning," he began. "I have been offered the church in Millburg, Pennsylvania, which is my hometown. Our family has certainly enjoyed the many years here at Springville, but naturally you can understand the attraction that this offer holds for me . . ."

Linda sat up straight and stared blankly at Pastor Baker. What was he saying? She could think of only one thing: if Pastor Baker left the area, it meant that Andrea would also leave. Andrea, who had been her best friend ever since . . . was it third grade? Dear lively and lovely Andrea, with her sweet personality. How could she ever live without her dear friend?

"Oh, Andrea," Linda gasped, turning to her friend as soon as the benediction was pronounced, "what will I do if you-all move away?"

Andrea clasped Linda's hands. "I've worried

about it ever since Daddy told us. And I didn't want to mention it to you, knowing how final it all sounds! Why, we'll be three hundred miles away—up in the mountains of Pennsylvania! My only hope is that the board of trustees will refuse Daddy's request. And yet, his heart is so set on it. Grandpa died and left us the farm, and Daddy always wanted to live on a farm. So he thinks this is a wonderful answer to prayer for him . . . being able to raise his family on a farm *and* preach."

"I'm sure he does feel it is an answer to prayer, and it probably is. Well, we still have today," Linda stated practically. "What shall we do? Want to come out to my house?"

And so, as soon as the lunch dishes were finished, the girls ambled out the long field lane. Taking a shortcut, they climbed over the fence and strolled across the pasture, where fat Jersey cows lay chewing their cuds in the lush rye grass. Soon they came to the tall pines at the edge of the forest and climbed over the fence again. As they entered the woods road, all nature was alive with song. Even the breeze was singing in the tops of the pines. They stepped softly along in the cushiony mat made by many seasons of fallen pine needles, chatting animatedly. Linda felt as if she must talk fast while she still had her friend near her!

On they walked to the river, where a little pier that Dad had made when the children were small jutted out over the slowly moving current. They sat on the edge, dangling their feet over the water, watching the sunbeams play on the ripples. Occasionally a sunfish or a perch would jump out of the water, creating a new circle of ripples. Dad's little motorboat rocked gently nearby, moored to the pier. Another wooden boat was upended against a nearby pine tree. Linda liked to use that one when she went out on the water because she could row it, and there was no motor to frighten the little mallards swimming with their parents over the endless ripples.

Softly Andrea quoted:

I have a rendezvous with beauty
    When spring comes back upon the hills;
I have a thousand new enchantments
    To fill my eyes and ears with thrills.

I'll hear the meadowlarks and bluebirds
    And listen to a laughing stream
Set free from winter's gloomy prison,
    Sparkling in the sun's warm gleam.

I have a rendezvous with beauty—
    A dream to hold through ice and snow,
That waits my ever-eager longing,
    Spring's wonders freely to bestow.

Will you who love the fresh, rare glory
　　On hill and meadow, flower and tree,
Come away in awe and rapture
　　To keep that rendezvous with me?
　　　　　　　　　*—Edna Greene Hines*

Andrea laughed. "The ice-and-snow part of that poem doesn't quite fit with this part of the country, but still it has a lot of pretty thoughts. It will fit better when we move to Pennsylvania; there we'll have hills, and ice and snow . . ."

"It is a nice poem. I enjoyed it too when we learned it in school—was it in eighth grade?" Linda sighed deeply. "I love it out here, Andrea. Everything seems so simple when you're in a quiet woods, on a Sunday afternoon, with the blue-green river flowing by."

"I know what you mean," Andrea said. "But I can't *say* it poetically like you can. I can only *quote* poetry!"

Linda looked dreamily out over the peaceful river, flowing calmly by in the stillness. "Why must life change?" she wondered soberly. "We have been so happy, going to school and church and everywhere together for so many years. Who will ever share all my little secrets and mistakes as you have? You have been a wonderful friend." A sob in her throat suddenly felt as if it would choke her. She must cheer up; this would never do!

"I will miss you too, Linda," Andrea replied

with sincerity in her voice.

"Oh, we can't spread gloom like this on such a gorgeous day! We can write letters, and we can visit each other, can't we?" Linda stated optimistically. "You aren't going to the other side of the world!"

"And we can still get together at the summer youth conferences . . ." Andrea began. Then she stopped short with a sudden remembrance. "You know what? I just thought of it—I don't think Daddy will care if I tell you. Daddy met a minister at the youth conference when we were there last summer that he thought would be just the man to replace him here, a Pastor Kelloway. Daddy turned his name in to the church board. I hope the board decides to ask him."

"But I don't really want anybody but your dad to be our pastor," Linda said. "Who else could take his place? Or yours?"

"You will grow to appreciate another pastor too, Linda, I'm sure. You will like Pastor Kelloway's family," Andrea assured her. "He has a kind-faced wife and four beautiful children. Not really children . . . the oldest boy, Steve, is probably seventeen."

*A pastor with a son my age . . . Steve Kelloway . . .* Linda sat thoughtfully. She thought about the boys at school. She knew them all—their possibilities or their lack of them. She could not think of one that interested her more than as a friend. As any normal girl, she wondered sometimes whom she might end up with in marriage. But she knew of no one who even remotely fit her ideal in that way! What kind of young man was this Steve Kelloway? Might he be a different stripe than the kind she was used to? Was he interested in the things that really mattered in life? Could he share in an intellectual way? Or was he, like most of the boys she knew, just another joker going over fool's hill?

# 4

Only two more months of school! Linda loved school, but when spring came with all its enchantment, there was no place like the farm. And so the days could hardly pass fast enough till once more she would be at home for the summer, basking in the joy of outdoor chores day after day.

But for now, there were studies. Then would come finals. And there must be no slackening in diligence, or someone else might take her place at the top of the class.

Linda and Andrea were chatting as they got their Latin books out of their lockers. "How many pages of Virgil did you get translated?" Andrea asked as she stuck the book *Aeneid,* by the Latin poet Virgil, on top of her stack.

"Mr. Taylor assigned four pages," Linda returned. "I did six because I knew I wouldn't have as much time this evening, with band practice after school."

"Who do you think will go to Williamstown for the statewide Latin tournament?" Andrea asked. "I know I have no chance for it. Virgil and

I aren't the greatest of friends!"

"I surely don't care about it; I hope Chester Dorsey gets to go. He's really good in Latin and deserves some claim to fame," Linda said laughingly.

They were joined by Mary Catherine Carmean and Patsy Jefferson. "What are you two planning now?" Mary Catherine demanded.

"We weren't talking to you, if you don't mind," Andrea replied tartly.

"You two country bumpkins have big ideas, don't you, talking about Latin tournaments? Ha! You should be talking about cows and forking manure and the likes. Oh, what lovely smells such thoughts bring to mind," Mary Catherine taunted, turning up her pert little nose. "Lovely farm perfumes like you and your wonderful brother wear to scent our city classrooms, Linda. Ha, ha, ha!"

Linda laughed. " 'Any fool will despise that which he cannot get.' " She quoted the moral from Aesop's famous sour-grape fable, knowing very well the reason for Mary Catherine's scorn of her brother.

Mary Catherine gave Linda a long look of indignation. "Oh, how brilliant we are today!" she returned scathingly. She paused and pompously scanned them both from head to toe. "And for your information," she continued, "*I* plan to be the one chosen to go to the tournament, and I plan to win first place as well!"

Linda glanced at Andrea, and together they began walking toward classroom 20. "Let's take the long way around," Andrea murmured, "and give her time to get to class before we get there."

When they were out of earshot, Linda sighed. "Oh, why did we even answer her, Andrea? We both know how mean Mary Catherine and her bunch are."

"Well, anyway," Andrea returned, "Mary Catherine is always picking on us—you especially. Because even with all her cheating, she can't get ahead of you. And I don't doubt at all but that she'll work things her way so that she will go to the tournament. You know how she keeps trying to work her way into Mr. Taylor's favor. And not only that, but Mary Catherine always knows how to get inside information as to what to expect on the test, as well!

"Well, here we are, for an hour of Virgil," she added in an undertone as the girls reached the classroom door. "I think I will welcome taking French for the next two years!" The girls slipped into their seats just as the last bell rang.

Mary Catherine turned around and fixed a mean stare on them. Andrea returned the stare coolly. *Andrea has a lot of nerve!* Linda thought, shivering to her very toes as she contemplated what revenge Mary Catherine might even now be plotting. *But then I, not Andrea, get the brunt of Mary Catherine's anger!* Mary Catherine had to turn to the front when Mr. Taylor called the class to order. But Linda knew they had not heard the last from her.

From Latin class, Linda went to geometry, while Andrea went to Algebra II. Red Ziller fell into step with Linda as they were leaving the geometry classroom. "Did you say something to your dad about whether he could use some help on the farm?" he asked Linda, his ready smile lighting up his cheerful face.

"Yes, I did, and he said you should call him. He seemed glad for the offer," Linda answered.

"Oh, great!" Red exclaimed. "I just love the farm and was sure hoping your dad would need help! That kind of work will keep me in shape for football tryouts next fall, eh?" He laughed, tossing a heavy lock of red hair off his forehead.

Linda laughed with him as she glanced at the hearty, stocky boy beside her. He surely did not appear to need farm work to build muscles, she was thinking. Red stopped off at his next class. "See you later," he said genially.

Linda walked down the hall to her next class, U.S. History, taught by Mr. Sharp. Linda thoroughly loathed both the class and the man. It seemed that no matter how hard she tried, she just could not enjoy history with a teacher who seemed to favor the dishonest students above those who conscientiously did their best. It was in this class that Mary Catherine excelled. Linda was thankful that not all teachers were like Mr. Sharp. His favorite pastimes seemed to be either curling the ends of his handlebar mustache or ogling the girls with his mean, close-set little eyes.

And then after that came music, her favorite class of the day. The days would alternate between music appreciation—a study of the classics as well as contemporary music—and glee club. Since music was an elective, most of the students in the class had a genuine interest in the study as well as in singing. Linda and Andrea sat together and shared this special time of the day.

"Isn't Beethoven wonderful?" Andrea said as a group of girls walked together from music class to the dining room.

"Give me Peter, Paul, and Mary," said Molly Westfield. "'How many times must a man look around . . .'" She sang several lines from a popular folk group.

"Frankly, I like the Beach Boys better," stated Lynne Johnson.

"Or Fats Domino," said Charlotte Carver, her face dimpling in a jolly laugh.

"I think much of their music is so empty and vulgar," Linda stated seriously and emphatically. "Besides, Dad would never let us children listen to it, and I'm thankful he drew some lines."

"What do you listen to then, if you don't listen to popular music?" Charlotte asked.

Linda thought for a moment. "Well, Dad always says he wants us to learn to enjoy 'enduring' music. Take the 'Hallelujah Chorus' from Handel's *Messiah* that we sang for the Christmas program, for instance. Where could you find anything more uplifting? The words say something—something wholesome and strengthening. Listening to such music brings out the best in a person, rather than the worst!"

"I know what you mean." Andrea sang some phrases, mimicking the singers of several popular songs. "What good is there in words like that? They should make decent people sick!"

"There is some truth in what you say. I'm sure my mother would agree with you," Charlotte conceded. "But something about the forlornness of country music, or the beat of rock 'n' roll, gets to me, and I want it more and more!"

"Those are reasons Dad always gave for *not* listening to it. Now that I'm older, I realize more what he meant," Linda said. "Another thing Dad said was that the beat and lyrics of rock 'n' roll act just like a drug and dull one's mind so that he can't even think decent thoughts."

"Didn't Mr. Cruz say one day in class that communist countries have outlawed rock 'n' roll because of what it does to the young people?" Andrea asked. "I think he said the leaders felt it takes control of the people's minds, and they don't want anything controlling the minds of their people except Communism!"

"Yes, I remember that," Linda said. Then she added, in a serious tone of voice, "Girls, I can think of much better ways to use my mind than to have it warped by such nonsense."

The girls leisurely strolled into the cafeteria, still airing their views. After getting their trays, they joined several other friends at a table in the back of the dining room. As always, Linda and Andrea bowed their heads in silent prayer. The other girls waited respectfully; then everyone started on their spaghetti and meatballs.

As Charlotte and Linda walked to home economics class after lunch, Charlotte confided, "Linda, I am so glad for a friend like you. You stick up for what you feel is right, no matter what others say. That is what makes you special to so many of us girls."

The warm feeling those words of praise brought to Linda somewhat helped to allay the dread of Mary Catherine's revenge. For Mary Catherine would seek revenge, of that she was sure! And it would be mean and hurtful.

The next class was English and literature. How Linda enjoyed sitting in Mrs. Whittleson's classes. She was a thorough and capable teacher, expecting and accepting nothing less than the best from her scholars. Today's assignment had been to write an original poem. For this class period, Mrs. Whittleson was expecting each student to read his own poem in class. But when Linda tried to find hers, she could not locate it anywhere. She looked through her literature book again and then in her notebook. But it just was not there! Had it dropped out of her notebook somewhere between here and her last class?

She had written it using the title "Faint Not But Face the Future Fearlessly" and was satisfied that she had done a good job. But where was it? And what would Mrs. Whittleson say when she did not have it to read?

"Linda Asbury," Mrs. Whittleson called.

Linda started. Of course she would be almost first, since her name started with *A*. "I'm sorry, Mrs. Whittleson. I had my assignment finished, but I cannot find it," she said simply.

Mrs. Whittleson looked at her sharply; it was not like Linda to lose her assignments. "We'll go on with the others, and we'll hear yours later after you find it," she said finally.

Linda sat inertly. Why look anymore? It simply was not there. She listened as others read their poems. Then it was Mary Catherine's turn.

Mary Catherine stood erect and read the title: " 'Faint Not But Face the Future Fearlessly.' " She glanced impressively around the class. Then she read the poem . . .

Linda stared at Mary Catherine in disbelief. *That's my poem!* she thought almost out loud. *How did she get her hands on it? And when?* As Mary Catherine sat down, she glanced triumphantly at Linda.

*Now what shall I do?* Linda wondered. *I can tell Mrs. Whittleson, but it's my word against Mary Catherine's. It's typed, so there is no handwriting to give away her lie . . .* Linda continued to ponder.

She left class, wondering what she could ever do about her assignment. Close behind her, Mary Catherine hissed, "If you say a word, you'll be in bigger trouble than you've ever been before in your life, Miss Linda Asbury! Remember, my dad is on the school board, and yours isn't!"

That touched off something in Linda. "Well, truth is truth, no matter who you think you are or who your father is! Of course I will tell Mrs. Whittleson," Linda said with vehemence. She turned and went back to the classroom.

Mrs. Whittleson listened closely. "I believe you, Linda," she said. "That poem didn't sound like the kind of thing that Mary Catherine would have written. Let me take care of this."

"Thank you so much," Linda said, relief spreading over her.

Linda hurried down the hall to the gym, hoping she would not be tardy for physical education class. Thankfully, Mary Catherine was not in that class. Some of her set were; but without Mary Catherine, they were bearable.

The girls enjoyed a lively game of field hockey and then hurried in to shower before their next classes. The time spent outdoors had been invigorating, and Linda went to chemistry class, ready to face its challenges.

Yesterday Mr. Lapseg had announced a lab class for today. He would give each student a beaker with an unidentified substance. Using the various tests they had learned through the year, they were to identify what was in the beaker.

To Linda's dismay, Mary Catherine claimed the spot next to her as everybody found a place to work in the lab. "You don't mind, of course, if I work beside the brain of the chemistry class?" Mary Catherine asked sweetly.

Linda wondered what she was up to, but decided to keep silent.

She did not wonder long. As she was concentrating on one of the tests, she suddenly felt a wetness and a burning on her arm that was resting on the counter. "Oh, Mr. Lapseg!" Mary Catherine wailed. "I upset my container of acetic acid, and I'm afraid some got on Linda!"

Linda rushed out the door to the restroom and yanked her arm out of her blouse sleeve. Quickly lowering her arm into a sink, she let the water run over the burning skin. It felt like fire.

She looked at her dangling sleeve and imagined that the acid would make holes where it had soaked through. But that did not matter so much right now; what was more important was, what would it do to her skin? At least it was the last class of the day, and she would not have to wear the ruined blouse for a day of classes! She could just put her jacket on for band practice after school.

Andrea came hurrying into the restroom. “What a mean trick!” she exploded. “Mr. Lapseg sent me over to see if you need help. And he sent this antidote to put on your arm,” she added.

“It *could* have been worse!” Linda laughed as she gently patted her arm dry with paper towels. “She could have spilled *sulfuric* acid on me!”

“And she would have been mean enough to do it, if she’d had access to it!” Andrea stated vehemently.

“Please do me a favor, Andrea, and don’t scold Mary Catherine for this,” Linda pleaded as Andrea carefully rubbed the ointment on Linda’s red arm. “Everyone in the class will know she did it on purpose, and she’ll get her punishment without our saying a word. Promise me?”

“Well, all right. But only because you insist!”

After school Linda and several friends walked to the music room as other students were rushing out to the waiting buses. Linda played the clarinet and Larry the trombone in the band, so neither rode home on the bus that day. "Have you learned the new song for music class tomorrow?" Lynne asked the girls.

" 'No man is an island . . . ,' " sang Raye Gibbons. The girls were singing their parts in harmony as they walked into the music room. Mr. Cruz looked up with a smile of approval as they got their instruments out of the supply closet.

As Larry and Linda drove home after practice, Linda told him about her day's encounters with Mary Catherine.

"What a character she is!" Larry exclaimed. "But don't do anything to her, sis. Everything will come out right in the end."

"I don't intend to try to get even. It wouldn't do me any good anyway," Linda responded. "I just wish Mary Catherine Carmean would *leave me alone!*"

Larry guided his little Corvair through the narrow back streets to the edge of town. "Well, don't let her meanness bother you," he said.

"I wish we wouldn't have to tell the folks at home," Linda said. She slipped off her jacket and, holding out her arm, looked at the frayed holes in her blouse sleeve. "But Mom will wonder what happened to this good blouse!"

"Well, maybe it would be good for Mom to realize that some of her hoity-toity friends don't have such nice daughters!" Larry responded with a short laugh.

They drove out the country road, and soon they were at home. It felt good to think of the security of home! *What a day this has been,* thought Linda. *I hope tomorrow is a better one than this!*

# 5

The next Tuesday morning in Latin class, Mr. Taylor made the announcement. "Linda Asbury has been chosen by the language department to represent our school at the state Latin tournament." He looked at Linda with a nod and a smile.

Linda sat in shocked silence. She did not want to represent Springville High School in a statewide language contest! Latin was not that easy for her in the first place. Nor did she relish the idea of being with so many strangers; she was sure she would forget everything she knew. More than that, most of the other contestants would likely be seniors, since most schools started Latin in ninth grade. Their county was the only one in the state in which the schools started Latin in seventh grade.

As soon as class was over, she went to Mr. Taylor's desk. "Thank you, sir, for the honor you have given me. But I really would prefer that someone else be chosen."

"What is your objection, Linda?" Mr. Taylor asked kindly.

"Your announcement came as a surprise to me. I had hoped someone like Chester Dorsey could go. He is good at Latin, and situations like this don't ruffle him. I'm afraid I would make an utter fool of myself and bring shame to our school as well."

"I appreciate your expressing yourself, and I understand your feeling, but as a faculty we felt that you would do well. Between now and the tournament, I will be coaching you as to what to expect. And you will do just fine," Mr. Taylor assured her.

"Well, if that is the way you feel, sir, I will try to do my best," Linda said, resigning herself to more study in her already crammed spring schedule.

"Deborah Riley will also be going, as the representative from the senior class, for French," Mr. Taylor added as Linda turned to leave.

*She will do well; she is really good in French . . . but ME!* Linda left the classroom in a sort of daze. *Why was I chosen when probably at least three in the class are better in Latin than I am?*

Andrea and Charlotte were eagerly waiting for her in the hall. "What an honor!" Charlotte exclaimed as the girls started for the next class. "I'm proud of you!"

"I should think you would feel honored," Andrea added.

"You wouldn't feel honored if it were *you!*" Linda stated. "I surely wish there were a way I could get out of it."

"I enjoyed the look of astonishment on Mary Catherine's face when Mr. Taylor made the announcement," Andrea said, laughing.

"Well, I'm not looking forward to what she will *say!*" Linda returned.

But the most astounding thing was that Mary Catherine did not say a word. Whether she was subdued after the apology that Mrs. Whittleson had made her give before the whole English class, or whether she was merely plotting another line of attack, Linda was not sure.

Linda settled down that evening in front of the fireplace with her Latin textbook and notes. The fire in the fireplace sizzled and crackled, curling around the pungent pine logs and making the whole room pleasantly toasty and cozy. Linda tried her best to think through verb conjugations and all the other rules and exceptions that she had learned the past four years. *There are so many other things I would rather be doing!* she thought ruefully. *I really must work on my term paper. It's due in a few weeks, and I still have the final copy to type up.*

Her term paper. Her mind drifted to her study on the Reformation, and how interesting it was to sort through the beliefs of the various churches that had emerged from it. She thought again about the group that had caught her attention—the Anabaptists. Linda had learned that when they started, others called them "Ana-baptists," which means "to baptize again," because they baptized only believers, not babies, and therefore rebaptized adult believers who had been baptized as infants. They said the Bible taught that churches must be made up of only those who are "born again" and who choose to be part of the church as committed followers of Christ and His teaching. Because of this, they were driven out of the state churches and had to meet in secret in fields and forests. The Catholics, as well as some Protestant groups, hated them. They read the Bible diligently and claimed the Bible as their only rule for belief and practice.

The Anabaptists believed that the church and state must be separate. They believed that Christians must not go to war or resist evil, because Jesus said His followers are to love their enemies. They did not swear, because Jesus said, "Swear not at all." Because of their firm conviction that Christians must be obedient to the Bible, they were persecuted by Catholics and Protestants alike. But in spite of severe persecution, their numbers increased greatly. A young Catholic priest from Holland was converted to their way. His name was Menno Simons. He became a powerful preacher who helped many to become faithful followers of the Bible. He was also a capable leader who helped to organize the many scattered groups of believers. After a while, many Anabaptists were called "Menno-nites."

Linda had read an account about a young Mennonite woman named Elizabeth, and she had included it in her paper. She could not help but cry as she thought that likely Elizabeth had been about her own age. It went like this:

> On the 15th of January in the year 1549, Elizabeth was taken. The examiner asked her on oath if she had a husband.
>
> She answered: "I cannot take an oath. All I can say is yes or no!"
>
> "What persons have you taught?"
>
> "I cannot tell you. I will confess my faith."
>
> "We will torture you."
>
> "I hope that with God's help I shall keep my tongue and not be a traitor."
>
> "What do you think of the Most Holy Sacrament?"
>
> "I have never in my life read in the Bible of a Most Holy Sacrament. I have read only of the Lord's Supper."
>
> "Why have you been baptized again?"
>
> "I haven't been baptized again. I have simply been baptized."
>
> "Do you think baptism saves you?"
>
> "No. All the water in the sea cannot save me. Christ saves me."

> Then they tortured her with thumbscrews till the blood gushed from her nails and she fainted. Coming to herself, she would not give in. Then she was sentenced in the year 1549 on the 27th of March to be put to death by drowning.*

Linda wondered if any such people were still around. Or had they all disappeared in the centuries since the Reformation? She knew about Quakers, and she had read articles and seen an occasional television program about the Amish. She had always thought of the Amish as a quaint, cultural group. But maybe they *were* spiritual, Bible-believing people.

Then Linda thought about the time last summer when she and Loretta had gone with Dad to the Delmarva livestock auction. Linda did not remember ever having been there before. While sitting in the auction barn, Linda had looked around and seen scores of black-hatted, strangely dressed men sitting on the bleachers.

Later when she and Loretta had gone to the restroom building, they encountered dozens of boys dressed in the same manner. She had also noticed girls who must have been of the same religious group as the boys. When Linda had asked Dad about them, he had said, "They are a religious group called Amish. No doubt they

---

* *The Church of Our Fathers,* by Roland Bainton

try to live in obedience to the Scriptures as they understand them."

*The Amish,* Linda thought now, *according to church history, began well. Are they a group with an Anabaptist background who* are *still faithful?*

Linda, sitting on the carpet as she watched the glowing fire, shifted restlessly. The floor did get hard after a while! With a sigh, she brought her mind back to the present and, picking up her Latin notebook, began to scan the pages of notes, wondering what she should be concentrating on for the coming tournament. But it was hard for her to focus on Latin. Thinking about her term paper topic was much more to her liking.

For the next weeks, Linda, along with the rest of her class, was busy getting her term paper ready to hand in. During the same time, the junior and senior classes were preoccupied with planning the annual junior–senior prom. The theme for that year was *Some Enchanted Evening.* And now, for the past week, preparations were going on full speed to change the gymnasium into a wonderland! As a senior, Larry was caught in the dizzy air of excitement all around him. But as the prom night drew closer, he seriously considered not attending. Even though the principal always saw to it that there was plenty of adult supervision, Larry knew from his experience the year before that things could get pretty much out of hand.

Ron Bradford was astounded that Larry would think of missing this last big dance of their high-school days. "You surely aren't going to stay home and play checkers on such a big night, are you, Larry?" he asked.

"Checkers? Well now . . . Tell you what, Ron. I know of a place where some big bass seem to be jumping. Bring your rod, and we'll make an evening of it."

Alberta was very upset, to put it mildly, when Linda told her that Larry would not be going to the prom, and that she herself did not plan to go either.

"What has gotten into your head lately, Linda?" she asked indignantly. Linda was the one at hand, and so she had to take the brunt of her mother's anger. "You seem to think that you know better what is good for you than your parents and your teachers!"

"But, Mom," Linda countered, "do you know what goes on at the prom? It might sound like a nice, quiet party to you. And maybe it was when you went to high school. But it isn't anymore. Do you realize how immodest some of the girls appear?"

"You can wear whatever you want to wear," Mom retorted heatedly. "You don't have to wear what the others wear!"

"But even worse than that," Linda went on,

"it is one night of the year that even many of the nice students do things that they later regret. Larry said that the party doesn't stop when the students leave school. And I've heard enough of the wilder students talking about the kinds of things that go on that I don't want anything to do with it! Many couples go and get drunk afterward and spend the night in revelry. Is that really what you want your children to be involved in? Don't you want us to behave ourselves?"

"Well, couldn't you come home after the actual prom is over at the school? You wouldn't need to be involved with all that goes on afterward." Mom was somewhat softened but still miffed that her children chose not to be involved in the kind of social events that were so important to her.

"Larry did think about doing that," Linda said. "But then he and Ron decided to just stay away, rather than be there and be caught up in the excitement of the evening and possibly be carried away with it. And I think their choice was a wise one."

Linda left the kitchen to avoid facing any more of her mother's anger and criticism. Her heart was heavy as she went outside to help with the barn chores. Were she and Larry, after all, being ridiculous in all this?

Mom may have been upset, but dear Dad

understood perfectly the way Larry and Linda felt. They shared their thoughts with him that evening as they worked in the barn together. He commended them for having the courage to stand alone. Linda's heart was set free of its questionings and again endeared to her father; he always understood and supported them when they followed their consciences rather than the crowd.

Loretta was another case. She lay across Linda's bed that night, her hair tightly done up in curlers for the next day. She watched as Linda combed out her long auburn hair. "Oh, Linda, I'm so jealous of your pretty hair! With your naturally curly hair, you don't need to mess around with curlers and perms like I do. Life just ain't fair!"

"Why, Loretta, how silly of you," Linda responded unbelievingly, feeling it was *Loretta* who had everything going for her as far as looks. "You wouldn't *have* to set your hair, you know."

"I'd look horrible if I didn't," she retorted.

Then she sighed. "I can't believe you and Larry," she continued. "You two are missing out on all the fun if you don't go to the prom! And to think that you, a sophomore, even had the privilege of being asked—and you refused! I thought you always loved to dance. Remember how after the May dance last year a lot of the students talked about you and Barry Engle dancing around the Maypole?" she said, laughing.

"Oh, please don't mention that!" Linda begged. "I was so ashamed later of how we showed off!"

"Well, anyway, I surely won't be the one to miss out on something so important as the prom!" Loretta assured Linda. "All the girls are talking about what goody-goodies you and Larry are. It embarrasses me!"

"Let them talk," Linda answered nonchalantly, assured of her stand after the encouraging talk with Dad. "Talk won't hurt Larry or me. And it won't hurt you either. Furthermore, if you don't learn to stand for some things, you'll get yourself into a heap of trouble somewhere along the way, believe me!" she added with feeling.

"And by the way, why are you wearing makeup at school? Don't you remember the principal's announcement at the beginning of the year that there is to be no makeup worn except for after-school functions?"

Loretta shrugged her shoulders. "Mr. Layman is so old-fashioned! This is '65, not '35! Besides, all the others are, so why shouldn't I?"

"They are not either, and you know it, Loretta Asbury!" Linda protested. "It's just a few wild ones that are trying to get away with it. And anyway, what makes you think that rouging your cheeks and painting your lips and putting mascara on your eyelashes makes you more lovely?"

"Well, you naturally have more color than I

do. I have to use something to make me not look so dead!"

"Look dead," Linda repeated in disbelief. "I always think when I see someone all painted up that they look like a painted corpse!" Linda looked closely at Loretta. "And you've been plucking your eyebrows too! Loretta, you should be ashamed."

"But mine aren't prettily arched like yours are! And besides, Mom plucks and paints hers."

"Oh, Loretta, I can't help what Mom does. But can't you see that you are thinking too much about yourself?" Linda spoke with deep compassion for her sister. "You are trying too hard to get attention. And I'm afraid you are getting it, but not the right kind nor from the right kind of people. I want you to take care! You're so young!"

Loretta laughed. "You're an old mother hen! I'm not worried. I can take care of myself." She tossed her head and slid off the bed. "Guess I'll go over to my own room. Good night."

"Good night, sis," Linda answered. Then she added softly, "I'm praying for you."

"What?" Loretta stopped short. "Did I hear you right? Are you a religious fanatic or something?"

"Yes, you heard me. I said that I am praying for you. I also read my Bible—nearly every day, in fact. I feel a need of God, of a power to help me, beyond myself. I wish you would realize you have that need too, Loretta." Tears that Linda could not stop came to her eyes.

Loretta's eyes softened. "I believe you really mean that, Linda. I do love you, sister dear. And I'll be good, for your sake. Night-night," she said kindly.

Linda watched her go. She was beautiful like Mom. She was petite like Mom too. Linda did not envy her; she only wished Loretta could see the many dangers that lay ahead unless she reined in those strong passions of hers.

Linda was glad when Saturday came again. It was nearly the end of April already, and there were so many wonderful activities to do outside—thinning perennials in the flower beds, replanting portulaca that were coming up as thick as hair in the rock gardens, and of course, pulling weeds. She hoped she could spend the day tomorrow doing exactly what she wanted to. Pansy was coming to clean, which meant that maybe even Mom or Loretta would help her with the flower beds. And she was going to lock up her schoolbooks and forget them for the whole wonderful weekend!

# 6

Promptly at eight o'clock, Pansy appeared at the side door. Linda ran to open it in response to her knock. "Good morning, Pansy. How are you this beautiful morning?" she greeted her, opening the screen door wide.

"Jes fine, chil', jes fine," Pansy said, her black face breaking into a bright smile.

"Come on in, Pansy," Alberta called from the dining room table. "Sorry, we're still at breakfast."

"Makes no matter. I done had mine and won't give ya no bothah! Jes show me where to start in dis mornin'."

"Pansy, you may not start cleaning till you sing with me a little," Linda coaxed playfully. "We learned a new song in glee club this week that I think you will like." Linda went to the piano and began to play.

Pansy followed her, her bright eyes shining. She loved to sing, and the occasional times around the piano filled her hungry heart with happy thoughts for days.

"Come here and help us, Larry; we need some bass for this song," Linda begged, the keys silent for a moment. Then her fingers flew again across the keys as Larry joined them.

"'Oh, glory, my soul is satisfied; Hallelujah, my soul is satisfied . . .'" Larry carried the bass part in the chorus. Pansy contributed her rich contralto while Linda sang the soprano.

"Sounds nice," Dad cheered from the dining room when the song was finished.

Linda swung around on the stool. "Enough for this morning, Pansy?" she asked with a laugh.

"No, no. Here, please play the 'Hallelujah Chorus' again," Pansy begged as she picked up a booklet of Handel's *Messiah* from the rack. As Linda played, Larry sang again, and Pansy chimed in on the parts she knew.

When Linda was finished, Pansy sank into a stuffed chair with a deep sigh. "Sho' is somethin' like!" she exclaimed in grateful appreciation. "But now, chil', I better get to my work, or I'll be at it all day! And 'sides, I'm keepin' de men from deirs." She pulled herself slowly up.

Linda hurried to the dining room to help Mom and Loretta clear the table.

Pansy picked up a stack of dishes and followed them to the kitchen. "Where does you want me to start, Miz' Albertie?"

"The upstairs had better be done thoroughly today, and then do whatever you have time for downstairs, I guess," Mom decided as she began running dishwater. "If you get finished, there is a pile of ironing to do. But maybe one of the girls will have time to do that."

"Well now, Pansy, I thought you were going to help me clean out the chicken house," Larry said, feigning surprise.

"Oh, go on now wid yo' shines," Pansy said, giving him a playful shove toward the back door.

"Well, seeing as I'm not getting any help, guess I have to go do it myself," Larry said forlornly, getting his jacket. He was soon going down the back walk whistling jauntily, " 'Oh, glory, my soul is satisfied . . .' " Tiny was running along at his heels.

Dad finished with the morning paper and came to the kitchen. "Does anyone have eggs ordered for this morning, Mother?" he asked. "There are a lot in the egg-packing room to be cleaned. Guess I will go do that first."

Alberta looked at the bulletin board. "Kroger needs two cases," she said. "Maybe I can deliver them if you let me know when they are packed. I ought to pick up a few groceries anyway."

"What shall I do, Mom?" Linda asked. "I was hoping to work in the yard and flower beds. But maybe I should help Dad do the eggs first."

"Well, now, I'd be glad for help," Dad said agreeably from the back hall, where he was getting his jacket.

"I'll soon be out to help then," Linda said, smiling at him.

"Remember, Linda, you and Loretta have piano practice this afternoon at three o'clock," Mom reminded her pleasantly.

It was nearly noon before Linda was able to get to the yard work. There had been a lot of eggs to pack, and then she used the pickup to haul some pine needles from the woods to mulch the raspberry patch.

After lunch, Loretta came out and helped pull weeds in the perennial and bulb beds. She had gloves on, just as Mom would, Linda noticed. Linda held her palms up and looked at them. They were stained with various shades of green and brown. She pulled her nails in. "Quite farmerly dirty," she chuckled to herself. Yes, she was a "country bumpkin," no doubt. But it surely was lots of fun!

"What's so funny?" Loretta asked, sitting back on her heels.

"Nothing much," Linda said, tossing a handful of grass to a pile beside the flower bed. "I was just thinking about how some girls at school like to call me a country bumpkin and how well the name fits! See?" Linda held up her dirty hands. "I suppose I should wear gloves like you and Mom do, but I love the feel of the soft, warm soil."

"Well, I don't. I only weed flower beds because I like things to look neat around here, that's all!" Loretta asserted. "Spending the morning baking is much more to my liking," she added.

"We need good cooks too," Linda encouraged her. "And we all love to eat your cooking. So please, keep it up, Loretta."

They worked in silence for some time, and then Loretta asked, "Have you and Larry really decided for sure that you aren't going to the prom?"

"It isn't a problem for me—I'm not a junior or senior, so if I choose not to go with a junior or senior, then I'm not invited. But Larry isn't planning to go either, as far as I know."

"What are you and Larry going to do that night?"

"I don't know about Larry, but Andrea and I will be getting together to do something. Maybe she will spend the night here."

"So Andrea isn't going either!" Loretta exclaimed. "She must be as queer as you are!"

Linda laughed. "I might be queer, but I don't think Andrea is! When Pastor Baker's heard about some of the goings-on the last couple of years, they didn't want Andrea to go. But she wasn't planning to anyway."

"Well, that sounds just like a pastor!" Loretta grumbled. "Never wants anyone to have any fun."

"I guess that depends on your idea of fun, Loretta," Linda said as she busily pulled grass from around the delphiniums. "There is a lot of good, clean fun available, without having to mess up our lives or the lives of others for it."

Loretta worked silently for a time. Linda wished she could know the thoughts that were going through the young teenager's mind. How could she help her sister to think more seriously about life?

Soon Linda stood up and brushed the sand off the knees of her jeans. She glanced at her watch. "It's nearly two-thirty! Guess we should get cleaned up for piano lessons, Loretta." Linda gathered the rest of the piles of grass and weeds and put them into the cart while Loretta picked up the garden tools and put them in the shed.

It was the next Friday evening—prom night. Andrea came along home with Linda after school to spend the evening. They brought the cows in together and fed the calves and heifers. "I love this kind of work, Linda," Andrea said as she scratched around the ears of a pretty little heifer. "If it weren't for leaving the area, I could really get excited about Daddy's farming ideas!"

Ron and Larry were doing the milking, and Dad spent the time grading and packing eggs. When Linda and Andrea were done with the feeding, they helped Dad finish.

Then the girls trooped to the house, where Loretta and Mom had started supper. They all worked together to finish the pizzas Loretta had started. Linda went to the garden and gathered fresh lettuce leaves, radishes, and green onions for a salad. *What a jolly suppertime,* Linda thought happily. *If only Loretta could see what true enjoyment is!* Mom had finally gotten reconciled to the idea that Linda and Larry would not be going to the prom, for which Linda was happy. Mom had fussed about it off and on for days, till Dad finally managed to calm her down with the thought that she ought to be thankful her children wanted to behave. And now she seemed to be enjoying the pleasant evening fully as much as the rest were.

After supper Linda and Andrea went horseback riding till dusk. When it was too dark to see, they put the horses in the barn and came to the house.

Mom and Loretta had mixed a batch of taffy and had popcorn balls cooling on the counter. "Oh, what fun!" Andrea exclaimed. "I hope the boys come in in time to help pull the taffy!"

Larry and Ron soon came back from fishing in the river. "No fish tonight; they just weren't biting. But the flies sure were!" Larry said in a melancholy tone as he scratched welts on his arms. Linda glanced at Andrea. She knew that Andrea would be happy to have no fish to clean. That was one job Andrea abhorred! Andrea winked at Linda, and they laughed together.

Soon everybody was pulling taffy, even Mom and Dad. Then Mom cut it and put some in boxes for Andrea and Ron to take home the next day. Dad had gone to the library and had his feet propped up in front of the huge, old-fashioned fireplace. "Well now, come on in here," he called when everybody started wandering out of the kitchen. "Let's have a couple of songs yet before we call it a night."

Mom came in, wiping her hands on her apron. The young people followed. "Let's try that new sheet music you picked up this week, Mother," Dad suggested.

Mom went to the piano. Soon she was playing "How Great Thou Art!" The young voices chimed in and sang along, all but Ron. Linda had noticed before that he did not seem to enjoy singing. While the rest sang, he paged through a book that he had taken off the library shelf.

"That is a beautiful hymn," Dad said reverently.

"A Mr. Stuart Hine translated the words from Russian, I think, and now George Beverly Shea is making it popular. He made a record with that hymn on it," Andrea said. She picked up another song folder from the bookrack. "This one looks interesting. Let's sing this, please," she said. She set the open sheets in front of Mom.

" 'They that wait upon the Lord shall renew their strength; they shall mount up with wings as eagles; they shall run, and not be weary; they shall walk, and not be faint. Teach me, Lord, teach me, Lord, to wait,' " they all sang together.

"Well, now," Dad spoke up after they had sung several more favorite songs, "it's time we're all getting to bed."

Long before the prom was over, the Asbury family and their guests settled down for the night. Larry and Ron took sleeping bags and went out to the woods to camp out for the night. Linda and Andrea settled down in Linda's room, but not to sleep. At least not for a while, for they talked long after only the sounds of tree frogs and peepers could be heard.

It seemed they were barely asleep when the phone rang in the hall. Linda glanced sleepily at her clock. Three o'clock! Who would be calling at such an hour of the morning? She ran to answer it. It was for Andrea, so Linda crawled back into bed. Soon Andrea came from the phone. "Oh, Linda!" she cried, tears filling her eyes. "Mary Catherine Carmean and Kenneth Taylor had an accident, and Kenneth is critically injured. The hospital called Daddy to come in, and he just called from the hospital because he knew we would want to know. Kenneth isn't expected to live."

"What happened?" Linda asked, wide awake instantly, her heart suddenly very heavy.

"I don't know the details for sure, but they both had been drinking, Daddy said. He said they were racing with another car, and Kenneth's car blew a tire. His car veered off the road to the left and hit the culvert over Poco Creek. Mary Catherine has broken ribs and a broken arm, but she isn't hurt nearly as bad as Kenneth. His skull is crushed, and he has a broken neck. Oh, it's too sad!" Andrea began crying again.

"This will really shake some people up, won't it," Linda said brokenly. "Nothing like this has ever happened before in our school. And Kenneth—he was chosen to be the prom king!"

Linda went to Mom and Dad's bedroom right away and, sobbing, told them about the accident. Mom came and hugged her.

"Well, now, Mom, aren't you glad Larry and Linda were safe at home in their beds?" Dad asked.

Linda and Andrea were not able to go back to sleep. Finally they got up and sat in the early morning stillness, looking out the bedroom window, watching the dawn beginning to lighten the morning sky. When they heard Dad stirring, they dressed and went out to help with the chores, sobered and silent as they thought of the tragedy of the early morning.

Andrea left right after breakfast to be with her family. Ron and Larry went to the hospital at Sharptown to see if there was any other information. It seemed to Linda that she could not think as she wandered listlessly from one thing to the other.

Then Larry called from the hospital to tell the family that Kenneth had died without ever regaining consciousness. *Death . . . and then what?* Linda wondered. She shivered. *Surely Kenneth could not have been a Christian. He didn't even go to church! And if the Bible is true, which I think it is, then he has gone to hell!* Linda groaned in her spirit. *And what about Mary Catherine? She certainly couldn't be a Christian either!*

Andrea's father had said that Mary Catherine sobered up fast after getting to the hospital. But now she was petulant and complaining, giving the doctors and nurses a hard time as they tried to work with her. Of course she must be in lots of pain, Linda knew. Mom had broken a rib once, and Linda knew how much that had hurt. But *several* broken ribs, as well as a broken arm! Linda's heart went out in pity to the poor girl.

The funeral was on Tuesday, and school was canceled that day. Many of the high-school students were there, as well as their families. The service was in the Episcopal church, and the rector, along with Pastor Baker, was in charge of the service. It was a sad service; many of the students were crying. They were sad because death had come so close: Kenneth was, after all, a teenager like themselves, with the right, in their minds, to many more years of life.

But to Linda, the sadness was much deeper. *Where is he right now?* Linda thought. *What hope can be given to his family?* She, along with her family, went to talk with Kenneth's family after the funeral service. To Linda's surprise, they talked freely about Kenneth being in heaven now, and how wonderful it was that he could look down and see them all here. They were sure he would want them to rejoice and not be sorrowful.

Somehow such words seemed meaningless and empty to Linda. What right had they to claim he was in heaven, when he had no interest whatever in such things when he was living? How could anyone who did not live in obedience to the Bible hope to go to heaven? And more than that, it had been his great delight to make a mockery of anything related to religion while he was still living. Surely their hope of heaven was a vain hope!

That evening, rather than going to choir practice, she sat with her Bible in the orchard, in her nest in the apple tree. She watched thoughtfully for a while as Dad ran the cultivator tractor through the rows of young corn. She saw Mom tying up raspberry canes in the patch beside the orchard. How she wished someone could answer her myriad of questions—could help her understand the mysteries of life and death, the mysteries of the Bible. If only she could talk to her parents. Did they know much about the Bible, more than the little that they heard at church on Sunday mornings?

"God, I don't know much about Your Book either. But I want to learn. I want to understand. Show me Your way," she prayed earnestly. She opened her Bible to John 14, the passage Pastor Baker had read that afternoon. She read verse 6: "Jesus saith unto him, I am the way, the truth, and the life: no man cometh unto the Father, but by me." She continued to read the chapter. She read that those who love Jesus will be loved by the Father. She read that the way to tell if one loves Jesus is if he keeps His words.

Linda leaned back against a branch and thought. *How can I love Jesus? When I learn to know people well is when I grow to love them. So then, I must learn to know Jesus well in order to grow to love Him.* She flipped back several pages to the beginning of the Book of John and began to read ardently. *Jesus was the Light. He came to the world, and the world didn't know Him; He came to His own people, and even they didn't want Him!* Tears came to Linda's eyes and silently ran down her cheeks. *He was full of grace, full of truth; yet so few knew Him or wanted Him! Why, O God, why? Why did so few know Jesus or, for that matter,* want *to know Him? But it is the same today. So few seem to know Him, or want to know Him . . . and, I suppose, even fewer love Him.*

Linda sat in thought as the birds sang their evening songs. Young rabbits played in the grass below her perch; everything was alive and aware in the wonderful world around her. Linda was deep in thought, in her search for God.

"God in heaven, teach me about You. And teach me about Your wonderful Son Jesus so that I can know Him and grow to love Him," Linda prayed aloud. A restful spirit settled over her, and happiness filled her heart. God would help her; she knew that. Had He not promised that if people seek Him, they would find Him?

# 7

Life settled back into normal patterns at Springville High School. Mary Catherine was still in the hospital and probably would not be back in school that year. To Linda, school was much more pleasant without Mary Catherine's caustic influence. But then, she did hope sincerely that Mary Catherine could soon be well again and out of the hospital. Linda had even visited her a time or two, along with Andrea and some of the other girls. Mary Catherine had been surprisingly pleasant and even happy for their visits. Maybe, just maybe, she would be kinder when she came back to school.

On one visit, Mary Catherine had asked Linda to get her things out of her school locker and take them home for her. *Why didn't she ask one of her friends?* Linda wondered. But she willingly did it. When Linda opened Mary Catherine's locker, there in bold letters glued on the back of the locker were words of a popular song: "Stop the world, and let me get off . . ." Linda shuddered. How nearly that had happened for Mary Catherine!

Linda was studying hard for the Latin tournament, which was coming up soon. She was thankful that her term paper had been completed and turned in. She was spending a couple of evenings after school each week with Mr. Taylor while he tried to coach her with the kind of questions and skills that were basic for competing in the tournament. The coming Saturday was *the* day! Mr. Taylor would be taking her to Williamstown, leaving early Saturday morning.

Linda knew that Dad did not like it that Mr. Taylor would be taking the girls to the tournament. But at least there were two who would be going—Linda and Deborah Riley. "I don't quite trust that Mr. Taylor," Dad told Linda on Friday evening as they cleaned eggs together. "He has such a congenial and pleasing personality, while he makes no secret about the fact that he has little time for God or Christianity. I feel uneasy about your being in his company for such a long time."

"I do too, Dad," Linda replied, "and I wish I could have gotten out of going, short of absolutely refusing. What should I have done?"

"We should have looked into it sooner, Linda. I only learned this week how you will be getting there."

Saturday morning came too soon for Linda. Sleepily she turned off the buzzing alarm at four-thirty and hurried to be ready by five-thirty.

Linda gathered her bags and nervously waited at the door till she saw Mr. Taylor's little red sports car turn up the driveway. "Good-bye, everybody. Wish me well!" she implored. Mom gave Linda a quick squeeze, and Dad's eyes spoke volumes of love and support as he told her good-bye. Even Loretta was up to see her off, and Larry and Red were waving their good wishes from the barn door as she ran out the sidewalk. Then Mr. Taylor opened the door for her, and they were off.

"You have a caring family, don't you?" Mr. Taylor observed as he drove out the lane and turned north on Route 104.

"Yes, I do. I have so much to be thankful for," Linda responded with vigor. "But . . . Mr. Taylor," she continued hesitatingly, "I thought Deb Riley was also going, and we're going the wrong direction to pick her up."

"Her parents decided yesterday that they would take her because they want to visit some relatives this weekend in the Baltimore area. They drove out yesterday already."

So she would be riding alone with Mr. Taylor for three hours! *What would Dad say? What can I do? God in heaven, help!*

But Mr. Taylor did not seem to sense her alarm. He was apparently still thinking about her family. "I lived with my mother as a child," he went on, "but seldom saw her; she was a member of the Senate for many years, and then was an ambassador to Italy.

"My mother was always busy; a governess really raised me. I never had the privilege of relating to a family, as such. A caring family would be a wonderful gift," he said musingly, as though talking to himself.

Linda was listening with only one ear. Why was she riding with a single man like this, and on a three-hour trip? No wonder Dad had been concerned! She knew he had not wanted her to be driving with him alone! But what could she do now? At least, she consoled herself, she would be coming home on the bus, as Mr. Taylor was planning to spend Sunday with his father in nearby Washington, D.C. Again Linda bowed her heart in silent petition to the heavenly Father.

Mr. Taylor chatted lightheartedly as they drove along. He told Linda about his life as a child, about going to Europe with his mother when he was a teenager, and about his high-school days, most of which he had spent in Italy. He had fallen in love with Latin, even though it was a dead language. And that was when he decided to pursue a study of languages. Linda knew he spoke at least eight languages fluently.

"What is your favorite language?" she asked politely.

"Spanish is probably the prettiest language. But I like the guttural tones of German, and the lilt of Italian. It's hard to say which one I like the best. Maybe you should ask me which one I *dream* in," he added, laughing.

Around eight o'clock, Mr. Taylor suddenly pulled into a restaurant parking lot. "I don't know about you," he said, "but I didn't take time to eat breakfast, and I am hungry."

"I was too excited to eat much," Linda admitted. But she was not sure she would be able to eat now either! She surely had not thought ahead to consider what all she was getting in for.

"What can I order for you?" he asked pleasantly.

"What are you going to have?"

"Probably orange juice, a sweet roll, and hot chocolate," he replied lightly.

"Then I'll have that too."

As Mr. Taylor chatted on congenially, his conversation gradually changed from items of general interest to personal questions that showed more than just a friendly interest. Linda hardly knew how to respond. She had never seen this side of him—the pleasant, sociable side—in the classroom. There he was usually stern: an excellent teacher, but one who tolerated no foolishness.

The waitress brought their order very soon, for which Linda was thankful. As was her custom, she bowed her head in silent prayer. Mr. Taylor waited quietly till she was finished.

"Is prayer a part of your homelife?" he asked with interest.

"Yes, at least at mealtimes. Occasionally we sing or pray or read the Bible together at other times too. As you know, our family attends the Mt. Olive Methodist Church."

Mr. Taylor nodded his head. "I have seen you there quite often," he said. "And listened with keen enjoyment to your occasional solos in the choir," he added with a smile.

Linda was thinking fast. He certainly appeared to have more than a casual interest in her. But surely he could not be serious about it. Teachers were not allowed to be on intimate terms with their students. Linda could remember a time or two when a teacher had been disciplined for such. And Mr. Taylor must realize that she could get him into trouble if she chose to report to the principal what he had already said.

The various types of testing employed during the tournament later that morning were, as Linda had anticipated, very difficult. High schools from all over the state had sent representatives. Linda felt quite sure she must be the stupidest person there.

"Well, how did it go?" Mr. Taylor asked as Linda walked into the lounge at noon, after the long morning. Deborah Riley was with her, having also just finished her testing.

Deborah laughed shortly. "Count me out for

putting Springville on the map! I didn't expect the exams to be anything like they were!" She sank wearily onto a bench to wait for her parents to come pick her up.

"I'm sure I didn't win any trophies for our school either!" Linda stated with conviction. "The oral part was especially hard. I couldn't understand the reader's accent very well, so very little of any worth got onto my test paper."

"Well, I'm sure you both did just fine. I'll be eager to get the results." He glanced briefly at his watch. "But, Linda, we'll need to keep moving to catch your bus in time. We'd better get some lunch first though." Mr. Taylor rose to his feet and picked up his attaché case.

Lunch was a pleasant time. Mr. Taylor made no mention of anything that put Linda on edge. But when they got to the bus station, the bus had already gone, much to Linda's dismay. Mr. Taylor looked at his watch; then he held it to his ear and listened. He shook it and listened again. "Well, it *has* stopped," he said unbelievingly. "Linda, I'm truly sorry." He stood in thought for a few moments. "What shall we do now?"

"Can't I wait here for the next bus?" Linda suggested, thinking anything would be better than subjecting herself further to Mr. Taylor's company.

"You, a country girl, wait here alone in a big city? I guess I wouldn't allow that—not when

*I* am responsible for your safety!" Mr. Taylor was emphatic. "Why don't we head toward Washington, and hope we can flag down a bus somewhere along the way."

Linda sat quietly in her seat as they drove on. She certainly did not like the turn of events, but what could she do about it? She was really at Mr. Taylor's mercy!

"I'm not such bad company, am I?" Mr. Taylor asked kindly, sensing her reluctance to be riding farther with him. "In fact, I'd be happy to take you to meet my dad. He would enjoy that."

"Please, Mr. Taylor, I prefer to go home," Linda said with conviction. "I'm sorry this is making you more bother, but my folks are expecting me this evening."

Suddenly the little red car slowed down and swung onto the shoulder. Mr. Taylor jumped out and waved his arms. A big Trailways bus pulled over onto the shoulder also.

Mr. Taylor opened her car door. "There's your bus, Linda!"

She quickly gathered her bags from the back seat and ran to the open bus door. Mr. Taylor had already made arrangements with the driver, so with a quick "Thanks" to Mr. Taylor, she climbed up the steps. With a sigh of relief, she settled down in a seat. Surely God had been watching over her, and she felt truly thankful for His care!

When Linda got home and told her parents how the trip had gone and that Deborah Riley had not been along after all, Dad was distraught. He did not place the blame on Linda but on himself. "Why didn't we think through this situation better, Mother?" he asked.

"I'm sorry we failed you in this, Linda. But we are thankful that God was looking out for you."

After the trip, Linda was dismayed to see that Mr. Taylor meant to persist in the friendliness that the trip had brought between them. He often stopped her after class for little chats or asked her to come back in after school for something he wished to discuss. She wished she knew more how to pray about such matters, and she wished that she could talk with someone who would give her sound, spiritual advice. She thought that she ought to talk to Dad about it, but what would he say? What *could* he say, when Mom had already made it plain that she did not see anything wrong with encouraging Mr. Taylor. More than ever, Linda looked forward to the end of school and the simplicity of farm life during the summer.

# 8

Red Ziller was coming out to the farm every Saturday now and working for Dad. He worked with a will, cutting back fencerows and trimming around pasture fences. Linda delighted in the cleaned-up appearance that the farm took on, and the farmyard fence glowed in its bright coat of fresh white paint. Linda and Loretta had helped with that as they had extra time.

Larry helped Red too when he was free from other chores. He and Red had gotten to be quite good friends. And Linda was enjoying the comradeship of another "brother" in the family.

As the weeks passed, Red became an invaluable help to Dad. Linda knew that it took a weight off Dad's mind to have someone whom he knew he could depend on to work on his own when Larry left for college in the fall.

Linda wondered, though, how long Red would be able to help. He would be eighteen in the fall, and then he would likely get his draft notice, as Larry and Ron had. They had been able to get deferments for education. However, Red would not have any legitimate reason unless he could possibly get a farm deferment. But it was not as if he were a son. *He will still be in school next year,* Linda suddenly remembered with a sense of relief. It was not that she cared for her own sake if Red stayed around to help; she knew that it took a lot of the burden of the work off Dad's shoulders.

Red always ate lunch with the Asburys, as the hired help usually did. Loretta was in her glory. She had always done well with cooking, but now everything she had learned so far in home economics classes was being put to the test. Here was a young man to impress, and she was doing her best! Linda, as usual, spent most of her Saturdays out-of-doors, weeding, working in flower beds, planting seeds in the vegetable garden, or working with the plants still growing in the sunroom. It was Loretta who was the belle at the lunch table, not Linda. But Linda did not care; her mind was preoccupied with deeper thoughts than impressing the boys.

Andrea was leaving—her dear bosom friend, Andrea! The church council had accepted Pastor Baker's resignation as of July 1. So it was final now. Linda thought she could somehow manage the summer without Andrea. But what about next year at school, and the next? Possibly after high school, they could go to college together. But till then how could she ever manage to get along without her closest friend?

But there was still a little time; there was some of May and still all of June. Linda and Andrea spent as much of that time together as possible, either at the Bakers' or at the Asburys'. Andrea enjoyed helping with the Saturday farm chores or working with Linda in the flower gardens or vegetable patch. Sometimes on Saturdays, if Linda could be spared at home and did not have studies, she helped the Bakers with their packing.

When Sundays were free, Linda and Andrea took long walks, often down the woods road to the river. Sometimes they took the rowboat out on the river, spending the afternoon dreaming or planning for the future as they rowed over the rippling water. Or sometimes they just sat on the pier, visiting and watching the white clouds float by in the blue, blue sky.

While Linda and Andrea used all their time together to the best possible advantage, Larry and Ron and the other seniors were preparing for graduation exercises. And then it was finals, and all the scramble of year-end activities—yearbooks, pictures, parties, and all the rest.

Graduation week finally came, the second week of June. Pastor Parker from the First Presbyterian Church had the baccalaureate service on Tuesday evening. On Thursday evening, one hundred fifty seniors with gowns and mortarboards sat on the auditorium stage for the graduation ceremony, filled with trepidation as the uncharted future lay ahead of them. Some had future plans made; they had been accepted at the colleges of their choice. Others were ready to enter the job market, hopeful of getting a job with sufficient wages to support themselves as well as a wife and family.

Ron and Larry would be going to a university in Charlottetown, come September. Ron had won a National Merit scholarship, but other than a partial scholarship from the local Favorite Sons Fund, Larry would have to pay his own way. He had been salutatorian of his class though, which was no small honor.

Linda thought his salutatory speech was wonderful. He had used the title from one of Shakespeare's poems, "To Thine Own Self Be True," and applied the ideals to his fellow classmates. At the close, he read the poem, which ended with these three lines:

> This above all: to thine own self be true,
> And it must follow, as the night the day,
> Thou canst not then be false to any man.

The people clapped a long time after he was finished. Amid many tears and good-byes all around, school finally was really over for the year. The Asbury family drove home together after the graduation ceremony. Linda felt strangely drained. How good it would be to relax on the farm for the summer. She was happy for her good report card, for the unbroken 4.0 grade point average; but there was a lot more to living than making good grades!

Linda took her armload of books, papers, notebooks, and reports to her room, eager to put them away for the summer. As she decided what to keep and what to discard, her thoughts were busy with the past year. She thought of the many good times. But there had also been perplexing times.

She thought especially of the past several months and of the many stresses that had been crammed into them: of going to the Latin tournament and earning only a seventh-place status for their school; of Mr. Taylor's continuing attentions—his frequent telephone calls and repeated offers to take her home from school in the afternoons—and her uncertainties about how to relate to him; of the prom and the accident following and then Kenneth Taylor's death; of her occasional visits with Mary Catherine as she recovered from her injuries; of Pastor Baker and his family, who were even now packing in earnest to leave in about two weeks.

But beyond all that, she still struggled with spiritual realities. Linda sat silently at her window, seeing only subconsciously the display of the coming summer spread over the countryside. Why must she struggle with such perplexities and with the continual gnawing inside her? It seemed no one else had such feelings! The more she read her Bible, the more she knew that somehow, or somewhere, there was something beyond what she and her friends and family were presently experiencing.

Pilate, ruler of the Jews, had asked Jesus, "What is truth?" And Linda felt the same question pressing inside her, begging for an answer. She had read in John 17 what Jesus said in His prayer for His disciples: "Thy word is truth." But what did He mean by that, and how could she understand the meaning of truth? Jesus had said God's Word is truth, but what did that mean? Was there anyone anywhere who really knew about truth?

# 9

It was haymaking time. The alfalfa was green and lush from the abundant spring rains, except where the field met the woods. There it had been cropped short by the herds of white-tailed deer that came out to graze each evening at sunset. Dad had mowed most of the back thirty acres, and it looked like many loads of hay.

Today he had gone out to finish mowing. Larry was feeding the chickens and packing eggs, and Linda was hoeing in the garden. As she worked, Linda wondered where Tiny was. Usually the lively little dog was chasing butterflies in the garden or finding rabbit trails in the nearby orchard. Linda hoped he was with Larry in the chicken house.

Suddenly Linda noticed Dad driving in the back lane. Surely he would not be finished with the mowing yet. But she thought little about it and went back to hoeing—that was, till Dad came across the yard toward her, carefully carrying something.

She flew to the yard. "What is it, Dad?" she asked, her heart pounding. But even before she asked, she knew. It was their little black Tiny. Dad had him on a fertilizer bag; she could see his mangled back legs sticking out at odd angles.

"He was running in the alfalfa, and I didn't even know he was around," Dad said with a catch in his voice. "I'm sorry, Linda, but the sickle bar got his back legs."

"God in heaven," Linda breathed softly, "he's just a dog, but please help us know what to do, and be able to do it!"

Mom came running out the back door. She took one look at Dad's stricken face and then one at the dog lying on the bag. "Linda, can you get me some peroxide, some clean bandages, and some tape? See if you can find something we can use for a splint too." This was Mom's realm, and she felt completely in her element. Dad, Linda knew, could hardly bear the sight of blood.

Tiny hardly flinched or whimpered. One back leg was only hanging on by a little skin; Mom took a sharp knife and carefully cut the skin. There was no use to try to save that leg. The other one was badly cut and broken, but could possibly be saved. Mom cleaned the wounds as well as she could with sterile patches. Then she poured peroxide over everything, watching it fizz and foam productively. Then Linda helped to hold the ends of bone together, while Mom put a tongue depressor splint on and carefully wrapped strips of cloth around it, taping it securely.

Loretta came then, bringing a clean and soft old blanket. Mom gently laid Tiny on the blanket and carried him to the house. "The laundry will be Tiny's hospital room for now," she said, glad to be finished with her tedious job. Linda brought him a saucer of water, and he lifted his head to drink eagerly. "He'll be all right," Mom assured the girls as they stood and watched.

And, sure enough, within a week Tiny was walking all around, balancing himself with ease on his two front legs, holding his bandaged leg and stump in the air. Then, his independence reasserting itself, he was ready to go outside again to see the world.

How everyone coming to the farm laughed at such a sight—a dog walking on his two front legs! Andrea brought her camera and took a picture; she wanted to be sure to have this souvenir from the farm, she said. Even a photographer from the *Democratic Messenger* came out to take a picture and do a write-up for the paper. Linda wondered whoever had told him about Tiny!

Tiny did well, and when his broken leg finally healed, he did everything on his three good legs that he had ever done on four. He ran after cats and rabbits, and he was still a splendid rat-and-mouse catcher. He could still run along after the cows and nip at their heels to keep them moving toward the barn. Linda rejoiced that the heavenly Father had cared enough to make it be all right—even if Tiny was just a dog. *He says in the Bible that He sees each sparrow fall; surely He does have an intense interest in all His creatures,* she mused.

By the time the hay was made, the grain was ready to be harvested. Then it was time for straw. Often Pug, Pansy's husband, came over to help with the haying or the straw making. His deep, jolly laugh made all the work seem less burdensome, Linda thought. Another neighbor, old Tobe, also came at times to help. Linda loved his wrinkled, leathery old face fringed all around by gray kinks of hair. He liked to tell stories about his grandmother, who had been a slave down South, and about how hard she had worked day after day, picking cotton in the hot sun.

When the black helpers came in for dinner, Mom always extended the kitchen table. Dad would never hear of having the blacks eat at a different table, as was the general custom in their area, so everybody sat down together at the kitchen table, which was where the black helpers felt the most comfortable. Linda loved Dad for that; it was exactly as she would have done. She loved her black friends as dearly as her other friends; in fact, she rarely thought about a color difference.

Linda enjoyed immensely the long afternoons on the wagons or in the barn, stacking the prickly bales, working side by side with the hired workers. Usually by evening, she felt like a true hayseed, as Mary Catherine had often called her!

One hot morning in late July, the family sat around the breakfast table visiting. "When are we going to do something special this year, Dad?" Loretta asked. The same thing had been on Linda's mind.

Usually one or two days each summer, the family would take a special family trip. Last summer they had taken the ferry across the Chesapeake Bay for one last time before the new bridge–tunnel opened. Dad had not said what they would do this year, but usually it needed to be something they could do between morning and evening milkings.

"Well now," Dad began in his typical drawl, "Mom and I thought that since Larry will soon be leaving, maybe we ought to take a bigger trip this year. Kind of a family trip, you know."

Mom was smiling.

"Where? Where?" Loretta asked quickly, her voice full of excitement.

"Well now," Dad drawled, "give me time and I'll tell you."

Linda was eagerly waiting to hear too what Dad and Mom were planning.

"We thought maybe we could take a couple of days and go see where Pastor Baker and his family have moved to, up in the hills of Pennsylvania—

at least if anyone wants to go along." Dad smiled at them all.

Now it was Linda's turn to be excited. Would she really have the opportunity to see Andrea again so soon? "Oh, Dad—and Mom too—that is so sweet of you to think of such a nice surprise! Do they know about it? Does it suit them to have company this soon after they moved?"

"Oh, yes, they know, and they are planning for us over next weekend," Mom said.

The rest of the week was spent in preparation for the big trip. Help needed to be lined up to take care of the chickens and to do the milking. Neighbors Shem and Louise would look after the chickens and the other small animals. Pug and old Tobe would help Red do the milking, since they had both helped with the milking chores before and were familiar with them.

Linda could hardly wait for Saturday morning to come. Loretta was a bit disappointed. She had informed them all that she could have found a dozen things more interesting than going to visit a former pastor's family!

Early Saturday morning, the big station wagon was packed to the gills and they were off. The milking crew stood in the barn door, waving as Larry turned the car around in the driveway. Pansy had come over early to see them off. She stood on the sidewalk as the car drove out the long lane; she was still waving as they turned onto the highway. Then she walked slowly to the house, where, Linda knew, she would do the weekly cleaning for the Asburys before going home to her own household chores.

Dad sat with Larry in the front. They were discussing the merits of various types of hay. Mom had settled into her corner, taking this rare opportunity to read. Linda held a book in her lap, but she was more interested in watching the passing scenery than in reading. Loretta, true to character, was already half asleep on her pillow.

The hours passed quickly, and the scenery changed from rolling farmland to metropolitan areas and then to sharply rising hills and deep valleys with farmsteads scattered among them. As they drove north, the air coming in their open windows was increasingly cool and fresh.

Near noon, they drove up a winding driveway along the side of a hill to a small farm nestled on the south side of a mountain. The barn was in need of paint, and the house and grounds were shabby. But the situation was beautiful. Linda gazed around her in fascination. She could see for miles, up and down a broad valley, out across some lower hills to mountain ranges in the distance. But there was little time for reflection. Out the side door rushed Andrea, and Linda greeted her happily.

"Oh, Andrea!" she cried. "We are really here.

It is so wonderful to see you again. And your place is delightful!" Linda scrutinized her closely. "Have you changed yet? No, you're just the same as always!"

Andrea shook her head, her eyes twinkling. "I don't think I have any silver threads among the gold yet," she teased. "And you haven't aged a great deal either!" Her tone became more serious. "But, oh, I have missed you so much, Linda!"

"Don't I even merit a 'hello'?" Larry asked Andrea.

Andrea went to him and held out her hand. "Welcome to my best brother," she said with a laugh.

Linda and Andrea walked off together, arm in arm. Mr. and Mrs. Baker and the Asbury parents were already strolling across the big yard, talking animatedly. Loretta was following them, playing with a yellow kitten she had found sitting on the porch rail.

One delight followed another during that whole wonderful weekend. Linda, Loretta, and Andrea wandered up and down the mountainside, often jumping from rock to rock over the creeks. For lack of other entertainment, Larry usually went with them. Andrea did not seem to mind, but Linda—as much as she loved her brother—could not help but feel that he was an intruder. She wanted to savor all these precious hours for themselves.

On Sunday morning, the whole family went to Pastor Baker's new church. It was a small country church and a small congregation. But Linda loved the warmth of these people. She noted with interest that they seemed poorer and not as well-dressed as the folks at home, but they were happy people.

The Bakers also seemed happy. Pastor Baker was enjoying his new role of farmer. He had several Jersey cows in the barn and even three pigs. There was a flock of chickens in the coop behind the garage. A neighbor was farming the fields this year, but Pastor Baker assured the Asburys that he hoped to work the ground next year, Lord willing.

That night Linda and Andrea whispered long after the others were asleep. There was a lot of news to catch up on about school friends and all the other things that girls like to talk about.

Katydids and tree frogs were making their night sounds in the maple trees outside the open bedroom windows. In the distance, Linda heard an owl. A whippoorwill sat on the porch roof and began to call, *Whip-poor-will, whip-poor-will*.

"Isn't it peaceful with all the wonderful night sounds?" Linda said wistfully. "I think I would love living in the mountains."

"I like it here," Andrea said. "But I do really

miss all the young people back home, and especially you-all. I haven't learned to know a lot of the youth around here yet. Probably I will once school starts, and yet I dread going to a new school and making new friends!"

"You will do okay; you've always made friends easily," Linda encouraged. "Just don't forget me!" she added.

"I could never forget you!" Andrea assured her warmly. Then she added, "Has the new pastor's family come yet?"

"I think they plan to move sometime in late August, before school starts. Pastor Kelloway has been there to preach a couple of Sunday mornings, but the family hasn't come with him yet. He said Mrs. Kelloway is getting over a bout with mononucleosis and isn't strong enough yet for packing and moving.

"I like Pastor Kelloway. His sermons are interesting, and he seems like a very kind person, although we haven't learned to know him well yet."

"I'm glad that the church council took Daddy's suggestion and asked them to come. You will like their family, I'm sure."

The girls were quiet for some time. "Are you asleep?" Andrea asked quietly.

"No, I was thinking," Linda answered.

"A penny for your thoughts," Andrea quipped.

"Actually, my thoughts were worth more than

that," Linda returned soberly. She paused and then added, "I was thinking about finding God's will for our lives. Do you read the Bible, Andrea? I'm sure you do, being a pastor's daughter. And I do too, and I want to know so many things. Every Sunday, your father preaches about God, about living for Him and being obedient to the Bible. But who listens? I mean, who is really doing that?"

"What do you mean, Linda? Do you think we are all heathens?"

"I'm not sure what I mean, only that I don't think most people that go to church every Sunday really are 'born again' as your father preached about. I don't know if any of us really understand what it means to be 'born again.' Neither do most of us live in obedience to God or to the Bible. We don't do what the Bible says."

"Like how?"

"Well, for example, I've been reading Jesus' Sermon on the Mount, from Matthew. These are Jesus' instructions to His disciples, and I suppose for us today too. He said, for example, that Christians are not to resist evil but to let others take advantage of them. If someone hits you on one cheek, let him hit you on the other one."

"That sounds far-fetched in our day, doesn't it?" Andrea injected.

"It sort of does. Jesus also said we are to love everybody, even our enemies, because anybody can love his friends. But it takes a real Christian to be able to love those who hate him." Linda paused briefly, hit by a sudden realization. "I guess that means I must love Mary Catherine Carmean, if I want to obey Jesus!"

"You could never do that, could you," Andrea remarked unbelievingly, "as mean as she is to you!"

"It would sure be hard!" Linda gazed out the window into the moonlit night.

Then she continued, "Jesus talked about not setting our hearts on riches and things of earth, and not worrying about what we are going to eat or wear. Then He ended His sermon by saying that those who hear His words but will not do them are like houses built on the sand; they will wash away when the storm comes."

"What are God's words that we are to do?" Andrea asked. "Does that mean that we are to go to church and do good works and things like that? We already do that."

Linda thought for a time. "I think it is more than that. Because Jesus said many will come to the Judgment, having called Him 'Lord, Lord,' and will expect to enter heaven because they have gone to church and done many good works. But Jesus will say to them, 'You never did the will of My Father which is in heaven. You are sinful workers; depart from Me into everlasting destruction!' "

Andrea shivered. "Sounds fearful, doesn't it?"

"I know!" Linda agreed. "So what I wonder is, how can we know what God's will is, and if we are doing it? How do we know if we are born again?"

Andrea yawned sleepily. "Oh, Linda, I'm too tired tonight to try to think through your deep, theological questions. But I do want to find answers too. I do think your thoughts are important, and knowing how to serve God is probably, as you feel, the most important thing in the world. Let's work together at finding answers!"

Linda stared at the soft moonlight illuminating the nighttime outside the window. *Somewhere out there, God is. He can see me as well in the night as in the day, according to Psalm 139.*

*God in heaven,* she prayed in her heart, *I'm so happy Andrea at least listened to me tonight. Please help me to find Your will and learn how to serve You. Help dear Andrea's family and my family too, so that all of us together can be Your own children, living holy, obedient lives.*

# 10

Saying good-bye the next morning was almost as hard as it had been when the Bakers moved away. But the morning was so beautiful and the birds were singing so cheerily from the hillsides and the treetops that Linda could not stay gloomy long.

Dad had planned to stop at Washington, D.C., for some sightseeing on the way home. But it was so hot, and everyone was too tired to have much heart for it. So after a stop at the Washington Monument and a White House tour, they headed home.

The summer days passed quickly. August came, and it was soon time to think *school* again. For Larry, that meant packing for college. And for Linda, it meant a long school year ahead without either Larry or Andrea.

She felt like moping. It was extremely hot and humid, even for August, so why bother keeping up with the flower beds or keeping the weeds out of the garden? Who cared whether the vegetables got picked or canned? Who would eat them anyway? She went out to the orchard and flopped face-down in the thick grass. *O God in heaven,* she prayed, *I'm sorry I'm so morbid. But the joy has gone out of life for me, it seems.* The tears ran down and watered the dry turf as she continued to struggle with her feelings of discouragement.

Suddenly the words of a Scripture verse came to her: "Rejoice in the Lord alway: and again I say, Rejoice." How ashamed she felt. She sat up, wiping her eyes on her skirt. *Please help me find joy in spite of circumstances, dear Jesus. You know everything. You know the sadness I feel, and surely You understand—You, who faced death alone because Your friends all forsook You. I'm sorry, Jesus, for moping, when I have so very much to be thankful for!*

Linda brushed the dry grass off herself and hurried to the garden shed. There was plenty of work to do, and she might as well get at it. Work would be a tonic for pitying herself, at least! Getting a wheelbarrow, she set to work picking off all the ripe tomatoes in the garden. Then she wheeled them to the back door. "Mom," she called at the screen door, "I brought tomatoes in from the garden."

After she heard Mom answer from somewhere inside the cool house, Linda went for a couple of baskets; there were green beans to pick. The stalks were hanging full, and in half an hour she had her two baskets full.

She sat at the picnic table in the shade of the maple trees and snapped beans. By the sound of kettles rattling that came from inside the house, she guessed that Mom and Loretta were washing and cutting up tomatoes to boil for spaghetti sauce.

Soon Loretta came out and joined her, carrying another dishpan. "Well, sis, school starts in two weeks! Are you ready for another year of cramming information into your brain?" Loretta asked as she sat down to help. "I'm not! But I am ready for the fun of being with my friends every day." She filled a pan with beans and began snipping off the ends. "Out here in the country we sure don't see much of the school crowd through the summer. Except Red. Oh, and Ron, of course. He's like a permanent fixture—translated *pest*—around here!"

"Yes, it will be nice to see more of our friends again. And I'm looking forward to studying this year too," Linda said. "It's always interesting to learn new things!"

She smiled in amusement at her younger sister, who was making a wry face, probably about the studying part. "You'll be in the ninth grade, and I'll be in the eleventh. We're getting old, aren't we."

"I'd say getting old *enough!* " Loretta stated with emphasis, rolling her big eyes and tossing her curls.

Linda let that pass. She knew well enough what was on Loretta's mind, but what could she say?

"There, these are finished," Linda said, gathering up the ends and scooping them into a basket. She set the two dishpans filled with cut beans on top of each other. "Do you want to take the beans in to Mom? I should go check if there are lima beans ready to pick yet." Linda handed the dishpans to Loretta, who took them, with a grimace at Linda, and went to the house.

Later when Linda walked into the kitchen, Loretta was nowhere around. "I thought Loretta was helping you, Mom," she said.

"Well, I thought she was helping you!" Mom returned, washing her hands and drying them with a paper towel. "I'll see if she went upstairs. She knows we need help here this afternoon, but she has her nose in a book every half chance she gets!"

Linda washed beans till Mom came down again, followed by an unhappy Loretta. "But, Mom, I wanted to see what happened in the story!" she complained. "I was at the best part of the book!"

"What were you reading?" Linda asked. "You're surely not reading one of those off-color novels again, were you?"

"Is that any business of yours?" Loretta retorted. "I got it at the library last week when we went to town, and I want to finish it before tomorrow so I can take it back!"

"Well, we have work to do now," Mom said with finality. "And you are not going to finish any book till the work is done."

That evening as Larry worked in the shop, Linda helped Dad wash up in the milk house. "Dad, I have a concern about Loretta," she said as she put the milkers through the washtubs. "I'm afraid she isn't reading the kind of books that are good for her, especially considering the weakness she already has for boys."

"What kind of books is she reading?" Dad asked.

"Well, right now she is reading some lewd novel, and last week I went in her room and saw another one on her nightstand. Earlier in the spring, she was reading one that Mom made her get rid of. But Mom didn't seem to have any problem with the one she was reading today.

"But those aren't the only books she has been reading. She seems to delight in finding ones with the foulest language. Or where the main character is wicked and his wickedness is then extolled—like *Huckleberry Finn*. Or ones with the most explicit love scenes. She checked out two at the library over my protests, just in the last month! I know what those books are, from what I've heard others say about them."

Dad nodded soberly.

"I worry about the influence this kind of reading is having on her," Linda went on. "Others consider her boy crazy and a flirt around school already! It really hurts me for her to have a reputation like that."

"It hurts me too," Dad echoed sadly.

"And, Dad, she runs around with some of the wildest students, and I'm afraid she's going to get into real trouble! Larry is worried about it too. We have talked about it, but we don't know how we can help her." Linda spoke with deep feeling.

"Another thing, Dad," Linda continued as Dad stood silently listening, "is that she has been wearing makeup in school. She knows you wouldn't approve, so she puts it on at school. I don't mean to be a tattletale, but I'm so afraid she is going to get in trouble and be expelled or something!"

Dad finally spoke. "Well, now, Linda, I'm glad you told me these things. I know she has problems, but I didn't realize all that is going on. I guess Mom and I must talk to her and also monitor her reading more closely," he said sincerely. "We thought we were doing the best we could by not allowing her to go to anything but family-rated movies, and by refusing to have television in our home."

"But she watches it at her friends' places," Linda said. "I did too when I was younger—not knowing then why you didn't allow us to have a TV when everyone else did."

Dad just looked sadly at Linda. "Well now, I see we have more work to do, and I'll need to talk with Mother about it," he continued, as though talking to himself.

"Thank you, Dad, for understanding!" Linda's heart felt as light as her feet as she skipped out the door and up the back walk to the house.

After supper, Dad and Mom took a drive. Loretta hid away in her bedroom, probably with a book, Linda thought. But she knew it was not the novel Loretta had been reading earlier, because she had seen Dad carry that one out with him. Linda quickly shelled the few limas she had picked earlier and set them in the refrigerator. Then she and Larry sat in the back yard, enjoying the cooler evening.

"I talked with Dad tonight about Loretta," Linda began. "He understood, and I wonder if he took Mom away so they would have time to talk things out between them."

"Good old Dad," Larry said with feeling. "Linda, not many families have a good father like we have. Do you realize that?"

"I do, and I'm so thankful for the way he's been a good example for us children. I often think that it's probably because of his deep interest in us that we are kind of different from the other young people at school."

"You mean . . . ?" Larry began.

"I mean, Dad has always protected us from the dangers of doing a lot of things that most people do without thinking. Like listening to rock 'n' roll, or watching TV half the night, or going to a lot of dances or the game rooms in town. Or even like going to the movies. He takes the family now and then, but he does not let us go by ourselves very often. He doesn't talk very much about being a Christian, but he must think like a Christian because of his interest in our moral character."

"I admit, I don't know much about how a Christian should act, other than living by the Golden Rule, and Dad does that," Larry said.

Linda sat pondering for a time. *Living by the Golden Rule . . . Is that all there is to obeying the Bible? Or is there more than that? But many a person can do to others as he would have others do to him*, she reasoned. *The truth from John 3 must go much deeper than that. "Except a man be born again, he cannot see the kingdom of God." But who can ever understand what that means?*

"Do you ever read the Bible, Larry?" Linda inquired. "I have been reading it every day for, oh, at least the last three or four months. And I have been feeling so burdened about some things. I think a lot about it all, about the things I read. And I wonder about so many things."

Larry studied the distant cornfields for a time. "To answer your question, I do read the Bible sometimes. I have thought a lot about what you asked me one time last spring. Something like 'How can we know God's will?' I have pondered over that, reading the Bible to try to find answers. There is more to Christianity, I fear, than most churches want to admit." Larry paused again, thoughtfully.

"And going to college isn't going to be without its temptations either," he added. "From some of the things I hear, anyone that wants to live a decent moral life has to pretty nearly stand alone. We've had a pretty decent high school, at least from what I've observed when we go for away-from-home games. But college will be a whole new arena!"

"You have Mom and Dad and me at home, Larry, to support you and pray for you," Linda encouraged.

"I realize that. And yet, I've begun to feel such a need for help beyond myself, to keep from getting into trouble. That is another reason I have been reading the Bible. I know God gives help to those who want His help. And I surely do want it!"

As Linda sat on the cool grass, feelings of great happiness sprang up inside her as she realized that Larry's burden was similar to hers—a burden to find answers to the questions of life.

Her dear brother was willing to talk over these deep and troubling things with her; surely together they could find some answers!

"Oh, Larry," she burst out, "I'm so happy you are beginning to understand how I've been feeling." Then a sudden thought came to her. "But soon you'll be going away to college. Then we won't be able to have our good talks together!" The happiness suddenly drained from her.

"Don't be downcast, Linda," Larry said kindly. "Ron and I plan to come home nearly every weekend, you know. And there is such a thing as letters."

"Of course. You are right, Larry. Sorry." Linda shifted her position on the grass as Tiny plopped down beside her. "This summer has been hard for me . . . you know, with Andrea leaving and all that. I doubt I will ever have a friend as dear to me as she has been. Andrea is very special to me, Larry. And now with you soon leaving too, I will have to make another hard adjustment!"

"Well, that's life, sis," Larry encouraged her. "We're growing up, you know, and changes and adjustments are just a natural part of that."

"Yes, I know." Linda nodded.

Suddenly, strains of harmonious music drifted across the yard. "Listen! It sounds like Shem and his quartet are practicing tonight!" Larry exclaimed.

Linda clapped her hands delightedly. "I

always love to hear them sing. They haven't sung for a while; at least I haven't heard them."

" 'Swing low, sweet chariot, comin' for to carry me home . . .' " The singing voices came clearly from the house across the road.

"I'm glad we have good neighbors, aren't you?" Linda said.

"Well, except for old Mrs. Davis!" Larry stated meaningfully. Linda thought of the vulgar old woman living in the little yellow house set at the edge of the pine forest, between their house and Grandpa's. She was supposedly a practicing witch, and Linda had always had a dreadful fear of her. She thought of how Mom and Dad had visited her on occasion in an effort to be neighborly. Once they had even invited her to come along to church. But she had rebuffed them, saying she did not need any neighbors snooping around in her business. And she did not need anything of God either! The thought of her saddened Linda's heart. She wished Larry had not mentioned her.

The car drove in the lane then, and Larry and Linda watched their parents walk slowly to the house.

# 11

"Pastor Kelloway told me on Sunday that his wife is feeling much stronger and that they have been packing their things," Dad stated at breakfast the next morning. "If possible, they would like to move into the parsonage this week."

"Do they need help with moving?" Mom asked.

Dad shook his head. "I asked him that. He said they hired a moving company. And some of his wife's family will be around to help them set up the house. But I did suggest that they stop in after they feel settled, and we will gladly supply the milk and eggs that they need for the first week. Pastor Kelloway seemed to appreciate that offer, so I expect they will. He said they are eager to get acquainted with the families in the church. I would expect, though, that they would call before they come, although I did tell him where we live."

Mom excused herself and started clearing the table. "If they call, we can invite them to stay for lunch or supper, whatever the case. We always have fresh vegetables and plenty of chicken and beef on hand, so a meal wouldn't be a problem. I'm eager to meet his wife," she said.

"Pastor Kelloway said he is eager for the family to be here with him," Dad went on. "And I can imagine he would be. He hopes everything will work out that they can be moved in before this coming Sunday."

*It's not unusual for people to stop in through the week,* Linda thought as she helped Mom clear the table. *But the Kelloways!* Linda hoped that they would call first before stopping in, if they did. *Farmers aren't always the cleanest,* she thought, thinking of the many chores around the farm that could be quite smelly or dirty, or both. And pastors' families were usually quite soft and did not know very much about the dirty side of farming. *Well, Pastor Baker was different. But he was an exception,* Linda thought. She remembered all the times through the years when Andrea had helped with whatever chores there had been on hand to do. Yes, Pastor Baker's family had been an exception; she was sure of that.

"What should I plan to do today, Dad?" Larry asked after excusing himself from the table.

"Well now." Dad scratched his ear. "I had told Red I'd like the ditch banks cleaned up before it's time to fill silo. So he is planning to work at that today."

"Good. I'll be glad for some vigorous exercise," Larry returned.

"It is to be a calm day, so possibly we can burn them off today too. Throw the brush on piles, and we can maybe burn the piles this evening."

Loretta clapped her hands. "Let's have a hot dog roast," she begged.

Dad grinned at her. "Well, now, maybe we could, if Mom agrees."

"If only Andrea were here," Linda moaned. "She was usually included in all such fun family doings. How I miss her!"

"Sometimes it's nice just to have the family together," Dad said. "But maybe we could invite Grandpa's over if you want somebody else. I'm sure they would enjoy that."

"That would be fun!" Linda agreed. "Then maybe we could sing around the fire."

And so the day passed with the extra incentive of an evening cookout. Loretta and Mom prepared a picnic menu for supper after the regular work was done for the day. Linda spent the day doing the laundry, working in the chicken house, and weeding the late broccoli-and-cabbage patch. All the time she was able to watch the progress along the ditch banks, thinking how much fun it would be to help with such cleanup. But at least Dad had a good helper in Red.

Friday dawned clear and warm. "What is there to do today, Mom?" Linda asked after breakfast. "It seems like the work is pretty much caught up."

"One of these times we'll need to get to some sewing," Mom reminded her. "But the weather seems too nice today to sit in the house, doesn't it."

Linda nodded. "I'm sure I can find *some*thing to do outside," she stated with a laugh. "Oh"—she turned to Dad—"I did see there are Rambo apples ready to pick."

"Red is planning to pick those today," Dad said. "He especially enjoys climbing the trees to do that job, so I'm glad to let him."

Mom ran dishwater in the sink. "I think the lima beans will need to be picked today. Then we will have them to shell and freeze."

"I guess I'll clean out calf pens today," Larry stated as he got up from the table. "That job should be done before I go off to school and leave you-all with the harvesting and silo filling and all the rest. Unless you have something more pressing for me to do, Dad."

"That should be done, and I'll be happy to have it done before you leave," Dad assented.

"Oh, may I help?" Linda asked eagerly. She thought it was wonderful exercise to fork out the strawy manure onto the spreader. And then what fun it was to watch the little brown heifers romp friskily in the fresh yellow wheat straw that she would put down in their clean pens. It would also be a great time for some brother–sister camaraderie—the kind that she was sorely going to miss when Larry went away.

"I'll be glad for help," Larry said, grinning jovially at her.

Loretta snorted. "What a stinky job! You can have it!" she stated with vehemence. "I'll help Red pick the apples."

"Well now, you will *not* help Red pick apples," Dad stated firmly. "You will help your mother pick and shell lima beans. And you won't go to the orchard to talk nonsense with Red either. You will stay at your work or take the consequences! A word to the wise should be sufficient."

Loretta looked startled, but did not respond. Linda was startled too. Seldom had she heard her father speak with such finality. But, to her mind, it was about time someone gave Loretta some firm direction.

Larry and Linda worked side by side, forking the manure into the spreader. After the spreader was loaded, Larry took it out to the mowed-off hayfield to spread. While he was doing that, Linda prepared the next pen for cleaning by moving the calves to another pen. Linda found there was little time or energy for talk. It was fork and throw, fork and throw. Any conversation was about the subject at hand—which pen to clean next, which calves were whose, and suchlike.

And it was a dirty, smelly job, just as Loretta had said. Linda looked down at her dirty jeans and Larry's outgrown gum boots that she had opted to wear rather than get her own boots dirty and smelly. "I sure hope no salesmen stop in today," she said with a laugh.

Larry scrutinized her. "You wouldn't fit very well in a fashion tableau just now," he agreed, laughing with her.

"We're going to be finished before noon at this rate," Larry commented later as they worked at the last pen.

"While you take this load out, I'll throw down the straw," Linda said. "Then we'll be ready for the fun part."

Larry threw the last forkful on the spreader, stuck his fork in the corner of the pen, and ran to the tractor. "I'll be in to help you bed the pens," he said as he climbed up.

Linda stuck her fork beside Larry's and then clomped to the ladder leading up to the barn loft. Quickly she started climbing. "Oh, these boots!" she exclaimed as she almost missed a rung with her too-big feet. But she made it safely up the ladder, and soon bale after bale went flying down the hay hole.

She started down the ladder again, and then, missing a rung, fell into the pile of yellow bales. Exasperated at her predicament, she struggled to free herself, pushing the bales aside till she was able to climb out of the pile. But her boots were still stuck at the bottom! Oh well, she would have to move more bales before she could dig them out. In her stocking feet, she started lugging bales to the back barn door and throwing them out into the barnyard.

Suddenly someone cleared his throat nearby, and Linda looked up, startled. There, standing near the front of the barn, she saw a young man. He was evidently very amused about something, judging by the big grin on his face. *Whoever can that be, and where did he come from?* Linda wondered, beating a retreat behind the pile of straw bales. *He's not a salesman that I recognize!*

"Hi there! How are you?" the young man asked in a relaxed and friendly manner when he saw Linda scrutinizing him.

"If you want to see my dad," she said tartly, trying her best to stay hidden as much as possible behind the straw pile, "he's in the chicken house."

"Well, I came out to see your brother, but I will help you take these bales wherever you need them, if you'll let me," he said, stepping closer, still with an amused grin.

"I don't need any help, thank you. And my brother is out in the field right now; you can go find him if you care to." Linda pointed out the back barn door toward the field where Larry was still spreading manure. She realized with shame that her temper was rising. How much had this grinning young man actually seen? Had he seen her fall down off the hay-hole ladder?

The young man seemed to take her cue. He picked his way carefully across the barnyard and stood at the gate, watching Larry drive the Farmall with the spreader from the field to the shed.

Linda looked at the pile of bales that still needed to be carried out and spread in pens. Larry could do that while she went to clean up for lunch. Leaving her dirty boots in the straw pile, she fled up the back walk to the house. She hastily washed up and went upstairs for a shower.

As Linda looked out her bedroom window, she saw Mom and Dad, with several other people, walking through the orchard, where Red was picking apples. *Wonder who that is?* she mused. Then a sudden thought struck her. *That must be Pastor Kelloway and his family! And that must have been their son that came to the barn!*

From the wonderful smells drifting up from the kitchen, Linda figured the Kelloways would be staying for lunch. She shrugged hopelessly. *It surely would have been nice to know what's going on,* she thought. She wondered why no one had bothered to tell her and Larry. A sinking feeling settled on her. *What an introduction to the new pastor and his family!*

She quickly showered and then washed her hair and dried it with the hair dryer. She brushed it out carefully and tied it back with a pink ribbon. Then she looked in her closet, contemplating. What should she put on? She finally settled for her favorite pink school blouse. She put on the burgundy denim jumper that she had made in home ec last year. Then she hurried downstairs.

Loretta was in the kitchen with Pansy. They were making a wonderful-smelling lunch—all sorts of nice things that were Loretta's delight.

Linda went to Pansy, who was cutting lettuce for a salad. "May I do this? Is there something else you can do?" she asked.

"What's de mattah, chil'?" Pansy wondered, her sensitive spirit feeling for Linda.

"Nothing much, Pansy," Linda assured her quietly. "I'm just a mite peckish feeling right now, that's all."

By the time everyone came in the front walk for lunch, the girls and Pansy had the table set with Mom's best table service, and everything was all ready. Larry had also come downstairs after cleaning up and had gone out the front door to meet the others. "Go on now and meet de folks," Pansy insisted, giving the girls a gentle push toward the front foyer. "I do de servin'."

Linda instantly liked Pastor and Mrs. Kelloway. They looked like folks who understood people and their needs. There were three girls, aged fifteen, twelve, and eight. Linda shook their hands and politely asked their names. Sharon was the oldest, then Lynette, and then Renae. Steve, Larry, and Dad were standing behind the girls. Steve had been watching Linda with an amused grin as she met and chatted with his sisters. He shook Linda's hand. "Have I seen you before?" he asked with a merry twinkle in his dark eyes.

Linda chose to ignore his comment. She was afraid of what she might say if she did respond.

Undaunted by her silence, he continued in an aside, "By the way, I brought your boots in and set them at the back door for you."

"Thanks," was her curt reply.

Lunch around the beautiful table was a delight, and Linda found it impossible to stay upset. Fresh Shasta daisies adorned the center of the table, and Loretta had tastefully planned her menu with complementing colors. Linda found herself gradually relaxing in the steady flow of pleasant and congenial conversation. Larry, Steve, and Red were chatting like old friends about school life, sports, fishing and hunting, and various other things that interest boys. Loretta and the two oldest Kelloway girls were comparing studies and favorite classes as well as books they had read through the summer. Mom and Dad were introducing the pastor and his wife to the community. Finally able to forget herself, for the time being at least, Linda joined the conversation.

Pansy insisted on doing the dishes and shooed the other women out of the kitchen. Everyone wandered out to the yard, to the comfortable lawn chairs under the maple trees by the pool. That was the coolest spot on the farm, Linda thought, except possibly out by the river.

Larry must have had the same thought. "Hey, folks, how about taking a ride out to our own personal river?" he proposed.

After some discussion, the older folks decided to stay where they were. "Take the pickup," Dad suggested. "Everybody can ride on the back."

It was perfect out by the river. A stiff breeze from the east was singing through the tops of the pine trees and roughing up whitecaps on the surface of the water. Loretta and the Kelloway girls sat on the end of the pier, chatting like old friends as they swung their feet over the water. Linda sat with them, watching the water and listening to the animated conversations going on around her. Steve and Larry were sitting by the river's edge, cypress and pine trees behind them. "This is beautiful out here," Steve said, leaning back against a tree trunk and sighing with pleasure.

Linda turned to look at him. *He must appreciate some of the simpler things of life too,* she thought, *even if he surely is not a farm boy.*

Barely an hour had passed till the faint sound of the dinner bell came on the breeze. "I think the folks are calling us in," Larry said.

"Oh, must we leave already? I wish we could stay out here forever," one of the Kelloway girls said, sighing regretfully.

Steve looked all around with appreciation. "It is so peaceful and quiet—not the sound of another human being! But we must go, gals," he said, helping his younger sisters up into the back of the pickup before he sprinted up. Linda climbed on too. Then Larry drove slowly back up the woods road to the open ground.

Steve seated himself facing Linda. "I feel I must have offended you today, Linda. I am so used to teasing my sisters that I did not think! But if I offended you, I'm sorry for that," he said, looking at her. "We're going to be friends, I hope."

"Sure, we'll be friends," Linda replied more calmly than she felt inside.

Larry had stopped the pickup at the fence gate. Linda jumped off to open the gate. "I'm going to walk in," she said to the other girls. "Want to come along?"

The girls all jumped off and walked up the field lane, scuffing along in the soft sand, talking and laughing. The pickup, with Larry driving and

Steve sitting alone in the back, was at the house long before the girls got there.

Feeding the calves that evening, Linda thought back on the day. *How childish I was*, she scolded herself. *Whatever made me act that way? It was not Steve's fault that he happened to catch me in an embarrassing situation. Why couldn't I just have laughed it off and taken it in stride?*

It did not help at all when Larry also scolded her for being so distant and cool. "Steve asked me if he had said something to offend you. I told him I didn't know." Larry smiled at Linda, the kind of smile that invites one to tell all.

But Linda could not bring herself to tell Larry how Steve had probably seen her fall down off the hay-hole ladder. Really, it all looked silly now.

She felt too miserable to read her Bible or pray that evening, but fell into bed, feeling totally ashamed.

# 12

Sunday was a rainy day. Linda thought the day was typical of the way she felt—dismal and dreary. Usually Sundays were pleasant family days, often spent with friends or with Grandpa Asbury's; but today she dreaded going to church.

How could she face the Kelloway family—any of them? They probably thought she was the world's worst snob!

The morning after their visit, she had told God how sorry she was for her pride and anger. But had He forgiven her? Would He forgive as long as she felt unforgiving toward Steve? Maybe Larry could help her know what to do. She doubted that even Dad would understand this predicament. *And Mom would not begin to understand!* Linda thought ruefully of how Mom had put in a good word quite often for Mr. Taylor. *No matter,* Linda thought, *if he is a full eight years older than I. Or if he has little regard for God or the Bible. To Mom, Anthony Taylor is the epitome of The Catch! Mom would certainly think it quite proper if I had put the pastor's son in his place.* But then, one could never tell for sure what Mom was thinking. She really seemed to be taken by the pastor and his wife and had spoken quite kindly of them and their family since their visit.

Linda watched the rain drip in front of her window. She noticed the cornfields beyond the orchard. The stalks looked as though they had grown a foot during the night, nourished by the gentle rain. Everything looked washed and clean. *God washed the world last night and hung it out to dry,* she mused, thinking of the poem. *Rather than feeling washed and clean,* she thought mournfully, *I just feel weepy, like everything outside looks!*

Pastor Kelloway's sermon that morning was titled "Jesus, an Example of a Godly Youth," taking his text from Luke 2. Linda forgot the burden on her mind and listened with rapt attention, caught up not only by his good delivery but also by the wonderful thoughts that he brought from the Bible. His first point was taken from verse 40: "The child grew, . . . filled with wisdom: and the grace of God was upon him." Jesus learned wisdom by listening to and speaking with His heavenly Father. God's grace was upon Him; His heart was a flame kindled by His Father; He spoke words of beauty, faith, glory, and hope.

From verse 49, Pastor Kelloway noted that Jesus loved to be in His Father's house. He loved prayer and worship.

Pastor Kelloway's third point was that Jesus was subject to His parents. He knew the Old Testament command to honor His parents, and He did that obediently.

The final point Pastor Kelloway gave was that Jesus advanced in wisdom and stature. All about Jesus were the strong influences that shaped His life—a godly home with faithful parental direction and teaching, the beauties of nature, the Scriptures that were read to Him in the home and synagogue. And above all, His love of the life and worship in the temple, His Father's house.

He closed his sermon with a plea to all youth to follow the example of Christ. Christ's life of victory and His death on the cross give all who desire His help, forgiveness of sins and the strength to live in victory over sin. " 'For even hereunto were ye called: because Christ also suffered for us, leaving us an example, that ye should follow his steps: who did no sin, neither was guile [deceit] found in his mouth,' " Pastor Kelloway quoted from 1 Peter 2. He also quoted 1 Timothy 4:12, which exhorts youth to be an example of the believers in word, in action, in love, in spirit, in faith, in purity.

Linda looked from her place in the choir loft over the congregation of some three hundred worshipers. How many of them, she wondered, had been touched by the sermon? How many really wanted to be more like Jesus, to follow the example of the life He had lived? Many, she guessed, came to church simply out of habit. Even now, it was easy to see that, for many, their thoughts were far away. Some were dozing, and some were looking around, no doubt observing who was wearing what.

She saw Mr. Taylor in a back pew, his look cynical as it usually was in any kind of spiritual setting. She noticed Red in the pew with his mother, listening with rapt attention, his usually merry face sober. Linda knew that under his jolly exterior he had a deep longing to know and do what was right. She knew he often went to Dad with many of the questions that boys normally ask their fathers. Dad did not talk about their conversations, but she had come upon them in deep discussion at various times. And always, after times like that, Dad would ask the family to pray for Red.

Here and there in the gathered congregation, various of her school friends were sitting with their families. Some seemed interested in worship; some seemed totally bored.

She stood up then with the choir to sing the closing number. " 'O God, our help in ages past, / Our hope for years to come, / Be Thou our guide while life shall last, / And our eternal home,' " she sang with all her heart.

Grandpa Asbury's had invited the family for

Sunday lunch. Loretta had plans to be with friends in town for the afternoon, but the rest went to Grandpa's. Linda thought it was so pleasant to visit again with Grandma and Grandpa, to be again in their quaint house that smelled of cedar and mothballs.

After lunch, everyone sat around the living room companionably. The house was warm, but with the rain through the night, it was still too wet to sit outside. "Well, Lester, what do you think of our new pastor?" Grandpa asked.

"Well now, I think he is a man of God," Dad responded. "He seems to have a burden to preach the Word in a way that Pastor Baker never quite did. Not that I didn't appreciate Pastor Baker," he hastened to add. "But there is a deeper dimension, or something, in Pastor Kelloway's sermons."

"That is the way Grandma and I feel too," Grandpa stated. "And yet we've been hearing some feedback that Pastor Kelloway is getting a little too radical."

"I've heard some of that too," Dad responded. "I don't like it. But you know, most people don't want to hear anything about sin. They want to hear that they are doing just fine and are on their way to heaven. Pastor Kelloway seems to believe that folks must have a new-birth experience in order to claim the promises of the Scriptures. And that after their birth into God's family, they must live daily as children of God."

Grandma sat on the edge of her rocker. "You know, we hear so much about being Christians; most of the people in town go to church every Sunday and would surely say they are Christians. But what difference does it make in most people's lives?"

"I think of that too," Dad replied. "For most, if they would have to choose between their money and God, or between their friends and God, or between their social standing and God, which would they choose? Questions like that bother me because I feel sure that God would lose every time! Most people—whether Christian in name or not—live for themselves and their own pleasures."

Grandpa took up the conversation. "The Bible says plainly that those who are Christians are new creatures in Christ; old things have passed away; and all things have become new. Christians are to set their affection, or mind, on God. They try, with God's help, to do only those things that please God—every day and all the time. The Bible is to be the guide for our lives."

Linda was intrigued with the conversation. She had never known that such spiritual searchings also bothered Grandma and Grandpa. She looked at the well-used Bible lying on the table beside Grandma's rocker. She knew that Grandma and Grandpa had Scripture reading every morning before they ate breakfast, and that they wanted to do what was right according to the Bible. But why did so few others? And why was there so little teaching about the deep things of the Bible? And now, when Pastor Kelloway was preaching the Scriptures, some were already complaining. She had heard it too.

Linda knew that among those not happy with the straightforward preaching were Pap-pap and Mam-mam Jones. Mom had spoken quite freely of how her parents did not approve of the "new" doctrines that Pastor Kelloway was preaching. They preferred to hear the kind of preaching they were always used to. Linda had often heard her mother on the telephone, talking with Mam-mam, and she knew the conflict.

Linda glanced at Mom now. She had not said a word. How was she taking this conversation?

Linda was soon able to draw a conclusion to that question. Mom was sitting very stiffly on her chair, her face a study in conflicting emotions. Suddenly she spoke up with some vehemence. "I don't know why Pastor Kelloway had to come here and upset a good thing! Why must he get everybody so unsettled? I wish he had stayed where he was!" Mom fidgeted nervously with her hands as the rest looked at her.

Linda turned quickly to Dad, who had a smitten look on his face. It was obvious to Linda that he must have been through some of these arguments before with Mom and that he wished she had not talked just now. Linda could also understand a bit how Mom must feel. Mom was caught in the middle. She knew that her husband loved and appreciated the new pastor, but what about her parents? Her very proper and socially correct parents! She certainly did not want to offend them!

Interrupting the suddenly stilted atmosphere, the telephone rang, and Grandpa got stiffly out of his chair to go and answer it. "For you, Linda," he called around the corner of the hallway.

It was Mr. Taylor. "I finally found you," he said. "No one answered at your house after I tried a number of times. I thought you just might be at your grandparents'." He paused briefly. "Could I see you this afternoon, Linda?" he asked, a note of urgency in his voice. "I wanted to talk with you this morning after the church service, but you were in the middle of a huddle of girls."

"Why don't you come out and join our family at Grandpa's?" Linda suggested, knowing quite well how interested he would be in such a suggestion.

"I'd rather go for a drive," he said.

Linda hesitated. "Let me say something to my parents," she said.

"It's all right with me," Mom assured her, as Linda knew she would.

But Dad suddenly got up from his chair and came into the hall. "Tell him to call back in ten minutes," Dad said firmly. Linda gave Mr. Taylor the message and hung up quickly, wondering what was on Dad's mind.

"Mom and I are going home," Dad said. "You can wait here for Mr. Taylor to call again, and you are to tell him that if he wants to visit with you, it will have to be in our home. Do you understand?"

Linda nodded her head, tears coming to her eyes. She felt bad to add to Dad's distress just now.

After saying their good-byes and thank-yous for the lunch, Dad and Mom went to the car to leave. Larry would wait and take Linda home after Mr. Taylor's phone call.

Mr. Taylor was not happy, to state it mildly, with the stipulations Dad had specified. But he decided to come anyway. "I have to see you, Linda, regardless of what your dad says," he told her.

"I'll be waiting at our house," she reaffirmed, hanging up the phone.

# 13

When Linda got home, Mom had gone to her room to rest. "Mother has a headache," Dad explained. "But maybe it is best if she is resting now. I would like to talk with Mr. Taylor sometime while he is here, and I'm afraid Mother would not appreciate what I have to say."

Linda straightened up the front porch, and set up chairs from the outdoor patio. Insects had been such a nuisance with the humid weather that it was not very inviting to sit in the yard. Inside the screened porch, she and Mr. Taylor could visit without needing to think about mosquitoes and deer flies droning their piercing music about them.

Soon she heard Mr. Taylor's car turn in the lane. She met him when he came to the door. Reluctantly he followed her in to meet Dad, who was reading in the library. Then Linda led Mr. Taylor to the lawn chairs on the pleasant porch.

The robins were singing cheerily in the maple trees around the house, as they usually did after a rain. Linda heard the pleasant songs of other birds and the bawl of a cow in the distance. But

Mr. Taylor was apparently distracted. He had not said a word.

Linda laughed in spite of herself. "Is this a Quaker meeting?" she asked, glancing at Mr. Taylor's sober face.

He smiled at her. "It's just that I'm not too happy with these arrangements and don't understand what is up," he said sarcastically. "I guess I would like to think I am a man in my own right!"

When Linda did not say anything, he continued, "I wish we could relate as friends, Linda. Why do you hold me off?"

"Do I?" Linda asked.

"Well, *I* think so! It's always Mr. Taylor this and Mr. Taylor that. Couldn't you at least call me Tony? It would sound so much more like we're friends if you would call me by my first name."

Linda did not speak for a time. She watched a robin in the yard as it cocked its head to listen for a worm. Then she watched it suddenly poke its bill into the ground and successfully pull the long earthworm out of its hole. Then it snipped it in half, characteristically, and flew off with its prize.

"Well?" Mr. Taylor questioned. "Am I more than a friend to you? Or am I even a friend?"

"You are a friend. And you are a teacher whom I respect and appreciate very much,"

Linda said earnestly. "I wish we could just continue the teacher–student relationship, and nothing more."

Mr. Taylor sighed deeply. "Did you know I'm not coming back to teach this fall?"

"No!" Linda turned to look at him. "Why not?"

"Someone reported that I was seeing you this summer. I think Mary Catherine Carmean probably did. But who it was isn't important, I guess. Anyway, the school board gave me the option to give you up or to give up my position. In the meantime, my father asked me to join his law practice in D.C. So, in hopes that you would not turn me away, I chose to give up my teaching position here, and told my father that I would take his offer." Mr. Taylor gazed thoughtfully into the distance. "I plan to rent out my mother's place here and move to D.C. within the next month."

"I didn't know you have a degree in law," Linda returned.

"I majored in languages, but at the insistence of my mother, I also got a law degree."

"I'm truly sorry that you will be leaving," Linda said sincerely. "I have appreciated you very much as a teacher the last two years. And I looked forward to having you for French classes for the next two."

"Thank you for that much at least!" Mr. Taylor stated crisply. "Might absence make the heart grow fonder?"

"Please, Mr. Taylor—"

"Tony."

"Well then, please, Tony, I am not ready for any involvement with you, or anyone else for that matter. I am not even seventeen yet—and will not be for two more months. And I have two more years of high school. I respect you. I admire you as a teacher. But—"

"Could you come to think of me as more than a teacher sometime, Linda?" Mr. Taylor asked eagerly. "If I gave you more time?"

Linda felt the trembling of her whole inner being. Certainly, she felt honored that he had singled her out—he, who could have had any one of a number of young eligibles around town. But it was an honor not worthy of consideration for one who wanted to be accepted of God—that she was sure of! How could she explain to him that he did not share this most important ambition of her heart—the desire to know and love God? How could she be happy with anyone who did not share that goal and desire? Furthermore, she felt it would be wrong for her to give him any hope. Even if he became a Christian, could she feel at one with him? He was so much older and moved in totally different social circles than she ever wished to move in.

She looked at Mr. Taylor, who was studying her face eagerly, waiting for her reply. How could she hurt and disappoint him?

"I would like to talk with my parents," Linda said finally, "before answering that question."

"Right now I don't care so much what they think. I want to know what your thoughts are," he answered, looking intently at her.

"Mr. Taylor," she began, trying to choose her words carefully, "what do you and I have in common? We are worlds apart on most issues. I mean, even besides our age difference, we do *not* have common goals or ambitions. What hope would there be that we could ever be happy together? We need to be realistic about all this."

Dad came to the porch just then, carrying a tray with a pitcher and three glasses. "I thought you might enjoy a drink of punch," he said as he set the tray on a table close to them. He poured them each a drink and pulled up a chair, sitting down next to Mr. Taylor.

"Thank you, Dad," Linda said, smiling at him, grateful for more than just the cold drink.

Mr. Taylor reached for his drink, shifting his feet uncomfortably. "We were just discussing that I will not be coming back to teach this fall," Mr. Taylor began as he sipped his punch. "I plan to move to Washington, D.C., and go into law practice with my father."

"I see," Dad returned.

"And I would like very much if Linda and I could stay in touch while I am away."

Dad sat up straighter. "For one thing, Mr. Taylor, she is only sixteen."

"I know that, Mr. Asbury," Mr. Taylor broke in quickly. "Like she said, she has two more years of high school, and then likely four more of college. But I am willing to wait; a girl like her is worth waiting for."

"But, Dad," Linda pled, turning to her father, "I told him we are so far apart in so many ways. And I wasn't thinking so much just then about my age or the years of schooling. I was thinking about our vastly differing views about God and His claim on people's lives.

"Mr. Taylor, we have talked about it before, and you know that my one ambition is to become what God wants me to be. You have expressed yourself plainly that such an ambition has no place in your life, that you are well able to look out for yourself!"

"And the Bible says that two people with such differing views toward life cannot be compatible in marriage," Dad said, taking up the conversation. "In Paul's letter to the Corinthian church, there is a verse that says that Christians are to marry only in the Lord—only marry other Christians. I believe that is very important to Linda, and it is of utmost importance to me as her father."

Linda looked at Mr. Taylor, who sat between them, his head bowed. She felt sorry for him, but what Dad had said was right, and what else could they say?

"Mr. Asbury and Linda, I wish indeed that I could share the faith that you have," Mr. Taylor said finally. "But all my educational background has been humanistic. I have been indoctrinated with all the foundational beliefs of humanism: that the time for belief in God is past, that the purpose of man's life is complete realization of human personality. All associations, all institutions exist for one thing—the fulfillment of human life, and that only! This is what college did for me. The textbooks are full of it, and the professors pour on all the cynicism and rebuff against faith that they possibly can. It is an anti-God world out there. And I was ill-prepared for facing the philosophies of such a world. I had no praying mother or caring family to stand behind me and support a faith in God." He paused in thought.

"But, Mr. Taylor, you can still have faith," Linda said sincerely. "Read your Bible with an open heart, and ask God to help you to understand His will for you. God always gives faith to those who earnestly seek for it."

"But how can I have faith when I don't even know if God exists? We have no proof that there is a God. I have never seen Him, have you? And this about the Bible. What makes such writing any greater than the writings of Socrates? Was he divine? Or was Plato? Or Aristotle? I wish I could believe, but how can I when there are no proofs of anything beyond what I can see or feel?"

"The Bible says that if we believe in God and in His Son Jesus, God will save us from our sins. He will change our lives from living to please ourselves to true joy in Him," Linda declared earnestly. "And the Bible does for me just what it says! I know there is a God. Furthermore, when I look at all this wonderful creation"—Linda swept her arm to include the beauty of the out-of-doors—"I know that some power much greater than I had to make it all! Faith is believing without seeing."

"I never studied about faith in any of my science classes," Mr. Taylor said with a dry chuckle.

"But *true* science complements faith," Dad countered. "Faith in God is not limited by the theories of men."

"Oh, Mr. Asbury, I wish I could be so simple as to believe as you do. Linda will change her mind too after she has a few years of college behind her. Everybody else does!"

"God forbid!" Linda stated with emphasis. "True education should draw men *to* God, not lead them away from Him." She looked out at the green lawn, wet and sparkling from the earlier rains.

"I do not doubt at all that the education that is offered by ungodly men leads people away from God," Dad added. "That is the will and desire of the evil one. But there is a true wisdom, the Bible says, and it comes from God."

Mr. Taylor sat gazing out over the rose garden that surrounded the patio. Linda noticed a pair of cardinals taking a bath in the fish pool and wondered if Mr. Taylor was noticing them too.

"I have been enjoying that lovely rose garden," Mr. Taylor said after a while, changing the subject. "The colors of the roses are beautiful, and the way they are planted in perfect symmetry makes the colors blend in a lovely scheme as they climb on those trellises. And I was admiring the skill with which someone matched and laid those rocks to make that patio. Someone around here must have some talent for art!"

"Oh, no," Dad said quickly. "You're wrong there. Nobody designed or made that rose garden! Those stones just kind of evolved into place, and the roses happened to start growing there, and they just happened to grow in those carefully patterned rows. The trellises sort of came together by themselves; don't ask me how! And after a while the fish pool formed, and somehow the fish got into it. Maybe the fish evolved from earthworms or something."

Linda turned quickly to Dad, wondering if he was okay. Dad's eyes twinkled at her, and

Linda sat back with a smile in her heart.

Mr. Taylor looked up with a dry laugh. "Okay, Mr. Asbury. I concede your point."

Dad just smiled. "Anyone care for more punch?" he asked as he got up to refill the pitcher.

"I believe I will, Mr. Asbury. It tastes very good on a hot day."

Dad went for more punch.

Seizing the opportunity, Mr. Taylor eagerly leaned forward. "Will you write to me, Linda?" he asked.

"I thought we had settled that question," Linda said. "You have made it clear that you do not desire to see things God's way. And I am not willing to compromise my faith in God for you."

"So you are saying that there is no hope for me? That you won't even write to me?" Mr. Taylor asked, his face emotional.

"I'm sorry, Mr. Taylor; this makes me truly feel bad for your sake. But, yes, that is what I am saying."

He got up and set his chair carefully back against the porch wall. "Well, then, I guess I will be going. And I guess this is good-bye."

"Aren't you going to wait for a drink?" Linda asked, hoping Dad would soon come back.

"I'll be going, Linda. Why draw this out? I do want to say this yet: thank you for being a continual inspiration in my classes. I will not forget you." He walked to the porch door, opened it, and went out.

"Good-bye, Mr. Taylor. I will remember you in my prayers," Linda said, getting up to stand by the screen as he went out the sidewalk to his car.

Mr. Taylor waved his hand and then turned to say, "If you ever change your mind about all this, will you let me know? Please?" Then he got into his car and drove slowly out the lane.

Linda entered the house, wondering where Dad had been so long. He was in the kitchen, mixing more punch. He turned to look at her as she came into the kitchen. "Mr. Taylor left," she said, tears coming to her eyes in spite of her great relief.

"I thought I heard his car leave."

"Thank you so much, Dad, for coming to my rescue," Linda said, truly thankful for her caring father. "I guess it's sort of an unhappy ending to an epoch in my life," she added sadly. "And yet I feel no remorse at what we told him; it had to be faced sometime."

"As much as we respected Mr. Taylor's skill as a teacher, he is not a Christian and, furthermore, seems to have no desire to ever be," Dad concluded.

Well, such was life, and life would go on. Linda would miss seeing Mr. Taylor, but only as an excellent language teacher, whom she had enjoyed in many ways. More than anything, she was thankful that God had been with her and had helped her to take a stand for Him in such a difficult situation.

Dad set the pitcher in the refrigerator. Glancing at the clock, he said, "It's almost chore time. Are you going to help this evening?"

Linda finished her drink and set her glass in the sink. "I may as well go get changed—" she began, but stopped short when Mom came into the kitchen.

Mom angrily pulled out a kitchen chair and plopped into it. "I would like to know what is going on around here!" she stated in clipped tones. "Did I just hear you two send Mr. Taylor off?"

"He left of his own choice, I think," Linda said.

Mom turned to face Linda. "You don't need to talk smart to me, young lady," she said huffily. "I heard you and your father turning away the most eligible man you will ever meet! And I want you to know you have gone too far this time!"

"Now, Mother," Dad said soothingly. "You must not be feeling well."

"I feel well enough, thank you. Although if I burst a blood vessel, it will be your fault!" Her voice was a stifled scream.

Dad went over and sat down across from Mom and motioned Linda to do the same. "Now I want to know what is bothering you,

Mother," he said gently.

"As though you don't know!" Mom's eyes flashed fire at Dad. "You know I fully approve of Mr. Taylor, and so do my parents. And now you work behind my back to send him off."

"Can you explain to me just why you approve of him?" Dad asked.

"He has money, distinction, class, looks . . . everything!" Mom was fairly screaming now. "Everything I would want for a daughter of mine!"

"And it doesn't matter to you that he has no use for God in his life?" Dad asked kindly.

"He's a good moral man. Isn't that good enough?"

"Not in God's sight. And not to me either. And I must say I'm very thankful for a daughter that wants more than that as well."

Linda looked from Dad to Mom, her heart burdened beyond words. She had never heard Mom this angry before. What was the matter?

Mom looked again at Dad. "I should never have married you, you religious fanatic! Now I know of only one way out! I'm packing my things and going home to my parents. You'll be hearing from my lawyer later." Mom jumped up and pushed her chair under the table with a slam.

Dad quickly got up too and took her firmly by the arm. "Let me alone!" Mom screamed, trying to jerk away from Dad.

"You are not feeling well, Mother, and I am going to help you to your room. When you are feeling better, we will talk more about this."

Turning to Linda, he added, "Could you and Larry start the barn chores, please?"

The pleading in his eyes was almost more than Linda could bear. She broke into soft sobs as she hurried upstairs to change her clothes. *O God in heaven, help Mom. And help Dad to know what to do,* she prayed, falling beside her bed.

It seemed like a long time till Dad finally joined her and Larry in the barn. Linda had brought the cows in from the pasture, while Larry had put the milkers together and started the feeding. Larry had been in the chicken house ever since coming home from Grandpa's and did not know what had gone on. Soberly Linda had tried to fill him in on the details.

Dad's face looked as if he had been through a tremendous emotional upheaval. "Mom will be all right," he told them as they worked together in the barn. "She is sorry for her outburst, as I knew she would be." Dad's words brought some relief to Linda, but still there was an indescribable ache in her heart. Perhaps it was all the stresses of the day combined.

After a light supper, Mom and Dad decided to go for a walk to the river. Linda was thankful that Mom had seemed like herself again at suppertime. But she had as much as threatened divorce. Did she mean it? Would she really carry out such a threat? It was a troubling thought. Linda was glad that at least Loretta did not know anything about it. Loretta had been with friends all day.

That evening the church youth had their regular Sunday evening youth night. Larry went, and no doubt Loretta would be there too, but Linda opted to stay home. She wanted to write a long letter to Andrea, and a quiet evening in a quiet house suited her purposes. As the evening wore on and page after page filled up, Linda felt a relief from the stresses of the day. To write everything to Andrea—all about the morning worship service, the afternoon discussion at Grandpa's, and even the time spent with Mr. Taylor—brought welcome relief. Andrea never had been able to figure out why Linda had not given him an emphatic "no" to begin with. She would be happy to hear that *that* matter was settled now.

She wrote about the new little calves in the barn, about the new kittens in the straw mow, about the great crop of apples that they had started to pick, and about the school chums that she had seen here and there. She even told her about the Kelloway family's visit and that they had stayed for lunch. But she did not say anything about the scene with Mom that afternoon.

Loretta came up to Linda's room after church,

full of chatter about her afternoon. "Everyone missed you at church, Linda," she went on to say. "I didn't know what to tell them when they asked why you weren't there."

"I guess you didn't need to tell them anything, Loretta," Linda answered from her desk. "It was nice to be home by myself and write a long letter to Andrea."

"Oh, wouldn't I love to read that letter," Loretta said, pretending to snatch it up from the desk.

"Go ahead, if you think you ought to," Linda returned.

"I was just teasing," Loretta admitted. "But you're too willing! Didn't you write about Steve and all the doings the last few weeks?"

"Well, no," Linda returned. "I only wrote as I would have talked to her if she had been here . . . and you or Mom or Dad had been overhearing. I didn't mention anything in particular about Steve."

"Would you believe," Loretta continued, "Steve *actually talked* with me this evening! He talked about the farm and how lovely he thought it was out here that day. He especially enjoyed being out at the river. Larry said Steve told him he wants to come out again soon!"

"I'm sure he was only being kind, Loretta. Please don't get ideas simply because a boy talked with you."

Loretta flopped across Linda's bed. "Larry said Steve asked him if we are related to that Bishop Asbury who was a bishop in the Methodist Church back in the early 1800s. He said he has read about him and his work with John Wesley in starting the Methodist Church in America. Steve must be a history buff or something. Larry said he really knows history."

Linda laughed. "You probably knew that much about Bishop Asbury too. Dad has talked about him a time or two. I think he was a great-great-great-grandpa of Dad's. He was the first circuit rider in America, having come to the New World as a missionary. During the Revolutionary War, he lived in Delaware. Some of his family stayed in the area, and those became our ancestors. Interesting?"

"To you, maybe! I'm no fan of ancient history! I much prefer the *interesting* 'history' that is happening right now."

Linda laid her pen down and spun around on her desk chair. What was the use of trying to write, with Loretta intent on chattering behind her! Then she saw Loretta's muddy shoes on her bed; they were leaving brown streaks across her clean bedspread. "Well, if you don't get your dirty shoes off my bed . . .!" she threatened with pretended ferocity.

Loretta jumped up and held out her shoes to look at them. "Oops, sorry, sis! Truly I am! I didn't know I had muddy feet!" She grabbed a handful of tissues out of Linda's box and started cleaning off the bedspread and her shoes.

"Are Dad and Mom home?" Loretta asked.

"Mom wasn't feeling so well today, so they went to bed early," Linda returned. Again, how thankful she was that Loretta had been away that afternoon. Such a scene would surely have unsettled her.

The next morning dawned bright and clear. The humidity had finally cleared after days of sultry, hot weather. Linda jumped out of bed and hurried to the window to get a glimpse and a sniff of the breaking day. The birds were heralding the new day with their buoyant songs. Linda dressed quickly and hurried to the barn. In the meadow, she heard the call of a quail: *Bob-white, bob-white, bob-bob-white!*

School would start again next week. She was eager for the learning experiences, but not eager to spend her days in the sticky, hot classrooms when she could be in the glorious outdoors! But the starting of school would get her mind off Larry's leaving, at least. He would be leaving on Wednesday for Charlottetown. Then Red would be helping Dad more with the morning and evening milkings, as well as general work around the farm. Red was like a brother, and Linda did not mind having him around, but he could never take Larry's place.

Linda savored each hour of the day, thinking about each little peculiar joy and sweetness that were hers on the farm and in the open air. The whole family was still around the table for these couple of days yet, at least! She often wondered why it was so hard for her to accept change. Some people—like Loretta—thrived on change. Loretta could change her bedroom furniture around every week, and she would have done the same with the living-room furniture if Mom had allowed her. Loretta often accused Linda of being too staid and proper. *I guess I find security in unchangeable things,* Linda thought. *Perhaps that is why God and His unchanging Word have such a strong appeal to me!*

# 14

Larry and Ron left early Wednesday morning in Larry's little blue Corvair, which was packed with all the things two boys would need in a dorm for a school year—at least all the things that their moms could think of. The parting had been a tearful one all around. Larry finally reminded everyone that it was only for ten *days,* not ten *years!* They would be coming home for most weekends, at least while the weather was nice. That did help to make the parting bearable. But after he left, Linda realized, with a sense of responsibility, she was the oldest of the children at home.

The next couple of days, Linda and Loretta sewed as fast as they could, trying to finish the dresses, skirts, and blouses that they needed for the coming school year. Loretta enjoyed sewing much more than Linda did, but Mom would not let Linda off from it. So the girls took turns at Linda's sewing machine, while Mom worked at more modest gym uniforms on hers.

Linda had been reading in her Bible that Christian women were to dress modestly and had finally gotten up enough courage to ask Mom about it. She had feared another outburst if her request happened to upset Mom. But Mom calmly replied that she thought Linda looked modest enough. Even so, she had conceded to Linda's wishes to make her new outfits longer, for which Linda was thankful. Still, she wondered if she should wear a gym uniform at all.

There were so many things to think about! As Linda continued reading the New Testament, she wondered if it was really meant to be taken literally. She surely had met no one—except maybe Dad and his parents—who acted as though he thought so! But if God did not mean what He said, then what *did* He mean? Linda thought that surely God, as great and all-knowing as He was, must have meant what He said and said what He meant. Had churches gotten so far from truth that no one was obeying the Scriptures anymore? Was there anyone, anywhere, who lived what the Bible taught? And if so, where were they?

She knew from history that during the Reformation some people had been serious about living what the Bible taught. They had, she remembered from the study she had done the year before, even been willing to die for what they believed was truth. What had happened to that kind of commitment? Was it as Jesus said at one point, "When the Son of man cometh, shall he find faith on the earth?" For her to obey the

Bible exactly would surely make her a total misfit in society!

Just the day before, she had been reading in 1 Corinthians 11 that Christian women were to have their heads covered when praying or teaching. *So that is why some of the older women wear hats to church,* she thought, the realization hitting her suddenly. *But why don't all Christian women do it?* But then, she was not a theology student, she concluded, and perhaps it meant something other than what it appeared to mean. She did not know.

When Linda grew tired of sewing, she bounced up and went out to the garden to pick a few vegetables. The canning and freezing were about finished for the summer; just the pumpkins to cook and can yet. And maybe some more pickled watermelon rind or some grape jam. But the garden was coming to an end.

Pug and Red were helping Dad with cutting corn for the first silo filling. Linda would have rather been out helping with that, but Dad had said he had enough help. He would enjoy having her help, he had said, his eyes twinkling at her, but she had better get her sewing done for school.

And so the summer ended, and school began again. Loretta and Linda boarded bus #15 and headed into town for the new school year.

Steve Kelloway was in Linda's homeroom. She

had thought he would be a senior, but then, she really did not know how old he was. He was also taking the academic course, so he would likely be in most of her classes, she soon realized. Linda thought it was going to be fun to discover if he would be a competitor or not; she always delighted in new challenges!

Linda sorely missed Andrea, but was truly glad for her other chums—Charlotte, Lynne, Raye, and all the rest. Mary Catherine was back again, and Linda did not know what to expect from her. She hoped that after the experiences of last spring, she would be kinder. Her father's hatchery business had failed during the summer too, and they had needed to move to a smaller house. But would such experiences make her meaner, or would they make her a little more sympathetic of others? Linda did not know.

Before many days passed, Linda learned that Steve was almost eighteen and a year behind most of his age group. Dad told her that. Pastor Kelloway had said that they had been in mission work in Africa for several years when the children were small. During that time the children were not able to keep up with their studies, because there just were no books. Their mother taught them the best she could, but even so, all of them were about a grade level behind, except Renae, who had not been in school yet at the time. Linda would be seventeen on October 14.

Steve would be eighteen on the twenty-eighth of the month, two days before Larry's nineteenth birthday.

Linda plunged into her studies again. In the first period, she had advanced biology. Then came American history, music, physical education, English/literature, French, and in the last period of the day, trigonometry. The new language teacher was a young and energetic lady teacher, Miss Palmer. Linda thought she would enjoy her for French classes. Many of her other teachers were old friends from previous years, except the advanced biology teacher. He was a young man named Mr. Larson, fresh out of graduate school, who seemed to think the world was his oyster. Linda was not sure at all that she would appreciate him or his egotistical airs.

It did not take Linda long to learn that in Steve Kelloway, she had met a challenge. He was not only smart, but had a tremendous memory to keep dates and facts in perfect order. How Linda studied, determined not to lose her rank of previous years. But it seemed that Steve breezed along without any great deal of effort—always on top, always alert and ready with the perfect answer.

"Well," Linda lamented to Charlotte as they walked to French class one day in early November, "guess I'll need to be content with second place this year. I can't keep ahead of that

Steve Kelloway, no matter how hard I try!"

Charlotte laughed. "Learn how the rest of us feel, Linda. We can't all be first!"

"You're probably happier than I am, is my guess," Linda admitted. "I don't know why getting good grades is so all-important to me. What does it really amount to? And yet, I do love to learn and I love to study."

"Well, just do it then without having to beat the rest of us out," Charlotte advised practically. "You know me; I could sit in a science class all day, every day for a year, and still not know whether I am an arthropod or an—uh—arachnid!" She laughed, and Linda laughed with her, knowing that Charlotte was not quite *that* bad off!

"But you know," Linda continued, "I can't be put out with Steve, smart as he is. He really is down-to-earth. I have enjoyed learning to know him at school as well as through church activities. And he's often out at our place when Larry is at home."

The weeks seemed to speed past. And after the Monday-through-Friday of school came the weekend, with Larry at home. Larry and Ron usually spent a lot of the weekend together. Usually they helped Red and Dad around the farm, but sometimes they had time for fishing, hunting, or playing sports with the boys in town. Often they included Steve in their weekend activities. The three made a jolly trio, and anywhere they were was sure to be enlivened! On Sunday afternoons, now that it was too cool for outside activities, Steve often played Scrabble with Loretta and Linda and Dad, while Larry and Ron played chess or table tennis. Here again, Linda found she had met her match. Then all too soon, the weekend would be over, and Ron and Larry would head back to college. But there was always the next weekend to look forward to.

*This year is not as bad as I thought it would be,* Linda had to concede. *If only Andrea were here*, she often mused, *then life would seem complete.* Linda was getting a letter from Andrea about every week. They were always full of the activities of her new school, happenings on the farm, and other things that she knew Linda would enjoy hearing about. One startling and exciting bit of information that Andrea shared in one of her first letters after school started was that there were quite a number of Mennonites in the Millburg High School. Soon she began to write about one of them in particular, a Kathy Yoder, whom she was learning to know quite well and enjoying her friendship. Their letters back and forth always included new spiritual insights or questions they had from Scripture passages they had read. The inspiration from Andrea's regular-as-clockwork letter writing was almost as good as having her there to talk to.

*Life is good,* Linda thought as she went about her work. *I guess I must be adjusting to the changes that growing up brings.*

Since Larry was away, Linda thought she and Loretta were closer as sisters. Maybe that was a small blessing that had come out of losing her big brother. She had gained a little sister! And Loretta was growing up too. Dad's efforts at taking her firmly in hand over the summer were bearing fruit, and Linda rejoiced to see a new maturity in Loretta's responses to various things. For one thing, she was taking her schoolwork more seriously. And for another, she often helped with the farm work without complaining. The two girls worked companionably together, grading eggs, feeding calves, or doing whatever needed to be done. Pansy was helping Mom more in the house, since Pug presently had no job at all and they had no other income. With Pansy's help two or three days a week, both girls were freer to help Dad outdoors.

Linda was careful not to fritter her time away when she should spend it in study. But somehow being at the top of her class had lost its importance; she wanted to study and work, not for the sake of excelling others but because of the wonderful privilege of expanding her mind and learning all she could. Somehow that view of learning seemed to fit better with pleasing

God than learning and studying and excelling for the purpose of defeating others.

Linda was packing eggs with Dad one wintry November Saturday morning. Larry had stayed in Charlottetown for the weekend, and Loretta was working on a term paper. Working with Dad alone was quite nice again; she had not had a good talk with him for months, it seemed. She had many questions about church that she was sure Dad would have answers for. It worried her to think that some people were still being critical of Pastor Kelloway. Could Dad explain why this was so? And what about some of his sermons? Did Dad understand if what Pastor Kelloway was preaching was actually truth or not?

It did not take Linda long at all to find out her father's feelings for Pastor Kelloway. Dad felt he was a man of God who was diligently teaching his congregation the kinds of things from the Bible that they ought to be hearing—not just the things they wanted to hear.

"Well, now, Pastor Kelloway has been good for our church, Linda," Dad said finally. "He has opened the eyes of many of us to our own needs and how we should be doing better."

"Is Mom feeling that way too?" Linda asked hesitantly, the scene from last summer still vivid in her mind.

"Yes, thank God, she is," Dad said. "And together we decided we need to give God His proper place in our home. I have failed in not being the godly leader in our home that I should have been, and I want to do better."

"Is that why you decided to have a family worship period before breakfast every morning?" Linda asked.

"Yes, partly. And partly because my parents always did when we were children at home. I regret that through the years we got so busy that we neglected the family altar too often."

"I really like it that we are reading the Scriptures together and praying and singing together more. It helps to make me feel prepared to face the day, and I know it is good for Loretta too. I think we feel closer as a family too, since we have been praying together. Thank you for caring about us so much, Dad," Linda said sincerely.

"I do care tremendously, Linda. I feel an awesome responsibility toward my family. I'm sorry that for years I didn't see the dangers of some of the things we allowed you children to do—like letting you go to the high school dances and to the theater. I thought that carefully monitoring the movies you saw was enough. But all of it belongs to the ungodly world, and the Christian should have no part with it. And taking mixed crowds of your friends to the beach . . . I know you girls made your own bathing suits, and they did cover better than the ones you could buy, but still it was not as it should have been. I have so much to learn!"

"If *you* do, imagine how *I* feel," Linda said. "But there has been a growing and burning desire in me to know God."

Linda looked eagerly up at Dad as she continued talking. "I have wanted to tell you this, Dad. Since Pastor Kelloway's sermon last Sunday on how to be born again, I feel that I am beginning to know God. I thought I was a Christian. But after that sermon I realized I wasn't, and I came home and gave myself over to God. Then I was reading that wonderful verse in Philippians 3 about the apostle Paul's desire to know Christ. 'That I may know him, and the power of his resurrection, and the fellowship of his sufferings, being made conformable unto his death.' I suppose it is a continual growing up in our knowledge of Him."

"You're right, Linda. Paul made it clear that we only learn to know Christ if we are willing to count all else but loss. I guess you would say the things of the world lose their appeal to us. Our relationship with Him gets so good that nothing else really matters. We press toward the mark for the prize of the high calling of God in Christ Jesus. Yes, Linda, it is a lifelong process. God bless you in your decision to live for Christ and to grow in your knowledge of Him!" Dad smiled at Linda; then he picked up the egg baskets and started up the steps to the chicken floors.

Linda continued to clean and pack eggs as Dad gathered more eggs upstairs. A song came to her heart and burst from her lips. " 'More like Thee, O Saviour, let me be . . .' "

Soon Dad came back with more full baskets and set them down to be washed. "Well, now, how is school going, Linda?" he asked as he lifted a packed crate onto a pallet.

"Real well, Dad. I really enjoy my studies—even history this year, since I have a different teacher—and I love French!"

"Do you enjoy Miss Palmer as much as Mr. Taylor for language?"

"I don't know. She is good, but Mr. Taylor was a natural for languages. He had a way of making you *want* to learn, that Miss Palmer does not quite have. But she makes classes interesting."

"In a way, I was sorry to see Mr. Taylor leave because he was an excellent language teacher. But with his cynical attitude about God and religion, it was good he did. He could have had a detrimental influence on the students in the end. I wasn't happy with his interest in you either, Linda, and I'm glad your mother sees it in the right light now too."

"I knew you were concerned, Dad, and I was so thankful you came and helped me to find my way through his arguments that afternoon last summer. Something was so appealing about him that made it hard to turn him down. I could have liked him real well; he was always interesting to be with. And I could talk intelligently with him, much more so than with some boys my age. But the fact that he didn't have any regard for God in his life really gave me pause. I did not ever want to marry a man like that! And, besides, he is old enough to marry now—he is twenty-five—and at seventeen, I have no interest in marriage for many years."

Linda stuck the last two filled egg cartons into a case and closed the covers. Dad picked up the case and set it with the other filled ones on the pallet. He then wheeled the pallet into the cooling room.

Quickly putting things in order, Linda waited for him to come out. "Is there anything else you want me to help you with?" she asked.

"Not that I can think of now," Dad responded. "Thanks for your help again," he added, giving her a warm smile of appreciation.

Linda grabbed her jacket and went out into the brisk, raw day. She thought fall was so invigorating, but she did hate to see everything die down for the winter. Only the evergreens still showed green against the grays of the coming winter. Most of the leaves were off the maple trees, and she and Mom had taken in all the flowers they possibly could to keep for planting next spring.

She walked toward the house. *What a lot of leaves to rake again,* she thought. Going to the shed, she got a yard rake and started at one corner of the yard, pulling the colorful maple leaves together onto great piles. An old blue car drove in the driveway and parked at the chicken barn. She saw that it was Steve Kelloway. *Um—probably needs some eggs,* she thought. He waved to her as he went into the barn.

Soon he was back out with four cartons of eggs. He put them into the car and then walked over to where she was busily raking leaves together. "Hi, Linda! Looks like fun! If you have another rake, I'll help you," he said.

"I don't pay very well for this job," she quipped.

"If I offer to do it for free?" he returned.

"You win." She laughed as she handed him her rake. She ran to the shed and got another one.

"I haven't raked leaves for so long," Steve said as she returned. "This is pure pleasure! The parsonage only has evergreens. Come to think of it, about every parsonage where we have ever lived has had only evergreens! It seems I can remember a house in the faint long ago where we had maple trees, and then, of course, we had leaves to rake."

"This is a job I enjoy too," Linda said. "It is something to do outdoors after the garden work is mostly laid aside."

The two raked companionably, pulling great

piles of leaves together to be gathered and taken to mulch the garden. They chatted as they worked, about school and various church functions.

"Is your family beginning to feel at home in Springville?" Linda asked after a while.

"We really like it here," Steve began. "But I'm not sure that all the parishioners appreciate Dad's preaching," he added seriously. "Sometimes we wonder what God has for us. Maybe we won't be staying here after our year of probation is up."

Linda looked up with apprehension. She had not considered such a possibility. Steve caught her look. "Would you be disappointed if we'd leave, Linda?" he asked.

"Yes, I would," Linda said. "I really admire your family. And I appreciate your father's sermons. It seems he preaches the Bible in the way that it ought to be preached—without fear or favor of man. My parents think that your father's coming here was an answer to prayer. We understand that a lot of others think that way too."

"But not everybody, lamentably," Steve added.

As they worked and visited, the piles of leaves grew higher and higher, and so did Linda's respect for Steve. *Here is a true kindred spirit,* she thought in amazement. *He feels the things of God deeply. He desires to know God as an intimate friend too!*

Dad came with the pickup and began to load up the piles of leaves. "Shall we help you, Mr.

Asbury?" Steve called.

Linda saw and understood Dad's look of appreciation for the fresh-faced, clean-cut young man. "Well, now, you may keep on with the raking," he returned. "Looks as if you two have been busy here the last couple of hours!"

"It was my pleasure, Mr. Asbury," Steve said. "But I guess I really should get home for lunch, or Mama will wonder if I got lost! She just sent me out for eggs, you see."

Steve handed his rake to Linda. "Thanks for letting me help, Linda," he said, smiling.

"Well, thanks so much for your help," Linda returned. "I'm sure I'd have been at this for most of the day!"

"See you tomorrow, Lord willing," he called back as he walked across the yard to his car.

Linda helped load leaves onto the back of the pickup. "Well now, Linda, that is one fine young man," Dad said, looking after Steve as he drove out the lane.

"I think he is too, Dad," Linda admitted sincerely.

Mom called for dinner, and Linda and Dad went to the house. Linda was ready to sit on a radiator and warm up a bit. The wind was raw and blustery, as if snow was on the way. But though she was cold on the outside, the happiness of that pleasant morning gave her a warm glow on the inside.

# 15

Andrea was coming for a visit! Linda read that part in Andrea's letter over again. Her folks were going south for a conference the week between Christmas and New Year and would drop her off for several days. That is, if she would be welcome, Andrea wrote. Welcome! Linda could hardly wait to answer her letter. Of course, she would be welcome, and *more* than welcome!

Linda felt they had so many things to talk about—the kinds of things she did not feel free to write in letters. But she had not known when she would ever have such an opportunity again. And now, here it was, almost at her doorstep.

There was so much to occupy her mind in the two weeks till Christmas that Linda barely had time to think about the time getting long. There was the Christmas program at school. The glee club would be singing again this year, and the students in the club were spending many evenings after school perfecting their numbers. Linda had been assigned a solo in one number, a lullaby to the baby Jesus.

After the Christmas program, as Linda

emerged from a crowd of friends, she was surprised to see a strange man waiting to talk with her. "Hello; my name is Patrick Nichols from radio station WICO. I was visiting here in Springville this week," he said, "and I decided to come and hear the local talent in your high-school program this evening. You have a lovely voice, Miss Asbury, and I would like to offer you a job singing on our radio broadcast."

Linda's astonishment almost overcame her power of speech. Finally she said, "You surprise me, sir. I have never considered such a thing. Let me talk this over with my parents. I'm certainly not ready to give you an answer this evening."

"No, no; I understand. Here is my card." He handed her a business card. "I'll be waiting to hear from you. Just remember, don't waste a voice like yours!"

Mom and Dad came then and helped to steer the shocked Linda out to the car. "Well now, what was that all about, Linda?" Dad asked.

"That man—I think he said his name was Nichols—offered me a job on his radio broadcast."

"What kind of broadcast is it?" Mom asked.

"He said WICO, I think."

"Oh, that is a live country music station out of Sharptown," Dad said. "You don't have an interest in such a thing, do you?"

"No, Dad, I don't," Linda said, regaining her

composure. "He said I should not waste my voice. But I suppose that would be the greatest waste—to sing foolishness that draws people's minds away from godly values—wouldn't it?"

"Well now, that is surely the way I would see it," Dad responded heartily. "Your voice is a gift from God. As His child, your responsibility is to use that gift for His glory."

The stars twinkled brightly in the dark winter sky as they drove out the country road toward home. Linda looked long at the beauty of the sky, thinking of that night long ago when Jesus was born in a stable in Bethlehem. *Shepherds under a sky probably just like this were treated to an angel chorus and the wonderful message that the Christ-child was born,* she thought dreamily. *Wouldn't it be marvelous to have such an experience? To hear the angel's announcement . . . But God does speak to us today; He speaks through His Bible. Dear God, help me to listen to what You say, and to do it just as willingly as the humble shepherds did.*

Linda thought of the words of one of the songs the glee club had sung that evening:

Under the stars one holy night,
    A little Babe was born;
Over His head a star shone bright
    And glistened till the morn.
        And wise men came from far away,

And shepherds wondered where He lay
Upon His lowly bed of hay,
Under the stars one night.

Under the stars one blessed night,
The Christ-child came to earth,
And from the darkness broke the light
Of morning at His birth.
And sweet hosannas filled the air,
And guardian angels watched Him where
The virgin mother knelt in prayer,
Under the stars one night.

Under the stars this happy night,
We wait for Him once more,
And seem to see the wondrous sight
The shepherds saw of yore.
Oh, Baby born in Bethlehem,
Come to us as You came to them
And crown us with love's diadem,
Under the stars this night.

—*Anna S. Driscol*

Tears sprang to Linda's eyes as she thought of the wonderful gift of Jesus that starry night long, long years ago.

She forgot all about Mr. Nichols and his business card in the happiness of preparing for Christmas Day and all Dad's family coming for the day. Then, just after that, Andrea would be coming! Linda and Loretta had ten days off from school. And Larry was home for two whole weeks. It would all be like old times.

Mom and the girls and Pansy were busy in the kitchen, making mincemeat pies, plum pudding, and all sorts of filled cookies and rolled cookies. Dad and Larry had set up a small spruce tree in the library, and Loretta and Linda had threaded long chains of popcorn to hang on it. Larry, Ron, and Steve had gone to the woods for holly. They had climbed to the tops of high trees to get mistletoe, which had then been placed as decorations on the windowsills and above the doorways. Weeks ago, the family had exchanged names, and a few small gifts were now under the tree, waiting for Christmas morning. Linda and Loretta had done their shopping on Springville's Main Street after school. The gifts they could afford were not extravagant, but would show their love for the recipients.

Linda had been reading the accounts of the birth of Jesus in her Bible from Matthew and Luke. For many years, she had gone through the Christmas season without thinking much about what it all meant. Now she began to realize that it was the day to remember the advent of the One who was willing to come to earth and identify with mankind and then to finally die on the cross in order to save from sin all who would receive Him! It was a beautiful thought to ponder.

Christmas Day arrived with the cousins, uncles, and aunts milling around the big house and yard. There were games and laughter in the house; and outside, the children played tag, hide-and-seek, and horseshoes. There was no snow, and the day was mild for December, so the older cousins took a walk through the fields to the woods and out to the river. Throughout the activities of the day, Linda had one consuming thought—she could hardly wait till tomorrow. For then Andrea would be coming!

The Bakers arrived in time for supper the following evening. They consented to stay overnight, rather than find a motel farther south, as they had planned. Dad was eager to feel Pastor Baker out about the planned merger between the Methodist Church and the United Brethren Church. The conference Pastor Baker was going to would be addressing that issue, and Dad was eager to hear the outcome and to learn how it would affect their present fellowship. Linda enjoyed listening to their animated discussions as they all sat in the library comfortably visiting together.

Everybody was up early to see the Bakers off the next morning as they left to head south to the conference. Linda and Andrea were up too, although it was hard for them to get up at five after having talked long into the night!

The five days of Andrea's visit passed rapidly. The girls worked, they played, they walked, they talked, and they rode horseback. Before either was ready for it, Pastor Baker and his wife were back, and Andrea needed to be on her way home with them.

But the memories . . . they were so sweet. Linda was afraid that Larry was shamefully neglecting his good friend Ron the last few days. But Ron assured them it was okay, that his married sisters were home and he needed to spend some time with them too. Steve was out a couple of days while Andrea was there. Larry, Linda, Steve, and Andrea spent those days doing things as a foursome. They went for long walks through the quiet woods, and they borrowed Shem's two old mares, so that with the Asburys' two, the four of them could go horseback riding on the quiet country roads. When they tired of the outdoors, they trooped to the house to play games and put puzzles together. One evening they made fudge and popcorn balls in the kitchen.

There was no grand announcement, but suddenly everyone knew that Andrea and Larry had begun a friendship. They seemed right for each other and were happy together. And Linda was very happy for them. But sharing Andrea with her brother did put a crimp on the time Linda had hoped to spend with her. The only time the girls really had to share alone was the quiet hours when everybody else was sleeping, or supposed to be.

"I appreciate Larry's way of starting a friendship," Andrea began one night as they lay across their beds. "He let me know that he cares for me, and we plan to write. But he knows and I know that we both have years of schooling ahead of us." Andrea sighed. "Those years look so long! Why must I go to college anyway, when all I ever wanted to do was to be a mother and a housewife?"

"Well, Andrea, you know that the guidance counselor and most of our teachers keep telling us that education is so important. Without it, no one can get a decent job. And even for girls, education, they say, is important so that we can support ourselves if we ever need to." Linda sat up on her bed and looked dreamily out the window. "You know, as I read the Bible, I see more and more that it wasn't the educated or the high-class people who came to Jesus. It was the simple—the fishermen, the tax collectors, the farmers, the day laborers."

"Paul speaks about that in Corinthians, doesn't he?" Andrea asked. "About not many mighty men or wise men being called. Christ's own disciples were fishermen—people who were called ignorant and unlearned by the scribes and lawyers. Jesus Himself was called ignorant, wasn't He? Something about, how can this man speak, having never learned letters?" Andrea sat up. "Probably putting so much emphasis on being educated and getting white-collar jobs is 'of the world,' " she observed astutely.

Linda laughed. "That makes me think of Mark Twain and his comment 'I never let schooling get in the way of my education!'"

"That's aptly put!" Andrea remarked, laughing with her.

Then Andrea sobered as she went on. "You know, I've written about that Kathy Yoder, the Mennonite girl in some of my high-school classes."

Linda nodded, eager to hear more.

"Well, she and I have talked about some of these things too. She is really a brain in science and is planning to go on into nursing. She'd even like to get a degree in social nursing. That surprised me because I didn't think her family would encourage that. She did say that many of their church families are farmers, but she wanted to be a nurse, ever since she was in the hospital one time as a little girl. And she has an aunt who is a social worker in a city mission. She just thinks that would be an ideal way to serve the Lord."

Linda thought about that for a time. "I'm sure that would be a way to serve, but who could bear to live in a city?"

"I asked Kathy about that," Andrea said. "She said her parents aren't encouraging her to follow the steps of her aunt, because she is 'liberal,' whatever that means."

"I know what the dictionary definition is, but I don't know how it applies here," Linda said.

Andrea shrugged. "The way Kathy has used that term, she is apparently referring to the kind of Mennonites who promote 'continuing education' and the professions, just as we are used to in our settings."

"I still wonder about 'continuing education,'" Linda said after a while. "I always wanted to be a farmer. Maybe that is the best occupation for a Christian to be in. It certainly has many continuing opportunities for 'education,' but without the hazards of being in such a wicked setting."

"This thing of education is something we need to think about and read in the Bible more to find answers to, isn't it," Andrea said seriously.

"There are so many challenges!" Linda added. "I feel like such a child when it comes to learning about God and His Bible! I am so happy for Pastor Kelloway's sermons. He has helped me so much in areas that I didn't understand. Like how to become a Christian, and many others. I mean, we can read these things in the Bible, but it is so much easier to understand if someone who *knows* can help us."

"Do you feel you are a Christian?" asked Andrea timidly.

"Yes, I do. For a long time I wanted to be one, and I thought I was. But then not long ago, Pastor Kelloway had a wonderful sermon on how to become a Christian." Linda paused briefly, trying to recall exactly the way Pastor Kelloway had put it all. "He said we need to first realize that we are sinners by birth; that all of us are, according to Romans—chapter 3, I think. We need to believe in Jesus, that He is God's Son and that He came to earth as the God-man. Then finally, we must believe that He died for our sins so that we can be forgiven and be justified in the sight of God. Our part in all this is to repent, confess our sinful state, and trust God to forgive us for all our sins by the blood of Jesus. He forgives our sins because He has promised to, and then we become His children! But it doesn't stop there. We need to read the Bible every day and pray. God's Spirit lives in our hearts and teaches us what is right, and He makes us feel bad if we do wrong. Pastor Kelloway said that we need to die to ourselves and become alive to God and that this must be a daily experience."

"And then what did you do?" Andrea ventured.

"I realized that I had never really repented of my sins or confessed my sins and by faith trusted God to forgive me for my sins. I came home and went to my own 'secret closet,' and I did all those things—looked to God for forgiveness and all that. And I accepted by faith that

He cleansed my heart. It gave me such a peace and joy! Then, almost right away, I felt condemned for how I have hated Mary Catherine Carmean. I knew I had to go to her and tell her that I was sorry for my meanness to her in the past. And, believe it or not, I did that. I told her I am a Christian now and that I want to love her as Christ loves me. She looked at me as if she thought I was crazy, at first. Then she kind of squeaked out, 'Linda, I believe you mean that! Oh, I wish I could be happy like you are.' I told her she could be, but she just turned away with a sob.

"It blessed my heart to know that I had done my part in relation to her. But I still have so much to learn. It seems that there are so few who really are serving God." Linda paused. "But I have talked a long time. What are you thinking?"

Andrea broke into sobs. "I don't know if I'm a Christian or not, Linda! I have always thought I was, because I was confirmed when you were, when we were twelve, along with a lot of others of our school chums. But I have never really repented or confessed my sin and trusted God to forgive my sins either; I guess I never thought of myself as a sinner. What can I do now?"

"Andrea, we can pray now," Linda stated with conviction. The girls knelt by Linda's bed, and Andrea prayed between sobs, confessing her need of Jesus to forgive her sins and make her a new person. Then Linda prayed, thanking God for making a way for people to be His children, and asking for strength for both of them to live like His children and to grow more like Him.

Later Linda thought back on those five wonderful days with Andrea. That last night with Andrea, they two alone with God, was the most wonderful part of the whole time! Sharing the peace of sins forgiven with her best and closest friend was an experience Linda would always cherish.

Andrea left with her parents the next morning. Larry went back to school. And Linda was set for the long winter with her studies. But the warm glow of the time spent with Andrea that Christmas season would stay with Linda for a long time to come!

# 16

The long winter with its periods of flying snow and slushy roads finally passed, and spring came once more. Once more the greens of the rye fields were showing, and the frisky Jerseys were turned out of the barnyard to graze the tender young shoots.

Life in the town was passing as usual. The weather was becoming warm enough for the loiterers to again lean against the sides of the Sinapuxent River bridge and pass the time of day, or to fish out the bass, sunfish, or perch from its blue-green rippling waters. A new business was being built on the east side of Springville. Linda had heard it was to be a General Motors plant. She supposed that would bring new faces to the town and to school. But Springville High School was already bursting at its seams. There was talk of building a middle school, which would alleviate some of the burden of the overcrowded elementary school as well as take grades 7 and 8 from the high school.

Mrs. Whittleson's husband, Warne, had sold out his five-and-ten-cent store to an enterprising younger man, which, Mrs. Whittleson said, gave her all day on Saturdays now to grade her schoolwork. And Mr. and Mrs. Gibbons, Raye's parents, were putting up a lovely restaurant south of town, the kind to which the high-school boys could take a first date and feel they had done well. So there were changes, and there was progress. The local newspaper, the *Democratic Messenger,* kept the townspeople informed about all the latest developments.

But with all the progress in Springville in the spring of 1966, things at the Mt. Olive Methodist Church on Townsend Street were not going well. It seemed that Pastor Kelloway's preaching was splitting the church wide open. Some parishioners avowed that he was preaching false doctrine; others were equally staunch in their conviction that he was preaching Gospel truth. Linda and her family, except Mom and Loretta at times, felt that he was preaching truth, and were firmly supporting him.

And yet, in spite of her love and respect for Pastor Kelloway, Linda despised the division that had come to their church. She did not like the continual undercurrent of discontent and the bickering among those who were dissatisfied. She did not like the stress that it brought between her and her friends. Her heart often ached for the Kelloways, knowing the suffering that this must be bringing to them. She was almost happy when, one Sunday in April, Pastor Kelloway announced his resignation, effective in one month. But even though his leaving would relieve the stress, what about him and his family? Where would they go, and what would they do now?

After the service, Steve met Linda at the back door. "Could I come out to your place this afternoon?" he asked. He smiled at her, but she sensed that his heart was hurting. In spite of the trauma of the morning service and the obvious hurt that Steve must be feeling, Linda felt warmly stirred. "You are welcome anytime, Steve," she said sincerely.

Although Steve had spent many Sunday afternoons during the past winter at the farm when Larry was home, he had never especially singled out Linda. But she had learned to appreciate Steve very much. His godly life in school and his continual good example as a Christian had touched the lives of many others as well as her own. And now, how could she bear to see their family leave? But more than that, how must Steve and his family feel about the obvious rejection by many in the congregation?

That afternoon, Steve and Linda walked down the woods road to the river. They sat on the pier, each feeling in silence the deep perturbation of the other.

Finally, Steve spoke reverently. "God is still

on the throne, Linda. Even though we cannot understand many things, we must just leave all to Him, who does everything according to His infinite foreknowledge."

"But where will you-all go?" Linda asked, her eyes filling with tears in spite of her best efforts to prevent them. "You will need to leave the parsonage. Will you also leave the community?"

"I don't know the answers to those things yet. But can we trust God to work out His will for my family? And His will for each of us, Linda?"

Linda turned to look up at him, and he gave her a kind and understanding smile in return. Linda tried to still the many qualms inside her, the insidious doubts that wanted to push to the fore and destroy her faith in God. If only she could trust God as Steve could. But the future looked so bleak.

But she must not let her own desires destroy her peace with God or her faith in His divine providence. She caught her breath in a sob as she tried to speak. "Oh, Steve," she said, "I want to believe that all of this is God's will—for our church, for your family, and for us. Pray for me, that I could learn to fully trust God!"

"I do pray for you," Steve assured her. "It isn't always easy for me to trust either, Linda. Life has many disappointments. When we moved here, I looked forward to being here a long time; we had moved so often. It didn't take long for this area to grow on me, and I thought I could spend the rest of my life here. The beautiful rolling countryside, the quiet country atmosphere, all the water nearby . . . I love it! And I have treasured the friendship of your family and the privilege of learning to know you." He looked down at her again with warmth shining from his eyes. "But, finally, God's will is the most important, and I want to submit to that. What are the words of Jesus quoted in the Hebrew letter? 'Lo, I come to do thy will, O God' or something like that. If we are to be like Jesus, can we say any less?"

The cool spring breeze whipped around them as they sat on the pier. Linda pulled her jacket tighter about her. "Are you chilly, Linda?" Steve asked. "We can walk back to the house, if you wish. Walking will warm us up too!"

They walked slowly back through the pinewoods, scuffing through the fallen pine needles. A blue jay screeched as it flitted from one tree to another. A flock of crows was calling to each other. In the distance, Linda heard a cow bawl for her newborn calf. What a pleasant spring day for a walk, she was thinking, and what a pleasant companion! Surely, God would work out all things according to His will and purpose.

Suddenly Steve started to laugh. "I remember another time in this woods," he teased. "*That* time I wondered if you would ever look at me, much less talk civilly to me."

Linda blushed as she laughed with him. "Oh, please forget that," she pleaded. "I don't know why I acted so immature!"

"Well, I'm glad I've learned to know you better since then," Steve said with a smile for her.

Soon they were walking up the field lane, sharing like old friends as they entered the farmyard. Dad smiled pleasantly in their direction as he passed them on his way to the barn to do chores. Then Steve changed into some of Larry's work clothes, and they went to the barn to feed the calves together.

Later as they walked to the house, Linda noticed that Steve was limping. "Did you hurt yourself?" she asked with concern.

"I don't think so. It's just that sometimes lately when I'm on my feet too much or play active games, I get this pain in my left knee. Mama is concerned about it. But I tell her it's nothing to worry about."

"I hope it isn't," Linda said sincerely.

Steve took Linda to church that evening in his old blue Ford. Loretta came with Mom and Dad. The youth were in charge of the service that evening. Several had talks from the life of Paul, and another group sang several numbers. Then Pastor Kelloway had a talk on "Finding God's Will for Our Lives." Linda thought it was such an appropriate topic, after the troublesome thoughts of the day.

After church, Steve sat with Linda's family around the kitchen table. Loretta and Linda brought out cherry pie and homemade ice cream.

"Who made this pie?" Steve asked as he ate it with delight.

"It is an attempt of Linda's at cooking," Loretta said, laughing.

"I would say it is a pretty good attempt," Steve returned.

" 'Can she bake a cherry pie, Stevie boy, Stevie boy?' " Loretta sang teasingly.

"If you want to sing, let's sing something worthwhile," Linda suggested. She carried some dirty dishes to the sink. "Shall we sing around the piano for a while?"

Mom sat down at the piano. "What shall we sing first?" she asked.

Steve paged through the hymnal. "I like this one," he said, setting the open book on the rack in front of her. "Shall we sing it?"

Together they sang the beautiful old song "'O God, our help in ages past, / Our hope for years to come . . .'" Then Linda chose "God Will Take Care of You." Her heart lifted at the beautiful promises of God's care for His children. Surely He was with them and would go with them through these experiences that they could not understand.

After Steve left for the night and Loretta had

gone upstairs, Mom and Dad and Linda sat around the kitchen table again.

"What is going to happen to our church now, Dad?" Linda asked, voicing her concern of the whole day.

"Well, now, I don't know exactly," Dad answered. "But I suspect that if Pastor Kelloway would consent to stay in the area and start a new church, he would have a good following."

Linda noticed that Mom did not have much to say. She thought back again to Mom's upheaval that day last summer. Gradually Mom had been changing in the months since then, she thought. But still she knew these changes were very hard for her. Mom had always been extremely concerned about being part of the socially proper in town and having her name in the society news column in the *Democratic Messenger.* But now, to side with Pastor Kelloway because Dad did put her suddenly on the wrong side of the issues!

Linda's heart warmed in a new love for her mother. Mom was truly trying to find her way in submission and loyalty to her husband, in spite of the ostracism it brought to her. Whether or not Mom was yet a Christian, she could not be sure. But she was coming!

Finally the significance of Dad's words hit Linda. Start a new church? Could Dad be serious?

She sat, her elbows propped on the table and her face in her hands, watching Dad. What was on his mind?

"Two of the other deacons very much favor keeping Pastor Kelloway, as I do. We have been discussing various possibilities. Though we are not eager to divide our church, the differences in thinking that have come up in the last year will hardly allow us to keep working together. Why not start another church out toward Ocean City? There is an empty church building about six miles from here, just off Route 104, that is available for rent."

"Do you think Pastor Kelloway would consent to being the pastor?" Linda broke in eagerly.

"We plan to approach him," Dad continued, "to see if he would be favorable to helping us start a church at a new location. I think there would be at least a hundred of our present members that would be willing to support such a move. And I feel quite sure that the rest of the deacons and also the church board would give an honorable release to those who wish to support another church work." Dad tapped the tabletop with his fingers, a habit of his when he was in deep thought. "Except possibly Deacon Tilghman. He has been quite vocal lately about Pastor Kelloway's preaching; he isn't too happy with it. I've seen another side of him that troubles me, and I feel almost sure he would not give his blessing. But he is only one out of seven."

Mom faced Dad, an anxious look on her face. "Such a move would be hard for me, Lester, you know, with my family feeling as they do."

Linda waited, hoping and praying that Mom would have the grace to control her feelings.

Mom suddenly broke into sobs and hid her face in her arms. Dad reached over and laid his hand over hers.

"I know this is hard for you, Mother, but God will give you the strength if you will only ask Him."

Dad reached for his Bible on the counter behind him. He opened it, looking intently for something. Finding what he wanted, he said, "Matthew 10:34–38 reads like this: 'Think not that I am come to send peace on earth: I came not to send peace, but a sword. For I am come to set a man at variance against his father, and the daughter against her mother, and the daughter in law against her mother in law. And a man's foes shall be they of his own household. He that loveth father or mother more than me is not worthy of me: and he that loveth son or daughter more than me is not worthy of me. And he that taketh not his cross, and followeth after me is not worthy of me.' " He paged again and continued, "And in Mark 10:29, 30, Jesus was speaking again: 'Verily I say unto you, There is no man that hath left house, or brethren, or sisters, or father, or mother, or wife, or children, or lands, for my sake, and the gospel's, but he shall receive an hundredfold now in this time, houses, and brethren, and sisters, and mothers, and children, and lands, with persecutions; and in the world to come eternal life.' "

He closed his Bible. "Do the words of Jesus apply to us today, or don't they? Can we expect to sail through life with no difficulties, no hardships, no testings, while true believers all through time have suffered intensely for their faith?"

He looked lovingly at Linda and at Mom, who still had her face buried in her arms on the table. "We don't ask for hardships or misunderstandings," he continued gently, "but if they come because we want to live according to the Bible, then God will bless us in spite of them. I think it is the writer of Hebrews that speaks of Jesus learning obedience by the things which He suffered. If Jesus needed to learn obedience by suffering, how much more do we."

All was quiet for a time. And then Mom lifted her head from her arms and wiped her eyes. "It will be hard, but, Dad, I will support you in whatever decision you make, whatever you feel is best for our children."

Deep joy flooded Linda's heart and made her feel like singing. A hallowed light also seemed to shine from Dad's face as he gazed at his wife.

Linda felt again the happy security in the love that she knew existed between her parents. How blessed she was to have a happy home and to know the love of a caring mother and father.

The clock in the living room struck eleven. Linda yawned and caught herself. "I'm sorry," she said. "I'm not bored—just awfully tired."

"It is time to get to bed, Linda," Dad assured her, "but I wanted to share these things so that you would hear them too. We must give ourselves to prayer, seeking God's will for us."

Linda was tired, but she lay awake a long time. Finally she got up and began a letter to Andrea. *May as well make my time worthwhile,* she thought, *if I can't sleep anyway.* She wrote about Pastor Kelloway turning in his resignation, the afternoon spent with Steve, and the discussion with Mom and Dad that evening. *I wonder what Pastor Baker would say to all this,* Linda thought. *Would he feel bad that the church he worked with for so many years has come to this? Or would he be thankful that the eyes of some have been opened to Bible obedience?* She did not know, but she hoped that he would be happy that some were choosing the way of obedience to all the Word of God. At any rate, whether he was happy or not, she knew that Andrea would understand that she was confident that God was overruling in it all.

# 17

Another school year ended, with its finals and yearbooks and end-of-the-year parties. Linda looked forward to the summer again, to having Larry home, to the restoration of all the normality of family life. And finally, one Thursday morning in mid-June, Larry and Ron arrived at home. The little blue Corvair was crammed so full that it had to be unpacked bit by bit.

"My head feels the same way!" Larry quipped as the family stood around, laughing at the stuffed car. "I'll sure be glad to think about making hay and milking cows rather than anatomy and physiology and calculus and the like!"

Ron looked at Linda and added, "Larry sure has been restless the last few weeks. Could hardly wait to get home. I think the finals were getting to both of us!"

Larry stretched. "Well, it sure is good to be home, anyway! I'm looking forward to a calm and quiet atmosphere once again, where there is still a little tranquillity in the world!"

Larry had not come home for at least two months. He had felt he had too many studies to make the run home over weekends. Linda wondered how much he knew of the way things were going at church. The family had written to him of what was happening, but it was doubtful that such information really registered when he was not home to actually live out the experiences. Perhaps he would not feel as though he was coming home to tranquillity if he knew everything.

Well, he would get filled in soon enough. That afternoon Dad and two others from the church board had an appointment to meet with the trustees of the unused Presbyterian church building near Northport. They felt confident that a contract could be worked out.

They had already talked with Pastor Kelloway. After a time of prayer and consideration, he had said that he would be willing to work with a small group in another setting.

The Kelloways had moved out of the parsonage in the middle of May. The new pastor, Pastor Marks, had moved in with his young family. The Kelloways had found a nice little farm to rent about three miles north of the Asburys. Steve and his father had put out an acre of cantaloupes and another acre of staked tomatoes.

Linda and Larry drove out to see the Kelloways' "produce operation" one day soon after Larry was at home. The girls and Steve were all out in the field suckering tomatoes and tying them up on the stakes. The girls had surgical gloves on to protect their hands, but Steve's hands were as farmerly green as Linda's had ever been, she noticed. Even Pastor Kelloway was out, using a hoe handle to gently lay cantaloupe vines on the row so that he could take the tiller through one last time. Steve was delighted to see them and happily showed them around the little place. Then Mrs. Kelloway brought a jug of iced tea and a plate of cookies out for them all to enjoy together before they parted.

The Asburys waved good-bye, but Linda observed that Steve was limping as he turned to go back into the tomato field. She had asked him about his limp a few times, but he said he usually minded it most after a hard day of work.

As the weeks passed, Linda became increasingly concerned about Steve's limp, especially when she observed that it seemed to be getting worse, rather than better. "Mom, what could be wrong with Steve's leg?" she asked one day as they were picking beans together. "He has been limping on it for the last couple of months. He says it really hurts him sometimes, but he figures it's nothing to worry about. But *I* worry about it!"

Mom thought for a time as she rubbed her weary back. "It most likely is the result of an injury from playing sports. But it could be something more serious, like an infection in the knee joint itself or in the lymph nodes. He certainly ought to see a doctor."

"He doesn't want to see a doctor and put that expense on his family. You know, they don't have any income right now, other than what they can make on their produce, and won't until the new church gets going. But I told him that it could be serious, and if it goes on too long, it might make more expense than if he had it taken care of promptly. But he just looks at me and laughs, as though I'm worrying uselessly." Linda sighed.

"I'll talk with his mother," Mom said. "Maybe I can find out what she thinks about it all, and give her some suggestions."

Linda hoped that since Mom had been a nurse, her suggestions would carry some weight. She was afraid something serious was wrong with Steve. She had seen the look of near agony on his face at times, when he thought no one was watching. And she knew that he was more listless at times and that his weight was dropping off, even though he claimed to be eating as much as always. He was more active, he would say, working from sunup to sundown, farming. But Linda knew that something more than that was going on. She only wished someone could convince him to get medical help.

Mom's suggestion must have helped, because Steve consented when his mother insisted he get an appointment immediately with Dr. Boyer. "Please let me know how things go, as soon as you get back," Linda had pleaded with Steve on Sunday as they sat on the porch steps. For the last several Sunday afternoons, when Steve came to the farm, he had not felt like taking the customary long walks or even playing games in the yard. "I must be working too hard through the week," he often said, laughing.

On Wednesday, the day of Steve's appointment, Linda waited almost impatiently for Mrs. Kelloway and Steve to get home. She felt sure that someone would call right away. She was hoping and praying that they would come home happy with a diagnosis of a simple infection or something like that, so that a treatment of antibiotics would be all Steve needed to quickly return to normal again. Aimlessly she wandered about the house and yard, waiting for the telephone to ring. Then it was chore time, and still no word had come. Finally, it was bedtime, but still no word. How could she go to bed without knowing what was going on?

Mom and Dad were sitting on the porch swing in the deepening dusk. Linda could hear their voices; they talked occasionally as they swung gently back and forth.

She went out to them, trying hard to conceal the deep concern she felt. "Mom, may I call the Kelloways and see if everything is okay with Steve?" she asked, a sob in her throat making it hard to talk. "I think I *have* to know something yet tonight! Steve's appointment was at one-thirty this afternoon. What could be taking so long?"

"Shall I call?" Mom asked Dad.

"That would be more appropriate than for Linda to call," Dad assented.

Steve's younger sister answered. Linda listened on the upstairs telephone as Mom talked with her. Sharon's voice sounded as though she had been crying. "Mama and Daddy aren't back yet," she said. "Mama called from Dr. Boyer's office this afternoon, wanting Daddy to come in too. She said they would be taking Steve to Sharptown Medical Center right away for some tests. Mama called again a little bit ago and said that Steve will need to stay in the hospital, but that she and Daddy will be home soon. Oh, Mrs. Asbury, it must be something serious, don't you think?"

Mom tried to reassure the sobbing girl, but Linda knew in her heart that Mom was thinking the same thing. When she hung up, Linda went back downstairs.

"Could we pray together for Steve?" she asked, trying hard to keep from crying herself.

"Well now, Linda, that is a good idea," Dad said. "Call Loretta from her room. And where is Larry?"

"Larry went into town to coach a Little League game this evening. But he should be home soon, since it's almost dark."

"Oh, that's right; he did tell me about that," Dad remembered.

By the time Loretta came downstairs, Larry was driving in the lane. "Any news about Steve yet?" he asked as he came in and saw them all sitting around soberly in the library.

"Not directly. I talked with Sharon," Mom said, "and she said they took him from Dr. Boyer's office right to Sharptown for tests. She said they are keeping him in the hospital."

"Well, I wonder if Steve's hunch is true. He told me a couple weeks ago that he suspects he has bone cancer," Larry said with reluctance. "Apparently he had done some reading and begun to realize how serious his condition might be. Maybe I shouldn't be telling you this. But I guess we should be prepared for the worst."

Mom nodded her head. "I've suspected as much myself," she said.

Linda started in alarm, her stomach suddenly tightening into a knot. Turbulent thoughts paraded in anguished rapidity through her mind. That would be too cruel. Surely, God cared more than that! He would not let such a thing happen to the Kelloways! Steve had already suffered so much . . . And if it was cancer, how could he ever live, or if he did, be normal again?

Somewhere inside her, a silent alarm sounded, and she recognized her rebellion. She must not feel this way! *Oh, dear Jesus, help us all,* she pleaded in her heart.

Dad looked around at the sober family. "We want to pray for the Kelloways, and for Steve especially, Larry. That is why we are all sitting here."

Quietly they all knelt. Linda buried her face in the sofa pillows, trying her best to keep her tears for when she was alone. Dad prayed, expressing so well Linda's heartfelt burden.

They were no sooner finished praying than Pastor Kelloway called, confirming the suspicions that they had all had. In his own grief, he tried to comfort them in theirs, reminding them that God's way is best even when we do not understand.

Linda kneeled a long time at her window that night. A cool night breeze fanned her warm cheeks and set the maple leaves outside her window to dancing. The tree frogs kept up a steady *ard-d-d-d-d-d, ard-d-d-d-d-d*. The sky was bright with stars as she gazed into the endless expanse of the heavens. Her heart had been somewhat comforted by Dad's prayer. But how her little world had been changed by that one awful word—*cancer!* For a long time, she prayed . . . for Steve's healing, for comfort for his family, for grace for all of them to accept whatever changes might come. Finally a sense of peace came to her as she realized again that God had them all in His care. Still she longed for the morning, hoping against hope that she would awaken to find that all this had been a bad dream.

Morning came at last. Wearily Linda dressed to go to the barn. Tiny skipped joyfully after her on his three legs as she plodded gloomily out to the woods for the cows.

Suddenly a song came to Linda's mind—one the choir had sung recently, which had touched her heart and she had especially enjoyed.

Under His wings I am safely abiding;
　　Though the night deepens and tempests are wild,
Still I can trust Him; I know He will keep me.
　　He has redeemed me, and I am His child.

Under His wings, what a refuge in sorrow!
　　How the heart yearningly turns to His rest!
Often when earth has no balm for my healing,
　　There I find comfort, and there I am blest.

Under His wings, oh, what precious enjoyment!
　　There will I hide till life's trials are o'er;
Sheltered, protected, no evil can harm me;
　　Resting in Jesus, I'm safe evermore.

*Chorus:*
Under His wings, under His wings,
　　Who from His love can sever?
Under His wings my soul shall abide,
　　Safely abide forever.

*—William O. Cushing*

Linda lifted her tear-stained face to the eastern sky as she softly hummed, thinking the words. *Oh, dear Father,* she prayed, *forgive my rebellion against Your perfect will. I do not understand why You are bringing this experience to Steve and his family or to me, but I trust You! I know You do all things well.* As she walked after the cows, she continued to pray for an abiding faith on her part, and again for strength for the Kelloways and especially for Steve. As the tears streamed across her face, she committed him and her blossoming love for him to God. *You know better than I do, dear Father. You see everything from beginning to end. May I rest in Your perfect knowledge and Your perfect will.*

*Arf, arf!* Tiny barked as the cows pressed into the loafing area and on into the barn. Linda looked at the little dog and smiled. He did not even know he had an infirmity! *We humans fret and worry over all our afflictions and trials, when God cares for us so infinitely more than He does for the animals,* she thought ruefully. *Oh, for a simple trust, to let everything rest in God's hands! Father, I trust You; I commit my desires, my all, to You. Do whatever You see best. Your will be done.* The peace of God so filled her heart that she could barely comprehend the great joy as she followed the last of the cows into the barn.

Linda gathered the buckets to feed the

calves. As she mixed their milk, she thought of the song "More Love to Thee." " 'Let sorrow do its work; / Send grief and pain; / Sweet are Thy messengers, / Sweet their refrain, / When they can sing with me: / More love, O Christ, to Thee, / More love to Thee, / More love to Thee!' " she sang softly as she carried the buckets to the calves' pens. Linda remembered Mrs. Prentiss's experiences from her book *Stepping Heavenward,* an old book that she had found at Grandma's. Mrs. Prentiss too had faced trying circumstances—the sudden death of her father, the death of her oldest son, her own poor health. *Could I come to that place, O Father, that I could* ask *for Your messengers of grief and pain?* She searched her heart and knew she would need to grow much in faith before she could honestly pray such a prayer. And yet, God was with her; He was upholding her. How faithful and kind was her heavenly Father!

Then her thoughts went again to Steve, and her heart filled with petition for him. Foremost in her thoughts was the prayer that he would find strength in God.

Mrs. Kelloway called Mom soon after breakfast. She and her husband wanted to leave shortly to go to the hospital again. But she was eager to have others know what was happening so that they could pray for them. "Dr. Boyer suspected bone cancer right away after seeing Steve's knee. His leg looked bad; there was a lot of swelling, especially around his knee. The doctor thought Steve must have endured tremendous pain, from the way his leg looked. But why did he never show it to us or even let on how much it hurt?" Her voice broke, and she could not speak for a time.

Then she went on, "Dr. Boyer called Sharptown right away and arranged for some x-ray studies and a bone scan. Then he told us to get there as fast as we could. The doctors there did the studies, including a bone biopsy, and were quite sure of the diagnosis. They plan to give us more information today, as far as treatment, more results of the tests, and so forth. Will you please tell Larry and Linda? I'm sure Steve would want them to know."

"I'm so sorry about all this," Alberta said with genuine sympathy. "I will tell the others, and we will be praying for you and staying in touch."

No one felt like working that day. Pansy came over to help with the laundry. When she heard the news about Steve, she went straight to Linda and hugged her with all her might. Linda and Pansy cried together, and Linda felt comforted by the sympathy of the motherly older woman. "You po' chil'," Pansy said when she could speak again. "You is young; you hasn't known sorrow. Pug and me lost three sweet chillens. Believe me, chil', when you got somebody in heaven, it sho' do increase de longin' to go dere!"

That evening Linda went out to the orchard and sat on the low-hanging branch of her apple tree. She had to be alone—alone to pour out the petitions of her soul to God. She was at peace in her own heart. But how must Steve feel? And his family? How they must be pondering and questioning in their soreness of heart! If only she could talk with Steve and be assured he was at peace and still trusting God. And his pain—how much he must be suffering physically! And if Steve did indeed have cancer, what would happen then?

Larry found her there sometimc later. "Linda," he said, sitting on the broad limb beside her, "I know this hurts you very much. But you just have to trust God, His love, and His wisdom for Steve and for you."

"Oh, I know, Larry, and I do want to trust God," she cried softly. "But it is so hard. Steve is so good; he doesn't deserve to suffer like this. And I feel so sorry for Steve's family. How can they bear this? Why must God let still more hardships come to their family?"

" 'For as the heavens are higher than the earth, so are my ways higher than your ways,' " Larry quoted. "Think of the experiences God allowed to come to His servant Job and to His own Son. We cannot see as God sees. He sees the whole picture; we see only a tiny part. We must just have faith that all He does is well done."

"I'm sure that Steve would say 'God is still on the throne.' That is a favorite saying of his," Linda said, brightening. "But surely we can pray for his healing, can't we?"

"Of course," Larry assured her. "But we must pray in God's will."

Things happened fast after that. All tests pointed toward bone cancer, and the biopsy confirmed the diagnosis. The specialists at Sharptown Medical Center felt they must remove his leg as quickly as possible in hopes of keeping the cancer from spreading to his lungs or other organs. Steve was staying at the hospital and being treated with anticancer drugs until further decisions were made.

Larry took Linda to see Steve one evening soon after the amputation. Steve was sedated heavily for pain, but joy lit up his face as he saw them come into the room. The tears came to Linda's eyes and flowed freely down her cheeks as she saw how thin and tired Steve actually looked.

He held out his hand toward her, and she clasped it in her own two strong ones. "Linda, don't cry; it's all right. God is with me," Steve assured her kindly.

Steve was not interested in the normal small

talk. "Get my Bible and read some Scripture verses to me, Larry, if you will," was his request.

Larry got Steve's open Bible off the stand and began to read where it was opened, at Psalm 88. *How much the sentiments of this psalm fit with how Steve must be feeling,* Linda thought. It was hard for Larry to keep his voice steady as he read.

> O Lord God of my salvation, I have cried day and night before thee: let my prayer come before thee: incline thine ear unto my cry; for my soul is full of troubles: and my life draweth nigh unto the grave. I am counted with them that go down into the pit: I am as a man that hath no strength: free among the dead, like the slain that lie in the grave, whom thou rememberest no more: and they are cut off from thy hand. Thou hast laid me in the lowest pit, in darkness, in the deeps. Thy wrath lieth hard upon me, and thou hast afflicted me with all thy waves. Selah. . . . Lord, I have called daily upon thee, I have stretched out my hands unto thee. . . . Thy fierce wrath goeth over me; thy terrors have cut me off. They came round about me daily like water; they compassed me about together. Lover and friend hast thou put far from me, and mine acquaintance into darkness.

"Please read Psalm 89 yet, to verse 18 at least, Larry," Steve requested as soon as Larry stopped reading. "We can't stop with God's chastening; we must read on and also see His great mercy, especially in verses 1 and 9."

> I will sing of the mercies of the Lord for ever: with my mouth will I make known thy faithfulness to all generations. . . . Thou rulest the raging of the sea: when the waves thereof arise, thou stillest them. . . . Blessed be the Lord for evermore. Amen, and Amen.

Somehow the summer passed. Linda knew the farm work got done, but she was not sure how, or who did it. She knew that Dad was thankful for Red's help, as well as all the help that Pug and Pansy were able to give. One thing Linda knew, and that was that the family did not have the free time that they usually did through the summer.

Even so, Dad was not ready to take up Clyde Tilghman's renewed offer to help them. Linda recalled with distaste how he had come to her after church one Sunday and asked if her "old man" had work for him. "Hey, you have work for that Ziller! Why not me?" he had said scornfully.

Linda had glanced at him and told him he would need to talk with her father about that. His smirking grin and hard gray eyes ruined what could have otherwise been good looks. How distasteful he had looked to her. She had tried to hide the repugnance she felt. He had then turned away with a hard glint in his eyes.

Linda had felt troubled for a time, but there was too much work to do in the coming week to think about it for long. She and Loretta were trying to do as many of the barn chores as possible so that Dad and Larry would be more free for other work.

Dad spent a lot of his time getting the old church building in Northport ready for services. Others helped too, especially Grandpa Asbury. He was retired and had a knack for carpentry, so he was just the man to be in charge of the other volunteers who came in to help almost every day. Pastor Kelloway's time was spent running between the church, his produce patch, and the hospital in Sharptown, where Steve needed to go on a regular schedule for chemotherapy treatments. Steve had not learned to drive with only one leg yet; nor would his parents have allowed him to, with the effects of the strong medicine on him. But he would gladly have done so if he could have!

One day when Linda went for the mail, she brought in an envelope with careless, unfamiliar handwriting. It was postmarked "Springville" and addressed to her father. Curious to know what it was about, she found Dad in the chicken barn. Dad opened it in his usual, slow way while Linda waited impatiently. As Dad read, his face took on a troubled look. "If you weren't standing right here, I wouldn't tell you about this, Linda. But perhaps I should, so that you can be in prayer. Someone must not appreciate our having part in starting another church. Listen to this: 'Trouble always comes to troublemakers! See what is happening to the righteous Kelloways. You will be next!' " Dad tucked the short note back into the envelope.

"No name?" Linda asked, her inner being all atremble.

"No. I don't know who would be mean enough to write a letter like that. But God knows. And we can trust our heavenly Father to keep us safe from the designs of evil men."

Linda was comforted by Dad's words and by his evidence of trust in God. Who could harm them if God was with them?

Later that week, Pastor Kelloway stopped in. He told Dad that he had received a similar letter. Then Grandpa came and shared one that he had received.

"What should we do, Pop?" Dad asked his father. "You don't think we should get the law to work on this, do you?"

"No, Lester; let's just leave these things in God's hands."

"That's the way I feel too," Dad calmly assured his father. They seemed to be of one mind.

Linda, working in the flower bed by the porch, overheard their conversation. Did Dad and Grandpa know about Jesus' teaching on not resisting evil? Was that why they were not going to call in the police to take over the case? Was that what that teaching meant? She did not know, but she knew that God could care for them better than any law officers on earth could. *Dear Father in heaven,* she prayed as she weeded, *You know all about who this is that seems to hate us. Just keep us in Your care, and help us to always trust You.* She could not imagine who would have evil designs against them, much less the Kelloways or her grandfather—kind, gentle old man that he was.

Several nights later, Grandpa's little horse barn burned down. He was glad that he saw the fire in time to lead the horse to safety, but all else was lost. There was no doubt in anyone's mind but that it was lit on purpose. And then the fire marshal, as he sifted through the charred remains, found an empty lighter-fluid can, which must have been purposely stuck under the new hay. Despite Grandpa's pleas for leniency, an intense search was begun at once for a suspect.

Linda feared for their own barn. As she helped unload the many wagonloads of hay through the next weeks, she often thought of such a possibility. How could she forget that awful night—the crackle of the fire, the sparks showering into the strangely illuminated sky as they sat on the grass nearby and watched helplessly? It was a horror she could not bear to think of having happen again. *Oh, dear Father, keep us from evil men,* she often pleaded in her heart as she unloaded bale after bale of fragrant alfalfa hay.

Grandpa's horse was still in their barn, stalled with their own two. Grandpa always hitched his horse to an old-fashioned plow or cultivator to work up and till his garden plot each summer. Spring planting was finished, so he did not need his horse at home so much now. And that was good because it might be a while before Grandpa could put up another barn, with the work of remodeling the church at Northport still taking so much of his time.

One night soon afterward, Linda awakened to hear Tiny barking frantically. She sat up suddenly, her heart in her throat. What should she do? She hurried over to knock on her parents' door. But by the time Dad was dressed and downstairs, Tiny was quiet again. Linda and her parents sat in the dark kitchen for some time, looking out across the moonlit yard and buildings. Larry glided quietly into the kitchen too and joined the watch. When nothing further happened, they finally went upstairs to finish their night of rest.

At breakfast the next morning, it suddenly occurred to Linda that Tiny had not been around the barn while they were choring. "Did any of you see Tiny this morning?" she asked at once.

"Well now, come to think of it, I don't believe I did," Dad said slowly.

"Neither did I," Larry said.

Leaving her breakfast unfinished, Linda hurried outside, her heart heavy. Tiny was just a dog, but he had been her pet for years. Had someone hurt him during the night—or even killed him? Fearfully, she looked around the buildings. "Tiny, here, Tiny!" she called as she walked from one building to another. After a fruitless search inside and behind buildings, she came back toward the yard.

"Tiny, where are you, Tiny?" she called again. Then she heard a whimper beside the fence. Quickly she looked under the rose of Sharon bush. "Tiny!" she cried as the little dog tried to sit up.

Taking in the situation at a glance, she ran to the house. "Oh, Mom, can you come?" she cried. "Tiny is hurt badly!"

Everyone followed her out the door to where Tiny was lying. "Someone girdled him with a razorblade, the way he looks!" Mom exclaimed, gently turning him. Tiny whimpered piteously.

"Oh, Mom! Will he die?" Linda and Loretta asked, almost in the same voice.

"Dogs are pretty resilient," Mom assured them. "But we'd better clean up that ugly cut. And he's lost a lot of blood." Linda could hardly bear to look at him, the way his skin was cut all around his body, exposing the muscle and tissue.

The question on everyone's mind was why anyone would have done such a thing. But Tiny did heal, and after a couple of weeks was again running around and acting as though nothing out of the ordinary had ever happened. The incident was soon only a dim memory.

Linda went to Pennsylvania with Larry one weekend to see Andrea and her family. She almost did not go along, because she did not want to miss any changes in Steve's condition. And she knew that her actual time with Andrea would be limited if Larry was also there. But once she was there, she was happy that she had gone. The weekend was refreshing; time with Andrea was always that! Mostly because Andrea was the only friend with whom she could share freely and feel a sense of release from pent-up emotions.

She came home, ready once again to tackle the heavy load of work that waited for all of them. And when their work eased off, there was always the church to work at or Steve's family to help.

Steve's sisters kept a produce stand going at the end of their lane. They sold bushels and bushels of cantaloupes and basket after basket of tomatoes. What they did not sell at the end of the lane was bought by some of the small local grocery stores or produce markets. The produce did help to provide a much-needed income for the family. At times, when the work was not so pressing at home, Loretta or Linda helped them to pick and pack and sell the produce, especially during the times that Pastor and Mrs. Kelloway needed to be away with Steve.

The day finally came when Steve was up and about again. He learned to use crutches and could get around quite well. But Linda missed so much the old comradeship of previous months, since they had had so little time together without hordes of other people around. Of course, Steve's high-school friends had often been out to see him, and various relatives of the family had spent time with them, visiting or helping as needed. Linda knew she was still Steve's "special girl"; she could tell that by the extra gleam in his eyes whenever she was with him. But how much she wanted to have a good chat with him again.

Dearest to Linda's heart, however, through that long summer was the wonderful assurance that she was God's child and that He was drawing her to Himself in His own special way. She spent more time than ever reading the Bible and praying, seeking for answers to the many questions that troubled her.

# 18

Fall came again with its splash of reds and oranges and the geese flocking south. The barn swallows had long gone, and the songbirds were gradually leaving for warmer climates as well. The dry cornfields rustled a music of their own in the brisk westerly breezes. On the Sunday afternoon of Linda's eighteenth birthday, the Kelloways and the Asburys ate lunch together. Afterward Linda and Steve took the pickup out to the river. Tiny had jumped onto the seat between them, always eager for a ride.

Now he skipped along beside Steve as Steve hopped on his crutches to the pier. Steve laughed. "Look, Linda, Tiny and I are in the same boat! But he sure seems to be coping better than I am. He doesn't even need crutches!"

Linda laughed with him. Hearing Steve's laugh made it seem like old times again. Steve and Linda sat down on the edge of the pier, and Tiny plopped down with a deep sigh beside them. Linda looked at Tiny, remembering the day last summer when she had found him so badly hurt. Now a faint scar around his middle was all that was visible to remind them of that scare.

Steve inhaled deeply of the aroma of fallen leaves and pine needles as he sat watching the water rippling by. "This is wonderful, to be out here again in the peace and quietness of God's creation!" he exclaimed happily. "Oh, Linda," he added, smiling tenderly at her, "it is good just to be with you again too! It seems like a long time since I have talked with you alone."

"It's really special to me too, Steve," Linda assured him, returning his smile. "God has been good to us, hasn't He?"

Steve sat silently for some time, gazing dreamily into the bright blue of the distant sky. A mild breeze played around them, ruffling Steve's dark hair and stirring gentle songs from the tops of the pine trees. Linda sat quietly, content just to have him near.

"I'm soon going to be with God, Linda," Steve said suddenly and softly. "It is a wonderful thought! And if it weren't for you and for my family, I would have no reluctance at all. I long to be with Jesus!"

Linda's heart seemed to stop; then it pounded as she stared at Steve. She had hoped for his complete recovery and had prayed for the same. However, she could not help but realize that he was merely a shadow of the vibrant, healthy young man he had been the year before.

Her tears, lately always near the surface, started again.

"Don't cry, Linda," Steve said gently. "Maybe I shouldn't have mentioned it. But I wanted you to know how I feel. God's ways are best. There is much I can't understand either, and naturally I would have loved to live a long time yet. But God has been so near and precious to me that I cannot rebel if He soon calls me home."

"I don't want to rebel against God's will either, Steve," she said through her tears, "but I would miss you so much. And I thought—I hoped you were getting better!"

"I would have liked to think so too, Linda. But I'm afraid I'm not. I have this pain so often just under my right ribs. The doctor suspects that the cancer has spread to my liver."

Linda looked longingly at the young man beside her. *O God,* she prayed once again, *help me to submit to Thee and to know that Thou doest all things well.*

She dabbed and dabbed at her eyes and blew her nose while Steve sat in sympathetic silence. Finally he said, "Can we change the subject for a while, Linda? Have you made any plans for after you graduate next spring?"

Almost relieved to be talking about something else, Linda replied, "Nothing definite. Mom is pressuring me to go into nurse's training, and I think I would enjoy that. Andrea and I want to be together, whatever we do."

"Would she enjoy nursing too?"

"She thinks so, although maybe it wouldn't be her first choice. She would have preferred to go to Peabody to get a degree in music, if anything. But"—Linda suddenly remembered—"she told me one time that all she ever *really* wanted to do was to be a wife and mother."

"Well, that would be according to the Bible, wouldn't it," Steve said thoughtfully. "Paul says in one place that women are to be 'keepers at home.' Other Scripture verses speak of women being in subjection to their husbands and that they should guide the house, bring up children, and such things. I don't know of any Scripture passage that suggests that godly women should be out working in public, at least married women. But I know that isn't what we hear at school. We are made to feel like social failures if we don't go on for higher education."

"Don't you think going to college is a good idea then?" Linda asked.

"I don't know what to say. I'm sure I don't know the answers in every situation. But I do know that the early Christians and other true Christians throughout history have often come from the humble walks of life. They weren't usually the educated, the sophisticated, or the emulated!"

Linda laughed softly. " 'You're a poet and

don't know it!' " she quoted.

"I can't even say 'My feet show it; they're "Longfellows" ' . . . because I only have one *foot!"* Steve laughed with her. "But back to our discussion, the push for education is probably part of what the apostle John calls 'of the world,' don't you think?"

"You're probably right," Linda agreed. "Education gives people social dominance and prestige, which is likely part of the 'pride of life' that he wrote about."

"Many in our own church would fit in that category, wouldn't they," Steve observed.

"Maybe even my family?" Linda looked up with a question in her eyes.

"I admit, I thought your family was quite cultured and well-to-do when I first knew you. But now that I know how hard farmers in our area need to work for a living and how little they get in return, I don't feel that way anymore! And you had horses. That was always a boyhood dream of mine—to have a horse of my own."

"Did you know Dad sold our horses?" Linda broke in. "He said, 'Why keep feeding them when they don't give any return?' And nobody has time to ride them anyway. I miss them, but I see Dad's point."

Steve chuckled. "And you had a maid—or that was the way it appeared to me. I know differently now." He smiled down at Linda.

Linda was surprised. "I never realized others looked at our family like that! I only know that we could never afford new cars or new equipment like some others. That didn't bother me; we were happy with what we had. And Pansy . . . dear Pansy! She helps us because she loves us, and we love her. I think she got started helping us years ago because Pug couldn't pay their rent any other way."

"Oh, Linda, you don't feel bad, do you? I was only telling you first impressions. But now I realize how much time and money your family uses helping others and how frugally you live yourselves. And I think that is wonderful!"

Linda smiled up at him. "Let's talk about something else," she said. "See . . . what were we talking about? Higher education?"

"I believe we were," Steve said, returning her smile. "One thing I thought of in favor of higher education is the ability to earn higher wages."

"Take the game Life," Linda interjected. "You can't get ahead in that game no matter how you try, unless you take the route of college education! I suppose games like that are part of Satan's strategy in the world to indoctrinate men's minds to ultimately bring *him* glory."

"It is a scary thought!"

"But thinking of the higher-income opportunities, the Bible says that having food and raiment we are to be content. So why would

Christians worry about 'earning power'?"

Steve sat silently, swinging his leg over the water. "I cannot answer all these questions," he said after a while. "But you know, there are some religious groups that discourage higher education. I wonder what their reasons are . . . if they are the same as the ones we discussed or if there are deeper reasons."

"What religious groups?" Linda asked.

"When we lived in Missouri, there was a new publishing work being started some fifty miles away by a group of Mennonites. Daddy met up with some of them occasionally and learned a lot about them. Many of their writers did not even have high-school diplomas. At that time, they were interested in writing a Bible-based Christian school curriculum. Daddy found it totally fascinating. They believed that true wisdom comes from God and that God will enable Spirit-filled writers. And really, that is what the Bible teaches. What Daddy learned from them has had a lot of influence on his life and preaching. He still subscribes to their periodicals. That group seemed to be truly Christian in doctrine as well as in their daily lives. He has often spoken of them and wished to meet up with them again. But Daddy had some problems with their dress standards, which he considered rigid."

Linda could hardly keep still. "I did a term paper in tenth grade about various religious groups during and after the Reformation period. I was fascinated then by the Mennonites and how their faith in Christ was so strong that they were willing to die for it. And many did! But I didn't know if there were any people who lived like that anymore. Andrea Baker has talked about Mennonites in her area, but I don't know much about them, other than what she has said."

"There are quite a few Mennonites in some areas—and all kinds! We have traveled quite a bit, you know. When we were in Africa, a Mennonite group had a mission there, and our mission worked closely with them. Since then, I have learned that that branch of Mennonites is considered liberal."

"What does that mean?" Linda questioned, wanting to hear his explanation.

"*Liberal* means that they are more progressive. There are liberals and there are conservatives—and all flavors in between. Then there are Amish, Old-order Mennonites, Brethren, Dunkards, Beachy-Amish, Hutterites, Quakers, and I don't know who else. They all descended from the Anabaptist heritage, if I'm not mistaken. I'm not sure if their present differences are in doctrine or only in practice. But from what I have observed, I think it is mostly in practice."

"I would love to learn more about them because in my study I found that they believed in holiness of life and in practicing everything the Scriptures teach. And which of the churches that we are familiar with live that way?"

"You said the key word—*live* that way! Many churches have good doctrines, even like our church. Our church emphasizes the New Birth, salvation through faith, and active Christian lives that include evangelization. Our church expects each member to publicly declare his faith in Jesus Christ. And it upholds the Bible as the supreme authority for man's religious practice. . . . That all sounds right on target!"

"But we don't live it!" Linda said. "We don't obey the Bible in everyday life!"

"You're exactly right. Daddy gets so disappointed sometimes. He preaches and preaches, and people tell him 'What a wonderful sermon!' and go home and live the way they always did! It's as though most people put their religious life into a box, and they only get it out and use it when it is convenient. They don't live out the Christian life in a day-to-day walk of faith, living by the power of the Holy Spirit."

"Do all the Mennonite groups really live like Christians ought to then?"

"I'm afraid you would be disappointed in some groups and some individuals within groups; no one is perfect, you know. Some of them are little different from the ordinary run of nominal Christians. And I think Daddy would say that for many of them, their religion is only a profession. But we have met many others that Daddy felt were truly Christian. They lived, as you said, in obedience to the Bible, and their everyday lives were holy."

"It would be wonderful to meet people and to be able to go to church with people who truly lived Christianity through the week, wouldn't it. I almost envy Andrea living among Mennonites and going to school with them. Would it be right to pray that I could meet some of that kind of people sometime?" Linda asked.

"Sure it would. I often thought that I would like to hunt up such groups again, once I was on my own, and spend enough time with them to learn what they believe. But it doesn't seem as though God will give me that opportunity."

Silently the river rippled by. *Just like our lives,* Linda thought. *We come, we pass by, we go on . . . and on and on, into an endless eternity.*

Linda noticed a sigh that escaped from Steve as he laboriously shifted his position. "Are you tired?" she asked with concern.

"Yes, I am," he admitted. "Much as I love being out here, sharing with you in this way and with the voices of nature all around, I guess I need to go back to the house."

He leaned his head wearily against the side of the door as Linda carefully drove back up the woods road to the farm buildings. Linda's heart was cut to the quick to see his obvious suffering. But he smiled at her, and in his smile she read his cheerful resignation to God's will.

And so the fall days passed. The silos had been filled, and now corn and soybean harvest was in full swing. Thanks to Red and old Tobe, the harvest was going on as usual. Red had graduated in the spring and had cheerfully asserted that he had had enough of classrooms. He loved the farm and fixing or making things in the shop, and he worked diligently day after day. Linda was happy that Dad had such a dependable helper. And they all were thankful that Dad had been able to work out a farm deferment from military service for Red. His brisk, sturdy stride carried him quickly from one job to another, and his cheerful, happy demeanor helped to lighten many a dreary day.

For there were dreary days. In spite of chemotherapy, it was soon obvious to all who loved him that Steve was going backward physically. He had had a couple of good months after recovering from the amputation and had started his senior year with the rest of his class, cheerfully hopping from class to class on his crutches. Linda and his sister Sharon helped carry his books and did all for him they could. But then, soon after the Sunday with Linda, he no longer tried going to school. His nausea and intense pain increased as time went on. Soon he was on painkillers continually. His weight continued to drop until he looked almost emaciated.

"Mom," Linda said one November Saturday as they cleaned out the flower beds, "is it the chemotherapy that is making Steve so sick, or is it like he thought, that the cancer has spread?"

"You may as well know, Linda, that his cancer has metastasized to his liver. The doctors were already suspicious of that a couple months ago, but now they can feel a mass on his liver." Mom spoke gently, looking with sympathy at Linda.

"Then his prognosis is not good," Linda guessed.

"I'm afraid not."

Linda marveled at how easy it had become to share with her mother. Was it a change in Mom, or was the change with herself, or both? "He told me, the day we were talking out by the river, that he thought the cancer had spread to his liver. He told me then that he thought he would soon be going to be with Jesus," Linda said, her voice heavy with emotion. She gathered dead flower stalks and loaded them into the garden cart.

"These dead stalks remind me of some verses I read in Isaiah, I think chapter 40, last evening," Linda continued. "Something about all flesh being as grass, and all the beauty of man like the flowers of the field. The Spirit of God blows upon them, and they wither and die. I know that death must come to everyone, but it is so hard to think about it coming to Steve, who was in the bloom of life."

"It is hard for all of us to accept, Linda. These have been difficult days," Mom sympathized. "But barring a miracle of God, Steve cannot live much longer. The doctors were amazed at how long he kept going with that bad leg. They thought it must have been his strong constitution and cheerful outlook on life. But now there is nothing more they can do. Perhaps our prayer now should be that Steve could soon be released from his suffering."

"Oh, Mom," Linda cried, "I will miss Steve so much. He has come to mean a lot to me since they moved here. I never met a young man like him . . . and likely will never meet another. He has always been so kind and unselfish, so tender, and yet firm in his beliefs, so appreciative of all God has given us to enjoy . . . just the ideal friend!"

"I know how you feel, Linda. And Dad and I would have gladly given you to him in marriage if it had come to that. Dad, especially, has a deep love and appreciation for him and his noble character. Your dad is as grieved about all this as Steve's own parents are, I believe. But we all, no matter how much we love him, must realize, as Dad says, that God loves him even more. And

God has everything planned according to His own perfect will."

Linda deeply appreciated that talk with her mother and often thought back to it in the months that followed, knowing of a certainty that she was not alone in her grief. Not only was God with her, supporting her, but her parents understood and supported her with their love and concern.

# 19

It was summertime again. In the cornfields, the corn stood knee-high, and soybeans were beginning to sprout in the fields where the grains had been harvested.

High-school days were finished for Linda. She had graduated. *The class of 1967!* She leaned on her hoe, thinking about her senior year. *By the grace of God,* she thought, *I made it through!* The year had been a difficult one for her, as one by one she had given up activities that she had enjoyed so much in previous years—first the class parties, then cheerleading, and then playing with the hockey team. She had been elected secretary of her class, but even that she resigned from. She did not feel right helping to plan things that she thought the Bible spoke against and that she herself could not do.

And then Miss Ducas, the guidance counselor, had called her into her office. "Linda," she had said, "some of the faculty have a concern for you. They sense that you are withdrawing from reality since Steve Kelloway's death."

"So the fact that I haven't been taking such

an active part in school life is the basis of their concern?" Linda had asked.

"Well, yes, that is part of it," Miss Ducas conceded.

"But that's because I have become a Christian, and I don't feel comfortable doing a lot of the things I used to do," Linda had told her. "I don't say this to judge others, but a lot of what goes on here in school is not according to what the Bible teaches."

"So you are getting a little fanatical about religion?" Miss Ducas had questioned.

"I hope not. Just trying to do what I think the Bible teaches."

Miss Ducas had not seemed to understand at all, Linda remembered. She had made a little joke then about Larry studying to be a doctor. "You'll have a doctor in the family so that you can be sick-for-nothing. Now *you'll* want to marry a preacher so that you can be good-for-nothing," she had quipped.

Well, Miss Ducas was not the only one who had not understood. Some of her old friends had given her a rough time too. How often through the year she was the subject of cruel and unfeeling jokes and teasing as she tried to live her new convictions. Her patience and sweetness had often been tried to the limit by the reproaches of former friends and even her beloved teachers. But had Jesus not warned His followers that the world would hate them? And the apostle Paul had said that "all that will live godly in Christ Jesus shall suffer persecution."

She thought of the struggles that her parents had also faced as the small group began worshiping in their remodeled church in Northport. Former church friends would openly snub them on the streets. It had been very hard for Mom to give up the social standing she had always been so proud of. Linda prayed often that her mother would have the strength and grace from God to live above the reproaches that came to her.

Linda thought too of the winter morning when she was in the barn loft, carrying alfalfa bales to the hay hole to throw down for the cows. She had uncovered a can and had picked it up to look at it more closely—lighter fluid! How the others had marveled when she showed them her find, realizing that God had protected them from the fire that apparently someone had planned for their barn. She could not help wondering if that can had been planted the night that Tiny was hurt. Probably they would never know.

The investigation into Grandpa's barn fire had continued through the winter, but so far the state police did not have a suspect. Whoever had done it had covered his tracks well.

She leaned over and pulled a weed beside a

tomato stalk. Little green tomatoes were already clustered on the stalk. It had been an early spring, and the garden things were well advanced for June.

Linda continued hoeing the row of tomatoes, her thoughts running through the past months. Graduation had been two weeks ago. She and Chester Dorsey, Miss Ducas had told her, had basically tied for head of the class. The faculty had given the honor of valedictorian to Chester. Linda could not help feeling that their decision was because of her not participating in senior class activities throughout the year. But really, what did that matter? She was happy to feel that she had done her best. And she was very happy that Chester had been valedictorian rather than she. In fact, she really had not wanted the honor, feeling that it would just direct more ill feeling toward her.

Linda felt more and more that honors and achievements were things of the world. The greatest victory for the year by far, Linda was convinced, was Mary Catherine's decision to follow Christ. Linda had been totally unprepared for Mary Catherine's coming to her in tears that day last winter and saying she wanted to be a Christian.

Linda could remember it like yesterday. It was the week after Steve's funeral—a cold, rainy Saturday. Mary Catherine had called, asking if it would be okay to come out to Linda's house. Linda had assumed she wanted to talk about Steve or maybe some studies, since she had been much friendlier during the last year. She had put some pine logs in the fireplace and had a cozy fire going, ready to chat in the pleasant library. But Mary Catherine had come into the house, her eyes tearstained and her heavy makeup smeared from the tears that had run down over her face, and had asked if they could go to Linda's room.

There she had burst out, "Linda, I want to be a Christian. I can't bear it anymore. Steve's dying is driving me crazy! He was so good and so unworthy of the horrible death he died. But he took it all so calmly and peacefully. We all were so touched! And you—you have been so kind to me, while I have been as rotten as I know how to be. You have something that the rest of us don't have; I could see it in the quiet way you accepted Steve's sickness and death. I can see it in the way you are kind and forgiving and loving, in the way you stick up for good morals, in the way you don't cheat or do things dishonestly to get ahead of others. I could say so much . . . but you are just—different!"

"Mary Catherine, I'm so happy you want to be a Christian," Linda had said, tears in her own eyes. "That's the only way any person can be what you say you have seen in Steve or me. I could never be anything by myself or in my own strength. It's only God working in me, showing Himself through me!"

Linda picked up her Bible from her nightstand. "This is the most important Book in my life." She smiled at Mary Catherine as she opened it to Romans 3. "First we need to realize that this is God's Word to us, and that it is all true. God tells us that 'all scripture is given by inspiration of God.' Then we need to realize that we are sinners. Romans 3 says that all of us have failed God; that every accountable person in the whole world is a sinner before God. But God made a way for us to be accepted with Him. He sent His beloved Son, Jesus, to die for our sins. Do you believe that?"

Mary Catherine nodded her head. "I heard all that stuff when I was a little girl going to Sunday school, but I never thought about what it meant! But I know I'm a sinner; nobody needs to tell me that! And I didn't used to care. But now I think, what if I would die—like I could have when Ken was killed. And now since Steve died . . . If it had been me, I'd have gone straight to hell, I know I would have!"

"God wants all people to be saved from sin and to follow Him so that they can spend eternity in heaven with Him. But many people do not care, and the Bible says that most people will go to hell, simply because they do not believe in the blood that Jesus shed for them."

"But, Linda, I want to be saved. Is there hope for somebody as wicked as I have been? You don't know all I've been into! Smoking and drinking and immorality—I mean, I've been a regular old sinner!"

Linda quoted the verse, " 'Him that cometh to me I will in no wise cast out.' That is Jesus speaking, and it means you. The apostle Paul, one of the writers of Scripture, said that he was the chief of sinners. Another time, a woman caught in the act of adultery was brought to Jesus by the religious rulers. They wanted her to be stoned, according to their Law. Jesus freely forgave her sins and told her to 'go, and sin no more.' God says that 'whosoever shall call upon the name of the Lord shall be saved.' "

Mary Catherine suddenly fell to her knees beside Linda's bed. Linda kneeled beside her. "God in heaven," Mary Catherine cried, "I'm such a sinner, God, but I want to believe You and accept Jesus' blood that was shed for my sins. I am so sorry, God, for all my sins. I have done so many wicked things, and You must hate me! But please don't, God, because I'm desperate. I need You, and I need Your help. So forgive me, if You can, and help me to live the way a Christian ought to live!" Mary Catherine continued to sob into Linda's pillow.

Then Linda prayed, "Dear Father, I thank You

for speaking to Mary Catherine and drawing her to Yourself. Cleanse her from her sins by the blood of Your dear Son, Jesus. And help her to live now as You want Your children to live. Thank You for hearing our prayers, dear Father. Thank You for all Your precious promises, and thank You that You are faithful in keeping them! Through Jesus' Name we pray, amen."

Linda would never forget the look of wonder and peace that shone from Mary Catherine's face as she rose from her knees. "Thank God!" she cried. "He heard my prayer. I feel so clean inside—like a new person!"

"The Bible says that now you *are* a new person," Linda assured her. "Do you have a Bible?"

"Not really. I have an old New Testament somewhere, if I can find it, that I used to take to Sunday school."

Linda handed hers to Mary Catherine. "Here, use mine," she said. "I have others to use. And you must have a Bible. It is God's road map to tell us how to get to heaven. Read it every day. Begin with the Book of John. Pray every day. Talk to God as you go about your work. Talk with other Christians if you have questions. And go to church where God's Word is taught, so that you can be with other Christians."

"Could I come to your church?" Mary Catherine asked shyly.

"Of course, Mary Catherine," Linda assured

her. "You are very welcome!"

And thus had begun a close friendship that Linda treasured. Mary Catherine had many questions as time went on, and the need to help her kept Linda studying and on her toes. So as Mary Catherine grew in her Christian life, so did Linda. Their close friendship helped Linda to cope better without Steve through the long winter.

Steve had died quietly the day after Christmas. The last words he had said to Linda were "I'm going to Jesus. Meet me there!" His mind was clear to the last, even though he had intense pain. But how Linda had suffered with him, till she had almost felt relief when at last his sufferings were over. And now, how could she wish him back? She often tried to imagine what joys he was experiencing in heaven; how she longed at times to join him there!

After the funeral, Steve's mother had come to Linda. "Here is Steve's Bible," she said. "Steve wanted you to have it." Somehow, when Linda read the special verses Steve had written on the back pages or the ones he had underlined that were special to him, it seemed to her that his spirit lived on in his Bible. Linda treasured that Bible.

She also treasured his letter to her that she found in it. Steve had written it a couple of days before he died. She had read it so often that she knew it by heart.

Saturday evening, December 24

My dear Linda,

I will never be able to tell you how much I have cared for you. All of my dreams for the future included you. I felt you were the girl for me soon after I learned to know you. Your noble and unselfish character shone from your life. And I knew you had much to give to the one so fortunate as to win your friendship. How much I wished to be that one!

But it will not be me. God has other plans for me. And I submit freely to His will; I long to be with Him because—even more than I love you—I love Him!

I am presumptuous enough to think that you will miss me. Here is a song that is precious to me, and I trust will help you to cope with the sorrow of parting:

"But for a moment"—this valley of sorrows,
Darkened with shadows and heavy with sighs;
Bright dawns the morrow, the glorious morrow!
Faint not! The sun shall with healing arise!

"Far more exceeding," the heavenly glory;
Sufferings here with it cannot compare.
Glory eternal, the guerdon for anguish;
Radiant crowns for the thorns, over there!

Temporal things like a vapor shall vanish;
Higher than earth lies the land of our choice.

Upward we press to the kingdom eternal;
  Jesus, our King, we behold and rejoice!

*Refrain:*
"But for a moment!" Only a moment!
  Light our affliction—'twill soon pass away.
"But for a moment!" Only a moment!
  Then comes the glory, forever and aye!

—*A.A.P.*

I am too tired to write more tonight. It won't be long now till I am with Jesus. Good-bye for now, my dear one. I hope and pray we meet again over *there!*

Praying that your strength fail not,
Steve

A special choir had sung the hymn at Steve's funeral, and Linda had often sung it since. To think of Steve with Jesus in the eternal glory . . . it was such a beautiful thought. No more pain or suffering. Yes, she wanted to meet him again sometime, over there!

But life goes on. And Linda had found that she needed to reinvest her interests in the things of life that were fruitful. She missed Steve tremendously. And many times she had gone to his family, and together they had shared the sorrow of his being gone. But as time wore on, the sharpness of the pain was wearing off; now the intense ache was replaced, most of the time, with a pleasant remembrance of the joys they had shared.

Linda had remembered Steve's talking about his parents getting periodicals from a Mennonite publishing company. She had asked Mrs. Kelloway if she might borrow them when they were finished with them. She so much enjoyed reading their youth paper, feeling that here were youth with whom she could identify.

One time she had gotten bold enough to write to the editor, asking a number of questions about their beliefs. He had answered her in a long, fatherly letter, helping her to understand why they believed and practiced various things as they did. He invited her to write whenever she had other questions, and he or his wife had always answered. She had shared the letters with her parents, who had also been impressed with the air of holiness and soundness that pervaded their theology. How she had often prayed for the opportunity to personally meet such people and, if God willed, to become a part of their group.

During the past year, instead of the extracurricular activities at school, she had taken up teaching a Sunday school class. She had also tutored some of the students who were struggling in English and French classes, as she tried to find activities more useful than some of her former, high-school ones. And then there were the times she had gone with Shem and Louise and helped teach Bible lessons to the poor children who lived along the railroad tracks in Springville. How dear those little black children had become to her!

She thought about that special Saturday morning in January when, during devotional time, Mom had told the family that she had made things right with God. She confessed to Dad and the children her many failures to be a good wife and mother in the past. She was sorry for not being the good example to the children that she should have been, and asked their prayer support to be a faithful and godly mother.

Larry had also expressed his desire to follow the Lord with all his heart and had asked the family to especially pray for him in his many spiritual struggles.

What a time of rejoicing that had been! Linda had only wished that Loretta would also be willing to come into the family of God. How often she prayed for Loretta, her prayer like a pleading thought rising to heaven during most of her waking hours.

Linda leaned on her hoe, thinking of Loretta and of her growth in spiritual knowledge over the past year. Loretta still was quick-tempered and flighty, but now, instead of moodily sulking after such an episode, she would confess her failures to the family and go on. Often she would come to Linda's room and ask to read her periodicals from the Mennonite publisher. Sometimes Loretta would ask questions: "Why do these people . . . ?" or "Why do they believe . . . ?" Linda did not know all the answers, but they would try to find answers in the Bible. She had shared with Loretta the letters that she had received from the publisher. These times of searching had brought them much closer together as sisters, and Linda cherished that.

Memories clung like soft shadows as Linda hoed on in the bright sunshine. The songs of the birds seemed to echo the deep joy in her heart as she thought about all that the Lord had done for her and been to her during the past year.

She wondered about the future, as she often had lately, especially now that she was out of school. She had been offered the coveted Springville Faculty Scholarship to the state-supported college of her choice. But her parents had advised her not to accept it. Larry was disillusioned with college—at least where he had been. He was planning to go to a church college in the fall. Ron was staying at the university, partly because that was where his scholarship was, and partly because he had gotten deeply involved in fraternity life, Larry had told her with regret.

Her thoughts continued to run on as she

hoed the last potato row. Next weekend, she was going with Larry to see Andrea. It would be so good to see her again. She had not seen her since Steve's funeral, and then they had had very little opportunity to talk. She was eager to talk over with her the things that she had learned about the Mennonites and to show her the letters she had gotten.

Linda surveyed the garden. She had hoed everything, and now she would run the tiller through it. Normally, Larry did that, but he was cultivating corn that day.

As she was walking the tiller to the garden, Red came from the chicken barn and intercepted her. "Let me do this for you," he said. "You're hardly strong enough to handle this beast!"

"Thanks, Red," she said, gratefully dropping to the cool grass. She was tired. She sat and watched for a while as Red expertly ran the tiller between the rows of potatoes, beans, and sweet corn. Faithful Red! How capable and sturdy he looked. His face and arms were almost as red as his hair, from all his time in the sun. Well, he loved to tease her about her freckles, but he surely had them too!

She got up and went to the house. Mom probably had work she would be happy to have help with. Mom was ironing, and Loretta was baking strawberry pies. Somewhere upstairs, she heard Pansy singing lustily at her cleaning.

On the side counter were ten or fifteen quarts of strawberries still waiting to be cleaned. They were end-of-the-season little ones, but were good enough for jam at least. Linda got a knife, sat down by the table, and began stemming them, humming along with Pansy's song, "'Oh, you gotta walk that lonesome valley; Oh, you gotta walk it by yourself . . .'"

Mom came through the kitchen to get more laundry. She smiled lovingly at Linda. "You happy, dear?" she asked.

She returned Mom's smile. How different Mom was since her conversion; how easy it was to love her now! And Mom was even teaching Sunday school at their new church. She had never done that before. She taught the ladies' class every other Sunday, and Linda had heard some comments about what a good teacher Mrs. Asbury was. Linda was happy that Mom was taking an active part in Christian service, not because she had to but because she wanted to.

Mom came back through the kitchen with more ironing. "Did you hear that old Mrs. Davis is sick?" Mom asked.

"Is that who you and Dad were talking about this morning?" Linda asked.

"Yes. Dr. Boyer had called and asked if Dad and I would go to visit her. He said she is on her deathbed. She has congestive heart failure and won't go to the hospital, so they have her on oxygen at the house. She's nearly crazy with terror about the possibility of dying. He didn't know if we could give her any spiritual help or not. As soon as we've had lunch, we want to drive over. You girls please be in prayer for us!"

Linda shivered. She could hardly imagine how it would be to relate to such a godless old woman. She knew from chance comments through the years that Mrs. Davis had lived a wicked life. Some thought she had the power to cast spells on people she did not like. Mr. Davis had mysteriously disappeared when Linda was small. Many thought Mrs. Davis had done away with him, but the authorities were never able to prove anything.

As soon as lunch was over, Mom put a fresh strawberry pie in a container, and she and Dad left for the unpleasant visit. Through the afternoon as Linda and Loretta made strawberry jam, Linda's thoughts often went to Mom and Dad and to the poor old woman they had gone to try to help.

"I can't believe Mom actually went to see that dirty old woman," Loretta said as she stirred jam. "You know well enough how fastidious Mom used to be about such things! She surely has changed."

"Yes, she has," Linda agreed happily from the sink, where she was washing pint jars.

"Mom has changed in a lot of other ways too," Loretta continued. "She is so sweet and a pleasure to be with!"

"That is what the grace of God does for us when we allow God to have control of our lives," Linda assured her with a loving smile.

Loretta turned away, intently stirring the jam.

Suddenly she broke out, "But, Linda, I can't be a Christian among my friends. I couldn't stand all the heckling that you took in school the last couple of years! And I don't want to give up all the fun things! Why must everything fun be sinful?"

"You don't understand the difference between true happiness and fun, Loretta," Linda explained, surprised that Loretta had said so much. "When a person has the joy of Christ in his heart, those other things look so empty! Christ gives us such depth of satisfaction that nothing else really matters."

Loretta said no more, and Linda wished she could read her thoughts. Or at least that she could know what was the right thing to say to lead Loretta to give herself up to God. *Father in heaven, continue to speak to Loretta.*

Mom and Dad were back by suppertime, and Linda was eager to hear how the visit had gone. Nothing was mentioned during the meal, but afterward Linda followed Mom and Dad to the porch. "How did your visit with Mrs. Davis go?"

she asked with concern.

"Oh, Linda, I almost cringe to think about it," Mom lamented. "She did seem glad to see us. But she was so filthy that the first thing I did was give her a bath. Dad used that time to clean and scrub at the grime in her house. She isn't able to walk anymore, but she is so thin and frail that it wasn't hard to move her around. But the dirt was nothing in comparison to her spiritual condition! Oh, Dad, you tell it!" Mom covered her face with her hands.

"Once she was cleaned up a bit and on clean sheets, we asked her questions about her spiritual condition: Does she know that she needs to get ready to meet God? That after death, all people must stand before God and answer for the things they have done in life? Could we help her to get right with God?" Dad stopped briefly.

"But she cried out, 'I've served the devil all my life! I can't find God now!' We read Scripture passage after Scripture passage to her about how God accepts all who come to Him, no matter how sinful. She said, 'You don't know how sinful I've been. I've sinned away the day of grace. There's no hope for me! No hope! I had a godly, praying mother, and she warned me I would come to this if I chose to go my own way. Oh, yes, I was the black sheep of my family. But I didn't care then; life was full and fun. I sinned every way under the sun. And finally I gave my soul to Satan! I loved the power he gave me to do strange things. But now I'm going to die, and I'm going to hell where he is—*and I don't want to!* But I can't turn to God; the devil has me by the feet and keeps pulling me down!' "

"We read Scripture verses all afternoon, between her ravings," Mom continued, "but it did no good. She just kept crying, 'He's got me by the feet, and he's pulling me down!'"

"Oh, Mom," Linda cried, "what a horrible way to live! And even worse, what a horrible way to die!"

A few days later, Dr. Boyer called again. "Won't you please go out to Mrs. Davis again, Mrs. Asbury? She just lies on her bed, screaming. The nurse who is staying with her is begging me to give her something to knock her out. But I don't want to give her morphine as long as there is any hope of salvation for the poor old woman!"

So Dad and Mom drove over again. Before they even got close to her house, they told the children later, they heard her hoarse screams of "Let me alone! Get out of here! Let go of my feet!" Intermingled were curses of the most horrible kind.

Mom had cringed at the door. "I can't face this again, Dad," she whispered. It seemed that the place was alive with the spirit of the devil. But while they stood at the door, she fell back on her bed and lay still. As they entered, she was gasping for breath, but soon she lay silent, her staring eyes fixed on the ceiling and a look of horror on her silent face. Dad and the nurse had pulled the sheet over her face, and the nurse had gone to call the doctor and the undertaker.

Mom wrung her hands with grief. "If only we had done more for the poor lady through the years," she said, her voice heavy with regret.

"You did do a lot, Mother," Dad comforted, "especially in the last year. But she never appreciated it nor seemed to have any interest in the Gospel. What more can a person do? Finally, it is each one's choice where he will spend eternity. And that choice needs to be made while a person is still alive!"

"What are we going to do about her funeral?" Mom asked after a while. "She said expressly that she didn't want that youngest brother of hers, with his 'pharisaic, religious airs,' snooping around her business."

"She has a brother? Around here?" Linda asked incredulously.

"Didn't we tell you about that?" Dad's face registered surprise. "Deacon Tilghman is her youngest brother."

Linda could hardly contain her shock. "Then that would make Clyde Tilghman her nephew?" she said in disbelief.

"Yes, it would," Dad replied. "We were quite surprised to hear all that too. But I guess Mr.

Tilghman never had reason to identify her as a kin to him, and she certainly didn't tell it either. They apparently didn't have much to do with each other, even though they lived in the same area for years. She did say, though, that Clyde seemed to take a liking to her and that he would come out to help her on occasion."

Linda's mind could hardly grasp such news. But somehow it did make sense, knowing Clyde as she did. Maybe there was a reason he could be so cold and unfeeling at times.

Mrs. Davis's death and funeral made a lasting impression on Linda. Apparently here was a person who had committed what the Bible calls the sin that cannot be forgiven. *How important it is to live daily in obedience to God's Word and the promptings of His Spirit,* Linda thought. *What promise does anyone have that he would not also come to the place Mrs. Davis did, after a lifetime of grieving the Holy Spirit of God?*

# 20

On Saturday morning, soon after six o'clock, Larry and Linda left for the Bakers'. It was already warm and humid when they left home. Linda was eager to get to the mountains, where she remembered it had been so refreshingly cool other times. She drove most of the way while Larry slept. He still was not caught up, he claimed, from all the sleep he had lost during finals! But Linda did not mind driving. As she drove, she sang softly, eager to be with Andrea again.

Soon they drove out of the metropolitan areas and into the rolling hills. Before long, Linda knew, they would be driving among the higher mountain ranges. She was anxious to see the beautiful mountains again. She remembered Dad saying when they were up there two years ago that they were lovely to look at, but he surely would not want to farm in them! She wondered if she could ever adapt from her native flatlands to these valleys and mountains, with the strips of farmland running across the sides of the hills. And the roads—how they curved, up and down and around between the hills! But Andrea loved it here, she knew.

As they drove up the long lane to the farm, Linda looked around in amazement. The buildings had been repaired and painted, and new siding covered the house. Shrubbery had been planted around the house, and the yard looked as if it had been recently reseeded. Linda was happy for the Bakers; she had almost pitied Andrea the first time they had visited, when the farm had looked so shabby. But Linda had soon forgotten about it because the Bakers did not seem to mind at all. They were all so happy to be on a farm.

Larry finally awoke and quickly groomed himself the best he could. Linda looked at him and laughed as he used his comb to carefully put the finishing touches on his dark, wavy hair. He made a wry face at her. Her silly big brother! All this effort to impress Andrea! She could hardly adjust to sharing her best friend with her brother. But that was not the worst; she was afraid her best friend was beginning to prefer the company of her big brother to her own! Oh well, whom would she rather have had Larry choose? And if all went well, perhaps someday Andrea would be more than a best friend; she would be a *sister!*

Andrea came out the door to meet them, not rushing as she had at sixteen, but walking sedately and calmly. She grasped Linda's hands tightly and then brushed away a few tears as she looked into Linda's eyes. "I'm fine," Linda whispered, sensing the reason for the sudden tears. "I don't envy you and Larry at all, but I'm very, very happy for you!"

"Thank you, Linda. You are truly a specimen of God's grace!" Andrea whispered back. Then Andrea went to Larry, and Linda left them and went to greet Pastor and Mrs. Baker, who had come out on the porch.

That afternoon, they all sat in the shade of the maples in the back yard. Pastor Baker loved talking about his little farming enterprises. That morning they had admired the neat, contoured fields of corn along the sides of the hills. Linda had walked around with them, looking into all the sheds and barns. There were chickens and goats and cows and pigs.

A rooster crowed now from the top of the chicken coop. "I can't keep the chickens in that coop for anything," Pastor Baker complained good-naturedly. "But I'd better figure out a way soon, or Mama will have their heads!" He glanced laughingly toward his merry-faced companion.

"You had better believe I will!" she returned. "They have scratched out half of my garden already!" She looked toward the garden. Linda looked too and was sure she saw several red hens vigorously scratching even now.

Mrs. Baker must have seen them too. She jumped up suddenly and ran toward the garden. "Shoo, shoo," she hollered, flapping her apron. The red hens made a beeline toward the coop, running first one way and then the other along the fence. Linda ran to help her. She and Mrs. Baker finally cornered them, one by one, and tossed them over the fence.

Soon she and Linda joined the group under the shade again, Mrs. Baker panting and puffing. "They are the dumbest critters," she complained. "They can figure out how to get *out* of the pen, but do you think they can ever figure out how to get back *in?*"

"Oh, Mama," Pastor Baker said, laughing, "you like your hens! And I know well enough you will never lay a hand on one of them in revenge!"

"I guess they're not as bad as your goats," she returned.

She turned to Linda and Larry. "Would you believe, those goats got out one night, early this spring, and chewed every bush on the place down to a couple of sticks! I didn't think the bushes would survive, and I *hoped* the goats wouldn't. Well, they all did, and neither the goats nor the bushes were any the worse for the experience! The lilacs didn't bloom though. Daddy could get rid of the *goats,* and I surely wouldn't mind if he did!"

"Oh, but the little kids are so cute," Andrea protested. "I love to watch them play."

Linda watched the growing kids running after their nannies, who were grazing the steep hillsides inside their fence. They were probably interesting as long as they stayed little, she decided.

"How about something to drink, Mama?" Pastor Baker asked after a while.

Mrs. Baker went to the house to make iced tea. Linda went with her. "May I help you, Mrs. Baker?" she asked as they entered the cheerful farm kitchen.

"That would be kind of you," she said.

"I'll go gather the tea. I saw where it is growing, I think," Linda said. "Was that mint growing behind the garage?"

"Yes, we can use that. I was just going to use tea bags. But fresh would be better. Here is a pan and a knife. I'll put water on to boil while you get the tea."

Linda went out to the mint bed and sniffed deeply of the fragrant smell. A big yellow cat rubbed against her legs as she cut the tea. She would have scratched him, but she was afraid of getting some of his long yellow hair in with the tea leaves. A red hen came around the corner of the garage but, seeing Linda, gave a startled cackle and ran the other direction. Linda noticed that it looked as though the hens had been in the tea patch as well as the garden. She pulled the long stems away from the wall of the garage. There, nestled close to the wall, was a tidy nest with ten large brown eggs in it. "I believe a hen has stolen a nest," Linda said to the friendly cat.

She took the mint to the house. Mrs. Baker was rushing around, getting trays and glasses and putting bar cookies on a paper plate.

"I found a surprise in your mint bed," Linda told her. "Want to come and see?"

Mrs. Baker hurried out the back walk with Linda. Linda pulled the long tea stems away from the wall again. "Oh!" Mrs. Baker exclaimed as she saw the hidden nest. "Last year a couple of hens set, and I didn't know it till they came around proudly leading flocks of little yellow chicks. They were so cute, but I had to catch them and pen them up, or the cats and hawks would have gotten them."

"Maybe the cat is waiting for this nest," Linda said, laughing. "He surely seems to be hanging around!" She bent to scratch the yellow cat that was again rubbing her legs.

"Oh, he's a pest. Go on, Goldie," Mrs. Baker said, giving a sharp *pss-s-st*. The cat took off around the garage.

"We have too many animals around here," she complained good-naturedly. "But Daddy likes every one of them!"

"Oh, I think your place is so interesting," Linda said as they walked back to the kitchen. "It seems like an old-fashioned farmstead!"

"We are happy here," Mrs. Baker agreed.

"I'm really looking forward to being here more when Andrea and I are in training together. Coming home to a farm on weekends should help me not be quite so homesick!"

Finally the tea was ready, and they carried it on a tray out to where the rest were still visiting.

"Did you have to wait for the tea to grow?" Pastor Baker asked. "We were awfully thirsty out here!"

"No, we were waiting for it to hatch," Mrs. Baker returned, with a wink at Linda.

In the evening Larry and Andrea went to a concert in a nearby town. Mr. and Mrs. Baker took Linda with them for a drive through the countryside. At several well-kept farms, Linda saw horses and buggies sitting in the farmyards. "Who lives there?" she asked, pointing out the buggies.

"They call themselves Old-order Mennonites," Pastor Baker returned. "One of them farms some of my land. They are honest people and good neighbors."

Linda was bursting with curiosity, but she did not want to ask too many questions. So this was one of the groups Steve had talked about. What was it that made them different from other

Mennonites? Using horses and buggies?

"Over there on that hill is their church house," Pastor Baker said, pointing. "They call it a meetinghouse. See the shed behind the church? That is where they tie their horses during church."

A horse with an open buggy came down the road beside the church. The horse was trotting briskly along. A strangely dressed young couple sat in the open buggy.

"I appreciate these people," Pastor Baker said. "Unfortunately, though, some of the young people sow their wild oats in the years before they join the church."

"Why don't they drive cars?" Linda asked.

"They consider that 'worldly'—I guess I may put it that simply. But they do hire drivers to take them places. They have called on me many times to take them here or there. They speak a German dialect from their ancestors. They call it Pennsylvania Dutch."

Linda continued to gaze as they slowly passed farm after farm where, Pastor Baker said, Mennonites lived. She saw large gardens, well-kept flower beds, and long clotheslines on pulleys, which often stretched high off the ground from house to barn. She saw horses, mules, and black-and-white Holstein cows grazing in the pastures and often a black buggy or two parked beside the house. She saw tractors with steel wheels rather than regular rubber tires. Several young children were often playing inside fenced yards, all dressed as miniatures of their parents.

"Are there other kinds of Mennonites in this area?" Linda asked after a while, remembering Kathy Yoder and not thinking she would be a part of this group.

"Oh, yes," Mrs. Baker said. "There is a church right outside of Millburg. We sometimes go there when they have special meetings, and occasionally some of them come to our services too. They dress differently—what they call 'plain.' Also they don't wear makeup or any jewelry, not even wedding bands. The women don't wear jeans or even skirts and blouses—just dresses. Some of their doctrines are a little different from ours too."

"For example, their young men go into what they term 'alternate service' rather than into the armed forces. They do that because they believe in what they call nonresistance," Pastor Baker added.

"Is nonresistance similar to Gandhi's pacifism?" Linda asked.

"I don't think they feel so," Pastor Baker said. "They feel that Gandhi, as a Hindu, was not a Christian, but used this nonviolent way of accomplishing his ends. Nonresistance to them is the Christian's application to Christ's teaching in the Sermon on the Mount of not resisting evil."

"I did a term paper on Gandhi one year in high school and would have to agree with their conclusions. He accomplished a lot of good, but it was by the use of silent force—like hunger strikes and sit-ins. Gandhi accomplished things by the use of his own power, not by God's power. I concluded from my study that nonviolence, whether passive or aggressive, often incites anger and hatred," Linda said, remembering her in-depth research for the required three-thousand-word theme. "So there must be a vast difference between true nonresistance and nonviolence, since one is practiced in obedience to the Bible and the other only as a method of getting one's way without actual warfare," she added thoughtfully.

"I never thought much about a comparison, but perhaps you are right," agreed Pastor Baker. "Nonresistance is a response from a heart of love for others, while pacifism is basically a selfish effort to get what one wants for himself or for a specific cause."

"You sound like you believe it is right yourself," Linda suggested, smiling at Pastor Baker.

"It does make sense in many ways, I have to admit. Even Jesus said that if His kingdom were of this world, then His servants would fight. And Paul talked about our citizenship being in heaven, implying that our 'warfare' is for the heavenly kingdom, not an earthly one." Pastor

Baker laughed shortly. "But to preach such a doctrine would mean a loss of my pulpit!"

How strange, Linda had to think, for Pastor Baker to profess to believe something that was obviously truth and yet not be willing to preach it because of fear of his people!

"Mrs. Baker, you mentioned that the Mennonites dress 'plain.' What did you mean by that?" Linda asked, remembering the statement Mrs. Baker had made several minutes earlier.

"That is a general term describing the conservative Mennonites' way of dressing. The men do not wear ties, but a suitcoat made to come up to their shirt collars in the front. The women wear dresses that have an extra piece of material to the waist that they call a cape. And of course, part of the plain dress is the head covering, also called a veil or veiling, that the women wear."

"Do you remember how some of the older women at the church in Springville would always wear hats to church? Maybe it was all for the same reason," Linda said. "What does that Scripture passage mean in 1 Corinthians which says that Christian women should have their heads covered when they pray or prophesy?"

"Oh, that," answered Pastor Baker. "That was a custom in the Corinthian church, probably. People don't practice that anymore."

"Oh," Linda responded. She did not wish to appear bold by saying what she thought. But she did wonder why, if wearing a veiling was only a practice in the Corinthian church, all churches still kept Communion, which was also mentioned as a practice in the same chapter.

Mrs. Baker laughed. "You probably wonder how we know so much about what the Mennonites believe."

"I did wonder," Linda admitted.

"In the couple of years we have lived here among the Mennonites, we have asked lots of questions."

"In many ways, we appreciate the Mennonites and what they believe," Pastor Baker said. "However, we think they take obedience to the Scriptures too literally."

Linda thought about that. How was it possible to take obedience too literally? Surely if God said it, He meant for His children to obey it, and without question. Was it each person's choice to decide which parts of the Scriptures he kept and which he disregarded? Did mere men—God's creation—think they knew better than God? She did not know the answers, she was sure. But she surely did wonder about a lot of things.

As Linda sat in her room that evening at the Bakers', waiting for Andrea to come home, she thought again about their plans for the fall. Part of Linda's reason for the trip to see Andrea was to try to iron out some final details. She and Andrea had applied for the three-year nursing program at the Harrisville School of Nursing, just twenty miles from the Bakers'. They would have to stay in the dorm through the week, but they were hoping for special permission to have weekends off to go to Andrea's home.

Linda looked out the window. A bright moon was casting shadows across the yard. Beyond the buildings, she could see the cornfields shimmering in its light. Then her mind went back to how she and Andrea had struggled to know what they should do in the fall. They had prayed, asking for God's direction. Linda sincerely hoped that they were doing the right thing. But she had to admit that she did have misgivings. For several months before they had graduated in the spring, they had been tossing the pros and cons back and forth as to whether to continue their education.

Linda knew what Steve's feeling had been about her going for further education. But now, what was she to do? She had no prospects of marriage in sight, as Andrea did. But even for Andrea, it might be years before Larry felt he could support a wife, at least if he still decided to go on to medical school after college. Andrea's parents had encouraged the girls to go ahead with nurse's training. And even though Linda's dad had seemed reluctant, he had finally given his approval. *Perhaps he gave his approval because he thinks it will help me to get on with my life now that Steve is gone,* Linda had thought at the time.

On Monday, Larry took Linda, Andrea, and Kathy Yoder to visit the school of nursing to finalize their plans. How delighted Linda was to finally meet this Mennonite girl about whom Andrea had written from time to time! From the first shared smile and greeting, Linda felt strangely drawn to this sweet girl, and it did not take many miles before Linda felt she had always known Kathy. She learned that Kathy was also a farm girl and loved animals and farming as well as she herself did. Linda was so eager to learn to know Kathy better and to learn about her beliefs as a Mennonite. She could hardly believe how God had answered her prayer to meet a Mennonite girl.

The girls were granted permission to have most weekends free, at least for the first six months. They chose their rooms, happy that the three of them could be close together.

How often Linda had prayed about this decision—was nursing school right for her and Andrea, or was it outside of God's will?—and had never seemed to get any really clear answer. She sincerely hoped that they were doing the right thing. At any rate, the decision was now firmly made.

Linda and Larry started home on Tuesday morning. "Are you able to drive home?" Linda asked slyly as Larry slid behind the wheel. "You sure you're all caught up with your sleep?"

She was thinking of how she had gone to bed alone each night and how, sometime later after she was sleeping, Andrea would come softly into the room.

Larry just laughed. "Oh, I have memories to buoy me up for many a day!" he quipped.

"Seriously now though," he continued, "it was a wonderful weekend. I'm so thankful for a good Christian girlfriend; what a treasure she is!"

"She told me she is so glad you're going to a Christian college this year instead of to the university. She worried about you—not because she didn't trust you but because she knows that so many have lost their faith while in college."

"Her concerns are valid, believe me!" Larry declared emphatically. "If it isn't one thing, it's another! Especially the last year. I was disagreeing with the professors a lot of the time. Philosophy class was terrible—humanistic through and through. I had to be on my guard continually for any teaching that ran counter to the Scriptures. Then English literature wasn't always the most pleasant. That professor seemed to take great delight in reading the lewdest poetry he could find. He was always taking any opportunity to make a mockery of sacred things.

One day in particular he was mocking something in the Bible. I knew, by the cynical look he turned on me, that he was trying to upset me. I got up and walked out of the class!"

"What a sacrilegious way for a professor to act!" Linda gasped. "Have such people no fear of God? Doesn't he think about a coming Day of Judgment or of punishment for sin?"

"I doubt it. One day when I had the opportunity, I challenged him about it. He laughed in my face!

"College biology was another challenge. It was so thoroughly saturated with evolution that I could hardly sort through what was right and wrong. I would answer my questions on exams: 'The book says . . .' The professor was not very happy about that, but he well knew I didn't believe the malarkey he was trying to teach."

"I know what you mean!"

"One day after school, we had a long discussion. I told him that evolution is based on one important tenet—that *simple* forms of life evolved to form *complex* forms of life. And I asked him if that is scientific. He said, 'In this case, it has to be.' I said to him that of course it isn't scientific, and he knows it. The law of science called *entropy* means that things get *less* complex with time rather than *more* complex! And yet science, as the world teaches it, holds as factual that complex forms of life evolved from simple forms of life over millions of years of evolution. According to that philosophy, man in his beauty and perfection evolved from some single-celled animal, given all that time!"

"What foolishness!"

"I know. And I told him that it takes less faith for me to believe the Bible than it would take to believe that. He really couldn't come up with an answer for me. I assured him that evolution is just wishful thinking for those who try to explain the existence of life apart from God. It is a counterfeit from Satan to frustrate the plan of God. He finally told me he admires me for what I believe and he only hopes I can keep my faith."

"We faced some of that in high school too," Linda remembered. "But not to the same extent, I'm sure."

"I don't know what was happening to Ron through the year. I tried to talk with him and keep him straightened out. But I'm afraid he has lost out. It really breaks my heart. After we had countless arguments about it, he finally said he was moving out of our room in the dorm and joining a fraternity. And he did."

"What happened then? Did you keep on seeing a lot of him?"

"Very little. The last I knew, he was smoking and drinking and running with the girls, like the rest of the fellows. He didn't come home this summer; he got a job in Charlottetown so he could be near his latest flame."

"I never had any great appreciation for him like you seemed to. I thought he seemed so shallow. But, Larry, even many that appear staunch will succumb to the pressures when they get to college; at least that is what Mr. Taylor told me one time. Thank God you could stand."

"There is so little encouragement to follow the Lord on a college campus! And the morals, even among some of the professors, are terrible. It helped me often to know I had a faithful Christian girlfriend at home, one who was praying for me and desiring my highest good. But without God and His sustaining help, I would have fallen as low as the rest."

"God's help is our only hope, isn't it," Linda inserted seriously.

"I've wondered sometimes what business we as Christians have in the world's institutions at all. I have thrown these questions around so much that I've almost gotten dizzy trying to think them through. Surely it is right to get an education, isn't it? Don't we need Christian doctors and Christian businessmen? But the education the world has to offer us is so dangerous!"

"So what are the answers?"

"That's what I would like to know!"

"You know, I've told you I wrote to the people at that Mennonite publishing company? Anyway, one question I asked them was why they don't believe in higher education. I asked them almost that same question: Don't we need Christian doctors and teachers and so forth?"

"And what did they say?"

"They wrote back with a lot of Scripture verses that support their view of only a basic, elementary education. . . ."

"Would they promote ignorance?" Larry asked in astonishment.

"Oh, no! They assured me that they are not opposed to learning. But they have a lot of problems with the training process that is available from colleges and universities of our day. They feel that that training process is too much of a threat to faith, to encourage Christians to become professionals. They would rather encourage Christians to be the laborers, working in the humbler stations in life. I think those were almost their exact words."

"Hmm . . . that's surely a new thought, isn't it," Larry mused. "Lots different from what we've always been taught!"

"When I asked how we would find work if we weren't educated, they answered that in our economy anyone who wants to work is always able to get and hold a job."

"Well, I have to admit they have a point there."

Larry drove silently for miles. Linda started singing, "'I would be true, for there are those who trust me; / I would be pure, for there are those who care. . . .'" She continued to the last verse: "'I would be prayerful through each busy moment; / I would be constantly in touch with God; / I would be tuned to hear the slightest whisper; / I would have faith to keep the path Christ trod. / I would have faith to keep the path Christ trod.'"

"Thank you for that appropriate song, Linda," Larry said thoughtfully.

Linda was glad to pull into their own poplar-lined lane late that evening. Mom and Dad were waiting up for them. They all chatted pleasantly about the Pennsylvania trip for a while, but Linda felt sure that something else was bothering Dad and Mom.

After a while, Dad pulled the daily paper off the counter. "By the way," he said, "today's paper has a write-up about Grandpa's barn fire. The state police have gotten enough leads that they feel they have a suspect. A hardware store in Sharptown reported selling several cans of lighter fluid to someone a week before the fire. With some of the police department's own evidence—fingerprints and so forth—along with various tips they received, the state police are ready to proceed with an arrest. The only problem is, the fellow has skipped the area and they can't find him."

"Who was it? Did it say?" Linda asked breathlessly, feeling from Dad's attitude that it was someone she knew well.

"They think it was Clyde Tilghman," Dad said slowly.

"Clyde Tilghman!" Linda exclaimed. "I knew he was hard and heartless at times, but I didn't think he would do something like that! I wonder what his motive was?"

"They haven't established a motive, because they haven't been able to talk with him," Dad answered.

"I wonder where he went?" Larry said, looking up from the article he was reading.

"That's a good question," Dad said.

"I just hope he isn't anywhere around *here,*" Linda said with feeling.

"Well now, Linda, I imagine he's gotten as far as he can from this area. But no matter. We will just need to forgive him for what he did," Dad reminded her. "I'm sure Grandpa won't press charges either."

"Think of how his parents must feel," Mom added with feeling.

Linda thought of her distaste for Clyde. She hung her head in shame; to hate someone, no matter how repugnant he might be, was sin. Surely God loved him just as He loved her! Yes, she must forgive and pray for him.

# 21

Linda walked up the street to the five-and-ten-cent store. It was a warm early-July morning, and likely would get warmer still. Dad had sent Linda to Springville to deliver the eggs to several little grocery stores and then to bring home some feed supplement from Southern States Feedstore. She decided that while she was in town she might as well pick up a few items she needed.

As she looked over the various shampoos, someone cleared his throat behind her. She turned around suddenly. A grinning Mr. Taylor was standing there.

"Mr. Taylor! I didn't know you were in the area. A quick business trip maybe?"

"Oh, I just ran home for a few weeks this summer. Wanted to do a little fishing and boating. I was hoping to run into you somewhere!"

He gazed at her till she was uncomfortable. "I saw in the papers that you graduated with honors," he said after a time, "and I was so glad for you. I wanted to be at the graduation but had an important case just then that I couldn't leave.

And I heard about Steve Kelloway. I was truly sorry to hear it, especially when I learned that you had been dating him. But there is so much to catch up on. Could we meet somewhere—maybe you would let me take you out to dinner?"

Mr. Taylor sounded so hopeful, and Linda hated to disappoint him. Why must she find him so appealing, when she knew it would be wrong for her to date someone who was not a Christian? The turmoil inside her tied her stomach in knots. *Lord, give me strength to do and say what I ought to,* she pleaded silently. She hesitated for a moment, hardly knowing what to say.

Finally she spoke. "I'm sorry, Mr. Taylor, but I cannot accept your invitation," she said kindly.

"You're still holding out on me, are you, Linda?" he asked, his smile slowly fading.

"But, Mr. Taylor, is there any reason I should feel differently than I did the last time I talked with you?" she asked soberly. "Have you changed your mind about God, about Christianity?"

"I must admit, Linda, I have thought a lot about your father's rose garden—uh—fable, would you call it? But don't ask such hard questions! I haven't talked with you for two years, and I guess I thought maybe you had changed." He hesitated briefly, and then continued, "But then again, I wouldn't want you to."

This discussion was pointless, Linda thought.

"Would you please excuse me, Mr. Taylor? I should finish the shopping I came in to do."

"Well, surely. I don't want to hold you up. I'll see you later," he said, walking briskly to the front of the store and pushing out through the swinging glass door.

Linda watched him pass the window as he walked down the sidewalk, his face sad. *I don't like to hurt him like this! And his continued interest in me is flattering. But dating him would be sin! O Father, forgive me and help me! I cannot let such feelings take control or override my better knowledge. I cannot give him any hope when he is not a Christian! Why can't he understand that I do not want a special relationship with him? Father in heaven, give me strength to stand against this temptation.*

When she was finished in the five-and-ten-cent store, Linda took the pickup out to the feedstore to pick up the supplement Dad needed. She waved at several black children fishing by the river. They had been in her Bible class. After the clerk had loaded the supplement, she hurried home, eager to get into the garden again, where Mom and Loretta had been picking tomatoes from the early patch.

They had finished picking, and a wheelbarrow full of tomatoes sat at the back door. Linda quickly changed her clothes and went to the kitchen, where Mom was getting out dishpans and canners and knives and all the rest of the paraphernalia needed to can tomatoes, juice, and spaghetti sauce. Then they set out some lunch before getting into the tomato project. Linda would have loved to share with her mother about meeting up with Mr. Taylor in town. But would her mother be able to handle graciously a reminder of that once-volatile situation? Linda wasn't quite sure, and so she chose to remain silent about it as she set the table.

The girls quickly cleaned up the kitchen after lunch and then sat down to cut up tomatoes. "Looks like we have our work cut out for today, doesn't it," Linda said laughingly.

"Today and maybe tomorrow too!" Loretta laughed with her.

"The tomatoes are earlier than usual this year, which is nice," Mom observed. "Gets them out of the way before the corn and beans come in." Mom and the girls worked companionably for the next several hours. Then it was time for Linda to help with the barn chores.

She skipped out the back walk. The day was so fragrant with freshness. Flowers were blooming in all the beds and lending their fragrance to that of the ripening early apples in the orchard. The smell of freshly mown hay blended with the other smells. *Someone must have been mowing hay today,* she thought as she looked out beyond the barns. *Maybe Red or Larry was mowing this morning.*

Larry and Red were already in the barn, getting ready to do the milking. "Where's Dad?" Linda asked as she went into the milk house, where Larry was putting the milkers together.

"He had a meeting with the church board, I think," Larry said.

Linda hurried to bring the cows in. As soon as she opened the door, they started filing into their places. She always marveled how each one knew her own stall from all the others and hardly ever did a cow get into the wrong one. If she did, the one that belonged there would try her best to squeeze in too! Quickly Linda went along both rows, snapping their fasteners shut.

As she worked, she sang the song that was on her heart:

O Jesus, I have promised
To serve Thee to the end;
Be Thou forever near me,
My Master and my Friend.
I shall not fear the battle
If Thou art by my side,
Nor wander from the pathway
If Thou wilt be my Guide.

Oh, let me feel Thee near me;
The world is ever near.
I see the sights that dazzle,

The tempting sounds I hear.
My foes are ever near me,
Around me and within;
But, Jesus, draw Thou nearer
And shield my soul from sin.

O Jesus, Thou hast promised
To all who follow Thee
That where Thou art in glory,
There shall Thy servant be.
And, Jesus, I have promised
To serve Thee to the end;
Oh, give me grace to follow
My Master and my Friend.
—*John E. Bode*

Linda looked around in surprise when she heard Red singing with her. What a lovely tenor voice! She had not known that he could sing. But then, she was not around him much. And she knew he did not sing in the choir or in the school glee club because he was too busy trying to earn a living for his mother. Larry was singing too, but that did not surprise her; he often sang with her as they went about their work.

She gathered her supplies to feed the hungry calves in the pens behind the barn, still humming the tune. It was easy to be happy here on the farm, with all the work she loved. How she would miss it when she needed to leave the end of August!

And for three long years! But she trusted that her dearest Friend would be there with her too.

When her barn chores were finished, she hurried back to the house. She was sure that Mom and Loretta would be happy for help again. Loretta had made meatloaf and scalloped potatoes and fresh beans for supper. There were sliced tomatoes nested on lettuce leaves, with egg salad on top. Linda looked appreciatively at Loretta's handiwork on the dining-room table. "You are a marvel, sis," she said sincerely. "I hope that someday I can learn to cook as well as you can!"

"Remember, you do a lot of things well that I can't, Linda," Loretta returned, a bright smile lighting her face.

"I'm happy for both my good girls," Mom said, smiling happily as she looked up from the tomatoes she was peeling at the kitchen table.

*Mom has aged the last year*, Linda thought, looking carefully at her. *The experiences our family has gone through, with the church and with Steve, have been hard for Mom.* She noticed the gray beginning to show in Mom's strawberry blond hair and the lines on her face that had not been there before. While Mom had stayed slim and girlish for many years, she was now showing definite signs of aging. *But Mom has changed so much in other ways too. She no longer needs the frequent social affairs with the elite from town to make her happy. She has come to know the joy of the Lord.* The thought filled Linda's heart with fresh joy.

After supper, the men went back outside, and Linda and Loretta went to the kitchen in hopes of finishing the tomatoes yet that evening. "Mom, you go and do something else, like sit on the porch," Linda said when Mom wearily followed them to the kitchen. "Loretta and I can finish in here."

"I believe I'll take you up on that," Mom said gratefully. "I guess I'm feeling my age these days."

"You are not old, just tired," Linda said kindly. "You've had a long day, and it's hot. You just go and relax for the evening."

The girls soon saw Mom walking through the orchard, checking the developing fruit on the fruit trees. The first apples would not be ready for another couple of weeks. By then, the green beans would be producing well, and other garden things would need to be taken care of. At least the tomatoes were off the list—or soon would be.

"Is Mom well?" Loretta asked with concern as the girls filled the last canner with tomatoes.

"I've wondered the same thing the last couple of months," Linda said. "But then I decided that she is just getting older and that we can't expect her to always act like a young girl anymore." Then she looked out the kitchen window and smiled.

"Dad's with her in the orchard now, and they're walking hand in hand. Isn't that sweet?"

"Did Larry go away this evening?" Loretta asked after a while. "I haven't seen him or Red since supper."

"They may have gone in to town to play ball this evening," Linda responded absent-mindedly as she washed kettles.

"Oh, I did hear Larry talking on the phone with someone before supper," Loretta remembered. "But he was telling them to find someone else—what it was all about, I don't know—because he wouldn't be helping anymore."

Linda looked up. "Now I remember. When we were coming home from Andrea's place the last time, he talked about playing sports. He and Red had been talking a lot about whether it was right, he told me. He said that they decided from principles they learned in their Bible reading that competitive sports belong to the ungodly."

"How could Larry ever give up sports?" Loretta exclaimed. "They were his life!"

"He said it was really hard to come to that decision," Linda assured her, "but there are many passages in the Scriptures that seem to condemn sports as part of the world. Like the verses that instruct Christians to be meek and lowly, not proud and assertive and competitive and trying to be the best. He also said the fact that the world so highly esteems sports should be a warning that

Christians should back off from such activity."

Loretta stared blankly at Linda, as though still not able to comprehend how Larry could come to such a conclusion.

Linda smiled at her as she continued, "Also, the Bible speaks about the world loving pleasures rather than God, and the fact that bodily exercise has only a little profit but godliness is always profitable."

"Surely there's nothing wrong with exercise!" Loretta inserted hotly.

"I wouldn't think so," Linda assured her. "We get lots of that here on the farm! But with sports, there were so many things that made him feel condemned. He said just the wild cheering during the games and the way the ungodly girls gloated over him made him feel he was doing something wrong. He said that he and Red have come to the conclusion, from their thinking and praying and study of the Scriptures about it all, that they want to leave sports with the world, where it belongs."

Loretta looked long at Linda, but said no more. Linda wondered what she was thinking, but felt she had said enough, knowing the hold that competitive sports still had on Loretta. Surely the Spirit of the Lord could take these things to Loretta's heart and help her to see her need in due time.

The rows of jars lining the counters when

the girls were finally finished were a lovely sight. "That looks like enough spaghetti sauce for the next five years!" Loretta exclaimed. "But it will go down fast enough, I guess, the way we use it for pizza and everything."

"Well, tomorrow we'll have the first picking of green beans for canning, and the first corn will soon be ready. But to me, this is a fun time of the year!"

"Is the kitchen cleaned up well enough for tonight? I'd like to go to bed," Loretta said, suppressing a yawn.

"You can go. I'll put a few of these kettles and dishpans away yet. Good night!"

Linda finished in the kitchen and wandered to the library. She sat at the piano and played for a while. Larry came in and stretched out on the recliner. He had gotten a special letter in the mail that day and was rereading it.

"Where were you and Red this evening?" Linda asked as she swung around on the piano stool.

Larry looked up from his letter. "We took a run out to the Kelloways' farm to see how things were going there. They were busy picking green beans, so we helped them for a while. It gave an opportunity for Red and me to talk with Pastor Kelloway about some things in the church that trouble us."

"Like what?" Linda probed.

"Well, for one, the lack of holy living among our church members. For another, the lack of any real difference between most of us and those who make no profession of godliness."

"Did he have answers?"

"Not really." Larry went back to ardently reading his letter, forgetting about all else.

For some reason, Linda felt restless. She wandered out on the porch and then walked out across the yard in the deepening dusk. Dad and Mom were just coming in, but they did not see her. She walked through the yard and into the orchard to her apple tree. She sat on its broad limb, listening to the night sounds around her. A whippoorwill called from somewhere near the house. She heard the katydids and tree frogs in the maple trees around the house. A bullfrog was croaking somewhere nearby, probably at the drainage ditch below the orchard. The chickens were making night sounds as they found their roosts for the night. The lights would soon go out in the chicken house, she knew, but how did the chickens know that? As she sat and thought, one by one the lights in the house went out. Everybody had gone to bed. *Everybody but me,* Linda thought wearily.

For some time, Linda's thoughts plodded relentlessly from one subject to another. A feeling of depression settled over her. What purpose was there for her in life anymore? *Am I missing Steve tonight?* she wondered finally. *Will I never be able to forget him or my love for him? What is there for me in life, since I don't have him anymore? Am I destined to be single? There could never be anyone else to take his place in my heart, could there? I surely wouldn't know who. I don't envy Larry and Andrea's happiness, but oh, I wish I still had Steve!*

Linda knew she was being perverse. But she did not feel like being good right now; she just wanted her own dear special friend back. She wished that she could turn time back to when he had been well and healthy and that everything else would be a bad dream.

The darkness deepened as she sat there, thinking over the past and wondering about the future. The moon came up over the eastern horizon. It was not quite full, but it brightened the night well enough that Linda did not feel quite so desolate. Suddenly an owl hooted, almost right above her, *Who-o-o-o!* She jumped, thoroughly frightened. How long had she sat there? She looked around in the quietness of the moonlit night, thinking about the protection of the angels, wishing that somehow she would have the spiritual sight to see them.

Suddenly she felt broken as she thought of the ever-loving presence and care of her heavenly Father. How unworthy she was! She humbly prayed, *Dear Jesus, I'm sorry. Forgive my rebellion against You. May Your will be done in my life. Help me to obediently submit to You and Your plan for me, whatever it is. Show me Your way, and help me to meekly follow.*

Her thoughts sweetened, and soon she began to sing, softly at first and then more loudly, the same song she had sung earlier at the barn.

"Yes, Jesus, I have promised," she said aloud to the twinkling stars, "I have promised to serve You to the end. Be forever near me, and keep me from the foes—around me and within! Draw ever nearer to me, and shield my soul from sin. Oh, give me grace to follow You, no matter how dark the way, and help me to trust You always, my Master and my Friend!" She put together broken parts of the song to express the feelings of her troubled heart. As always, Jesus brought comfort to her again and the assurance that He was with her and would be with her "unto the end of the world."

Slowly she found her way back to the house. She was tired too. Why had she not gone to bed when Loretta had? Then she would be in a good sleep already. But she had needed that time with her thoughts, a time to sort out and readjust her priorities, a quiet time when God could speak and meet her needs.

The house was quiet and dark. She softly climbed the stairs and went into her dark bedroom. How hot it was! She opened the windows wide, hoping for a breath of fresh air.

Outside, Tiny barked suddenly and sharply. She looked out the window into the darkness and drew in her breath sharply. Someone was walking in the orchard! She could see a figure occasionally come out of the shadows and pass through a moonlit area. Her heart beat wildly; who could it be? and what was he doing out there? She was quite sure it was not any of the family.

She continued to watch. Whoever it was continued to walk stealthily among the trees and then out the back driveway till she could no longer see him. After a while she heard a car start out on the road and take off quietly into the night.

She puzzled over this mysterious event as she dressed for bed in the darkness. Should she tell Dad and Mom about it tonight yet, or should she wait till morning?

Finally she decided not to awaken them, since the person, whoever it was, had apparently already left. She fell wearily into bed, so thankful for the protection her heavenly Father had again given her.

# 22

"Linda," Dad said, drawing her aside at the barn the next morning, "your mother needs to see a doctor. She hasn't been feeling the best since spring. Could you be in prayer for her?"

Fear flew through Linda. Surely not her mother now, was her first thought. "What is the matter, Dad?" she tried to ask calmly. "I thought she has seemed unusually tired and pale."

"She thinks it may be her gallbladder, but she isn't sure. She hopes to get some answers soon. She has a doctor appointment tomorrow."

Linda finished her barn chores and then hurried to the house, eager to allay her fears by seeing Mom's cheerful bustling about the kitchen. But only Loretta was getting breakfast.

"Where's Mom?" Linda asked.

"Dad got me up before he went out. He said that Mom isn't feeling well and that I should go ahead with the laundry and breakfast. What is wrong with her?"

"Dad didn't seem to know when he mentioned it to me this morning. He just said she has a doctor appointment tomorrow."

"I hope it isn't anything serious," Loretta said, voicing the fear that Linda also had.

Linda did not know how she could go off to nurse's training in less than two months, with Mom not feeling well. And besides, there was so much work to do! But maybe Pansy would come over to help them today with the green beans if Linda would run over to ask her.

Pansy did come over, and while Loretta and Linda picked, Mom and Pansy cleaned beans. Then Pansy began filling jars; and when she had enough full jars, she loaded the pressure canner. When the girls were finished picking, Linda sent Mom to rest, and then she took over the trimming and cutting. It was not long before all the beans were in jars, waiting for the canner. Then Pansy walked back home, taking a bagful of garden goodies for her and Pug's lunch.

Dad and Larry and Red came in promptly at twelve o'clock for lunch. There were green beans, of course, fixed with mushroom soup, along with broiled steak and new potatoes, fried in their skins. Linda had sliced some cucumbers and put a cream dressing over them. Loretta, in spite of the busy morning, had managed to bake fresh cherry pies.

Somehow in the middle of all the work and the concerns for Mom, Linda forgot about what she had seen in the orchard the night before. That is, till after supper that evening when Dad was reading an account from the *Democratic Messenger*.

"Listen to this, Larry!" he exclaimed, his face troubled. " 'Ronald Bradford, from Springville, was arrested early this morning in Northport, after he left the scene of an accident.' Apparently he sideswiped a car as he was going through the town, and drove on. A police officer happened to see it and stopped him. He also had been drinking, it says."

"Does it say a time?" Linda asked, peering over Dad's shoulder and suddenly feeling sure that it was Ron who had been in the orchard last night. Now she recognized his familiar walk and build.

"Shortly after midnight," Dad answered, wondering at Linda's question.

She proceeded to tell them what she had seen in the orchard after coming in to bed.

Dad's next words were solemn. "For some reason," he said, "Mother and I were awake just then; and through our open window, we heard you singing. We felt the urge to pray for you, and we did. How glad we are that we did!" Linda had seldom seen such emotion on Dad's face as she saw now. "How merciful God is!" he exclaimed.

"I didn't know Ron was home," Larry said.

"I did," Red said from where he was still relaxing at the table. "I saw him yesterday morning at the Esso station when I filled up my car with gas. He wondered if I was still working for the Asburys. I said I was. Then he asked me if Linda was still around, and I said she was. He seemed to have been drinking, so I didn't take his comments too seriously. Now I wish I had told you all about it!"

"It's okay, Red," Dad assured him, his voice thick with emotion. "God did more than any of us could have done!"

"Oh, I do thank Him," Red said gravely.

Mom and Loretta were looking on soberly and wordlessly. Dad turned to Linda. "Perhaps you had better keep your wanderings for the daytime, Linda. God has been merciful, but we need to use wisdom and do our part too."

A sober Linda went back to the kitchen to check the beans in the canner. She was more thankful for God's protection than she could express. At the same time, she felt so sorry for what Larry's friend of many years had come to. That was what college had done for him; God forbid that it would do that to Larry too!

The next morning Larry drove the pickup beside the sweet-corn patch. He and Red pulled hundreds of ears of fresh corn, loading them onto the back of the pickup. Dad had taken Mom to the doctor, and the girls and Pansy were all set for a big day of freezing corn. Larry backed the pickup beside the cement ledge at the barn, and the girls took the dishpans out and got busy husking.

"Shall we help with the husking?" Red asked Linda.

"Pansy is here to help, so we can probably manage," Linda said. "But thanks anyway."

"I say, let them help if they wish," Loretta said, laughing. "I never turn down an offer of help."

"Oh, well, there isn't that much other work just now. Shall we give them a hand, Larry?" Red asked. He set to work pulling off husks, exposing the bright kernels, and then hung some of the yellow silks over Larry's ears. It looked so comical with his dark hair that everyone had to laugh.

"Hey, put them on Loretta! They would match her hair to a tee!" Larry attempted it, but Loretta was quick; and as soon as she saw him coming, she dashed around to the other side of the pickup.

It could have been a jolly morning, but always in Linda's mind was the undercurrent of concern for Mom. The boys worked fast, pulling off the husks and throwing them over the pasture fence to the row of cows that kept pushing and jostling, waiting for a share in the treat. They filled dishpan after dishpan with the short yellow-and-white ears. The girls carried the first dishpans to the house, where they began cleaning and washing the tender ears of corn.

Pansy filled the big canners with cleaned corn to blanch. After cooling the first blanched ears in the laundry tubs, she sat at the kitchen table to cut off the shiny, juicy kernels. The boys kept bursting in the back door with fresh panfuls, and the girls kept cleaning and washing the corn and filling the canners. Finally all the corn was husked, but the girls had barely begun the long job of cutting it off and freezing it.

"Thanks for your good help," Linda told the boys when they brought in the last of the corn.

"Our pleasure," Red said cheerfully, following Larry back out, where they were soon busy with outdoor chores.

Mom and Dad were back before lunch. Linda looked closely at them as they came in. She thought she detected an air of mingled pleasure on Mom's face and a genuinely joyful look on Dad's. Relief like a cleansing fountain poured over her spirit. Everything was going to be all right! She felt again that she could laugh and feel the freedom of a teenage girl rather than the responsibility of an uncertain future.

While Pansy and the girls prepared lunch among the pans of corn, Dad went upstairs to change into his everyday clothes. A few minutes later, Mom slipped into the library to rest. Linda caught Loretta's eye, and they both followed Mom. "And so, what was the doctor's verdict?" Loretta demanded.

Mom answered, a mysterious twinkle in her eyes, "Would you believe it? The doctor says I'm going to be a mother again!" She laughed softly.

Loretta for once appeared to be at a loss for words as a look of total disbelief and amazement swept over her face. Then she burst out, "Are my ears deceiving me, or am I dreaming? Why didn't this happen about ten years ago, when I was begging for a baby to play with?" While Loretta's tone was almost hysterical, Linda could see the look of joy and pleasure on her face. Now she lapsed into silence and just gazed happily at Mom.

"Oh, Mom!" Linda began, glad to get a word in. "I—I can hardly grasp such a thought! What a surprise!"

"It took me by surprise too, when Dr. Boyer told me the 'simple' news, as he called it!"

"But . . . are you too old, Mom?" Linda asked a little hesitantly. "Will all go well?"

"I'm only forty-two, Linda. Sarah in the Bible was ninety, wasn't she?" Mom laughed. "Dad is the one most concerned, and I'm afraid he won't let me turn a hand at anything for the next six months!"

"Did I hear someone talking about me?" Dad asked jovially as he came around the corner buttoning his shirtsleeves. "Did you hear our news, girls? I'm as excited as a—a—a kernel of popcorn in hot oil!"

They all laughed together. Life looked so good after all, Linda thought as she went back to the kitchen with Loretta to finish preparing lunch.

# 23

Larry left the last week of August for Wesleyan University in Grandville, Pennsylvania. He took Linda farther north to the Bakers' before returning to get settled in at Wesleyan. He had decided on Wesleyan for more than one reason, but perhaps the biggest one was that it would be closer to Andrea. He had also decided to change his major from premedical to science. Linda was very happy at the thought of having someone of the family closer to her. She and the Bakers, where she would be staying, would be only an hour's drive away from Larry. And during the week, when they were at classes, they would be only twenty miles apart!

Linda had found it hard to leave home for nurse's training, realizing that this was the beginning phase of leaving home for good. As they drove through Springville, she eagerly looked at all the old familiar places, trying to rivet all the dear memories in her mind. There were the little black children, some with their daddies, fishing in the river. There were the places she always liked to shop. There went some of her high-school friends, walking up the street to do some shopping. . . .

And she had not liked leaving the farm and the work she enjoyed so much. With Larry and her both gone, how would the work ever get done? At least, Dad had good help with the farm work. Red had assured her that he would take good care of things till she got back.

Linda sat now at her window in the cheerful bedroom that was to be hers while she boarded with the Bakers. Her thoughts were of home and how much she would miss her family. And all the old routines. And the animals. And the familiar chores. *Red assured me that he would take good care of things till I got back.*

*Yes, dear Red. I will miss him too,* her thoughts rambled on. *But he will be an invaluable help to Dad with all his native skills!* He definitely had not been a brain in school. If he managed to get on the honor roll, he thought he had accomplished something. But was book intelligence all that important? There were other gifts that probably counted more in the course of life. She thought about how Red could fix anything or make anything or improvise parts when something broke on the machinery. She thought of the little handmade gifts he had given her each year on her birthday and for Christmas—unique little works of art that he had designed and made with great care. She thought of how indispensable his capable management of the farm work was to Dad.

Linda got up from the window seat and decided to run downstairs and see what the rest were doing.

"So there you are," Mrs. Baker said as Linda came into the kitchen. "Are you settled in your room? Supper is almost ready."

"I should have been down here helping you. I'm sorry," Linda said. "But here, let me pour the water anyway." She took the water pitcher to the table and filled the glasses. She saw Larry and Andrea coming up the back walk. Pastor Baker came from doing the barn chores and joined them at the back door. Larry would need to leave yet that evening to get settled at Wesleyan for opening exercises the next day. But he was making good use of what time he had yet with Andrea, Linda was thinking.

The girls did not need to register for classes till Thursday, so they spent Wednesday shopping and doing last-minute chores. It was so good to have this time with Andrea again. But Mama Baker (as she wished Linda to call her) was insistent that the girls get a good night's sleep. So she saw to it that each went to her own room when they went upstairs for the night. Linda did not mind too much, as there would be lots of time to visit—like old times. And she was tired from the day of shopping and the days before of busy preparations and packing.

Breakfast was at six-thirty the next morning so that the girls could leave by seven o'clock. Linda was surprised that the Bakers did not have morning worship. She would need to ask Andrea about that sometime.

Andrea drove first to Millburg to pick up Kathy Yoder, who would be traveling with them to Harrisville. The girls visited pleasantly as they drove to the nursing school. Already Linda felt that Kathy was a kindred spirit, and they were able to share freely together. Most of all, Linda was thankful for the spiritual insights that Kathy appeared to have about many issues.

The weeks passed quickly. Linda was happy for the weekends that Larry spent with the Bakers too. And he even spent some time just visiting with her! They were always eager to compare their letters from home. Linda, especially, was concerned about how Mom was doing. Larry's concerns were always centered more around how the farm work was going. He often heard from Red as well as from Mom and Dad.

One Sunday in October when Larry was at the Bakers,' Linda and Larry and Andrea decided to visit the Mennonite Church in Millburg. Kathy had often invited them to come. As they drove into the churchyard, Linda could hardly see things fast enough. She saw the kind of cars they drove and the people walking into the church.

The women wore veilings on their heads, some larger and some smaller. Most of the men wore what Daddy Baker had called plain suits, a few wore regular suits and ties, and a few others wore regular suits with no ties.

She was impressed to see how large most of the families were. Quite a few fathers and mothers walked into the church with six or eight children of various sizes and ages walking with them. There were younger couples as well, sometimes the father and the mother each carrying a small child.

As they entered the large auditorium, Linda noticed that the men sat on one side and the ladies on the other. Larry went to the men's side and found an empty seat at the end of a bench. An usher came and showed Linda and Andrea a place to sit. Kathy smiled happily at them from the other end of the bench.

Linda looked around for a piano or an organ; there was none, she concluded. And there was no choir loft either. She wondered if they did not sing at all. But about that time, a young man walked to the front. He held up a songbook and announced a number. Linda quickly reached for a book in the rack in front of her and found the number. Then the young man blew the pitch on a pitch pipe. *How interesting to see a pitch pipe in this setting!* Linda thought. *We used them in music class.*

The young man drew his arm up, and everyone started in singing. Linda could hardly believe her ears. They sang four parts; where did they get their training for that? She listened carefully. There were a few discordant notes, but most of the people were singing on tune, and Linda thought it was quite lovely! She joined eagerly in the singing. It was a song they often sang at home too: "Come, Thou Almighty King." A lady on the bench in front of Linda turned around to look at her. Was she doing something wrong by helping to sing? Oh well, why shouldn't she sing if she knew the Lord too?

After another song, a middle-aged man read a passage of Scripture and commented on it. Then he asked the congregation to kneel, and he led them in prayer. Then offering baskets were passed. After another song, the Sunday school classes were dismissed to their places. Larry, Andrea, and Linda went to the youth class. An enthusiastic, middle-aged man taught their class. He seemed to have a good knowledge of the Scriptures, Linda thought. After Sunday school, they again went upstairs to the main auditorium, where they again sang a song. Then the minister got up. He was dressed in a plain suit like many of the others wore, not a special clerical robe.

Linda listened intently to the message. She thought he preached much like Pastor Kelloway, and it made her feel at home. He took his message from Acts 9, the conversion of Saul, and tried to impress on his listeners the need for a genuine conversion—a turning around in their lives to serve a new Master.

Linda appreciated the message very much; but as she looked around at times, she was disappointed by the lack of reverence among a few of the young people. A couple of the girls in front of her kept touching their hair or adjusting their veilings. *They act as bad as the young people act at our church,* she thought, feeling shame for them. She felt regret that some of the youth had no more spiritual interest than what they seemed to display. *Would I despise my heritage too, if I had such a rich heritage as these young people have?* she wondered. *Don't they realize the blessing they have?*

After the service, Linda was astonished when many of the women began shaking hands and greeting each other with a kiss. She noticed that the men were doing the same thing. Then she recalled several verses in the apostle Paul's letters to the churches that spoke about "greet[ing] one another with an holy kiss." Apparently, they were trying to obey that command!

Many came up to the three after church and spoke with them. The lady that had been sitting in front of Andrea and Linda, who had turned around to look at them, came and introduced herself. "I'm sorry for seeming to be rude," she apologized. "But I heard these two lovely voices behind me, and I wondered who our visitors were. I'm so glad you came, and I want you to come again!"

Two women—"sisters" was what these women called each other—even invited them along home to lunch! Linda thought that they seemed to show a genuine love and concern. They seemed so much like Kathy, to whom Linda had been drawn by her loving and caring heart. She remembered reading a Scripture verse that said that all men would know who true Christians are by their love for each other. Was that the test for finding a church that obeyed the Scriptures? Linda appreciated also the spiritual interest that Kathy seemed to have and her consistent, godly life.

Several little girls clustered around them, staring at them intently. When Linda smiled at them, one little girl whispered loudly to the others, "They must not be Christians; they don't wear coverings." Then they all scampered off to find the young mothers with babies. But the words Linda had overheard took a little of the sweetness out of the visit.

There were a number of church papers on a table in the back of the auditorium. Someone invited Linda to take all she cared to. She looked through them, picking up a number of issues of a paper for youth, and several of one for the unsaved.

As Linda and Andrea were reading the youth papers that afternoon, Linda said, "These stories are surely different from the stories in the youth paper I get from the other Mennonite publisher! These stories seem like the ones in our own church publications or even like something I would have read in *Seventeen* magazine! How can the young people read things like this and maintain a spiritual interest?" She was disappointed that the people she admired would endorse such reading material.

Nearly every week after that, Andrea and Linda went to the Mennonite Church in Millburg. They both increasingly enjoyed the fellowship. Linda enjoyed the orderly services and the spirit of love that she sensed among most of the membership. She especially enjoyed the challenging discussions in the youth Sunday school class, taught by Kathy's father.

She and Andrea were impressed with and blessed by the Sunday evening services. They had been used to drama and games and other forms of entertainment. But Millburg Mennonite Church usually had a preaching service. Sometimes they had a song service, during which most of the evening was spent just in singing. "Such evening services make me feel like I have been fed," Linda said one evening as they drove home from church, "not just entertained."

"I know what you mean," Andrea responded. "Just like the sermon this evening: 'Facing the Pressures of the World.' A sermon like that makes me feel ready to face a week of tests in training again!"

There were some things that Linda and Andrea could not understand though. They puzzled over a small group of young people that seemed to always be pushing against the "fences," not content or happy inside the boundaries that their parents and church leaders had set for them. Linda often wished she knew a way to help them realize what a wonderful heritage they had, and to appreciate it! But they enjoyed things like volleyball and swimming, deer spotting and eating out, much more than a good spiritual discussion.

They often invited Linda and Andrea to their gatherings. But after accepting the invitation one time, the girls did not go again. "I couldn't believe how rebellious some of those girls acted!" Linda said as she and Andrea drove home together. "Did you see them in the one girl's bedroom, trying to style their hair? They may have veilings, but I do not believe they understand or care what their purpose is!"

"The way the boys and girls carried on together was surely not appropriate! I was embarrassed. It does not surprise me that Kathy's parents do not allow her to associate with them."

"I was so put out by a couple of the fellows trying to flirt with us! I suppose they'll consider us stuck-up, since we didn't appear flattered by their attention. I was very thankful, Andrea, that you had the presence of mind to suggest we go inside to get away from them. Then I overheard two of the girls, when they were in the kitchen getting snacks ready, mocking Kathy and her folks. Probably they are mocking us too.

"I just had to think as I watched that group," Linda continued, "that they reminded me of Kenneth Taylor and Mary Catherine Carmean—before she was a Christian—and their wild set. It was the same spirit, to my mind. It surely will end up at the same place.

"But the saddest part is that they are church members and probably feel a false assurance that they are on the way to heaven. I imagine it is hard to help people like that to realize that they are living for themselves just like the rest of the world."

"I couldn't believe the parents were there and were allowing what was going on," Andrea said after a while.

Linda sighed softly. "I noticed that the little girl who thought we weren't Christians because we don't wear coverings was a part of that household. I found that interesting!"

"I guess that poor child has never had the

opportunity to learn that real Christianity begins by a changed heart," Andrea observed a bit huffily.

"Well, genuine Christianity certainly can't be put on by wearing certain clothes or doing certain things, can it. I sincerely hope and pray that, by the grace of God, our Christianity will always be more than something external like that!"

"A few of these young people need our prayers," Andrea concluded earnestly.

Regardless of such disappointing inconsistencies, the girls felt increasingly drawn to the Mennonite Church. They asked many questions, both of Kathy and of the pastor. Pastor Martin gave the girls a book called *Doctrines of the Bible*. The girls pored over it night after night, looking up Scripture verses and praying with open hearts about what they found and read.

"See here, Andrea, the Mennonites believe in Feet Washing just like Communion!" Linda pushed the *Doctrines of the Bible* book across her desk to show Andrea. "They take the teaching from John 13 and practice it literally."

Andrea read silently along with Linda. "The funny part is that we have read that passage many times before, and it never occurred to us that it should be taken literally!" she commented when she had finished the article.

Linda opened her Bible to John 13 and read the passage about Feet Washing. "See, here in verses 14–17," Linda began, holding her Bible so that Andrea could see it, "it says, 'If I then, your Lord and Master, have washed your feet; ye also ought to wash one another's feet. For I have given you an example, that ye should do as I have done to you. Verily, verily, I say unto you, The servant is not greater than his lord; neither he that is sent greater than he that sent him. If ye know these things, happy are ye if ye do them.'"

Andrea looked wide-eyed at Linda. "It really says that, doesn't it."

"So why don't churches do it?"

"Maybe because it's like it says there at the end of the chapter in *Doctrines of the Bible:* It would be too hard for the rich to stoop to wash the feet of the poor."

"It would probably be too hard for them to stoop to wash *anyone's* feet," Linda corrected.

That weekend at the Bakers', the girls had another opportunity for study from the Bible doctrines book. The next Christian ordinance that the book talked about was the Devotional Covering.

"Now maybe," Linda said happily, "we can understand from this Scripture passage in 1 Corinthians why the Mennonites wear veilings."

The girls read ardently, looking up all the included Scripture verses as they read, especially noticing that the ordinance was based on the fundamental fact that God created man as the head of the woman.

"Obviously, this Scripture is meant to be obeyed; don't you think so?" Linda observed after more than an hour of careful study.

"It would seem so," Andrea admitted. "And yet, how queer I'd feel to start wearing a veiling! What would our friends say?"

"See, what did that last objection say?" Linda said with a chuckle, reaching for the book. "'I would be ashamed to wear it.' And the writer answers, 'You have probably revealed the secret of most of your objections. It is safe to say that most of the objections to the devotional covering would vanish immediately if it were fashionable or popular to wear it.'"

Andrea looked long at Linda. "That statement hits the nail on the head! Now what are we to do?"

"I think we should pray about it and then talk with our parents. We are young, and I know that my father, at least, would have good advice for us."

Andrea made a doleful face. "I think I know without asking what *my* parents would say!"

So far, Daddy and Mama Baker had not said much about Linda and Andrea's relationship to the Mennonites. Nor had they seriously objected to their attending the Mennonite worship services. But, as Andrea expected, when the girls asked them what their feeling was about the Scriptural teaching of wearing a veiling, Daddy Baker got indignant. He felt it was high time to put a stop to their nonsense.

"Girls, Mama and I are responsible for you. We wonder if you are doing a wise thing by going so often to the Mennonite Church. We cannot look favorably on a church that is so legalistic in its interpretation of the Scriptures. Also we don't approve of their not being patriotic and not supporting community affairs and not serving as elected officials. Sure, they are good people, but so are a lot of other people—without being so extreme!"

Linda listened quietly to his concern. It was not that she did not appreciate the Bakers, but they did not look at things with a spiritual viewpoint as she had been used to her parents doing. And she had only realized how shallow his sermons were after having gotten accustomed to the much deeper ones that Pastor Kelloway preached.

The girls did decide to wait for a while, though, before starting what the Mennonites called the instruction class. Linda wanted to talk with her parents about it all first. But both girls began to let their hair grow long, as they felt the Scriptures taught. Linda's always had been longer than Andrea's, and she soon began to wear it up in a French twist.

"I'm going to stop going to the hairdresser

too," Andrea said soberly one Saturday, after canceling an appointment her mother had made for her. "I know some of the Mennonite girls set their hair, but it seems to me that to perm my hair tells God that I am not satisfied with the straight hair He gave me."

"I admire you," Linda told her from a happy heart.

They also decided not to wear their shorts or jeans anymore, but just wear modest and simple dresses. And their jewelry and makeup—what little they had worn—were put away in boxes till they could decide what should be done with them.

When Linda talked with Andrea about whether or not her parents had family devotions, Andrea had informed Linda that they rarely did. So the girls had devotions together when they were home for weekends, just as they did at the nursing school dorm, before they went for breakfast.

Andrea had asked her father one weekend when the girls were home if they could have devotions together as a family. But Daddy Baker had said, "Solomon talked about not being righteous over much, and such a practice might well fall into that category." Linda had been distressed that a preacher of the Gospel would consider being "righteous over much" even a remote possibility for anyone! It was at that time that the girls—

Linda, Andrea, and Kathy—had decided to start their own "family devotions." They felt that when they did this, the Lord blessed them and strengthened them in a special way for the temptations that they faced each day.

And they did face temptations. The teachers and the teaching were probably not unlike what Larry had been exposed to at the university. "One thing in our favor though," Linda stated one day as they were driving home, "is that we can go home every weekend. At least we don't need to be exposed to the social life that goes on over the weekends."

"And our class is all girls," added Kathy. "I like that. But did you think about it that after we get into clinical service, we won't be able to go home every weekend anymore?"

"That's right! I had forgotten about that," Linda said soberly.

"I have wondered, why does the one instructor always think he has to tell filthy jokes?" Andrea injected. "I get so tired of his crass humor!"

"He probably thinks he's breaking us in to the realities of life, as we will face it once we get out on the floor," guessed Kathy.

Linda enjoyed the studies, but she was looking forward to going home for Thanksgiving. She was so eager to feel her parents out, in person, about her wearing a veiling and joining the

Mennonite Church. She felt confident that they would have wise counsel; Dad always did! She did struggle, though, with uncertainties over how her mother might react to such a proposition. Even so, Linda wanted to talk with her; she and Mom were so much closer since Mom had become a Christian.

Thanksgiving vacation finally came. Larry came for Linda on Wednesday morning, and they left from the Bakers' at noon. Even with good driving, it was still after six when they drove in the familiar lane at the home farm. Linda rushed to the house before Larry got his car put away. Tiny jumped up off the porch step and wiggled so hard Linda was afraid he would break himself in half. She stooped to pat him quickly before rushing in the door. How good it was to see the old familiar pattern on the kitchen linoleum and to smell the familiar smell of—what was it? Soap and spice? She was not sure, but it was so wonderfully homelike! But where was everybody? She had thought they would all be waiting to greet them.

She had seen lights in the barn. Was everybody still out there? But Mom would not be! She rushed back out, running smack into Larry coming in the door, his arms loaded with suitcases. "Oh, I'm sorry," she gasped when she got her breath again.

"Why the haste?" Larry asked.

"There isn't anybody around! No one! But I saw lights in the barn, so I'm going to find out where everybody is."

She ran down the walk and out the lane to the barn. Rushing inside, she saw Pug, Loretta, and Red doing the milking.

"Oh, you're home!" Loretta happily hurried to hug Linda, barn smells and all. "We weren't expecting you yet! Dad took Mom to the hospital this afternoon, but we haven't heard any news yet. And we're late getting the milking done because Red had all the chickens to do too."

Red and Pug waved their welcomes from the other end of the barn.

"Mom?" Worry inched into Linda's heart. "Is everything all right?"

"As far as I know."

"Oh, I hope so. But how much of the chores are there to do yet? Shall we go change and help you finish? I'd love to get my hands in the barn work again," Linda said as Larry walked in.

"I just started the calves, but I would go get supper if someone else would finish them."

"I'll go change," Linda stated, hurrying out of the barn. She found her old clothes and got into them; but feeling smitten, she quickly sought out an old dress.

Soon she was feeding the calves, a new set from what she had been feeding before she left. She found out that her cow had had a calf—

another cute little brown heifer. She would have to think of a name, but not tonight.

She heard the milker pump stop before she was finished with the last pen of calves. Soon Red came out, a bright smile lighting his face. "Would you like me to finish or at least to help?" he asked.

"Oh, I'm enjoying this too much to give it up," Linda said, laughing. *How good and dependable Red is,* she thought.

"It's good to see you again, Linda. Nothing seemed right around here without my best sis," Red said as he carried her full buckets to the next set of calves.

Linda followed him to the waiting calves. "I have missed you too, Red," she said sincerely as they each held a bucket for a hungry little heifer. "But I was happy to think of you here, faithfully helping Dad, doing the things that Larry and I couldn't, since we were away. Thank you!"

"I like the way you have your hair combed, Linda," Red said after a while. "Larry wrote to me that you-all have been attending a Mennonite Church. Is that why you don't have your class ring on either?"

"Yes, partly. Also because I read in the Bible that women are not to wear gold or pearls or costly array. In another passage, it speaks of women not adorning themselves by fixing up their hair, or wearing gold, or putting on extras.

Instead they are to show by how they are dressed that they have a meek and quiet spirit, which is in the sight of God of great price."

"The Scriptures certainly speak pointedly about many issues, don't they," Red responded. "If only professing Christians would be willing to simply obey, rather than trying to find ways to excuse themselves!"

Linda gazed with wonder at Red. She was so thankful for his apparent comprehension of spiritual things.

"I've been studying the Bible too, Linda," he said seriously, "looking for answers to many of my questions."

"Oh, I'm so glad, Red! God will honor your search for what is right."

Later as Linda hurried to the house, Loretta rushed out to meet her. "Dad called," she said breathlessly. "The baby is here, and all is well! Born at three-thirty this afternoon."

"Oh, thank God!" gasped Linda. "Boy or girl?"

"Boy! Dad said he is a little fellow, but he'll grow. Just under five pounds. I can hardly believe he is so small. Dad said they didn't decide on a name yet. He said that Mom wants us to come in tonight yet if we can, to meet our new little brother!"

"I am so eager to see him, I can hardly wait! And Mom and Dad too!"

No one felt like taking time to eat supper. As

soon as everyone had cleaned up, they hurried off to Sharptown. Mom and Dad were eagerly awaiting their arrival.

"You look like a happy mother," Linda said as she bent over to kiss Mom. "And you even have some color in your cheeks again! How do you feel?"

"A little tired, but so happy!"

Dad came around the side of Mom's bed and gave the hand Linda held out to him a tight squeeze. "I've missed you so much. And you too, Larry," he said as he gave him a hearty handshake. "God has been good to us!"

"Where is this little fellow?" Loretta asked impatiently. "That's who I came to see!"

"We'll have to walk down to the nursery," Dad said. "Mom wants to walk with us."

He turned to her and asked tenderly, "Are you ready to try the walk down the hall?"

"If you help me," she said.

The curtain was open at the nursery, and Linda and Loretta pressed close to the window. They were trying hard to pick out *Boy Asbury* among all the babies. Suddenly Loretta exclaimed, "What is going on here? I see two *Boy Asbury*s. Do we have relatives around here or something?"

Behind her, Dad chuckled, and then Linda knew. "Mom, did you—did you have *twin* boys?" she exclaimed incredulously.

And the surprise was out!

"We were as surprised as you are, believe me," Dad said, his eyes shining. "We are just so thankful that all is well and that the babies are healthy."

Loretta was so excited that she did not say a word. She just kept looking, as though not believing her eyes. Finally, she spoke with a happy tremor in her voice. "Guess I have my work cut out for me for the next few years. I didn't want to go to college anyway."

"God willing, I'll be able to take care of them, now that I'll surely be feeling better," Mom said with a chuckle.

Linda went to Mom and put her arm around her tenderly. "They are wonderful little boys, Mom dear. I'm so happy about it all that I can hardly contain it! And I can hardly wait to hold them in my arms!"

Thanksgiving weekend was different from what Linda had imagined it would be, for Mom was not there. She and Loretta made Thanksgiving dinner. Dad invited Pug and Pansy over, since they had no family to be with, and also Red and his mother. Of course, Grandpa Asbury's were there too. Dad excused himself and left to be with Mom, as soon as dinner was over, but everyone understood. The rest had a pleasant day of singing hymns around the piano, playing games, and just visiting.

"You know, all the time Red has been working

for us, we have never had his mother out for a meal!" Loretta exclaimed to Linda as they cleaned up later that afternoon. "She must have been lonely often, all by herself."

"I'm glad Dad thought of it. I really enjoyed Mrs. Ziller. She is quiet, and I had never learned to know her well, but she is such a sweet and cheerful person. It isn't hard to see where Red gets his cheerful personality."

"And Pug and Pansy—they are always a delight to have around," Loretta said, laughing.

While riding with Dad to visit Mom each evening, Linda was able to tell him about many of the things that she and Andrea had been pondering. She had written a lot of the things home already, so it was not entirely new to him.

"Kathy loaned me some books that she said I could leave at home for you-all to look at, at least till Christmas," Linda said. "One is *Doctrines of the Bible,* the book that I had told you we've been studying. Others are about Mennonite church history. One is called *Mennonites and Their Heritage*. I thought you and Mom would find the books interesting."

"I am eager to read them," Dad assured her. "Mom will have extra time to read now too, while she gets her strength back."

"Andrea and I have been doing a lot of thinking and praying about what we are reading, and we are concluding that what the Mennonites believe and practice is according to the Bible. But we are young, and we want to be open to how older Christians feel too."

"I appreciate that, Linda. The Bible says that at the mouth of two or three witnesses every word shall be established. It also states that in the multitude of counselors there is safety. Sometimes we can be misled when we rely solely on our own judgments."

"One thing does bother me, Dad. I feel guilty when I have my devotions without a covering on my head. First Corinthians 11 says that Christian women are to have their heads covered when praying or prophesying, and what else does it mean but just that?"

Dad was thoughtful. "Whatever you do, Linda, I would counsel you not to enter into anything hastily. Search the Scriptures with an open heart, asking for God's Spirit to guide you. Jesus promised that the Spirit will guide us into all truth. And I accept that by faith! If we live in obedience to what we know, then God will honor our desires to grow in Him. And He will show us the right time to make changes in our lives, if changes are called for."

"The Bakers don't approve of our going to the Mennonite Church in Millburg, and they have tried to discourage us from going. They aren't forbidding it, but I know they would be very happy if we would change our minds."

"Certainly you want to respect their wishes. But ultimately, we must please God rather than men."

"Would you and Mom feel comfortable with our decision if Andrea and I started to wear veilings? We thought maybe we could just wear special scarves, if you would prefer that we not wear veilings like the Mennonites use."

"That is a hard question, Linda. I have pondered that Scripture in 1 Corinthians often, especially since you have exposed us to Mennonite teachings, and it seems very obvious that is what that Scripture passage is teaching. I'm sorry to say that Mom has more of a problem with it."

Linda looked quickly at Dad. "So Mom has expressed herself about the veiling already?"

"I'm afraid so. She told me point-blank when you first wrote about it that she would never wear a veiling and that I could just 'hang up' the idea of joining the Mennonites. But I think that with teaching she will see it right too. Mom has already come a long way. I have rejoiced often at her openness to Scriptural teaching the last couple of years."

"And Loretta has changed too," Linda rejoiced.

"Yes, she has, since she gave herself up to God. What a struggle she had till she finally came through to victory!"

"It made me so happy when Mom wrote

about it. I just thanked God over and over; I was hardly able to contain my thankfulness."

Dad smiled at Linda as he stopped for a traffic light in Sharptown. "Loretta will probably always be more happy-go-lucky than you though; she doesn't have your serious nature. But she will fill a place too in God's service if she continues to grow in Him. She's a bright and cheerful sunbeam about the place!"

"I wish Pastor Kelloway would feel about the Mennonites like we do," Linda said wistfully. "I talked with him some when I visited them yesterday, but he feels the Mennonites are too legalistic in their practices. He says he has a lot of respect for them. But he feels the grace of God should tell us how to live, not a church discipline."

Dad laughed a little. "Perhaps Scriptural church discipline in our church would be his answer at times. He often comes to me, perplexed about how to relate to the many who don't live the way he preaches. I tell him that without firm guidelines for membership, people are pretty much going to do what is right in their own eyes. That is just the way human nature is!"

"I have appreciated them so much since they have been here, and yet he does seem to have a blind spot in that area, doesn't he," Linda added. "Steve talked about it at times too, how he wished his father could see the need for a more-regulated church membership. Steve would say how he'd tell his dad that even John Wesley came to the point where he regretted he hadn't set firm guidelines for the churches."

"I've read that too about John Wesley," Dad agreed.

"Steve liked the order he saw among the Mennonites they learned to know in Missouri."

Dad turned the car into the hospital parking lot.

"Of course, Pastor Kelloway's group as a whole doesn't believe in nonresistance as the Mennonites do—although Pastor Kelloway says *he* does. Or in being a separated people in all of life," Linda continued. "I wonder why they don't, when those seem to be such apparent teachings of the Scriptures."

"Well now, Linda, we have not been exposed to some of these teachings, and they come as new thoughts to most of us. All of us have a lot of room to learn and grow. And I venture to say that if you learn to know the Mennonites well, you will find areas where they aren't totally consistent either. You may discover they have some blind spots too. The most important thing is that we are teachable and pliable, willing and wanting to know and do God's will," Dad said as he carefully backed the car into an empty parking space.

"I'm sure you're right, Dad, and I'd have to

admit to you I've already seen some inconsistencies. But despite that, they seem to live the closest to the Scriptures of any church group that I know about."

Linda opened her door, saying eagerly, "But now I'm ready to go see Mom and those dear little fellows!" Dad smiled in agreement as he got out on his side.

# 24

Larry and Linda left early Monday morning to get back in time for Tuesday's classes. Linda thought Mom just *had* to be home before they left. However, the doctor thought she should stay in the hospital another few days at least, even though she insisted she was getting lazier by the day. "And these little fellows should weigh at least five pounds before we let them go home," the doctor had told Mom when he came in to see her on Sunday evening.

The babies were doing quite well, and Linda had been allowed to hold them that last evening when she was in. How it stirred her mother-heart! They were so precious! She had held one, and Larry the other; she watched Larry as he sat gazing intently at the little one in his arms. Was it stirring a desire in him for his own too? she wondered.

They had finally decided on names: Leon and Loren. But they looked so much alike that Linda did not know yet which was which. Hopefully when she was home for Christmas, she would learn to know them better.

They were driving silently along. Finally Larry broke the silence. "Are you glad or sorry to be going north?" he asked with a grin in Linda's direction.

"I was thinking about Mom and her babies. And wishing I was home with them!"

"I'm torn between two," Larry admitted. "I was surely drawn to my new little brothers. But I'm drawn northward too!"

"In a hurry to get back into the halls of learning, no doubt!" Linda teased.

"Wel-l-l-l," Larry drawled.

Linda sobered. "Has Andrea talked much with you about the things we have been thinking and talking about—I mean, in relation to church?" she asked.

"We have talked quite a bit. And we have read and studied the Bible together. I have even gotten commentaries and other books out of Pastor Baker's library to read and study. But somehow, books don't fill the bill."

"They are so contradictory that it isn't hard to tell they weren't Spirit-inspired," Linda injected.

"You're right. And so we go back to the Word and pray for open hearts to find there what God wants us to do. And I admit, it isn't easy to give up our own ways of thinking for what is obviously truth. But we want to! We desire God's will more than anything else—His will for us individually and His will for us as a couple."

"Has Andrea talked with you about wearing a veiling?"

Larry nodded soberly. "We have talked at length about it. At first I thought that it couldn't be right if so few others are doing it. But then I realized that Jesus said the way is narrow and 'few there be that find it.' If we choose to live in obedience to the Scriptures, there won't be many in sympathy with us; that is the whole consensus of the Scriptures!"

"You're right. I come across terms in my Bible reading like 'strangers and pilgrims,' 'peculiar people,' 'gazingstock,' 'holy brethren.' The writers are describing true believers living in the midst of professing Christians and total unbelievers."

"Anyway, I told Andrea that if she decides to wear a veiling, I will support her in that. And I will say the same to you, sis," Larry said sincerely.

The next week was one of intense struggle as Linda and Andrea weighed the decision of whether or not to wear veilings. Larry and Dad would support them. But besides that, they felt quite sure they would have to stand alone in their new conviction. At this point, they could not expect support from any other members of their families.

*Maybe I ought to talk with someone from the Mennonite Church at Millburg. Maybe they could help me understand some of the details that I am not sure about.* Taking courage, Linda called the pastor's wife one day. "I hope I'm not interrupting something, Mrs. Martin—"

"I'm just Ann. What's on your mind, Linda?"

"Just a fine point, Ann, about—about your covering. Why do you wear it all the time? First Corinthians 11 just says when praying or prophesying. Am I thinking right?"

"That's what it says. And that's when I'm especially aware of the need to cover my head. But let me collect my thoughts. I was letting my mind relax this morning. Hmm—when do you pray, Linda?"

"I have my special times to pray every day. But it seems I've been praying all morning."

"Very good. And when do you prophesy?"

"What is that?"

"It's a general term. The apostle Paul defines prophesying later in 1 Corinthians, I think in chapter 14, as speaking to others to edify, to exhort, or to comfort. Are there times that you might do that through the day—say to share a spiritual insight with someone?"

"Oh, yes," Linda agreed. "I might do that any time of the day."

"So you pray any time, and you prophesy any time," Ann noted. "So when should you be veiled?"

"I guess any time."

"Any time and every time; that's the way we

look at it. Does that make any sense to you, Linda?"

"Thank you, Ann. I want to think about this some more. Pray for me. And for Andrea. She's going through this too."

"We have been praying for you," said Ann Martin, so warmly that Linda half expected her to add "dear chil'," as Pansy would have.

After spending a lot more time in prayer and careful consideration, by the next weekend Linda and Andrea were ready to ask the pastor's wife for veilings. Ann was able to find one that fit nicely for each of them. Linda's hair was thick and naturally wavy, and it was hard for her to get it up to fit under a veiling. But with Sister Ann's help, she was finally able to get her hair up neatly. Linda could not explain the feeling of peace that came to her as she put her veiling over her carefully combed hair. She felt that what she was doing was honoring God and bringing Him glory.

She looked at Andrea—her straight blond hair combed back modestly, neatly put up, and covered by her veiling. How sweet and angelic she looked, how much like a submissive follower of Jesus. Linda smiled tearfully at Andrea. "It surely is a major step in our lives, isn't it," she said.

"I only wish my parents could see that this is a teaching of the Scriptures," Andrea said regretfully. "But perhaps they will still come to believe it if we keep praying for them."

"It seems to be such an obvious teaching of the Scriptures," Linda remarked, "the acknowledgement of God's order of headship—that I wonder why so few believe it or practice it. And the teaching that women are to be covered is so clear in 1 Corinthians 11 itself. And all through church history, I've read, till the last century, nearly all Christian churches practiced it without question."

"I suppose the true meaning of it had been long lost though, which made it easy to quickly lose the practice also," Ann said.

One weekend Kathy invited the girls to stay at her home. Kathy had one older brother and six younger brothers and sisters, all lively and cheerful, but obedient. Her parents were Mark and Debra Yoder. They were pleasant and friendly, making Linda and Andrea immediately feel at home. The girls spent the morning cleaning and baking. In the afternoon, they took a walk out through the fields to a creek flowing along the far edge of the farm. It was a cold December afternoon, and the feel of snow was in the air. They wrapped their coats more tightly around themselves as they sat on the bank and watched the water flowing over rocks and small falls.

"I'm so happy to be here this weekend," Linda said. "I feel so free and at home!"

"Things aren't the same at my house anymore since we decided to wear veilings, Kathy," Andrea confided. "Daddy about hit the roof when we came around with coverings. It isn't that I don't want to honor them—he accused me of that—but finally, Linda and I felt that we needed to do what the Bible teaches in spite of what others say."

"My family has been praying so much for you girls," Kathy said sincerely. "And I know others are too. We don't understand altogether what you are facing, but we do know it isn't easy to do what is right in the face of opposition. We want you to know that you have the prayers and support of our church."

"We feel your love and support," Linda said.

"Have you thought about joining our church?" Kathy asked.

"We have given it a lot of thought," Andrea acknowledged.

"Larry and I want to talk about it more with my family when we are home over Christmas," Linda added. "Dad told me at Thanksgiving that he doesn't think we should hurry into a decision about something so important."

"I think that is probably wise," Kathy said.

"We still have so many questions," Andrea added. "Some of the doctrines your church believes are completely new to us. Like nonresistance. Our church always taught that Jesus' teachings were for *individuals.* For example, *individuals* weren't to kill, but if we were doing it for the state, that was different. We never had teaching about not taking part in the affairs of government and so forth; rather, we were taught that to be patriotic was almost synonymous with being Christian."

"But you understand now, don't you, that Christians are not a part of the world system, that we are citizens of a different country?" Kathy asked. "As Jesus said, 'If my kingdom were of this world, then would my servants fight.' And the apostle Paul wrote in Romans 13 that we should obey our government and pay our taxes. And 1 Timothy 2 says that we should pray for our leaders. That is the Christian's responsibility in relation to the government."

"I remember so well when President Kennedy was elected," Linda said. "He was a Catholic, which was really scary to Protestants. A lot of our local churches got all worked up about the possibility of a Catholic man being elected president."

"I remember that too," Andrea inserted. "Daddy sort of spearheaded that protest in Springville against Kennedy. They mailed out flyers and campaigned strongly against him. But Kennedy was elected anyway."

"I remember Dad's surprise when Kennedy was elected in spite of the widespread opposition to him," Linda continued. "Dad at that time quoted the verse from Daniel, that God sets up whom He will and puts down whom He will. When I think about these things, I wonder, How do we know God's will in political issues? How do we know if we might be working against the plan that God has, if we get involved in politics? I can understand why your church feels as it does, that the Christian does not belong in politics."

Andrea was thoughtful, her cheeks pink in the cold mountain breeze. After a while, she said, "Another thing I haven't been able to completely think through is why you have certain ways of dressing. Can't a Christian woman dress modestly without having to use a certain pattern? And why do men need to wear a certain kind of suit?"

"That is a good question," Kathy admitted. "And I'm not sure I can completely answer it. Father could tell you better."

"Do you think he would be willing to answer some of our questions if we'd ask him this evening?"

"I'm sure he would! Just remind me to say something to him after supper."

The girls sat quietly for a time. A Carolina wren sang high in a treetop near them. Several titmice were calling in the distance. Crows were cawing over the treasures they had found in a nearby cornfield.

"Did you know, Kathy," Linda said after a time of quiet reflection, "that Mrs. Miller called Andrea and me into her office after we began wearing veilings? She wondered why we were just now beginning the practice of wearing 'Mennonite' veilings. We tried to explain to her our growing conviction that it is a teaching of the Scriptures. Then she wondered what we plan to do at the capping ceremony. It struck us both as a new thought! What are you going to do?"

"I just figured I would take my veiling off for the nurse's cap," Kathy said. "The style of cap they wear at Harrisville is large, and I figured it would work for a head covering as well as my regular covering."

"Mrs. Miller said that is what all the Mennonite girls do. But somehow that doesn't seem right, Kathy," Linda said with conviction. "But I haven't figured out yet why I feel that way."

"I would rather not need to do it either, but they will not make any allowances. Father checked into it. Some hospitals allow their Mennonite nurses to wear their coverings instead of caps, but only after training."

"I'm cold!" Andrea shivered as she pulled her parka around her tighter.

"I am too. But I was enjoying the interesting conversation too much to say so!" Kathy laughed.

The girls walked slowly back to the farm buildings, their blood circulating a little faster again, making them feel slightly warmer. They stopped at the barn, where Kathy's father and brothers were doing the evening chores.

Linda watched with interest as they milked the huge Holsteins with big DeLaval milkers. It would be a whole new experience to milk in this kind of situation.

The boys working carefully and quickly reminded her of Red and Dad working at home in their barn. A wave of homesickness hit her, a longing to be at home again in the familiar surroundings with Mom and Dad and Loretta and the dear little babies.

After supper, they all sat around the dining-room table and sang. The Yoder family obviously enjoyed singing, and the singing was hearty and uplifting. Kathy's father read the Sunday school lesson after a time of singing, and then they had prayer together.

The younger children were excused, and they ran off to play for a little before bedtime. Linda was still thinking about their afternoon discussion. "You asked us to remind you, Kathy . . ." she started to whisper to Kathy, who was reading a periodical beside her.

"Oh, yes." Kathy looked toward her father. "Father, we girls were having a discussion this afternoon, and we would like you to answer some questions for us."

He smiled fondly at Kathy. "I will be happy to answer anything I can," he assured her.

"One thing Andrea and Linda wondered was why we have a certain pattern of dress. Couldn't we dress modestly without a specific pattern? And why do the men wear a certain type of suit?"

She looked at Andrea. "Were those your questions?"

"Basically," Andrea agreed, smiling.

"Well, let me begin this way. Through the years, our church has been interested in preserving agreed-upon practices. This helps to give stability in our teaching programs and to the oncoming generations. For years, the cape dress, as Mennonites wear it, has been a pattern for our women. It has changed slightly from time to time and in different places. But the purpose continues to be for modesty as well as uniformity of practice."

"Actually," he asked with a twinkle, "did you ever consider why student nurses wear uniforms? Why do they?"

Andrea smiled thoughtfully. "Well, uniforms look nice, and . . ." She looked at Linda for help.

"I guess uniforms prevent a lot of questions about what's acceptable to wear," Linda said, feeling her way. "And they identify a student nurse for who she is."

"You said it well. And in the same way, our uniform way of dressing answers many questions for us before we ask them. We don't have to continually reinvent practical ways to—be modest, for instance. Also it identifies us as godly people. Those who see us don't have to be confused about what we stand for.

"As for your comment, Andrea, about looking nice, that wasn't a bad observation. There's something beautiful about uniformity, and it is right for the church to require a certain amount of it."

"That's interesting. I suppose you would say the same thing about the plain coat?"

"Basically. I might add this: we believe a necktie is superfluous, and so the plain suit came to be used among conservative Mennonite men. The way it is made makes being dressed-up complete without adding a tie.

"There are a number of principles from the Scriptures that influence our patterns," Mr. Yoder continued. "One is from the Old Testament; God commanded the Jewish nation to dress a certain way so that they would remember God's commandments and be a holy people. Modesty, covering our bodies to conceal our form, is a teaching all through the Scriptures. It began, of course, with Adam and Eve. After they sinned, they sewed fig leaves together to cover themselves. But God made them more-adequate clothing. He made them coats of animal skins. Throughout the Scriptures, being modestly clothed was a sign of righteousness, while not being clothed modestly was a sign of sinfulness.

"The New Testament has a lot of pointed

verses pertaining to dress. First Peter 1 says, 'Not fashioning yourselves according to the former lusts in your ignorance.' And there are verses about modesty in 1 Timothy and 1 Peter. Jesus said in Matthew 6 that the world is worried about their clothes, but the Christian should not be."

Mr. Yoder smiled at the girls. "That was quite a long speech. Did it make sense at all?"

Andrea nodded her head. "I followed your thought."

Linda was trying to remember a passage from the Old Testament that she had read lately. "I read in one of the prophets somewhere—I believe in Isaiah—how God was so displeased with His people, the Jews. They still claimed to honor and love Him, but God said they had backslidden. And He was going to punish them because they were haughty, walking around with stretched-out necks and deceptive eyes and mincing feet. The chapter talked about all the ornaments they were wearing like the heathen around them wore—chains and bracelets and spangles and earrings and rings and nose jewels. It talked about the hair curlers and well-set hair and perfumes and clothing added for ornamentation. Then it mentioned the 'changeable suits of apparel.' I was astounded to find that Scripture passage, and I read it over and over! I wondered how any true child of God could ignore the obvious revealing of God's mind there."

"That passage is in Isaiah. I have wondered the same thing," Mr. Yoder agreed with feeling. "And yet there are so many even in the Mennonite Church that feel they are right with God while they keep on ignoring what they know to be the simple teachings of the Scriptures. They say, 'Oh, that Scripture passage does not mean *that!'* Or 'Times have changed, you know.'"

"I've heard that too," Linda agreed.

"As though God wasn't great enough or intelligent enough," Mrs. Yoder said, entering the discussion, "to make a Bible that is applicable to all times! And they look on those of us who choose to live in Gospel simplicity as being antiquated and out-of-date. Or perhaps simply lacking in intelligence. They say *we* are living under law, while *they* are living under grace. But they forget that grace is not a license to do anything a person pleases. They feel that Christianity is only a condition of the *mind*—being 'transformed by the renewing of your *mind,'* they often quote from Romans 12."

"That sounds like deliberate blindness," Linda said unbelievingly. "Why, Roman 12:1 mentions specifically that we are to give our *bodies* as a living sacrifice. Living for God involves us totally! Also, I found *grace* defined in *Strong's Concordance* to mean the divine influence on the believer's heart, which has its reflection in his life. Wouldn't that teach a change in all areas of life as well as a change of heart?"

Mr. Yoder nodded in agreement. "That's the way I would understand it. But you've probably noticed that even in our church here at Millburg, there are differences. We are thankful for concerned Christians within our conference who are taking a stand on some of these issues. I expect that before long, either the more liberal among us will leave, or else the more conservative of us will go elsewhere and start a new church. I tell you that so that maybe it will help you to understand if you see things that seem contradictory."

"I can identify with that," Linda said sincerely. "It happened to our church at home."

"But back to our other discussion, there is a Scripture passage that speaks about people being deceived in the last days," Mr. Yoder continued. "I think it's 2 Thessalonians 2. It says that many people will perish in the end time 'because they received not the *love of the truth,* that they might be saved.' And because of that, God will 'send them strong delusion, that they should believe a lie.'"

"In other words, they will think they are on the way to heaven, while all the time they are disobedient to the Word," Andrea said with understanding.

"Right. In another place, it says that the people who will do God's will shall know the doctrines of truth. But those who reject what they know will be deceived and finally receive the same condemnation as the world. It is really a sad thought and one to make us think seriously about the Christian life." Mr. Yoder looked kindly at the girls. "Have we answered any questions for you?"

"Oh, yes," Linda assured him. "We appreciate your help in explaining some of the things that were not clear to us."

"Maybe we can visit more tomorrow afternoon," Mrs. Yoder suggested. "The children should be getting their baths and going to bed soon."

The younger children went upstairs with their mother, and the older ones gradually drifted to a variety of tasks that needed to be finished yet before Sunday. Soon the girls went upstairs to their room.

"I was never in a home that reminds me more of my own," Linda told Kathy as they prepared for the night. "But I do wonder—and may I ask—Why don't you have a piano?"

"We used to, and Mother played a lot. But then as we children got older and began to play it, Mother and Father wondered if it was having the right influence on us. So they sold it. Some in our churches do have pianos or organs. But Father thinks that musical instruments belong in the same category as fine estates, and manicured lawns with statuaries, and fine paintings and antiques—"

"But David, a man after God's own heart, played a harp," Linda interrupted.

"That was in the Old Testament, remember, Linda?" Kathy said kindly. "During that time the people used a lot of objects to worship. Think how beautiful the temple was, with gold and ornately embroidered tapestries."

"I thought about that when I was reading from Leviticus lately," Andrea agreed.

"And remember the beautiful, symbolic clothing that the priests were to wear? Their worship was intended to appeal to the soul (the part of us that is emotionally touched by the beautiful). But Jesus spoke of us, in the New Testament era, as worshiping 'in spirit and in truth.' Our worship now is spiritual rather than soulish. There is no mention made of instruments being used in the New Testament worship services; they simply sang. Other than in Revelation, that is. But that will be still another new era!"

"I have so much to learn," Linda sighed.

"I do too," Kathy assured her. "And you have taught me a lot!"

"I notice you don't have a radio either," Andrea observed.

"No, we don't. Father doesn't think it has much value, but it does have lots that could lead us the wrong way."

"I *can* understand that," Linda said. "We had a radio, but seldom listened to it, other than for the news or weather. Dad thought it was mostly foolishness, and he detested rock 'n' roll!"

"But he always encouraged your interest in classical music, didn't he?" Andrea asked.

"He used to. But lately he has begun to wonder if that kind of music glorifies God or just the composer. And listening to it really isn't worshiping. It simply is gratifying to the ear. And I am beginning to see his point."

There was a gentle knock on the door.

"Come in," Kathy called.

Her mother opened the door. "Girls," she reminded them kindly, "tomorrow is Sunday. You really should get to sleep soon so that you feel awake and alert in church. You will have more time to visit tomorrow."

"Thanks for the reminder, Mother. I guess we weren't thinking," Kathy said respectfully.

Linda glanced at the clock. It was ten-thirty! Where had the time gone?

After a time of Bible reading and prayer, the girls fell into bed. Linda lay awake for a while, her mind trying to sort and assimilate the many things the girls had talked about that day.

*I have so much to learn,* she thought sleepily. *Dear Lord, help me to learn what You have for me, and not to grow weary or give up in the process.* She looked out the window, where the curtain was pulled aside. The yard light shone on flakes of snow drifting softly to the ground—the first snow of the season. *Father, I thank You for the pure white snow. And thank You that because of the blood of Your dear Son, Jesus, Your children can be as pure in Your sight as the snow.*

# 25

One of the girls in the nursing class, Starla Weaver, was a Mennonite from another area. She was eager for Andrea and Linda to come along home with her for a weekend. "Would you like to come along and go to the Christmas music concert at the Mennonite high school that I graduated from?" she asked one day.

"That sounds like fun!" Linda responded. "You must know how much we like singing." She was also thinking it would help the time to go faster till they could go home for Christmas vacation.

But the weekend turned out much differently from what the girls had imagined. As Andrea traveled with Linda and Larry to Virginia for Christmas vacation a week later, she and Linda told him about it.

"Starla and her friends were completely different from the Mennonites at Millburg," Linda informed Larry.

"Well, except for a few 'wild' young people at Millburg," Andrea injected.

"How was that?" Larry asked.

"I don't mean to judge them by what I say, but these were my impressions," Linda began hesitantly. "Somehow they seemed 'of the world.' They hustled and bustled about their many chores, pushing buttons to do a lot of their work, with the latest technology. And they must have a lot of money. The house and grounds looked like a picture out of the *Good Housekeeping* magazine."

"Perhaps they were patterned after *Good Housekeeping,*" Andrea contributed. "I saw a number of those magazines lying around."

"And I got the feeling," Linda continued slowly, "that making money and being in style with the latest gadgets and keeping up with the neighbors were the most important things in their lives. They didn't have family worship at all while we were there. But maybe that was not the norm. There was no mention of God either, except on Sunday at church. At first I was puzzled, and then I began to feel sorry for them. They seemed to feel so self-sufficient and even proud. But maybe I shouldn't draw such conclusions!"

Larry chuckled a little. "They probably were laughing at you-all, thinking how laid-back and slow you were! But you said you went to a concert Friday evening. Did you enjoy that?" he asked, changing the subject.

"The numbers they sang were mostly very

pretty, but their actual singing style disappointed me," Andrea stated.

"What do you mean?" Larry inquired.

"Well, their manner of singing and the airs they seemed to put on impressed me as though they were trying hard to sound and act professional. That surprised me. Why would Mennonites want to mimic the world? Then after the concert, I heard some of them congratulating themselves on how well they had done. That sort of took me aback and, I guess, contributed to my earlier impression.

"I enjoyed the music program, but I was troubled by the general spirit that I sensed in the students we mingled with. They probably were dressed according to the regulations of the school. But I sensed, by chance comments I heard and by the kind of extras they wore, that for many of them it was because they *had* to."

"Not because of any conviction or commitment to it on their part," Linda added.

"Really, Larry, I thought many of them acted just like the young people at public school," Andrea continued. "Some of them were boisterous show-offs. And I heard slang expressions. I thought that if I had been blindfolded, I might not have known the difference between their school and a public school. That's saying it strong, but I really was greatly disappointed," Andrea said sadly.

"That surely *would* be disappointing," Larry agreed thoughtfully. "When people profess something, you expect them to live up to it."

"I thought, though, that likely the young people we were around were the less spiritual ones because Starla took us with her when she mingled with *her* friends," Andrea added. "So maybe we didn't get a true picture of how *all* the young people are."

"Did you notice how the girls had their dresses made, Andrea?" Linda asked. "I noticed a few who were truly modest and simple, as if the girls understood the spirit of the Biblical teaching. I would have liked to talk with *those* girls—but apparently they weren't in Starla's inner circle. Starla's friends, it appeared to me, were trying their best to follow the world's styles in their own way. Even though cape dresses were required, they had them made in such a way that they looked very much in line with fashion."

"One thing I noticed about their dresses was how skimpy a lot of the capes were," Andrea added. "I thought, what good is a cape if it's made so tight and narrow?"

"Or with darts in the bottom and in the sides."

"And there were many showy and sheer materials, and skirts that were formfitting. I was embarrassed by the way some of them appeared."

"Oh, Larry, you probably think we are really critical, but we got such an eyeful! It was all so disappointing and hard for us to believe," Linda stated.

"We just didn't expect to see anything like what we saw!" Andrea agreed. "I guess we thought most Mennonites appreciate their church and want to obey the Bible."

"You do sound critical," Larry acknowledged. "But if we want to be Mennonites, I hope we can learn from those who don't appear to appreciate what they have."

"On Saturday we spent part of the day shopping in the area. I was so astounded by all the Mennonites of all kinds, rushing here and there, in stores and everywhere, going this way and that. And they didn't even look at us as we passed on the sidewalk! At home, we speak to everyone, Christian or non-Christian, whether we know them or not. And if we would see a Mennonite on the streets of Springville, I'm very sure we would introduce ourselves, ask about them, and . . ."

"Probably even invite them to lunch!" Andrea finished.

They all laughed. Then Linda said, "I asked Starla why they don't speak to each other or even recognize each other. She said she never thought of it. She guessed that is just what they are used to."

"I suppose that is partly a difference in culture between our area and the north," Larry contributed.

"As we drove around," Linda continued, "Starla pointed out where this friend of hers or that one lived. The farms were prosperous and carefully tended. But many of the operations looked to me like an unnecessary collection of wealth. Starla even pointed out various places where several farms belonged to one individual. I had to wonder if those people give to the Lord as they should, or if they keep it all for themselves."

"And so many grew tobacco for extra income," Andrea added. "I was surprised that so many Mennonites would grow something like tobacco!"

"I wondered what they do for God, if they spend any part of the day just for Him—like visiting ungodly neighbors or witnessing in the towns."

"You would wonder how they could even *think* about God when their minds must be so filled up with their own work and planning. I know how that can be," Larry injected knowingly.

"I know we all have room to grow in these areas," Linda continued. "But couldn't they be content with less and spend time as ambassadors for God, as the Bible says is the Christian's first obligation? I have really been troubled about that since we were there."

Larry sat thinking. "That is one troubling thing that I observed too about some Mennonites," he said. "Do they support mission work, I wonder? Or are they, like many families of the world, raising their children to help them create a financial empire? Are they or their children willing to go to foreign missions?"

Linda nodded her head. "What did Christ Himself teach? He called His disciples to leave *all* to follow Him."

"Jesus had no place to lay His head," Andrea added.

"It is something to think about, isn't it," Larry said. "Just how much do earthly things mean to us? Would Jesus possibly say to some of us, 'One thing thou lackest: go thy way, sell whatsoever thou hast, . . . and come, take up the cross, and follow me'?"

"And Starla talked about how many of the women—even some mothers—make elaborate quilts and other crafts to sell to tourists," added Andrea.

"Well, the Scriptures still say, to them as well as to us, that we cannot serve God and mammon. Neither can we have the best of both worlds. To selfishly desire wealth is covetousness, and that is a sin listed with all the others that will keep people out of heaven," Larry concluded soberly.

More miles passed by as the little blue Corvair headed south. Andrea had picked up a book and was trying to read. But Linda was still thinking about their earlier conversation. "I guess we didn't paint a very nice picture of the Mennonites in Starla's area, did we. But I'm sure not all who live in that area are that way," Linda said. "There are surely true Christians there too.

"I did decide, though, that I don't think I would ever want to live where there is such an accumulation of all kinds of Mennonites!" she continued.

"What else did you do over the weekend?" Larry asked as he watched the highway, with heavy traffic on each side of him.

"They had some kind of a young people's gathering on Saturday evening," Andrea recalled as she laid her book on the seat. "After a quick devotional period, they played games. One was called 'flying Dutchmen.' For another one, they all stood in a circle, touching shoulders—boys and girls together—and were passing something behind them. Someone in the middle had to guess who had the object."

"Then they played 'guard your partner'—holding hands and swinging their partners around, like in a dance. Their games didn't seem any different from our own earlier youth activities," Linda observed.

"Linda and I asked to be excused from playing the games. They probably thought we were oddballs! Then after those games, they brought out card games. Again, we were shocked. My daddy and your dad never allowed us to play cards."

"We were tired anyway from all the goings-on," Linda filled in, "and we asked Starla if she would take us back to their place. She was very disappointed with us and acted ashamed of us. But what else should we have done? She took us back to her house, and then she returned to play cards. I don't know when she came home, but I doubt that it was before midnight."

"Your tone sounds a bit cynical," Larry observed.

"I'm sorry. But the whole weekend was very stressful; there just wasn't a feeling of Christian peace or relaxation," Linda said, trying hard to express the frustration and doubt that she had felt. "My heart was so heavy after coming back from that weekend. I wondered if we were making the right choices. Did I want to be a part of a church that seems so secure in its earthly assets? Or one that feels so smug about its spiritual standing (because their fathers and grandfathers were Mennonites—and *they* are church members)? Or one that does not seem to be passing on to its young people a commitment to truth?"

"I know just how you felt, Linda. I struggled with the same doubts. I was so glad to get back to the dorm Sunday night," Andrea stated. "And there was sweet, unselfish, humble Kathy to greet us and welcome us back—so totally different from what we had been with all weekend!"

Linda thought again of how comforting it had been to see Kathy. It was then that the Lord had helped her to remember there were faithful and consistent Christians in the Mennonite Church.

Larry's little blue Corvair continued to head south as fast as legally possible. Linda became increasingly eager to be at home again to share with her parents and to hold those dear babies. She was eager for Andrea to see them too. Andrea had been as excited as they were when Larry had called her on Thanksgiving Day with the news. And now she was giving up Christmas with her family to go along home with them.

However, in all her eagerness to get home, Linda was more than a little apprehensive about what her mother would say when she saw the girls' veilings. Would she appreciate their convictions, or would she feel their decision had been out of place? Surely, she would not get upset and angry in front of Andrea! *Oh, please, heavenly Father, help Mom to accept our decision in this. You know we did it in response to the teaching of Your Word.* She did not worry about Dad. He would concede that they had done the right thing.

The porch light was on, shining a welcome. Then Mom came to the door as the car drove in the driveway. She was holding a baby. Soon Dad joined her, holding the other one. *What a welcome!* Linda thought as she hurried up the walk to greet her smiling parents. She noticed that Mom looked long at her, but there did not seem to be any ill feeling in the look. How her heart lifted in hope!

"Whom shall I relieve of a baby?" Linda asked after she had greeted her parents. She looked first at one baby and then at the other. They were both eyeing her intently. Then the one Mom was holding gave her a crooked grin. She reached for him, delighted.

"Welcome home, sis!" Loretta called from the kitchen.

"We're surely glad to be here!" Linda answered Loretta. She continued looking into the sweet little face of the baby she was holding. "Which baby do I have?" she asked after a while.

"That is Loren; he is the quicker one to respond," Mom said.

"You look like yourself again, Mom dear," Linda said. "I'm so happy to see you looking so well and bright and happy."

"You look nice too, Linda," Mom said sincerely, looking with meaning at her veiled head.

"Yes, you do," Dad added.

"Thank you, Mom and Dad."

Tears of relief and thankfulness came to Linda's eyes at Mom's words of approval. She must have been more concerned about how Mom would accept her than she had known. She bowed her head to kiss little Loren, hiding her face in his blankets, loving the sweet baby smell.

Andrea and Larry were coming in the door, Larry's arms full of luggage. Linda handed her baby to Andrea with a smile and hurried back out to bring in her luggage. She did not want Larry to have to bring hers in too.

But somebody was already there. Red was lifting the last suitcases out of the car when she got there. "I saw you-all drive in and saw you make a beeline for the house! But I could have brought these things in; you didn't need to come back out," he said with his merry smile.

"I didn't even see you out here, Red." Linda laughed. "I was so eager to see the little ones! And Mom and Dad. But I'm happy to see you too," she added sincerely.

"I am glad I hadn't gone home yet when you-all got here," he said.

Linda reached for some of the luggage. "Here, let me carry some of this stuff; you don't need to take it all."

"You look good, Linda, with your veiling over your hair," Red said as they carried the luggage in. "I'm sure that wasn't an easy decision to make."

"No, it wasn't. But I have such peace about it, feeling sure that it was the right decision."

"I would like to say 'God bless you,' " Red said seriously.

"I appreciate that, Red. Thank you," Linda returned, opening the door so that he could go through with his loaded arms.

Linda casually meandered through the downstairs, this time carrying little Leon. She looked in each room, noting the changes that Loretta had made. *She surely likes to change things around,* Linda thought, noticing that the living-room furniture had been totally rearranged. But it looked nice. She saw the familiar holly and evergreens, and the mistletoe over the doorways. She went into the library and noticed the little spruce tree in the corner, with the Christmas gifts stacked under it. Linda sat down on the rocking chair with little Leon. She talked to him as he eyed her, trying to get him to respond. Finally he also gave her a crooked grin, just like Loren had—and both just like Larry's, she thought. She laughed delightedly and gave him a warm, gentle hug. "You darling baby," she crooned, rocking him gently as he continued to gaze at her.

Loretta soon came in to her, and after a while Mom and Dad. A pleasant fire was going in the fireplace. "Are you and Andrea coming in?" Dad called out to Larry, who was raiding the refrigerator. "Tell Red to come in too, Larry," he added.

"We're finding a little nourishment; then we'll

be there," Larry called back.

Linda went over to the sofa and sat beside Mom. She compared the two babies. "How can you tell them apart?" she asked. "Oh, I see, Loren has two dimples, and Leon has only one."

"Loren also has darker hair. See, his hair will be dark like Larry's, but Leon's is light, almost red," Mom added.

"Oh, Mom, they are such darlings! How can you contain all your joy?"

"I just thank God, Linda. He has been so good! Dad and I often think what a blessing these two little fellows will be in our old age, even though we weren't expecting the Lord to give us more children. And we are enjoying them so much now too. God's ways are best, we often tell each other."

Larry and Andrea sauntered into the library, followed by Red. Red came over to Mom. "I would love to hold one of these fellows, Mrs. Asbury, if you would let me," he said, holding out his arms.

Tenderly he cradled the little one in his strong arms. He sat down nearby, looking with longing into the little face. Linda saw Loren look at him and give him a smile. Red's face lit up. "You sweet baby," he said, "you want to tell me a story, don't you."

Linda enjoyed watching the interchange between Red and the baby. No doubt, since he had never had brothers or sisters, this little fellow touched a tender chord in his heart.

This Christmas, Uncle Bob and Aunt Evelyn had invited the Asbury family to their house. Linda was glad Andrea would be along so that there would be two of them to help the rest of the relatives understand why they were choosing to be Mennonites.

Grandpa and Grandma were as sweet as ever. "God bless you, Andrea and Linda, my dears," Grandma said from her heart. "I believe you are doing right, and God will reward you for your obedience." Linda looked at Grandma with her heavy mop of graying hair, pulled into a bun at the back of her head, as usual. Grandma usually wore a hat to church, but that was the only time Linda had ever seen her with any kind of head covering. Today she had a heavy hairnet pulled over her hair. Linda purposed to ask Grandma about that sometime, but she felt quite sure she knew the reason. Her heart rejoiced at the growing spiritual understanding of her dear grandmother.

Uncle Bob ambled on the scene. "Ho, what have we here?" he teased laughingly. "The nurses, with a new style of cap?"

"Now, Bob," Aunt Evelyn said gently, "you know better. The girls are joining the Mennonite Church. And I think it is wonderful. The Mennonites are good people."

The day went a lot better than Linda had dared to hope. The cousins were respectful and even supportive. She was so happy for the time to visit alone with Grandma as they prepared a midafternoon snack together in Aunt Evelyn's kitchen.

But Linda was happiest for the days at home after Christmas Day. She was happy to be out in the barn, to work around the familiar animals, to help Dad with the chickens.

She and Andrea spent some time shopping in Springville and Sharptown, looking for appropriate dress material as well as other items they needed for school. They met many of their old school friends. Some were kind, but others made mocking comments as they saw the girls' neatly veiled heads and modest appearance. Miss Ducas met them as she was coming out of Silco. She looked intently for a bit, ready to pass by them. Then she stopped suddenly. "Why, it's Linda Asbury and Andrea Baker!" she exclaimed unbelievingly. "What has nurse's training done to you two? Does your school require special uniforms, or what?" She continued to look inquiringly at them.

Linda knew that Miss Ducas would not understand, no matter what they would say. She answered simply, "We aren't dressed as nurses but as Christians. Our veilings are to cover our heads, as the Bible teaches in 1 Corinthians 11. We wear these dresses"—Linda indicated with her free hand their simply made dresses—"to obey the Bible teaching of simplicity and modesty for Christian women."

Miss Ducas continued to stare, dumbfounded. Then finally she said, "Well, I never thought such of you two—two of Springville's most promising students! . . . But . . . well . . . I guess you're smart enough to know what you're doing. God bless you!"

As Miss Ducas left them and headed down the sidewalk, Linda was sure she heard her muttering, "Mennonites, that's what! Indeed!" Linda could not help but smile at Andrea, who seemed a little wilted by the encounter. Somehow Linda felt a bit like the apostles who rejoiced for the privilege of being misunderstood, because it was for Christ's sake.

After accumulating an assortment of simple dress materials, the girls settled down to a couple days of sewing. With Loretta's help, they hoped to be able to make several new dresses for each of them, to help fill out their meager wardrobes.

"Why are you cutting these dresses so much bigger than your pattern?" Loretta asked, watching as Linda was cutting carefully around the pattern, allowing extra inches at various places.

"I want them fuller and longer than some of my old ones, so they are more modest," Linda explained.

Surprisingly, Loretta did not say more. But Linda noticed that she looked a lot. She often felt Loretta's eyes on her veiling too, and she wished Loretta would say what she was thinking.

Evenings were often spent in the library, a cozy fire flickering in the fireplace, the pine logs giving off the compressed heat of a hundred summers. With everyone sitting together and visiting in the dusky firelight, the atmosphere seemed so cozy and peaceful. Linda treasured these days, knowing that as she grew older, they would probably occur less and less.

Most evenings, they would pop corn or roast marshmallows over the glowing fire. But tonight, New Year's Eve, they were just sitting in companionable quietness. Linda and Loretta were each holding a twin.

"Well now, Larry, how is school going?" Dad asked in his usual drawl.

"I must say, better than the last two years. But still, Dad, to be completely honest, I feel out of place there. I could probably count on my fingers the students there whom I would consider truly Christian. I guess human nature is about the same everywhere—as long as it is not under the power of Christ. The administration has much better control over the students though, for which I am thankful. That is partly because it is a much smaller student body and also because there is still some Christian principle among the administration."

"What about the textbooks?" Dad asked.

"Basically I am studying the same textbooks that I did at the university. The professors don't push the theoretical part of the studies though, as they did at the university. So there are some pluses."

Larry studied for a bit. "I guess I haven't been there long enough to really make a fair evaluation. But one thing I have thought of is that in a Christian college it is easier to let your guard down, which actually makes the potential for deception greater."

Dad looked thoughtfully at Larry, studying for some time before he spoke. "Well, Larry, we want you to know that we don't feel you must stay in school, if you feel the study or environment is a threat to your faith. Getting more education may have its benefits, but never at the expense of faith."

Then Dad turned to Linda and Andrea. "And how is nursing school going?" he asked.

"I'm enjoying the studies," Andrea responded. "But not necessarily the associations," she admitted honestly.

"We pretty much need to stand alone, along with Kathy Yoder," Linda added. "But I do really look forward to working on the floor when we have clinical practice. I think I will enjoy the patient involvement best."

"The capping ceremony is in early March. Will you all be coming up for that?" Andrea asked.

Dad looked up suddenly. "What will you girls do about your veilings?" he asked, as though it was a new thought to him.

"I wish we knew, Dad. We asked Kathy Yoder what she is planning to do, and she said she will take off her veiling to put on the nurse's cap. She thought she would still be veiled that way. But, Dad, somehow that doesn't seem right to Andrea and me."

Dad studied for a few moments. "I would agree with you that it wouldn't seem right. The nurse's cap is a symbol of being a nurse. It relates only to nursing, and nothing else. The Christian woman's veiling is a sign of submission to Christ and of the headship of the man over the woman. I don't see how the nurse's cap could take the place of the Biblical veiling. If it did, then any kind of cap would do. And men would be 'veiled' too when they have a work cap on their heads."

"Oh, Dad, what should we do?" Linda asked, certain that she did not want to compromise her new conviction of the importance of being veiled as the Bible taught.

"Well now, girls, I don't know. We will need to think and pray about it," Dad said.

The fire made big moving shadows on the walls. Loretta jumped up suddenly and switched on some lamps. "I don't like those shadows," she said. "They make me feel creepy!"

"Well, Andrea, I don't know how your parents feel about it all," Dad began again, "but for Mother and me, we still aren't sure that Linda is where she ought to be. This weighs heavily on our hearts." Dad bowed his head and sighed deeply.

Linda felt sorry for Dad and Mom. She knew they felt torn between the simplicity of life that the Bible taught and the social norms as they had always known them.

Suddenly Dad sat up straighter. "I just remembered something," he said. "Recently when I was in Sharptown, I saw a man dressed like a Mennonite in the Sears store. I was curious where he was from and what he was doing in Sharptown, so I got bold enough to walk up and talk to him. He told me that seven families have moved into the Sharptown area and have started a church there. They are renting a building south of town, toward Springville. He said his name was James Hertzler.

"When he learned I was from Springville, he wondered if I knew of any folks in this area who would be interested in knowing about their church. I told him yes, that our daughter was hoping to join a Mennonite Church, but that she was in Pennsylvania in nurse's training right now. He wondered if she was associating with any church. When I said Millburg, he said that he knew the pastor there and that his family has been there for services in the past.

"So this opens new options for us, children, that I want us all to be thinking and praying about. We have appreciated our church in the past and especially what Pastor Kelloway has done to help us. But Mother and I have decided that we want a church that makes holiness of life a necessity for membership, for the Bible says that without holiness, men shall not see the Lord."

Linda's face lit up with joy, and she thought her heart would burst with thanksgiving.

"This is changing the subject somewhat," Mom said. "But I was thinking about being with my folks tomorrow, and the special strength that we may all need, to face the tests of the day. I have a feeling that they will be extremely upset with Linda and Andrea."

"No doubt you are right," Dad agreed. "'To be forewarned is to be forearmed,' girls," he quoted. "Let's have a time of singing and devotion together this evening yet. I know it is late, but many others are out passing the time till the New Year comes in, doing things that are not profitable. Surely it would be right to spend time in prayer for the coming year. Shall we sing first? What shall we sing?"

"Let me put the babies in their cribs first, Dad," Mom said. She gently took a sleeping baby out of Linda's arms and carried him upstairs. Loretta followed with the other one.

Andrea reached for a songbook. "Do you mind if I pick a song?" She paged briefly till she found the one she was looking for. "Here, I like this one: 'Now Thank We All Our God.'"

Everyone gathered around the piano as Mom found the song. Then they sang the old hymn together, joyfully and prayerfully.

Now thank we all our God
    With hearts and hands and voices,
Who wondrous things hath done,
    In whom His world rejoices;
Who, from our mothers' arms,
    Hath blessed us on our way
With countless gifts of love,
    And still is ours today.

Oh, may this bounteous God
    Through all our life be near us,
With ever joyful hearts
    And blessed peace to cheer us;
And keep us in His grace,
    And guide us when perplexed,
And free us from all ills
    In this world and the next.

All praise and thanks to God
    The Father now be given,
The Son, and Him who reigns
    With them in highest heaven—
The one eternal God
    Whom earth and heav'n adore—
For thus it was, is now,
    And shall be evermore.
        —Martin Rinkart

**Then Linda chose Frances Havergal's old hymn "Another Year Is Dawning."**

Another year is dawning!
    Dear Father, let it be,
In working or in waiting,
    Another year with Thee;
Another year of progress,
    Another year of praise,
Another year of proving
    Thy presence all the days;

Another year of mercies,
    Of faithfulness and grace;
Another year of gladness,
    The glory of Thy face;
Another year of leaning
    Upon Thy loving breast;
Another year of trusting,
    Of quiet, happy rest;

Another year of service,
　　Of witness for Thy love;
Another year of training
　　For holier work above.
Another year is dawning!
　　Dear Father, let it be
On earth, or else in heaven,
　　Another year for Thee.
　　　*—Frances R. Havergal*

Dad read the familiar Psalm 90. Then they knelt to pray, each one in the family circle taking a turn. While they were praying, they heard the town fire sirens heralding the New Year.

Even though she was extremely tired, Linda could not sleep immediately. Andrea was already sound asleep in the spare bed. But Linda sat at her window seat, looking out into the moonlit night. The moon on the snow made the night almost bright. She saw the trees in the orchard with their naked branches stretching out. Everything looked barren in the wintry blue light of the night.

She thought about the past and the many experiences that were behind her. She pondered the fact that this week last year had been the week of Steve's funeral. How many things had changed since then. It would be so wonderful if time could be rolled back and he were still with her—vibrant, healthy, and happy! But how much more wonderful to think that he was with the Lord—*supremely* vibrant, healthy, and happy! She thought about the unknown future, wondering what God had for her. "'LORD, thou hast been our dwelling place in all generations. . . . O satisfy us early with thy mercy; that we may rejoice and be glad all our days.'" She mused over the verses that Dad had read from Psalm 90. A gladness overwhelmed her as she claimed God's promise to be her dwelling place—her refuge, forever.

# 26

It seemed like a long time since Linda had been at Pap-pap Jones's. She noted with new interest the beautiful and elaborately kept grounds and the well-maintained old stone house. The ivy that covered the stone walls was now a deep maroon rather than the summertime green.

Dear old Mamie came in answer to their knock and welcomed them in. She took one look at Linda and Andrea. "God bless ya, honey," she said. "Ya look like one of God's angels." Then she led them to the parlor, where Mam-mam and Pap-pap were waiting for them.

How Linda pitied the stiff old couple. If only they had the joy of the Lord in their hearts! But all their lives they had lived for their riches and the pleasures of the world. *Such shallow ambitions . . . How empty life must seem to them,* Linda thought often that day.

The dinner prepared by Mamie and her daughter was wonderful. There were all sorts of delicious things—oyster stuffing, ham glazed with pineapple sauce, sweet potatoes swimming in brown sugar and butter, sour-milk biscuits, fig preserves, and quince pie. But during the meal, Linda thought that love would have been the best "sauce."

After dinner the four young people wandered out to the gardens behind the house. Ornate walkways meandered through plantings of shrubs and trees. Stone benches were placed at intervals, and birdbaths or fountains adorned the centers of many of the particular groupings. A light snow brightened the shadows under the evergreen trees.

The green rye grass on the garden plot behind Joe and Mamie's quarters was also sprinkled with a covering of snow. Even the greens—the collards and the kale as they stood tall in their rows—looked fresh and bright against the contrasting whiteness. Linda thought of the many years Mamie had canned and frozen and preserved fruits and vegetables out of that garden for Mam-mam's freezer and pantry shelves, much like most of the other townspeople were used to doing.

"I don't think I ever saw more than the front of your grandparents' estate when we passed on the street," Andrea said. "It surely is beautiful back here among the trees!"

"We spent a lot of time out here with old Joe when we were children, didn't we, Larry and Loretta," Linda said. "He was always wonderfully kind; he taught me a lot of what I know about flowers and their care. But, oh, Andrea, this is all such vanity! What does all this work and expense amount to for eternity?"

"I was thinking the same thing," Andrea replied.

The back of the grounds sloped gently down to the river. There they found Joe industriously working in a shed near Pap-pap's pleasure boat, cleaning up and mending his fishing nets. He jumped up and greeted them profusely. "Well, well. Miz' Albertie's chillens!" he exclaimed. "I ain't seen ya fer so long. But de ol' folks waren't too happy y'all left de church in town! But y'all look good. And who is dis?" he asked, looking at Andrea.

Larry happily introduced Andrea. "This is my girlfriend, Andrea Baker. Remember Pastor Baker that used to be at Mt. Olive Methodist Church? She's his daughter."

"Glad to know ya, glad to know ya! I'se so happy to see y'all again!" Joe exclaimed enthusiastically, his dark face crinkled in a smile. Linda and Loretta sat down on a bench in the shed and watched as he continued his work. He chatted happily about the past, about his remembrances of them as little girls.

"Did you know Mom has twin babies?" Linda asked after a while.

"Well now! Ain't that somepin! What do she have? . . . Boys! I has to go see 'em," he exclaimed.

So when the girls walked up to the house later, Joe walked with them. *Dear old soul, his age is telling on him,* Linda thought tenderly as she noticed how he limped along.

When they all got home later that afternoon, Red was already doing the chores. Larry and Dad went to help him finish up, while the girls made a quick, simple supper.

Linda could tell that something was bothering Mom, but decided not to say anything in front of Andrea and Loretta. After Loretta had gone upstairs and Larry and Andrea had gone to visit Grandpa Asbury's, Linda, Mom, and Dad settled down in the library. A bright fire crackling around pine logs was casting its warm glow around the room. Linda and Mom were playing with Leon and Loren. Dad, with his feet up on a footstool, was reading his Bible.

"How did you enjoy the day today, Mom?" Linda asked after a while, almost fearful of broaching the subject. Would Mom have taken her and Andrea's part if there had been a conflict, or would she have sided with her parents?

But her mother's answer warmed and gratified Linda's heart. "Oh, Linda, it makes my heart hurt to see my parents' coldness. It seems they just have no spiritual interest whatever. Their hearts are totally wrapped up in *things.* It is so sad. Do they think they will be able to take their riches with them when they die? Or do they think they will live here forever?" Tears threatened to spill from Mom's eyes. "The poor old people! How empty their lives must be!"

Dad looked up from his reading, his eyes luminous. Linda wondered if it was from happiness for Mom's testimony or from sadness for her parents.

Finally he spoke. "They didn't want to say anything in front of you girls—probably because they didn't want to hurt Andrea—but they were very upset about your 'fishnets,' as they called them. They wondered whatever you girls thought you were doing, to get involved with a false cult like the Mennonites. Mam-mam said they would disown you—and all the rest of us, if any of us join that church. And Pap-pap backed her up."

"I don't know if they really would if it came down to it," Mom continued. "But I don't need their wealth, and if they choose to give it all to my two brothers—as they threatened to do—I'm sure I don't care. What really hurts me is that they thought they could move us from our resolve by using money as a handle. Is our profession of Christianity no more convincing to them than that? Believe me, Linda, it was not a very pleasant day of visiting. I just thank God that He gave your father and me the grace to be calm and charitable in it all."

"Yes, thank God!" Dad exclaimed. Linda looked at his happy face, knowing that his thankfulness was as much for Mom's stand of faith as for anything.

"It was so good to see dear old Mamie and Joe again," Linda said after a while. "They are just as sweet and kind as ever. It was worth the visit today just to be with them! I think about it so much, that it is the simple in heart, the uneducated, that seem to understand the fear and love of God. They are the ones who are willing to just accept the Word by faith."

"Just like Pansy," Mom said.

Linda nodded, thinking how impressionable Pansy was and how she had wanted to see "from the Bible" the reasons for the changes that Linda and Andrea were making. Then she had said from the depths of her simple heart, "God bless ya, my dears. It's all dere, right in de Bible, and why doesn't folks do it?"

"It has always been that way," Dad was saying, "from the time of Jesus, when He was on earth. Did He go into the high priest's palace and the rich Sadducees' estates to call men to Himself? No, He went to the seashore and called fishermen; He went to the out-of-the-way places, to the poor and the lowly, and called the sinners and outcasts to Himself. And those are still the ones who hear Him most freely today. The apostle Paul says that 'not many wise men after the flesh, not many mighty, not many noble, are called: but God hath chosen the foolish things of the world to confound the wise; and God hath chosen the weak things of the world to confound the things which are mighty; and base things of the world, and things which are despised, hath God chosen, yea, and things which are not, to bring to nought things that are.' I was just reading these verses from 1 Corinthians 1."

"It's so sad that so few people are willing to give up themselves and live for God," Linda said soberly. "It seems that the whole world would come running to Jesus, eager to find forgiveness for their sins, and joy and rest!"

"Jesus said that the way to Him is narrow and few will find it," Dad added. "I often think of that. Then I think how important it is to be in a church fellowship where people are serious about living for the Lord and serious about getting to heaven."

Linda thought for a moment. "Perhaps that is why I feel so drawn to the holiness of life that I see in Christians in the Mennonite Church."

Mom shifted baby Loren on her lap. Tears filled her eyes and coursed down her cheeks. She groped for a handkerchief in her apron pocket. "Dad, it has been so hard to give up my own will in this situation. But if the Bible teaches that Christian women are to be veiled—and I've come to see that it does—I want to obey that teaching."

"I prayed you would come to see it that way, Mother," Dad said, looking tenderly at her.

*How happy this must make Dad!* Linda rejoiced, seeing his loving gaze. *Thank You, dear heavenly Father, for answering our prayers for Mom!*

"Is the church at Sharptown already having services?" Linda asked. "Could we attend there on Sunday? I would love for you-all to have the opportunity to worship in a Mennonite service. It is such an uplifting experience!"

"Yes," Dad answered. "I understood from Mr. Hertzler they have been having services since late last summer.

"How about it, Mother? Would you like to go there? We would need to start the chores earlier on Sunday morning."

"Whatever you say, Dad," Mom agreed.

As they talked over plans later with Larry and Andrea and Loretta, Larry was quick to think about Red. "What about Red? He would want to go too, I'm sure," he said.

"Why don't we call Red by his given name," Dad suggested, as if a new thought had just entered his mind. "After all, he is a young man now and deserves the respect of a decent name! Do you think he would mind?"

"He'd probably appreciate the change!" Larry replied, laughing. "He was dubbed 'Red' by his schoolmates from first grade, I think, and he likely would be happy to be 'John Ray' again! Why don't you ask him about it—or do you want me to?"

*John Ray Ziller.* Linda thought it would take some getting used to, to call him by his right name after all these years. But it did sound more respectful.

Dad called Pastor Kelloway about their plans to go to the Sharptown Mennonite Church on Sunday. "I almost envy you," Pastor Kelloway said sincerely. "They are a people I admire immensely. I wish I knew their knack for having obedient families and obedient church members. And I envy them their Christian school."

Dad was telling the family about the call at the supper table Saturday evening. "If only the Kelloways could see their way clear to come with us," Dad said, troubled in heart for them.

"I feel sorry for them," Loretta spoke up. "Did you know that Lynette has been running with the wild set at school? And Sharon isn't too much better. Sharon is in my class, and we used to be good friends. But this year, that has changed. She's real popular with the fellows, and she takes advantage of it! I'm afraid her reputation isn't too good. The girls aren't at all like Steve was."

"Oh, the poor Kelloways!" Linda gasped. "I wish there was a way to help them!" Such news made her heart feel heavy. How must Pastor and Mrs. Kelloway feel to have their own girls turn away from their teaching?

Linda was up early on Sunday morning helping with the chores. She was so eager to see what the day would hold in the unfolding of the will of the Lord for her family.

They pulled into the church parking lot at nine-fifteen. Linda noticed that there were not many cars in the lot yet. But then maybe there were not many members, she thought. And she was right. There were only the seven families whom Dad had mentioned. The people were all dressed simply, like the more conservative ones at Millburg. She was happy to see that. The Asburys were welcomed warmly by the small group that was gathering. James Hertzler remembered Dad and was delighted to see him there with his family.

The singing group was small, but their faces all shone with the joy of the Lord as they sang several songs at the beginning of the service. Linda shifted tiny Loren so that she could help Andrea hold a book. Then she joined in singing the familiar songs, and her heart filled with joy. What would her family think of this—their first Mennonite service? She and Andrea had tried to tell them how it would be as they drove to church that morning. Even so, Linda noticed, Mom was looking around in wonder and surprise. But Linda rejoiced to see that she looked happy.

What would Loretta think of all this? She had a bewildered look on her face, as though she could not quite comprehend what they all were doing there. *Ah, the beauty of simplicity,* Linda thought. *Will Loretta be willing to submit to the modesty and simplicity that the Bible requires for godly women?*

Loretta was no longer cutting or setting her hair but was letting it grow, at Dad's request. She had it neatly tied back that day in a blue ribbon. She also had on a new soft-blue seersucker dress that she had been willing to let Linda help her make with a lot of gathers and fullness, the way Linda was making her own. Linda breathed a prayer in her heart that Loretta would also desire to walk with the Lord according to the Scriptures.

Linda looked across the aisle at Dad and Larry, who were sitting together, holding a hymnal between them. Red, or John Ray, who had been delighted at the invitation to come along, was singing heartily on the bench behind Father. How manly and dignified he looked, dressed up in a dark suit, with his hair neatly trimmed and in place. Linda felt such joy to see all her loved ones in such a service, that she could hardly contain it!

The Sunday school classes were small. The youth and adult classes were together in the auditorium, taught by a capable, serious young man. The lesson was on discipleship, taken from the teachings of Christ in Luke 9. "If any man will come after me, let him deny himself, and take up his cross daily, and follow me. For whosoever will save his life shall lose it: but whosoever will lose his life for my sake, the same shall save it. . . . For whosoever shall be ashamed of me and of my words, of him shall the Son of man be ashamed, when he shall come in his own glory, and in his Father's, and of the holy angels."

Linda listened with rapt attention as all the men and youth boys took part in discussing what it meant to walk with God. Someone brought in the verses from Luke 14:26–33 that spoke of being willing to leave all close family ties for the sake of the Gospel. He emphasized that Jesus said in that passage, "And whosoever doth not bear his cross, and come after me, cannot be my disciple."

Another man spoke of what the Christian's cross is, from Romans 6. "The apostle Paul said that the Christian is to trust Christ to put to death his selfish nature, just as Christ was put to death on the cross. Then the Christian rises in newness of life, no longer to serve sin, but to serve God. By faith in the power of Christ, we become 'alive unto God,' servants of His, doing His will from our hearts! To my mind, that is where discipleship begins."

Linda noticed that Dad was following the discussion with intense interest. Finally he spoke, hesitantly, as though not sure if he should. "Could part of the Christian's cross also be the reproach, the misunderstanding, the loss of reputation that comes with the choice to follow Christ? The cross was such a demeaning thing, an understood curse for the one who died in such a manner. True followers of Christ will still stand out as a spectacle; they don't blend in with the mainstream of humanity around them; they are viewed with derision and disdain by an ungodly society."

"I believe you are right," the young teacher agreed. "Paul told Timothy that '*all* that will live godly in Christ Jesus shall suffer persecution.' "

He skillfully led the discussion with questions and appropriate comments to direct the thinking of the class. Linda felt blessed to be there and hoped that the rest of the family was enjoying the class as much as she was.

The pastor was Brother Daniel Shenk. He was middle-aged and looked like a patient, fatherly man. His sermon was on "The Church." Most of his thoughts were taken from Ephesians 4. Linda could not remember ever having heard a sermon like that. The church was pictured as a body, with each part contributing its own special gift and each member working for the perfection of the body, till every member in the church comes "unto the measure of the stature of the fulness of Christ."

Brother Shenk emphasized several reasons why each believer needs the church. Some thoughts that stood out most to Linda were that the church provides spiritual nourishment and that it is a shelter for God's people.

Linda appreciated the sermon very much. Then the congregation knelt for prayer, which helped to establish in Linda's mind how important humility and fellowship with other Christians really were.

At the close of the service, the leader led a song that was pasted on the inside front cover of the hymnals. As she helped to sing, the words brought tears to Linda's eyes.

My Shepherd will supply my need;
Jehovah is His name.
In pastures fresh, He makes me feed
Beside the living stream.
He brings my wandering spirit back
When I forsake His ways;
And leads me, for His mercy's sake,
In paths of truth and grace.

When I walk through the shades of death,
Thy presence is my stay;
One word of Thy supporting breath
Drives all my fears away.
Thy hand, in sight of all my foes,
Doth still my table spread.
My cup with blessings overflows;
Thine oil anoints my head.

The sure provisions of my God
    Attend me all my days;
Oh, may Thy house be my abode,
    And all my work be praise.
There would I find a settled rest,
    While others go and come;
No more a stranger nor a guest,
    But like a child at home.

*—Isaac Watts*

Linda quietly wiped her eyes. *What wonderful provisions our Good Shepherd makes for His sheep—the church!* she was thinking. She read again the last phrases of the song before she put her book back into the bookrack. *"There would I find a settled rest, / While others go and come; / No more a stranger nor a guest, / But* ***like a child at home****"!* How much, with all her being, she craved that experience, to find a rest with the people of God.

The James Hertzler family invited the Asburys along home for lunch. Having a lunch invitation from someone at church was a new experience for Mom and Dad. Dad decided that since it was a thirty-minute drive home, they would take the offer this time. "That is, Mother, if you feel up to it," he said. "The babies aren't very old yet."

"If we don't stay too long, Dad, I think I can take it," she responded, cuddling Loren. Linda was happy for the opportunity to learn to know these people who, because of a love for the lost, had left their familiar surroundings—their homes, farms, and businesses—to bring the Gospel to this area. And Linda sensed that Dad was eager also to have more time to visit with the Hertzlers.

As they drove in the short drive, Linda looked around with interest. The Hertzlers apparently did not farm—there was not enough land for that—but they had a few acres that looked as though vegetables might have grown there the past summer. A small barn sat on the back edge of the property. The house looked new, as did the barn, but both were simply built.

Dad was looking around the small farmstead as well. "I believe Brother Hertzler said he is a carpenter by trade," he said. "Before they moved here, they bought this piece of land. Then Brother Hertzler and the two oldest boys built the house and barn. The oldest son, David, who taught the Sunday school class, is the teacher for their Christian school. Brother David says he has twenty-one students in six grades. So he is a busy teacher!"

Linda and Andrea and Loretta helped Sister Sarah set out the lunch while the men visited in the living room and Mom fed the twins. Sister Sarah had a simple casserole prepared for lunch. She brought a jar of pickles from the pantry and got a Jello salad and a head of lettuce out of the refrigerator. For dessert, she brought out several cherry pies to cut in pieces and homemade ice cream to dish into a serving bowl. Loretta, as always, quite capably went ahead in the kitchen, arranging the salad on lettuce leaves with flair. They all chatted companionably as they finished up lunch preparations. There were two Hertzler girls helping in the kitchen: Donna, Loretta's age, and Elaine, several years younger.

Soon the two younger Hertzler girls came into the kitchen, gently carrying Leon and Loren. How excited they were to have live dolls. They sat on the sofa and cuddled and talked to them. The babies, their tummies full, responded with their crooked little grins.

As they all sat together visiting around the bountiful lunch table, Dad suddenly asked, "I wonder about something. I noticed that you-all don't have any Christmas decorations in the house. Is it because you don't observe Christmas, or is there another reason? Or maybe you took them down already?"

Brother Hertzler answered pleasantly, "We do remember Christ's birth—that is, we enjoy singing carols, and we usually spend time reading the accounts in the Bible about His birth. But we can do that any time of the year, not just at the time the world observes Christmas.

"If we have the opportunity, we enjoy going to a church service on Christmas Day. In our home community, we usually had services. We haven't started that yet since we are at Sharptown because some of our families travel to family gatherings over that time."

"What about greenery from the woods? Is there a Scriptural reason for not decorating with that?" Dad asked.

"We don't bring in holly or cedar, nor do we have a tree, because we feel that such things do not really have any part with Christ's birth. They are practices introduced by the world. Just like the Santa Claus idea and lights and other decorations."

"This is all very interesting," Dad said sincerely. "I wonder then if you give gifts, or is that also part of the world's practice?"

"We give our children the things they need throughout the year, when they need them. Some Mennonite families give small gifts to the children at Christmas. And we would find no fault with that. However, the excessive gift giving the world indulges in does not belong in Christian homes. We feel it encourages covetousness and materialism and waste."

"Recently we realized there is an Old Testament practice that sounds much like the world's practice of the Christmas tree," David contributed. "Let me read it out of the Bible; I can't remember it well enough to repeat it." He reached for a Bible behind him on the buffet. "Here it is in Jeremiah

10. The Lord was speaking to His people Israel. He told them not to learn the way of the heathen. The heathen cut a tree out of the forest, decked it with silver and gold, and fastened it with nails and hammers. God said that His people were to worship only Him and to fear His Name; they were not to be caught in idol worship like their heathen neighbors." He closed his Bible and laid it on the table.

"Of course, as you said, that's not speaking of Christmas trees exactly—"

"You're right. I simply mean that just as God's people had to be careful not to learn heathen ways back in those days, they have to be careful today. The veneration people give Christmas trees definitely detracts from the worship we want to give to Christ."

"I never knew this Scripture was in the Bible," Dad said reflectively. "This is new teaching to us. But I believe these Scriptures are something to pay attention to."

*How interesting,* Linda thought. *We surely have a lot to learn; we don't want to be identified with the ungodly!* She reflected some more. *Is it because people don't know the Christ of Christmas that they feel the need to waste so much money and time on lights and decorations and gifts? And is Santa Claus Satan's counterfeit for Christ?* She would have to think more about all that. She remembered that in Starla

Weaver's home they had had candles in every window, an elaborate manger scene in the living room, and lots of greenery. And yet there was no mention of Christ; they lived as though they did not need Him at all.

The afternoon was so pleasant. The young people sang for a while. Then David decided to take the boys next door to see his little schoolhouse. Linda, Loretta, Donna, and Elaine helped the younger children to play a couple of games. Then, leaving the younger children playing Memory, they went back to the living room, where the older folks had a lively discussion going.

"Oh, here are my girls," Mom said as Linda and Loretta sat down near her. "I was just asking Sister Hertzler if it would be appropriate to get a veiling. I don't feel comfortable praying anymore without one. She said that she has some extra ones here and that I may try one on to see if it fits. So she was about to take me to her bedroom and help me arrange my hair. Maybe you want to help, Linda."

The four girls followed Mom and Sister Hertzler to the bedroom. Sister Hertzler set a chair in front of her bureau mirror, and Linda began to comb out Mom's soft, wavy hair. She arranged it carefully, holding it in place with extra hairpins that Sister Hertzler gave her. Then Sister Hertzler brought a veiling, and Linda put it on Mom's neatly arranged hair. Tears came to Linda's eyes. How lovely Mom looked, neatly veiled as the Bible taught. Tears were in Mom's eyes too.

"This has been a hard decision, but I feel it is the right one," Mom said, her voice quivering. "Truly we want the Lord's will in our lives. Life is too short to trifle with truth!"

Loretta suddenly ran out of the room and across the hall to the bathroom. A startled hush fell on the others in the room.

Then Linda quietly followed Loretta. Loretta opened the door in answer to Linda's knock. "What is the matter, sis?" Linda asked kindly, seeing Loretta's tearstained face.

Loretta could hardly speak at first for the sobs that shook her body. "Oh, Linda, I know I should wear a veiling too!" she finally blurted out, tears streaming across her face. "But what would my friends at school think? I would be the scorn of everybody! I just can't do it! It's asking too much!"

Linda remembered vividly the struggle that Loretta had had when Dad had asked her to let her hair grow and would no longer allow her to go to the hairdresser. And now, another struggle! But Loretta just did not understand the quiet rest of submitting all to God.

Linda spoke gently. "No one is saying you have to wear a veiling, Loretta. That must be your decision. But can you say no to something that the Bible so plainly asks of God's children? God will give you grace to meet your friends. And if you are willing to do His will, He will give you such peace that nothing else will really matter! I know, because I have been through the struggles of this same decision."

Linda got a paper towel and handed it to the sniffling Loretta. "But shall I leave you alone?" she added. "I don't mean to meddle, Loretta. But I do love you, and it breaks my heart to see you so distressed and troubled."

"Stay with me, Linda," Loretta said brokenly. "I want to do what is right. Would you pray for me, that I would have the strength to do what I know I ought to?"

"Let's pray right now," Linda suggested. She kneeled by the side of the tub, and Loretta kneeled beside her. "Tell the Lord how you feel, Loretta. He stands by, loving you and wanting you to choose His way because He knows that is how you will be the happiest."

Brokenly, Loretta committed her will to God. Linda prayed too, quietly, asking the Lord for strength for all of them to continue to follow in the ways of truth.

Loretta sat up on the edge of the tub, the tears still streaming but a look of joy on her face. "Thank you, Linda, for coming to me. God has given me peace in my heart; I know He will give me strength to do what is right."

"Here, Loretta, wash your face," Linda said, wetting a clean washcloth for her. "Then let's go back to the others. They will wonder what's happened to us!"

Soon Loretta too was fitted with a neat veiling. What a difference it made in her, Linda thought, as she looked at her in admiration. *Now Loretta is truly lovely—with the beauty that God appreciates!*

As the women walked back to the living room, the men stopped their conversation and looked up with interest. In a choked voice, Dad said, "Thank God for my godly women!"

"Amen!" Brother Hertzler echoed.

After a little, the men were deep in a spiritual discussion again, and Linda turned her attention to what they were saying. Too soon, it seemed, it was time for the Asburys to leave to go home and do the chores.

She sat that evening in her window seat, attended by a glad contentment. God had been so good to them! She could never have thought that He would work in such a wonderful way in the lives of all of them, to bring them to a fuller understanding of His ways. But had He not promised that all who seek will find? And truly they were seeking! Above all else, she desired the will of God in her life, and she knew this was the desire of each of her dear ones.

Tomorrow she and Larry and Andrea would be leaving again to go back to Pennsylvania—back to an uncertain future. But God was in it all and would show them the way.

# 27

It was late February in Pennsylvania. The day was one of those tormentingly springlike days in the middle of winter. Usually on Saturdays, if the weather was pleasant, the girls liked to take a walk outdoors. Walking in the fresh air was such a welcome change from the classroom atmosphere of the week in nursing school.

Linda and Andrea sat out in Daddy Baker's woods by one of the rushing mountain streams. They watched the water sheeting over the rocks on the hillside, following the path of the stream as it wound down to the valley. Abundant melting snows and the higher-than-normal temperatures had made the stream run over its banks.

"Remember that time several years ago when we were sitting out on the pier by the river at your place?" Andrea recalled. "I quoted that poem about spring. About the 'laughing stream / Set free from winter's gloomy prison, / Sparkling in the sun's warm gleam.' Do this stream and the songs of the birds make you think of poetry too?"

"They do! And I'm glad for this little bit of poetry in our lives, amid all the prose," Linda said seriously. "But I guess as we get older and have more responsibilities, life doesn't seem like a big lark anymore, does it. 'Life is real! Life is earnest.'"

"Life becomes more serious when you think of people like Starla Weaver and what she has gotten herself into," Andrea said soberly.

"Remember how we told her, when she started dating that divorced doctor, that she should know better? The Bible says that to marry a divorced person is to live in adultery. Then her church excommunicated her when they learned about it. But she didn't even care. She just laughed and said, 'I always planned to marry a doctor!' Now she has turned aside from everything Christian and is as worldly as anybody could be! It's so sad."

"Someday she will look back with regret," Andrea said.

"It's hard to believe that someone with such a wonderful heritage of faith is willing to drop it for a little pleasure."

"I think of that too. But you know, she never really valued her heritage, nor did she seem to have any sense of commitment to serving the Lord. She did what she did because she had to or because her church expected it of her, not because of a firm conviction that the Bible teaches it."

"Oh, Andrea, I'm so thankful that the Lord

has brought us to a people who believe the Bible and live holy lives. I can't appreciate it enough or thank the Lord enough!"

"And to think, we are in the instruction class for church membership! I'm so happy that the ministers here sacrificed for us so that you and Larry and I could have our classes on Saturday evenings."

"It would be so nice if my parents and Loretta and John Ray would be in our class here too," Linda commented, "but at least they are also taking instruction at the church at Sharptown."

"And we can share experiences!"

An early-spring bluebird was warbling its song on a nearby fence post. Deeper in the woods, a cardinal was whistling. The girls sat in silence beside the rushing water, which was nearly drowning out the songs of the birds.

"We should probably get back to the house," Andrea suggested after a while. "Larry said he would be coming in time for supper. Then we will need to get ready for instruction class. Do you have your lesson finished?"

"I do; what about you?" Linda responded as they got to their feet and started the long walk back to the farm buildings.

"I need to look up a few things yet in a Bible dictionary."

The field lanes were soft on top, and the girls had to step carefully to stay out of the mud.

"Tonight's lesson sounds interesting: 'Separation From the World.' I'm eager to learn more of what the Scriptures say about separation," Linda declared.

"The Scripture verses included in the lesson make it plain that there is a clear line of distinction, in every area of life, between the Christian and the unbeliever."

"That's right," Linda agreed. "The doctrine, I think, is based on those verses from one of the Corinthian letters that say, 'Come out from among them, and be ye separate, saith the Lord, and touch not the unclean thing; and I will receive you, and will be a Father unto you, and ye shall be my sons and daughters, saith the Lord.' But the fact that we are daughters of God makes any little sacrifice worth it, doesn't it."

"Oh, it does! The apostle Paul also said that the world was crucified unto him, and he unto the world; it works both ways. And Jesus said that because He has chosen us out of the world, the world will hate us."

"There is so much to think about, so much to learn! But it is so wonderful to be children of God and to have the assurance that as we desire to know *all* His will, He will lead us into all truth."

The girls continued to pick their way carefully along the muddy lane as they neared the buildings. Daddy Baker was just walking to the house after milking his three Jersey cows. He waved at the girls, and they waved back.

"Isn't it wonderful how your parents have accepted our decision to be Mennonites? It is an answer to prayer!"

"I know," Andrea replied. "But it's like Daddy said, when he learned it wasn't a passing whim, but rather that we had the support of your family, he thought differently about it. It was so good of him to come and apologize to us for his display of anger that time when we first asked him about wearing veilings. And the even bigger display when we actually came home with veilings on!"

"At least we have a much better relationship again. But I still pray that they will also come to see that this is the way of truth."

"I wish I could believe they will see it. Maybe my faith is weak. But they still feel sure that we are being too radical in our Christianity."

Larry drove in as the girls walked into the yard. Andrea hurried to his car. Linda waved to him and then walked to the house to help Mama Baker finish putting supper on the table.

As the three drove to Brother Martin's home that evening, Larry suddenly remembered something. "Oh, Linda," he exclaimed, "Dad called this morning and said that Red—John Ray—is sick!"

"John Ray is sick?" Linda echoed in concern.

"He wasn't feeling very well for a couple of weeks, had an awful sore throat. Dad said he told him to get an appointment with Dr. Boyer, but John Ray said, 'Ah, it's nothing. I've never been sick in my life, and this will soon go away too.' But before long, he was limping around with a sore knee. That scared him because he thought of Steve. And Mom told him, 'You get to a doctor immediately! You probably have strep throat, and it will be rheumatic fever soon, if it isn't already!' "

"Did he go?" Linda asked with concern.

"Yes, he went as soon as he could get an appointment. But by then he was running a high fever and was really sick—swollen joints and the whole picture. He's in the hospital on IV antibiotic therapy now, but Dr. Boyer thinks he might have some heart valve damage because he let the strep infection go so long."

Linda sat as one stunned. Andrea and Larry were talking more about it, but Linda could only think that Steve had gotten sick and died, and now John Ray was sick! Would he die too? Why must God deal with her family in this way? John Ray was like a dear brother to her! Her eyes filled with tears as she contemplated the situation. *What does God want to teach us through these hard experiences? What does God want to teach me? Is there some sin in my life, or something that does not please Him?*

But she could not go on with this heavy burden on her heart. *How must John Ray feel, and his mother, who has only one son left to her?*

*Dear Lord, I'm sorry for my rebellion and my selfishness,* she prayed. *Please be near to John Ray and grant him Your strength and healing, according to Your will. Be near to his mother during this time. Thank You for the example in the Bible of the son that You brought back to life for a lonely mother's sake. I trust Your mercy for John Ray and for his mother.* The peace of God filled her heart as the car pulled in at Brother Martin's house.

As they drove home after the class, Linda was still thinking about John Ray. "Did Dad say who is helping him since John Ray is in the hospital?" she asked.

"Right now, Pug is, but he can never fill the place that John Ray filled. I feel like just going home now! I have had enough of fighting the 'wolves' at college anyway. I suggested that to Dad, but he thought they could manage till school is out. But he said he wouldn't forbid my coming home if I really feel that is the thing to do."

"Oh, I wish I could go with you," Linda said, her heart aching to be at home to help ease the situation. She thought of John Ray, the healthy, lively redhead that for almost three years had been such a cheerful ray of sunshine around their place.

*O heavenly Father, please spare John Ray,* she pleaded again. She knew that John Ray's father had died young with heart problems. Could Mr. Ziller have had a similar problem—an untreated strep infection that led to permanent heart damage?

Before Larry left on Sunday evening to go back to the campus, he and Linda decided to call home and see how John Ray was doing. Dad answered the telephone. "There really isn't any change," he said. "The doctor was hoping he would be turning around for the better by now."

All week, John Ray's condition weighed heavily on Linda's heart. When Larry called the nursing school on Thursday evening to talk with her, they decided to make a quick trip home over the weekend. It took some shuffling of plans, but they were able to leave on Friday after classes.

Linda had not been home since the holidays. She was so happy to see how much the twins had grown. They were responsive and jolly, happy babies. Linda thought she would have enjoyed spending the whole weekend playing with them. But uppermost in her mind was John Ray's condition. She could hardly wait till they could get away on Saturday afternoon to go to Sharptown Medical Center to see him.

Dad had said he still was not doing as well as the doctors had hoped. But when Larry and Linda walked into his hospital room, he looked up at them with undisguised pleasure. "What a delightful surprise!" he exclaimed, beaming.

Larry squeezed the hand that John Ray held out to him. "Sorry it has to be my left hand!" John Ray quipped. "They have the other one tied up!" Linda glanced at the IV tube, wishing she knew how to make him hurry up and get better.

"Linda, how good to see you too."

After they had visited for a while, John Ray asked if Larry and Linda would sing several songs for him. "Do you have a suggestion?" Larry asked.

"I was thinking of the song 'Take the World, but Give Me Jesus,' " he said. "Mother brought me a songbook. It's there in that drawer—number 385, I think."

Softly Linda and Larry sang. John Ray joined them at times as he was able.

"Another one?" Larry asked.

" 'I Must Tell Jesus,' " John Ray suggested. "I think that one is number 344."

After they were finished, John Ray said, "Do you have time yet to read a Scripture passage? I was thinking about Hebrews 12—at least the first part of the chapter."

Larry read slowly and reverently.

"I don't mind the chastening; I'm a *son*!" John Ray said exultantly.

"Thank God for that privilege," Larry added. "Well, John Ray, we should be getting home; Dad needs help with the chores. We'll try to stop in tomorrow again either after church or on our way back to Pennsylvania." Larry again squeezed John Ray's hand.

"I hate to see you leave. My days get so long in here. Mother spends as much time as she can with me, but that isn't a lot, because of her cleaning jobs. The folks from the Sharptown Mennonite Church get in regularly too, and I'm so thankful for their loving concern. But I miss you all; do come again tomorrow if you can."

Linda returned to the bedside also to say goodbye. "I'm praying for you continually," she said sincerely. "I pray that the strength and the healing of God will be upon you."

"Thanks, Linda," he said. "Your concern means so much."

As Larry and Linda walked out into the hallway, they met Brother Shenk, who was just coming in for a visit with John Ray. Smiling kindly, he held out his hand to Larry. "Let me see, this is Larry and Linda Asbury, isn't it?" he greeted them.

"Yes, it is. And you are Brother Shenk."

"That's right. I want you to know how much we appreciate your parents and the spiritual growth that we have been seeing in their lives. And I want you to know too," he said with tears in his eyes, "that we are remembering you both in our prayers."

"Thank you. We appreciate your concern,"

Larry said sincerely. "We surely do feel a need of prayer."

As they walked to the parking lot, Linda could not help remarking, "What a caring and godly man Brother Shenk is! Doesn't it make you long to be part of a group of *holy* people?"

"I know what you mean," Larry agreed.

As the family sat together in the library that evening, Linda could hardly contain the joy of being at home once more. "It is so good to be home," she said happily. "I miss you all so much when I'm away!"

"By the way," Dad said, "Mother and I have been much in prayer to learn what God would have you do about the capping ceremony."

"Oh, Dad, did you figure anything out?" Linda asked breathlessly.

"We called your nursing supervisor and asked if there was any way you girls could continue to wear your veilings. She said, no, she was sorry, but their school had never made that allowance. I told her that our daughter and Andrea Baker did not want to take off their veilings to wear nurse's caps, and I asked what we should do about it. She responded that you should have thought about that before you entered training."

"What can we do?" Linda asked, hardly knowing how to think.

"I assure you, Linda, Mother and I have prayed about this and struggled with the issue.

And it seems clear to us that you should drop out of training. I know that the social stigma attached to dropping out is not pleasant. And I know you will lose the investment of your tuition for one year and the cost of your books. The books you can possibly sell and recover some of your cost."

"Oh, Dad—"

"I don't know how this sounds to you," Dad continued, interrupting Linda. "And I don't know how Andrea will feel about it. I am afraid that her parents will be quite upset if we influence her to stop her training."

"Oh, Dad, I think in many ways it would be a relief! Not that I don't enjoy the study, but my conscience bothers me so often with the kind of things that go on in the dorm and elsewhere, that aren't Christian. And the kind of exposure we have to the raw world has not been very pleasant either."

"The capping ceremony was to be March 18, wasn't it?" Mom asked. "You still have a couple of weeks to take care of details and to pack up your things."

"And I will call and talk to your supervisors about this decision so that you won't need to be the one to tell them," Dad offered kindly.

That evening, in spite of the cold, Linda went out to her favorite apple tree. These changes were all so sudden, but somehow she felt a strange and wonderful sense of relief. *Dear Father in heaven,* she prayed as she sat on the broad limb with her coat wrapped tightly around her, *I just thank You and praise You for the way You have made Your will plain to us. Help me to humbly accept the changes that this will bring, and give me grace to face the social ostracism as well. O God, I thank You for the wonderful privilege of being Your child. May the world be crucified unto me, and I unto the world! Nothing else really matters!* Then her thoughts turned to John Ray, and she again interceded with the Lord for his healing according to God's will.

On Sunday when they stopped in to see John Ray, the nurse had him sitting out on a chair. "They say I'm getting better," he said with his cheerful smile. "Lord willing, I can soon go home, and then soon be back at the farm work!"

The nurse stepped in the door just then to take his temperature and blood pressure. "It won't go quite *that* fast, Mr. Ziller!" the nurse said crisply. "The doctor says you'll have to take care of that heart for quite a few months yet."

But John Ray winked at them behind her back. Linda was quite sure he thought he knew better than the nurse!

After a short hour of visiting, Larry and Linda knew they must leave to make the six-hour trip north. "I'll be home for the summer, John Ray," Larry said. "Then you and I will work at the farming together, and it will be like old times!"

John Ray glanced at Linda. "And will you be at home this summer too?" he asked.

"I plan to be," she replied, choosing not to say that she would likely soon be home to stay.

Larry drove in silence, busy with his thoughts, as Linda was with hers.

Finally Larry spoke. "Linda," he said seriously, "how can you hold John Ray at a distance like you do? You aren't being fair to him; he's every inch a fine young man and worthy of you in every way!"

"But, Larry, what do you mean? I agree with you one hundred percent—that he is every inch a fine young man. And he's worthy of someone better than me. He is noble, good, and unselfish. He's twenty—old enough to ask a girl for her friendship if he is interested in her, don't you think?"

Larry drove in silence again for several miles. "I know!" he said with a grin. "Maybe he's afraid to ask you, so I could say something to him like 'You should write to Linda; I think she would be overjoyed to hear from you. She misses you so much!' "

"Oh, Larry, please don't do such a thing! Can't we just pray about it and let the Lord work things out according to His will? I would rather see how the Lord unfolds His plan in the days ahead. Besides, John Ray might not have any intention of asking me."

Larry drove in silence for a few moments, and then he said simply, "I will concede that my suggestion was out of place. Yours is better—to pray about it and leave it all in the Lord's hands."

They again drove in silence for some miles. Linda watched the now familiar scenery as they passed through the various towns and villages. Soon, she knew, they would be crossing the Chesapeake Bay Bridge. Then there would be heavy traffic in the metropolitan areas for the next hour or more; then back to the more pastoral scenery of farming country and rolling hills, and finally the mountains of Andrea's home area.

Larry's thoughts must have been running in the same vein. "This route is getting familiar enough to drive by heart, isn't it," he said, laughing. "But one of these times, God willing, we won't be making this drive so often anymore."

"And what are you telling me by that?" Linda asked, quite curious.

"Well, for one, someday our schooling days will be over. And for another, I hope to get married sometime so that my lovely lady will be with me and I won't have to drive six hours to see her."

"Am I being too nosey to ask if you and Andrea have plans for marriage?"

"We haven't made definite plans; we felt we couldn't as long as she was in training. But now that will change! Andrea is still young; she was just nineteen in January. I'll be twenty-two in the fall, and I feel like I'm getting quite old. But I would like her to be at least twenty, and both our parents feel that way too."

"It seems as though you have been special friends for a long time!"

"I know. Andrea was only sixteen—too young, I realize now. The Mennonites recommend not beginning special friendships till eighteen at least, which is so different from what we were used to. But it is wise. I'm glad our parents held us back from a lot of early dating. But even so, we got into some things we should not have."

"But, oh, Larry, God has been merciful! When I think back to what we became involved in when we were so immature, I realize that it was only because of the mercy of God that we were spared from permanent scarring."

Larry nodded his head soberly. "I know what you mean," he agreed. "I thank God often for His mercy. And we owe a lot to a firm father, who drew lines as to where we went, and when, and with whom. I look back with a lot of appreciation for all the guidance he gave us, even though it often ran counter to what others were doing or allowing."

"I just think it's so wonderful how we are all growing and learning together now! One in faith and practice. . . . Won't it be a blessed experience to be baptized and taken into the church as members this fall? I wish we could all be together at the Sharptown Church. Somehow they seem more like home folks."

"This is changing the subject, but when is your summer break? Will you be able to drive home with me after this semester at Wesleyan is over?" Larry asked.

"Have you forgotten? I'm coming home as soon as I can get my bags packed!" Linda replied eagerly.

# 28

Linda took a deep breath of the balmy spring air. How wonderful to be home and out in the garden with the early vegetables growing prolifically all around her. How glad she was that she would not be going back to school again, to be enclosed in those four walls, to learn chemistry, physiology, pharmacology, and the like. But best of all, she would not need to be constantly exposed to the ungodly people and the temptations that such exposure had brought to her. Home was where she belonged, with the wonderful smells and sounds of nature all around her! Loretta, at the other end of the garden, stopped her hoeing to laugh at Linda. "You can't get done daydreaming since you're home," she called teasingly.

"It's just so good to be here!" Linda returned earnestly.

Linda could hear the tractors running in the fields. She thought Dad was mowing first-cutting hay, and probably Pug was planting corn. It was so different not to see John Ray busily hurrying from one job to another. He was much better and was at home now; she was so thankful for that!

But he would not be coming back to help on the farm. After a lot of prayer and consideration, Father, along with James Hertzler, had helped John Ray find a small farm near Sharptown for him and his mother. Father had cosigned the mortgage for him, and now Brother Hertzler was building a shop on the acreage behind the farmhouse, where John Ray would be doing woodworking. They had felt this would be much easier than heavy farm work and would still give him a way to be productive. And his mother could have a large garden with even the possibility of selling produce along the busy highway that bordered their property. It had seemed like a wise decision all around. They hoped to move to their farm soon, and Linda was eager to see it.

But how sorely she missed seeing his cheerful face about the place. It was as if a vital member of the family was missing. He had been a part of their family for so long.

She saw the mailman go and hoped there would be a letter from Andrea. She missed her dear friend keenly. Poor Andrea! What a scene her parents had made when she told them of her and Linda's decision to drop out of nurse's training. Linda was glad she had been there with Andrea at the time to help shield her from some of the blame. But it had been a difficult session.

Since then, Andrea had gotten a job working at a private old people's home that one of the Millburg members operated. She had written once to Linda since then and said how happy she was to be doing something to serve others, even though it was menial work, for the most part. Linda was glad for her, that she was doing something she found fulfilling.

Kathy was still in training. Andrea and Linda had sat in the audience during the capping ceremony and felt so sad to see Kathy take off her veiling and put on the nurse's cap. Linda often prayed for Kathy, that this would not be a turning point away from God. They had been so disappointed that neither Kathy nor her family seemed to sympathize fully with their decision to drop out of training. Had they done the wrong thing? But, no, they could not feel that way. They felt they had done what the Lord had directed them to do.

And then, the coming *home!* Linda thought again of how her heart had swelled with happiness the closer they had gotten home. The old familiar towns and landmarks . . . and then finally Springville! They had crossed the river bridge, and all the twinkling lights shining out from the homes and businesses had seemed to beam a "welcome home!" just for her. Yes, this was home, and she would gladly always live here, if this was God's will.

*A letter from Kathy! How nice!* Linda thought as she paged through the mail later. She hurried to her room to open it.

> . . . I am beginning to see the wisdom of your and Andrea's choice. Since we are doing clinical practice, my eyes have been opened to so many things! There is so much wickedness behind the scenes. Many of the doctors and nurses have no moral conscience, it seems, and carry on in a way that is very repulsive to a sheltered farm girl or any Christian. And often the patients are neglected shamefully while nurses are flirting with doctors or simply visiting among themselves at the nurses' station. I'm glad they aren't all like this. There are some good doctors and nurses that seem to be here for the good of the patients and not just to collect wages.
>
> I often wonder if I could become calloused and vulgar like so many of the ones I work with on the floor. Pray for me!

Kathy's letter mostly set her to rejoicing again that she and Andrea were out of the school setting. But her heart grew heavy as she thought about her good friend Kathy. Could Kathy remain faithful under the constant pressure of such an environment?

Tomorrow was Sunday. As Linda fed the calves that evening, she thought about the last couple of Sundays and how much she had enjoyed being with the Sharptown congregation. There was a warmth and a depth to their Christianity that was even sweeter than what she had experienced with the congregation at Millburg.

And going along with her family on Thursday evenings to Sharptown for instruction classes was also a blessed experience. John Ray was also in the class, and usually Brother Shenk conducted the class. Some of the lessons were repetitious for Linda, since she had been further ahead in the instruction booklet at Millburg. But she did not mind that. It was simply an opportunity to have truth more firmly implanted.

This past week the discussion had again been on separation, and Linda enjoyed Brother Shenk's in-depth approach to the study. Brother Martin at Millburg had taught the lesson very well, Linda had thought at the time. But it seemed that Brother Shenk had a deeper burden for the preservation of Biblical conservatism than what Brother Martin had. Of course, it helped too to have Dad and John Ray in the class to join in the discussion. Linda marveled at John Ray's growth in the knowledge of truth. Apparently, he had been applying himself to intense Bible study since he was not supposed to work so hard.

And tomorrow Mary Catherine was planning to go with the Asburys to church! Linda was still surprised at how quickly Mary Catherine had consented when she had invited her to go along with them. She thought about it again as she washed up the empty calf buckets. She had seen Mary Catherine in Springville when she delivered the eggs to Kroger on Wednesday. Mary Catherine had asked about her veiling, thinking it must be her nurse's cap. When Linda had explained what all had happened since they had last seen each other, Mary Catherine had hardly seemed able to grasp it all.

"My family has been going to the Mennonite church near Sharptown. Would you go along to church with us on Sunday, Mary Catherine?" Linda had invited. "And then you could spend the afternoon at my house. That would be a pleasure again!"

Linda thought happily about tomorrow as she went to see how the milking was going. Dad and Pug were just finishing up the last cows. While Pug let the cows out, she helped to wash up in the milk house, happy to be working with Dad again.

"I'm so happy to be home to help you, Dad," Linda bubbled. "I feel this is where I belong! Especially now since you don't have John Ray's help. I think this was all planned by God—the timing and everything!"

" 'All things work together for good to them that love God,' the Word says," Dad answered, giving her a special smile. Linda knew he was especially grateful for her help again, and she rejoiced to be filling her role as a faithful daughter in the home.

With the barn work done, she hurried to the house, eager for the coming day.

Sunday dawned bright and clear. As Linda walked to the woods in the early morning stillness, she had to think back over the years. How wonderful to see how God had led her family. *Thank You, Father in heaven, for Your goodness to us. Thank You for all the experiences that You have brought that have drawn us closer to You. Continue to lead us in ways of truth. Thank You for giving us the privilege of being a part of a godly church. Keep us faithful to You till death.* She felt the presence of Christ with her in such a real way.

The sun came up, a huge red ball over the eastern horizon. Its glorious rays shone through the pine trees and pointed across the pasture like beacons, drawing her to the heavens. *Surely Christ still walks with His children on earth!* she thought exultantly. *He's walking with me now!*

She tried to hurry the cows, eager to get on with the work and eager to get on with the day.

Mary Catherine sat in open-mouthed eagerness as she heard the Sunday school lesson taught and the Word preached that morning. Linda rejoiced to see her enjoying the service. Linda was also happy to see Mrs. Ziller sitting with Sister Hertzler near the front of the auditorium. There were others there also from the local community. Surely God was working to build a church in that area, Linda thought joyfully.

Mary Catherine went along to the Asburys' for lunch. Linda felt that she had shamefully neglected their friendship since she was out of school. But she was happy that Mary Catherine still seemed to have a genuine interest in spiritual things and was obviously growing in her understanding of the Word.

The three girls took a walk through the orchard, where the blooms were just beginning to show pink and white on the bare branches. Then they walked out the field lane, past the farthermost fields, and on to the pine forest at the south edge of the farm. It had been a long time since Linda was out that way. She remembered a little island in the marsh that she hoped they could get to. Tiny skipped happily after them, always ready for a lark in the woods.

"What is that old house sitting there beside the woods?" Mary Catherine asked as they drew closer to the woods road that was the border between their place and Grandpa's.

"Oh, that's where old Mrs. Davis used to live," Loretta said. "She died some time ago. I almost forgot about this house. It is so desolate out here; we hardly get out to this side of the farm."

As the girls neared the house, Tiny suddenly started to bark. His hackles stood up on his back, and he barked more ferociously than Linda or Loretta ever remembered hearing him bark.

Linda stopped and looked at the others. "What is it?" she asked. "What does he see?"

They all strained their eyes toward the old house, where Tiny's eyes were fixed. In silent agreement, the girls veered out in a wide circle away from the house, walking along the edge of the Asburys' woods till they got to the woods road. Tiny continued to growl under his breath at times as he skipped after them.

"Should we go on?" Linda asked.

"He can't possibly see or smell anything that would hurt us," Loretta asserted cheerfully. "There are no wild animals around here big enough to worry about. Except deer, and they're harmless!"

The girls walked on, entering the forest by a little path. It was lovely, damp, and dark in this part of the woods. Only a smattering of sunlight filtered through to make bright spots on the forest floor.

"Do you remember where our island is, Loretta?" Linda asked.

"I think I do."

"Look!" Mary Catherine said excitedly, pointing ahead. Several white flags were vanishing quickly among the trees and brush.

"Whitetails," Linda said. "We don't often see deer when we walk in the woods—probably because we make so much noise. But do you know what? This would be just the place for the does to hide their fawns! Wouldn't that be wonderful if we found one!"

The girls continued to walk softly, looking carefully under the low-hanging evergreen branches. Soon they came to the marsh. Linda walked along a flowing stream till she saw the little island she was looking for.

"Now we have to jump the stream," she said, suiting words to action. Loretta and Mary Catherine followed. They found themselves on a small island with only a big leaning oak tree in the center.

"I used to love to come out here," Linda recalled. "But since I'm older, I haven't been here as much. See, here on the tree we all have our names scratched!" The girls laughed together as they saw the scrawlings of young children, which had grown with the tree and now had grotesque proportions.

"And here"—Loretta indicated some half-rotten stumps—"are the remnants of the seats we used to sit on. Dad and Mom used to walk back here with us a lot before we had the other lane opened to the river."

"This is all so interesting," Mary Catherine said. "You-all are fortunate to have so many good family memories!"

"Then we would walk back up through the woods there," Linda said, pointing, "till we came to where there were sassafras trees growing. We would always dig a few roots and take them to the house to make tea."

The girls jumped back across the stream and followed the woods road to the edge of the woods. How bright it seemed again as they walked along the edge of the woods beside the newly planted fields.

"What's this?" Loretta asked, bending over to pick up some paper.

"Candy wrappers! Where did they come from?"

"There's a soda can," added Mary Catherine, pointing to a can that was glinting in the sunshine.

"Someone else must have found our trail!" Linda guessed. "I hope they aren't around now."

"Do you think that's what Tiny was growling about?" Loretta asked.

Linda looked at the little dog. He was still growling occasionally as he hopped around stiffly on his three legs, sniffing the ground.

"Well, let's get going!" Loretta stated, starting off at a brisk pace. She dropped the candy wrapper beside her. Linda stooped to pick it up, curious as to how it had gotten there.

*Hmm! A Milky Way wrapper. How did this*

*get here?* She knew there had been an almost full carton of Milky Way bars on the milk house shelf at the barn, but they had all disappeared last week. She had not thought anything of it at the time. But none of their family had been out here lately that she could think of. Well, it probably was none from their pack. She stuck the wrapper in her jacket pocket.

"Are you all tired of walking? Would you like to head for the house?" Linda asked.

"Oh, I love it out here! You've talked sometimes about going fishing. Where is that place?" Mary Catherine asked.

"That's on the other side of the farm, and a good long walk. Do you want to walk it?"

"Oh, yes! That is, if you have time."

The girls walked along the edges of rye fields, and then the alfalfa field, where the deer often came out in the evenings to graze. They walked under huge, spreading oak trees and watched as busy squirrels scampered up and down the trunks.

"We can enter the woods here, on this little trail, and it will bring us out on the lane that goes to the river," Loretta suggested.

As the girls walked farther into the forest, they came upon a patch of lupines just beginning to bud in the shadows of the pines. Huge patches of creeping cedar and crow's-foot covered the forest floor beside the path where the girls were walking. "This is beautiful," Mary Catherine gasped. She walked among the lupines and picked a handful. "It's not hard to believe we have a wonderful and loving Creator, is it?" she added as she examined the beautiful lupines. "And to think I used to despise the thought of a God!"

"I often think how good God was to make so many different kinds of flowers for us to enjoy!" Linda exclaimed.

"And all the different birds and all the different kinds of trees and so forth," Mary Catherine added.

Loretta laughed happily as the girls stepped along. "Think of how it would be if God had only made one kind of bird or one kind of flower! How different our world would be!"

"But God is interested in our happiness, and so He created a beautiful, colorful world for His children to enjoy," Linda added.

Before long they reached the woods lane that went to the river, and began the walk along the pine-needle-carpeted lane. Reaching the clearing and the river, they all dropped wearily onto the pier. "Whew! That was a walk!" exclaimed Mary Catherine. "But I enjoyed it so much." She swung her feet over the water. "For a town girl like me, it is really special to get out into the quietness of the country."

"Steve Kelloway always especially enjoyed it here at the river," Linda said, remembering the times she had spent with him here. "He always thought it was so peaceful and quiet."

Loretta looked dreamily out over the rippling blue water. "Our family used to spend a lot of time here, especially in the summer, fishing or just enjoying the quietness. But we don't have as much spare time now. I miss it."

"Don't you miss Steve a lot?" Mary Catherine asked.

"I do," Linda admitted. "But as time goes on, I don't think about it nearly as much."

"He was a nice boy. They don't come like that very often!"

"I know."

"Don't you miss dating? You aren't dating anyone now, are you?"

"No, I'm not. I can't say that I don't miss it, but I am content to wait on God to lead in my life. If I am to get married, there will be someone, sometime, who will come into my experience."

"I wish I could have the faith that you do," Mary Catherine said wistfully. "I would love for a fine Christian young man to ask me out, but they seem awfully scarce to me! I think Red Ziller is awfully nice. But I don't think he would ever look at me. He knew me too well in school!"

"I'm sure that if John Ray is the one for you, he would be willing to overlook your past. You are a Christian young lady now, and just be the best one you can be," Linda encouraged. "If it's God's will for you to marry, some fine Christian young man will find you. And if it isn't God's will for you, then He will give you peace and happiness where you are. Just wait patiently on the Lord."

"It sounds so easy for you," Mary Catherine sighed.

"Oh, but it isn't, Mary Catherine! I've had my many struggles too. Believe me, I have spent much time in prayer over this very thing, wanting my own way and not wanting to give up my own desires. But God does give a deep inner rest if we just submit to Him."

"Tell me again why you girls are wearing those veilings," Mary Catherine said earnestly. "I know you said it is a teaching of the Scriptures, and I looked up the passages that you mentioned."

Together Linda and Loretta explained the order of headship that God established for mankind, as they remembered the teaching.

"That helps me to understand it better. But why don't preachers in all the churches teach that? It's in the Bible, clear as day."

"Probably because they know no one would want to hear it," Loretta guessed. "And most preachers these days preach to tickle the ears of their hearers because, after all, they won't get a paycheck if they don't!"

"The Mennonites don't have trained pastors. They call their leaders from among the local group. That seems to be a much safer way than to call someone in, from who knows where, that you don't know anything about," Linda explained.

"I loved the beauty and solemnity of the service this morning at that Mennonite church," Mary Catherine said thoughtfully. "I am so glad you invited me to go along with you. Do you think I could be a Mennonite?"

"I'm sure you could. But it isn't a light decision. Why don't you spend time in prayer about it? And we can give you some books that explain the Bible reasons for the things they do. You should study them and compare what they say with the Bible. Living in obedience to God's Word is not easy, and it requires a total commitment to do the will of God."

"How would your parents feel about such a decision?" Loretta asked.

"Don't mention it!" Mary Catherine responded emphatically with a grimace. "I have a feeling they'd think I was crazy!"

"But you should share with them, Mary Catherine. Be open and honest with them, and God will honor your witness. We will pray for them and for you too as you think and pray about all of this."

"You know, one struggle I have all the time is with the songs I used to know," Mary Catherine said after a while. "Do you think I will ever forget those awful words and music? They haunt me! I used to live for rock 'n' roll and Elvis. It was actually easier for me to give up smoking than to give up listening to that music. And the books I used to read . . . Some of those lurid scenes just stay in my mind. I beg the Lord to give me victory over them, and to *make* me forget!"

"I can sympathize with you," Loretta affirmed. "I'm so glad, though, that my parents caught on to what I was doing before I had any more memories to unsettle my mind."

"The Lord forgives us, Mary Catherine," said Linda. "And yet there is still a reaping, the Bible says, for the seed we have sown. Claim the grace of God to give you continued victory, as well as to erase such memories from your mind. God is faithful. The Bible says that He who has begun a good work in you will perform it till Jesus comes. What a promise! But we must do our part and *want* His work to be done in us."

Mary Catherine helped the girls do their barn chores. Then, after a light supper, they all got ready for the evening service at the Sharptown church.

"Thank you for the wonderful day!" Mary Catherine stated sincerely when the Asburys dropped her off at her house that night after the service. "My legs sure ache, but my heart is as light as a feather!" she added laughingly. With a wave of her hand, she ran up the walk to her house.

"Who would have thought that someday Mary Catherine Carmean would become one of my best friends?" Linda marveled as they drove out in the country toward home. "She was the bane of my existence through most of my school days!"

"A miracle of the grace of God!" Mom said sweetly. "Just as we all are!"

It was not till the next morning that Linda thought of the candy wrapper and Tiny's strange behavior on their walk the day before. She was hanging out the laundry on the lines in the back yard, marveling at the beauty of the opening apple blossoms in the nearby orchard. Across the fields, she noticed Mrs. Davis's old house. Once the crops were tall in the summer, they could no longer see it from their buildings. The house looked little and tumbledown from where she stood. What if some strange wild animal were hanging out there? It was such a wild and remote place! She would have to tell Dad about it at the first opportunity.

When the sheets were all on the line, she ran to the chicken barn, where she knew Dad was cleaning eggs. He was in the egg-packing room, getting ready to wash the baskets of eggs he had just collected.

"Are you hurrying in to help me? Or has something remarkable happened?" he asked, his eyes twinkling at her as she entered breathlessly.

"Nothing remarkable, I don't think," Linda

said, not noting the double negatives in her excitement. She pulled the candy wrapper from her pocket. "We girls found this on our walk yesterday, back by the woods, near Mrs. Davis's house. Also, when we got near the house, Tiny really carried on frantically. His hair stood up on his back, as if he was really scared about something. I don't know if it all goes together or not, but I thought I should tell you."

Dad looked thoughtful. "I think we should look into this," he said finally. Linda thought his manner betrayed more than what he said. But she did not ask more, figuring that Dad would tell her more, if and when he thought it proper.

She hurried back up the walk to the house, grabbing her laundry basket on the way. Another load was finished. How splendid to hang laundry out on such a perfect spring day!

That afternoon as she took the fragrant wash off the lines, she noticed several police cars at Mrs. Davis's house. She thought she could see people walking around. Whatever was happening?

Dad must have seen too, from where he was cutting hay. He soon drove the tractor in, jumped into the pickup, and drove hurriedly out the field lane to the old house.

Linda wished he had said something. She watched till the police cars left, one by one. Soon the pickup came back in, and Linda ran out to meet it.

"What is going on?" she asked, hardly able to contain her curiosity.

"Clyde Tilghman has been hiding out back in that house for the last month or so. He's in custody now, and I am thankful for that. Even though we don't plan to press charges, he is a dangerous individual. It seemed right for me to let the law know where he was."

"But how did you know someone was there?" Linda asked, shivering in spite of the warmth of the spring day.

"I suspected it for the last while because eggs were disappearing, as well as milk. Then when that nearly full carton of candy bars disappeared last week, I was pretty sure that someone was holed up somewhere around here. I was keeping a close watch for anything around our buildings, but could not find anything unusual. I even spent an afternoon climbing through the haymow, looking for hiding places. When you told me what you did, I was sure I had my answer."

"Oh, Dad," Linda said, her voice trembly, "I'm so thankful the Lord was watching over us! We three girls were so close to that house yesterday! No doubt Clyde saw us, with all the commotion that Tiny made."

"'The angel of the LORD encampeth round about them that fear him, and delivereth them,'" Dad quoted reverently.

# 29

Summer came on in a flurry of busyness—planting, harvesting grain, haymaking, and all the rest. Larry came home in June, ready again to tackle the heavy end of the farming. Linda helped outside all she could, as well. Still they all missed John Ray and all the help he would have contributed to the summer work.

One evening as they worked in the barn together, Larry and Linda were discussing what solutions there could be to Dad's need for help—especially that fall, when Larry would go back to school. "Sometimes I feel like dropping out of school," Larry said. "There is no way Dad can carry on here by himself. He is getting older, for one thing, and so is Pug. So who does that leave for the heavy work?"

"Dad has talked about selling the cows, but I can't bear that thought," Linda stated. "I'd sooner have him sell the chickens. He says the eggs hardly pay more than for the feed anyway."

Larry looked surprised at Linda's suggestion. "I can't imagine that he would seriously consider selling either. I would sooner expect him to rent out some of his land."

"Renting land won't help this year," Linda reminded Larry. "It's already all planted for the summer, other than the late soybean crops."

"Maybe the Lord is giving me an answer as to whether I should go back to school this fall," Larry said meditatively. "If Dad needs help, I should be the one to be here to help him. And I have had plenty of doubts anyway about whether college is the place for me."

"How would Andrea feel about that?"

"I really don't think she would have a problem with it, but we'll need to talk about it when I see her again."

The first weekend in July, the Bakers came, bringing Andrea for a visit while they went to a conference in the area. That Saturday evening, Andrea and Larry went to visit Brother Shenk. Larry had told Linda they wanted to discuss a number of things with him, among them how their church would feel in relation to Larry's continuing his education.

Linda was eager for Andrea to get back, to hear how their discussion went. But Andrea did not come back with Larry; Brother Shenk had invited her to stay with them overnight. Linda asked where she was, when Larry came home without her.

Larry explained. "Brother Shenk said that usually they recommend that dating couples do not stay at the same house. 'Not that we would not trust you,' he told me, 'but to avoid the appearance of evil.' It was a new thought to me, but I appreciated his fatherly concern."

It was also a new thought to Linda. She pondered it as she sat at her window seat alone that evening. *It makes sense,* she concluded finally. *Surely we need all the help we can get to avoid temptation! Besides, she can learn to know Brother Shenk's family this way.* Linda thought of the Shenks' two sweet and conscientious teenage girls, Dorothy and Louise. How much she had enjoyed learning to know them, and how much she had profited by their godly example!

The Mast family invited the Asburys to lunch the next day. In the afternoon, they all visited together on the Masts' front porch, shaded from the bright summer sun. The porch did not have the benefit of being screened in, but thankfully, the insects were not bad. The men reviewed the morning sermon and the Sunday school lesson, highlighting main points in a way that helped the spiritual instruction to stay in Linda's mind. She thoroughly enjoyed these times of sharing with other families about spiritual things. She found it a help in her Christian life and an impetus to propel her through a week of daily duties.

The girls also spent some of the afternoon wandering over the Masts' lot, looking at the flowers and the garden. "Did you girls ever think of going to Bible school?" Joy asked as they stood at the garden fence.

"Bible school?" Andrea asked.

"Yes. Our conservative church group has a Bible school in Ohio, in a little town called Carbon Hill. I was there last year for twelve weeks, and it was a great experience."

Excitement rose in Linda. "What kind of studies did you have?" she asked, the old love for study coming back to her.

"Um . . . let me see. Last year I took some book studies; I think they were 'Titus, Philemon, and James.' I also took a study called 'Types and Shadows,' another called 'Life of Christ,' one on 'The Bible and Science,' and . . . 'Christian Writing,' and 'Personal Evangelism,' and . . . I can't think of the others right now."

"That sounds very interesting!" Linda exclaimed. "I would love to go if possible."

Andrea nodded her head eagerly. "I would too. At least if I could get off that long from my job."

"I would like to go, but I doubt Linda and I could both go the same year. And since she is quite a lot older, I guess she should go first," Loretta said teasingly.

Joy looked at them happily. "Maybe you could each go six weeks. The Bible school is arranged in three-week terms. I'll see if there are any more Bible school brochures in the house," she said.

When they went to the house later, Joy found several brochures on her father's desk. Linda took them eagerly, praying in her heart that there would somehow be a way that she could go to Bible school. *What an experience in Christian growth that would be,* she thought.

There was no church service at Sharptown that evening. So after the chores were done for the day, the Asburys sat in the front yard under the maple trees. Grandpa and Grandma came over to sit with them for a while.

"Let's sing!" Linda suggested.

"Oh, please, let's do," Grandma agreed.

Linda ran inside for books, coming back with six *Church Hymnals,* which Dad had just acquired through Brother Hertzler.

"You don't need the piano?" Grandpa asked curiously.

"We can sing without it, don't you think?" Dad said. "God gave us each a natural 'harp' that is able to bring Him glory in a way that an instrument cannot!"

Larry gave the pitch, and they sang song after song. Linda marveled at the beauty of the perfect harmony. How much they had missed by always having accompaniment!

Grandma kept paging in her book. "I don't want this to stop," she said, looking up finally with a glowing face. "I think this must be a little bit like heaven!"

"Can we sing just one more yet?" Grandpa asked. "Number 633?"

"'Shall We Gather at the River?' A good song to end with," Dad said after they had sung all four verses. "God grant that we can all be faithful so that we can gather someday at the throne of God!"

Larry stood up. "The Shenks are expecting Andrea to spend the night at their place again. So I guess I should be leaving to take her there," he said.

Good nights said all around, the happy evening together was over. Linda went to her room, eager to read the Bible school brochure and to be alone with all the new thoughts from the day.

As Linda hung out the laundry the next morning in the bright July sunshine, she saw Larry mowing the pastures. How eager she was to talk with him again, to ask about his visit with Brother Shenk on Saturday evening.

That evening as they milked together, they were able to share. "I'm so curious what advice Brother Shenk gave you about continuing your education," Linda said.

"I guess they counseled Andrea and me about the way we thought they would," Larry replied. "Brother Shenk said he does not have a problem with learning, if it is the right things and in the right environment. However, because of the humanistic approach to learning in the colleges and universities of our time, he does not recommend higher education to their young people."

"So he thought you should quit?" Linda asked.

"He didn't expressly say that, although I know that would be his preferred choice. He said that I do have a few things in my favor—that I could be at church every weekend, that I have a Christian girlfriend, and that I am older than many students. He said if I do choose to go, he would certainly recommend that I commute rather than stay in the dormitory."

"Did you decide what you are going to do?"

"Not for sure. But Andrea and I both lean pretty heavily toward my quitting, especially since Dad needs help on the farm."

"What do you think Mom will say if you quit one year short of your degree?"

"I thought of that. She has had her heart set on my getting a B.S. in science."

"Maybe she has changed her mind about that. She has changed in so many other areas," Linda suggested.

"No doubt she has," Larry surmised as he carried his milker to another cow.

Grandpa and Dad had occasionally driven the twenty-six miles to John Ray's little place to help with building his shop. One Tuesday Dad asked if the girls could ride along the next day.

The house needed a cleaning before John Ray and his mother moved in. Other sisters from the church would also be there and would provide a lunch for all the helpers.

How happy Linda was to finally have the opportunity to see the Ziller place more closely! They had driven past a time or two. But now they were actually driving up the driveway to a quaint little cottage.

She instantly loved the charming setting. The buildings were set back from the road, with a spacious yard between. Mature trees and shrubs surrounded the house. The shrubs were badly in need of trimming. Close to the house, hydrangeas, peonies, and a variety of other blooming bushes added their beauty. Linda's hands fairly ached to get at the flower beds, where she saw petunias, snapdragons, larkspur, and other flowers trying to bloom among the weeds. So far, the vegetable garden had been the only thing tended. And it was growing well with its rows of beans and tomatoes and melons and all the rest.

Soon the Masts and the Hertzlers also arrived. Joy Mast, just Linda's age and already a close friend, decided to help Linda clean up outside, which was much to Linda's liking. They found a hedge trimmer in one of the nearby sheds and went to work. Then Joy raked the lawn while Linda worked at weeding the flower beds. Other women from Sharptown came as well, and Linda heard lots of pleasant chatter inside the house through the wide-open windows. How happy it made her to hear Loretta visiting cheerfully as she worked. Loretta and Donna Hertzler were quite good friends, and Linda was sure Donna was a good influence on Loretta.

By late afternoon, the house was sparkling and the lawn had taken on a much more appealing look. Linda and Loretta stood on the lawn with the other sisters and admired the fruits of their labors. Dad and Grandpa soon came on the scene. "Well, girls, guess we'd better get home to chore. It surely looks like something got accomplished today!"

"Thank you so much for your help," Sister Shenk said sincerely as they got ready to leave.

Dad asked her, "Do you have any idea when the Zillers will be moving?"

"They're thinking of next week, Lord willing," Sister Shenk responded.

"Well now, let us know if we can help," Dad offered.

The next week Linda and Loretta went with Dad to help John Ray and his mother move into their new place. What fun Linda thought it was to arrange the kitchen for Mrs. Ziller and to help hang pictures and curtains! What fun it was to watch the empty house become a cozy home! "I have never helped anyone move before," Linda confided to Joy Mast. "It has been delightful and fascinating."

"You haven't!" Joy was astounded. "I always think moving is fun. But I'm ready to stay put for a while!"

Now when the Asburys drove to Sharptown to church services or to other meetings, they often took the road that went past the Ziller farmstead. Linda liked to observe what was happening there. She was so happy that John Ray and his mother had such a convenient place of their own. John Ray was busy in his shop making tables and chairs to sell to a Mennonite furniture dealer in Delaware. He was thankful for the training in woodworking he had received in shop in his later years in school.

Summer was a busy time of learning to know the families at the Sharptown church. As the summer passed, the Asburys had the opportunity for a visit to each of the seven homes. Linda especially appreciated the times at the Shenk home, where many issues were discussed—issues they faced as a family as they found their way in oneness of conviction with the conservative way of life.

One Friday evening in late August, Brother Shenk and his wife came to visit the Asburys. They sat on the screened porch, sharing congenially.

"Part of the reason for our visit this evening," Brother Shenk began after a while, "is to see how you-all are feeling about our church by now. Your instruction lessons are finished, and you have told us that you would like to become members. And, of course, as a congregation we very much desire that." Brother Shenk smiled kindly at the family sitting with him. "Is there anything that you feel stands in the way of your being members with us?" he asked then.

Dad thought for some time. "Well now," he said finally, "I don't think of anything. Perhaps you do, however."

"I understand that you got rid of your radio, and we appreciate that. We noticed your baby grand piano and are wondering how you feel about that."

"As for the piano," Dad said, "we no longer have it. We decided that we did not want to have such an expensive-looking piece of furniture in our house, and because the church feels that New Testament worship should not include instruments, we got rid of it," he said simply.

Linda glanced at Mom, knowing the struggle it had been for her to accept it when Dad decided to get rid of the piano. Not only because it had been a wedding gift from her parents, but because of the personal enjoyment that it had always been to her. But Mom's face now showed nothing but serenity. Linda rejoiced again in this obvious manifestation that God's grace is sufficient.

Brother Shenk looked gratified. *He's probably happy that he does not need to suggest that we do that now,* Linda thought.

"Thank God for your growing convictions," Brother Shenk said sincerely, looking at Dad with a glowing face.

"Is there anything else?" Dad asked. "Anything that we are not seeing that we ought to? Our desire is to be open, to be willing to learn whatever we ought to know, to help us be more like Christ."

Brother Shenk shook his head. "I can't think of anything at this time," he said.

After visiting for a time longer, Brother Shenk suggested they spend some time in prayer together before the Shenks left. Linda somehow felt that the time of sharing and kneeling together in prayer must be a little like heaven, where everything is love and harmony. How eager she was for the time that they would be taken in as members! Brother Shenk had said it would be sometime in October, when it would suit the bishop, Brother Miller, to be there. Oh, the time could not pass fast enough!

# 30

Fall had come again. The leaves on the maples around the house were a myriad of colors—gorgeous reds and yellows and browns. The flower beds were still beautiful with zinnias, asters, cleomes, and snapdragons. The orchard was nearly picked clean; only a few apples hung on yet, waiting to be picked and stored for the winter. The garden was basically bare too, except for a few big orange pumpkins.

Some of the corn had been harvested for the silo, but the rest of the cornfields stood tall and brown. The dry leaves rustled a music of their own in the slightest breeze. The soybean fields were also turning yellow. It was a glorious time of the year, Linda thought as she pulled weeds in the strawberry bed, glancing up occasionally at the deep blue sky overhead.

But the most wonderful consideration by far was that this Sunday her family and John Ray were all going to be taken in as members at the Sharptown Mennonite Church! Was she ready for that big step, she wondered again, as she often had in the last months since their instruction was finished.

She searched her heart again. Yes, it was what she desired. And she felt certain that it was God's will for her. Together she and her family had studied the doctrines that the Mennonite Church believed the Bible taught. They were convinced it was all truth. And, furthermore, they were convinced that here were a people who not only *taught* it but *lived* it as well.

Linda, as well as Larry, was eagerly waiting for Andrea to come for the weekend. By special arrangement with the Millburg ministry, Andrea would be baptized and taken in as a member at Sharptown too, since that would be her home church after her marriage. Pastor and Mrs. Baker were coming and bringing Andrea with them. Larry had convinced them to come to be at this special service. Linda was happy for Andrea's sake that her parents were willing to come.

Loretta was even now busy in the kitchen, making lots of food in preparation for the busy weekend. Pansy and Mom were helping her, between tending babies and cleaning and whatever else needed to be done. And Linda was trying her best to get the flower beds and garden cleaned up to look presentable. She really had not had much time in the yard that summer. Since John Ray had not been there to help, she had needed to spend more time in the fields, helping Dad and Larry.

Linda thought of John Ray. She missed seeing him around the farm. She seldom saw him other than at church services. She had seen him at the weekly instruction meetings, but those were finished now.

She thought with admiration of John Ray's developing interest in Christian service, especially for the interest he was showing in Clyde Tilghman. Clyde was in prison in Sharptown, and John Ray spent many hours there, teaching him from the Bible. Sometimes Dad went along with John Ray, and sometimes one of the brothers from the Sharptown church went. So far, Clyde had not made a commitment to Christ, but they were all praying for him, hoping for the day when he would give his life to the Lord. Dad had as much as told the family that, if the time came, he would be willing to take Clyde on parole. Linda still had a little anxiety about that, but continued to pray for love in her heart for Clyde.

And she thought of Pansy, with her many and continued questions as she helped them each week. "I would love to come to yo' church," Pansy had confided once to Linda. "But Pug would nevah come wid me—nor let me eithah. He laks his sinnin' too much." Linda had encouraged Pansy to keep reading her Bible and serving the Lord the best she could.

Saturday came. And the Bakers finally arrived with Andrea! Linda and Andrea sat out in the orchard on Linda's favorite apple tree branch, in the fresh October blueness, happily catching up on all the news in each other's lives.

"Are you still enjoying your work in the nursing home?" Linda asked.

"Oh, yes! The old folks have become so dear to me. As I serve them, in their lowly needs, I feel I am serving the Lord. It is a wonderful feeling."

"Have your parents accepted your dropping out of training?"

"They basically have, and Daddy again apologized for getting so upset with me. I think hearing about Starla Weaver helped them to change their minds. And Kathy Yoder had some really serious struggles."

"Oh, no! What happened to her?" Linda asked in real concern.

"In the pediatric ward, she met a male nurse that wanted to take her out. She worked with him a lot and was really tempted to fall for him. But she was willing to share with her parents and ministry, and they all joined in praying for her, that she would be faithful."

"And was she? Oh, I hope so!"

"So far, she is," Andrea assured Linda. "Her parents came to Mama and Daddy and told them that they so much admired what we girls had done, and that they wished they had insisted on the same for Kathy. At that point, they were still trying to decide what course they should take. They knew that Kathy's heart was really set on nursing."

"She's on my mind so much, and I pray that she can be faithful." Linda sighed. Then she added, "Have you heard more about Starla?"

"Starla isn't doing so well. Remember how she was so determined to marry a doctor? Well, she will never have the happy family life she thought they'd have—the doctor dropped out of her life. Probably to find another unsuspecting victim."

"How sad!" Linda gasped.

"We can only thank God for His mercy! We surely don't deserve it any more than anyone else."

"You're right. And I'm so thankful God is still working, drawing true seekers to Himself. Did you know that Mary Catherine is under instruction right now to join at Sharptown? And also Mrs. Ziller, as well as several folks from the Sharptown area?"

"Mary Catherine! I can hardly imagine it. But I know you had written how she became a Christian. And I know that God is able to change lives! He surely did ours! I'm so happy for her."

"Tell me about your plans," Linda entreated Andrea after a while. "Larry said you have some."

"Lord willing, we plan to get married next summer. You know how Larry struggled with whether to follow through with his plans and go ahead and graduate from college. Last spring when he counseled with the Millburg ministry, they felt it would need to be his decision."

"I didn't know he talked with them," Linda said.

"He did. But then we talked with Brother Shenk here, and Larry felt his advice was much more fitting with Biblical conservatism."

"He told me some about your visit with Brother Shenk."

"Your mother wasn't too happy at first about his decision not to finish, but your father was, of course."

"But Mom feels now that it was right. I know, because she told me just lately how happy she is to have Larry home to help Dad."

"I'm glad to hear that," Andrea said happily, looking up with tears in her eyes. "It bothered me a little, wondering how she could join the church if she still felt that way."

"What do you plan to do after you are married?"

"Larry and your father have talked about a partnership on the farm here."

"Wonderful! Then I will see more of you too!" Linda exclaimed. "Where will you live? Are those plans made yet?"

"You won't believe this!" Andrea laughed. "We are thinking of buying Mrs. Davis's house from the county! It will be fun to fix it up, and it will be close to Larry's work if he works with your father."

"What fun! It will be a challenge, all right; but won't it be fun to see what you can make of that old house?"

Andrea laughed. "That's what Larry and I both thought!" Andrea sat dreamily for a time, looking across the harvested fields. "Larry has talked about teaching too, and I think he'd make a wonderful teacher. But I don't know where he would find such an opportunity in a Christian environment. He thinks too that he ought to have a couple years to learn before he would be capable of teaching in a Mennonite school."

"Maybe he could teach sometime at our church school at Sharptown," Linda suggested. "I think David Hertzler is planning to help his father in carpentry after this year."

"He thought about teaching there if he was asked to. Maybe after we have been members for a few years."

Linda sat quietly for some time as she looked off into the distant blue. Then she sighed.

"Something troubling you?" Andrea questioned kindly.

"Not really much," Linda said, her mind coming back suddenly to the present. "It's just that I was thinking about my twentieth birthday next week. It is hard to comprehend that I am actually getting that old! Imagine, I will be out of my teens, never to return to them again!"

"I think about that too. Of course, I won't be twenty yet for a couple of months." Andrea laughed as she looked at Linda's doleful face.

"You can laugh! Your future is all down pat, but I don't foresee anything for me, other than the routine of farm work for the next fifty years!" Linda was determined to be difficult.

"Oh, Linda!" Andrea protested. "Someone will come along one of these times and claim your affections, just you wait!"

"It isn't that," Linda objected. "It's just that . . . well, what is there for me to do that is really useful? You will be a wife and likely a mother . . . and . . ." Linda paused briefly. "Maybe that *is* the problem. I must admit, I desire to be a wife and mother too, more than anything else. What if it isn't God's will for me?" Linda felt tears threatening to spill over. Frantically she groped for more cheerful thoughts. Whatever ailed her, to sit here and cry at such a joyous time for their family!

"Linda, Linda!" Andrea chided gently. "You surprise me! You have always been the one that encouraged me on in faith. And now—what has happened? Can't you trust that God does all things well? Can't we wait upon Him to bring His will to pass for us?"

"Oh, Andrea, you are right, of course. I don't know *what* is the matter with me. But pray for me, that I will continue to be a faithful, submissive, and useful child of God."

"I do, Linda. And you have the blessing of caring and supportive parents. Be strong in faith! God will show you His will in His own time. And it will be *good!"*

Linda reached over and squeezed Andrea's hand. Then she jumped off the branch. "Shall we go in and see what the rest are doing?" she asked.

"We probably should see if there is something we can do to help," Andrea said. "I think Loretta was baking apple pies for tomorrow."

The girls meandered slowly through the orchard to the house. They each picked a Red Delicious apple to eat on the way in.

No one was in the kitchen, but a delightful smell of baking pies came from the oven. Linda found Mom in the library, rocking Leon to sleep. Loren was still busily crawling over the floor. Linda stooped and grabbed him up. "It's hard to believe these fellows are nearly a year old," she said, squeezing Loren till he giggled.

Andrea had followed her into the library. "Where's your piano?" She whispered, noticing that Leon was nearly asleep in Mom's arms. She looked at the corner where the baby grand had always stood.

"We sold it," Linda answered.

"Did you need to before you could become members at Sharptown?" Andrea asked.

"They didn't need to tell us to; Dad thought having such an expensive piano in our house didn't really fit with a simple lifestyle, nor does it fit with worship the way we have learned to understand it. And we cleaned out our record cupboard," Linda added, opening the cabinet to show only a few records left. "But again, it was because we felt we should, not because someone told us to. They wouldn't have known what was there, but our consciences did!"

"We have needed to do some other house-cleaning too, Andrea," Mom said softly. "The Goodwill store in town got a boon when we began to clean out our clothes closets. Maybe we should have just burned the clothes. We did burn a lot of other things—books, makeup paraphernalia, and suchlike. Dad took our jewelry in to Gus, the jeweler, for whatever he chose to give us for it. It's been a time of soul-searching and cleansing as well as a house cleansing!"

"I needed to do the same, but on a much smaller scale, I'm sure, than a family would," Andrea responded.

"Oh, I look forward so much to tomorrow!" Linda exclaimed. "I don't know how I'll be able to sleep tonight. We've looked forward to this for so long, and now the Lord is bringing it to pass!

"Remember, Andrea, how I told you—I think it was in tenth grade, when I was doing that term paper about various churches—that I was praying to meet a people who were willing to die for their faith? And to think, God has answered that prayer!"

"He has been faithful to us," Mom exclaimed softly. "How can we ever thank Him enough?"

"By the way, where are my parents?" Andrea asked.

"They are visiting some friends in town this afternoon. Then I think they will be eating out with some other friends this evening."

Mom took Leon to his crib; then she took Loren from Linda to feed him and put him to sleep.

"What should we girls be doing, Mom? I feel somewhat disjointed today! Maybe you can help me to think logically."

"Well, there really isn't a lot to finish up. We were planning for a light supper, since there is a service at church tonight. I'm sure Dad would be happy for help in the barn, once it's time to start chores.

"Maybe you could pick a half-bushel of Red Delicious apples to have around for tomorrow," she added.

"That sounds like something I would have the presence of mind to do," Linda said, laughing.

That job was soon finished, and the girls decided to change into barn clothes and start the chores. Dad and Larry were still working in the chicken barn when the girls went out later to bring the cows in and put the milkers together.

"What is the service this evening about?" Andrea asked as they were feeding the cows grain.

"It is called the preparatory service. They usually have this service before Communion. You know, tomorrow is the Communion and Feet Washing service, as well as Baptism."

"Larry had told me that."

"So your parents will see a truly Biblical Communion and Feet Washing service. I wonder what they will think about it."

As Linda had expected, she found it hard to sleep that night. It had been late by the time they got home from church, and she thought she should be able to fall into bed and sleep like a baby! But, no, here she was, still awake, and her alarm clock had said 12:25 the last time she looked.

The next thing she knew she was wide-awake and it was morning. She jumped up quietly and dressed to help at the barn. It was going to be a mild, sunny day, she thought as she looked at the brightening sky on her way to bring the cows in from the pasture.

When they arrived at church some hours later, Linda looked around the parking lot in surprise. There must be visitors, she thought, seeing the unusual number of cars. The auditorium was already well filled. And they had thought they would be early!

There would be no Sunday school that morning, and Brother Shenk had told the applicants that the baptism would take place during the first part of the service. He had told them that the bishop, Brother Miller, would be there and would want to meet with them before the service.

Linda and her family gathered in the classroom to the side of the main auditorium. She looked at each one. Mom, Loretta, Andrea, and she were all dressed in navy blue cape dresses, with their hair neatly arranged under their white veilings. Dad, Larry, and John Ray all had dark plain suits. How serious everyone looked! And she knew she felt that way herself.

After a briefing as to what to expect, Brother Miller prayed with them and wished them God's blessing. Then he asked the men to sit on the front bench on the brethren's side, and the ladies to sit on the front bench on the sisters' side.

After a time of singing and devotion, Brother Miller conducted the baptism. First, each one was asked several questions, in which he committed himself to live for the Lord all his life. Then Brother Miller sealed their commitments by pouring a little water onto the head of each kneeling applicant. How solemn Linda felt as she thought about the vows she was making, and about the baptism symbolizing the baptism of the Holy Spirit in the new birth experience and signifying entrance into the family of God. She wondered how the rest felt, if they felt inspired to worship and fear God all their days, as she did.

Then Brother Miller gave his hand, inviting each one to stand, welcoming them into the local congregation. He greeted the new brethren with a holy kiss, and his wife came to greet the new sisters with a holy kiss.

It was all so new that Linda felt trembly inside. But at least now the attention would be off them, and they could all relax and enjoy the rest of the service—and their first Communion!

Brother Miller preached a sermon on "The Sacrifice of Christ." As Linda took notes, she marveled again at the tremendous sacrifice Christ had made to come to earth, to live among men, and then to die as a sacrifice for the sins of the world. Often she thought of the Bakers sitting somewhere in the audience behind her, and her heart breathed a prayer for them, that their hearts would be open to the whole teaching of the Word.

What a blessing to join in the Communion service as Brother Miller and Brother Shenk passed the bread and the grape juice to each member. Then came the wonderful time of kneeling to wash each other's feet in obedience to Christ's command: the sisters with the sisters in the nearby classroom, and the brethren with the brethren at the front of the auditorium. It was also an expression of humility and a symbol of the desire to help each other keep their walk clean. Linda wondered if her heart could contain it all. But this was just the beginning, she thought with joy. All this was hers to enjoy, as part of God's family, for the rest of her life! And it did not even end there: for all eternity she could share in the joy of being part of God's family!

After the service, as her family waited in the front of the auditorium, she believed that every church member who was there came forward to greet them and welcome them into the fellowship. Many had tears in their eyes as they assured them of their prayers and support. What love! Linda's heart overflowed with joy.

Kathy Yoder and her brother Robert, who had made the trip south for this occasion, came and shook hands with each of them, greeting them. Kathy was crying openly, her heart sharing the joy they felt. Then Pastor and Mrs. Baker came to them. They went first to Andrea and assured her of their continued love. Then they shook hands with each of the others, all of them former parishioners. Linda wondered what the Bakers were thinking. Could they not see that here were a people who were truly serving the

Lord? A plea rose from her heart for them. Then Mary Catherine came, and Mrs. Ziller, each one with joy in her face, eager for her own experience of belonging to God's family.

It was late when the Asburys got home from church. The Bakers had come for lunch, as well as John Ray and Mrs. Ziller, and Kathy and Robert. Brother Miller and his wife had also consented to come. Dad and Mom were eager to learn to know them better, and they to know the Asburys.

Meat loaf and scalloped potatoes and corn were in the oven and only needed to be set on the table. The girls soon had the salads out, and preserves and pickles in serving dishes.

Linda looked around the extended table at all her loved ones, at the twins in their high chairs, at Loretta and dear Mom and Dad, at Larry and Andrea, and the Bakers, at John Ray and his mother, and their bishop and his dear wife. How precious that they could all be together in this way. She was happy too to have Kathy and Robert there, to share in this special time.

At the head of the table sat her father, his face a study in solemn joy. "Are you happy, Dad?" Linda asked as she looked up at him.

"Yes. I feel so full of joy I can hardly contain it," he responded. "What about you?"

"To say I feel overwhelmed with how the Lord has worked in our lives would be stating it mildly!" she replied. "Somehow I feel I have come home! I'm part of the family of God!"

*Yes, I have come home, in heart as well as in spirit!* she thought. *"No more a stranger, nor a guest, but like a child at home."* What rest she felt as she thought of the wonderful way that God had led her and her dear ones in the past years. And she trusted Him for the unknown future, knowing that He would continue to faithfully show them the way.